RAVE REVIEWS FOR *WITH EYES OF LOVE*!

"Wicked Regency fun from Corey McFadden. The staid city of Bath has never been so treacherous—or so romantic!"

—Mary Jo Putney, *New York Times* bestselling author

"Brilliant fun! Bright, wonderful characters!"

—Cathy Maxwell, *New York Times* bestselling author

"Well written with an impressive command of the Regency time period, Corey McFadden's *With Eyes of Love* is clever, sexy, and delightful."

—Susan King, national bestselling author

"Deliciously witty! If you love the English Regency era, don't miss Corey McFadden's *With Eyes of Love*."

—Hope Tarr, author of *A Rogue's Pleasure*

VISIONS OF LOVE

"Ah, Miss Quinn, again you allow me to understand I present myself as a shallow, self-absorbed fellow. Indeed, I find nothing the least bit trifling or dull about you."

Did he mock her again? How could she know if he was making sport of her if she couldn't see his face? "Would you mind terribly if I put on my spectacles, sir?" she asked. "I find it difficult to converse with dark blurs."

"As do I, ma'am. You may wear yours if I may wear my own." He reached into his waistcoat pocket and settled them on his aquiline nose. She fished hers from her reticule and, her own now similarly situated, they peered carefully at one another.

"You are even more beautiful than I realized," he said softly.

Her heart knocked about a bit in her chest. Then someone's laughter rang out, reminding her of the game that was played among the "Quality." "You flatter me, sir," she said simply, looking away. "It's not a good idea, really. I am woefully ill-used to such remarks and quite apt to take you far too seriously."

She started when his gloved hand covered hers, but she did not draw away. "I am guilty of the foolish repartee of the Beau Monde, Miss Quinn. But not with you. There is something about you that calls out the better in me—such as it is."

"Weston-under-Lizard," she said, in a shaky voice.

"I beg your pardon?"

"I live in a little town called Weston-under-Lizard. I am the eldest of five in my family. Papa died a little less than a year ago, and we are rather modest in our demeanor and society. Not at all interesting, you see." She finished nearly breathless.

WITH EYES OF LOVE

COREY McFADDEN

LEISURE BOOKS  NEW YORK CITY

A LEISURE BOOK®

June 2003

Published by

Dorchester Publishing Co., Inc.
276 Fifth Avenue
New York, NY 10001

ISBN 0-8439-5217-2

Printed in the United States of America.

WITH EYES OF LOVE

"The waters of Bath are an acquired taste. And the only place one can acquire it is here."

—Audio tour of the Roman Baths, Bath, England

"There is to be a grand gala on Tuesday evening in Sydney Gardens; a Concert, with illuminations and fireworks; to the latter Eliz. & I shall look forward with pleasure, & even the Concert will have more than its usual charm with me, as the gardens are large enough for me to get pretty well beyond the reach of its sound."

—Jane Austen's letter to her sister Cassandra, 2nd June, 1799

Chapter One

"But, Mama, Aunt Bettina loathes us all. She has made that quite clear for years."

"I know, I know, my dearest. But this is an opportunity for you that we dare not decline. Imagine! Bath in its high Season! And Bettina promises to bring you out as if you were her very own daughter."

"She has her very own daughter, Mama, I might remind you," Elspeth said, gently, not wanting her words to sting, "and my cousin Caroline makes her mother seem the very soul of human kindness. Caroline will have nothing to do with poor relations like us, I assure you. She as much as told me at Papa's funeral that we were an embarrassment to the rest of the family, and that they had come only out of a sense of duty and condescension."

Elspeth's mother's usually smiling mouth thinned into a slit, and Elspeth instantly regretted her words. "I'll admit the chit has no manners," Mrs. Quinn, replied, "but she comes by that fault honestly. I'll never understand why your father's brother married such an ill-tempered woman."

"I imagine Aunt Bettina's rather magnificent marriage settlement played something of a role in helping him to reach that decision, Mama," Elspeth said dryly. She held the nightcap she was mending up to the thinning light from the window. It wasn't much use. In a moment the twilight would have faded past her ability to do close work. She settled her spectacles firmly upon the bridge of her nose and sent the needle flying again.

"Well, it certainly wasn't her appearance," Mrs. Quinn said with a little giggle, then, turning beet-red, she added quickly, "Oh, dear, I should never have said anything so unkind. I'm sure Bettina was a lovely girl in her day." The effect of the gracious remark was rather spoiled when Elspeth let out a snort, and Mrs. Quinn's eyes began watering at her inadequate effort not to laugh.

"I hope that when you are presented to society in Bath, my dear, you will make a better show of your good manners than you have ever learned from me," Mrs. Quinn said at last, dabbing her eyes with her lace handkerchief—too-oft mended, Elspeth noted with a pang. Everything in the cottage was too-oft mended, she thought, looking around the snug room. Had it always looked so bedraggled, or was she seeing her home, now, through eyes saddened and grown more mature over these last, difficult six months? Heaven only knew the size of a marriage portion had not been a factor in Papa's decision to marry the girl he loved beyond all things. The third son of a marginally situated family and the third daughter of a downright impecunious one, Louis and Margaret Quinn had carefully and cheerfully raised four daughters and a son in the small dwelling that had once been the steward's lodge on a larger estate.

Papa's death in a hunting accident nearly a year ago had been a devastating blow to children and wife alike. Mrs. Quinn was still a loving mother, but some of the light had died in her eyes, and Elspeth had lately overheard some awkward conversations with local tradesmen, who couldn't, after all, be expected to carry the family's outstanding debts forever.

Perhaps that was why her mother was so eager for Elspeth to accept the unlooked-for offer that had just arrived by post from the haughty and disdainful Aunt Bettina, herself widowed long since, when Uncle Harry had gone to his early grave, some whispering that he was happy to go.

"I suppose it would be a help to have me gone for a few months at that," Elspeth said, adjusting her spectacles farther up on her nose again. Dratted things never stayed up, but she was bat-blind without them, at least for close work.

"Oh, never think that, my darling!" exclaimed Mrs. Quinn, patting her daughter's hand. "I shall miss you most dreadfully—you know that! Why, I shall have the other four to care for all by myself and you know your sisters aren't much help yet. Too dreamy to keep their minds on any task."

They were a family of dreamers, Elspeth thought, carefully folding the still-unfinished nightcap and stowing it back in her mending basket. A family poor by financial accounts but wildly rich in imagination and good will. Not commodities, unfortunately, with which to settle debts with tradesmen.

"I don't know what I'll do with Harry, though," her mother said, thoughtfully. She frowned over her embroidery and shook it out into the light. Weakness of vision seemed the very plague of this family, as least as far as its females were concerned. Nine-year-old Harry, though, took after Papa. Near or far, tiny and tinier, Harry could see everything down to infinitesimal detail. No spectacles for Harry. "The boy is such a handful," she sighed, folding her embroidery in her lap. "You're the only one he'll listen to now that Papa's gone."

"That's because I take no nonsense from him, Mama. You should show him a little less indulgence and a little more discipline." It was an old argument, and one Elspeth never expected to win.

"Oh, but he looks so like your father did at his age, Elspeth, when I very first met him. Such an angel! Golden curls, beautiful brown eyes. When I looked at him that very first moment I knew right then we would marry. He was already the perfect gentleman."

"That's because he caught you falling out of a tree, Mama, and then didn't run and tell on you," replied Elspeth, laughing. She had heard the story a thousand times, and Papa grew handsomer and handsomer in the telling.

"And Harry's an angel, too," Mrs. Quinn finished with a decided pronouncement.

"A fallen one, I'm afraid, Mama," Elspeth said, laughing. "Lucifer, Son of the Morning, that's my little brother."

"Oh, hush! Don't say such a thing," cried Mrs. Quinn, hurriedly looking over her shoulder as if Elspeth's very words could conjure up the devil himself.

"Still, Mama, the similarity you find between Papa and Harry seems a wish born more of hopes than truth. I wonder. . . ." Elspeth paused as an interesting idea took hold.

"Mmmm?" her mother asked absently. She had picked up a piece of paper and, dipping her pen in the small inkwell that stood on the table next to her, started to jot what appeared to be some numbers on it. It seemed she was always jotting numbers these days, thought Elspeth sadly, and one column always outweighed the other.

Elspeth made up her mind in that moment. "I'll go to Aunt Bettina, if—"

"If?" her mother asked, looking up, hope in her eyes.

"I wish to take Harry with me. He needs to learn a little about society. More than I do, indeed."

"Oh, dear me, I don't think . . . Bettina is not likely to agree to take on the burden of Harry, too. You understand, she wishes you to be companion to your cousin Caroline."

"Probably because Caroline can keep no friends of her own," Elspeth remarked drily.

"That's unkind, dear," Mrs. Quinn remonstrated, the chastisement falling short because of the twinkle in her eye.

"Roderick is close in age to Harry, isn't he?" Elspeth asked.

"Well, older by a bit, some eighteen months, as I recall." Mrs. Quinn frowned with the effort to remember. "Yes, that's right, because I remember Bettina suggesting to me that it was unseemly to be increasing at my age, and she a good half year older than I! The very idea!"

"Well, then offer us as a duo, two companions instead of one. If Roderick is anything like his sister, he could use a friend, too, I'm sure."

"To tell the truth, my dear, I'm a little concerned as to what bad habits Harry might be put in the way of acquiring from his cousin," Mrs. Quinn said, doubtfully. "I recall the boy was something of a trial to his father."

"More so than our Harry? My, that's rather difficult to imagine," replied Elspeth, laughing. "Besides, I recall Roderick's behavior involved just the usual 'bad boy' things."

"He put a dead mouse in Cook's boots," Mrs. Quinn said with a sniff. "I had to bribe her to stay on, and me trying to bury your father with some feint at family dignity."

"Well, yes, the mouse was unfortunate, Mama. Cook peers carefully into her boots before donning them to this day, now that you mention it."

"As do I," Mrs. Quinn said shuddering.

"Well, if Harry comes with me, I can keep an eye on him. And, who knows, Roderick might learn a thing or two about deviling sisters from our Harry."

"I don't know how I'd manage him without you here, at that, my dear."

Good. The point was won. The more Elspeth considered the matter, the better she liked the idea of bringing Harry along. She didn't care a fig for her own Season, quite a lot of nonsense *that* would amount to at her advanced age of twenty-three, but Harry—now here was an opportunity to bring him to the notice of some of his better-set-up relatives. When she thought on it, late in these long nights since Papa's death, Elspeth was troubled for them all. There was not much money, nor much opportunity to acquire any. She had conceived a scheme long ago whereby the family could purchase Harry his colors, although the wherewithal had yet to manifest itself, even in her dreams.

"Good, that's settled then," Elspeth announced. "I'll go, and take Harry with me."

"Not so fast, miss," cried her mother, holding up her hand. "There is the matter of convincing your Aunt Bettina that she truly wants another mouth to feed.

She's a stubborn woman, as you know," she finished with a shudder of distaste.

"You leave Aunt Bettina to me, Mama. I shall pen a reply that will have her all but begging for the pleasure of our little angel's company."

"Oh, dear. You won't . . . ah . . . misrepresent him, will you, dear? I shouldn't want any unpleasantness, after all. We would eventually be caught at it, you know," she finished timidly.

"Why, Mama, you said yourself Harry is a perfect angel. How ever could I misrepresent him?"

Caught in a trap of her own making, Mrs. Quinn satisfied herself with a harrumph and betook herself to the kitchen to check on Cook's progress with supper.

" 'And I am sure Roderick would enjoy having his younger cousin to tutor in the finer arts of becoming a gentleman—a clean slate upon which your dear boy can make such a good and profound impression.' Nicely put, at that, isn't it, Caroline? You might do well to emulate your cousin Elspeth's pretty style. And, indeed, we would be showing such condescension in having both these misbegotten poor relatives for an educational visit. I cannot think why Harry's brother would have married such a negligible woman. Poor as church mice, her family was. No real refinement at all. A most unsatisfactory union in my humble opinion, as we can all now appreciate, although certainly no one would listen to me at the time."

"Mama," Caroline put in, exasperated. "You cannot be thinking of saddling me with another brat to contend with. Roderick is trial enough to me, as you well know. Why, yesterday, he switched my rouge pot with the kohl, and I was quite unpresentable for the better part of an hour. Nellie half scrubbed my face off. I gave her quite a dressing down for being too rough."

"You shouldn't use so much paint, darling. It suggests you are trying to hide your age."

"I *am* trying to hide my age, Mama."

"Nevertheless, it's no good being obvious about it. One of the biddies commented on it the other day. Sly old witch thought she could disguise her remark as a general witticism, but I know an insult when I hear it. Veiled or not."

"What did she say?" Caroline asked, sulkily. She stood glancing out of a small gap where the heavy silk draperies did not quite close. Today was her "at home." Was no one going to call, her mother wondered?

"Oh, just some bon mot about how one could compare a girl with the rings of a tree, telling the number of years she had been in the marriage mart by counting the layers of paint on her face."

"Which one of the old harridans said that?" Caroline asked, turning, her face suffused with anger.

"That Mrs. Peterson. Too loud. A bit vulgar. Pay her no mind, dear."

"That Mrs. Peterson has three daughters, one of whom has been out longer than I," Caroline said, stalking toward the center of the room. "And a positive Antidote she is. The woman has her nerve criticizing me."

"Well, perhaps she was speaking of her own daughter at that, Caroline. Now that I think of it, there was a young woman with her who blushed mightily at the comment. Nevertheless," Bettina went on hurriedly, anxious to get back to the subject at hand, "give the matter of your cousins some thought. After all, with his little cousin here, Roderick will have someone upon whom to focus his energies besides you and me. To spare us his pranks for now."

"It's my fourth Season, remember," Caroline warned darkly. "Any more after this and I'll be branded a wallflower forever. Oh, how I wish Lord Rokeby had come up to scratch last Season. I was almost certain of having secured his affections, and then, for no reason that I could see, he simply left town. Made quite the laughingstock of me, I vow."

"Oh, nonsense, Caroline. The man's stable burned to the ground and all his cattle with it. Naturally he was called away. Indeed, I understand he is to return for the Season this year. Perhaps you will find it amusing and profitable to reattach his sentiments. He is quite wealthy, you know."

"Of course I know, Mama. Else I'd not have wasted all last Season encouraging him to the exclusion of the rest. Quite a waste of my valuable time that was." She flung herself up from the divan she had only just flung herself down upon, and stalked to the window again. "And if I am so much the toast of the Season, where is everyone?"

"Now, Caroline, you know the Season has not quite begun. No one is calling yet. It simply isn't time. We're only here early to get settled in this house before things do get underway."

"I still say the whole idea is dreadful, Mother," retorted Caroline, turning from the window with a pout. "Elspeth is entirely unpresentable. Bookish and plain, an absolute country bumpkin. Why she's at least twenty-five, isn't she? Quite nearly a spinster. I shall be trapped beside her at every function, and no one will come near us, save the old men, widowed and senile. Everyone will think we are two old crows standing together hoping for carrion to feed upon! I declare, if that malodorous old fool, Sir Richard Sommers, requests a dance of me one more time, I shall kick his cane out from under him! The very idea that I might be desperate enough to dance with the likes of him!".

And that was precisely what Bettina feared—that Caroline might indeed grow desperate enough that the likes of Sir Richard was the best she could hope for. And, Bettina thought, suppressing a shudder, the rank old goat was her own elder by several years.

"Ah, but you are not looking at it from quite the right perspective, my dear," said her mother with a conspiratorial smile. "It is exactly Elspeth's slightly shopworn appearance that I seek. You are, even if it is I who say it, a splendid-looking girl—or, at least,"—she raised an eyebrow—"you would be if you didn't pout so. At any rate, no girl in the marriage mart today can approach you in beauty." She ignored the rolling of Caroline's eyes. What she said was true—as far as it went. Still, there was that certain, indefinable quality that a young woman took on after perhaps one too many years on display. Perhaps it was really there, perhaps those around her simply relished thinking it was, but after a few Seasons a demoiselle began to look rather—well—desperate. It was just this look Bettina wished to avoid at all costs for her beautiful Caroline. "But, as you say, you have just past one-and-twenty, and your age is something from which to divert attention. Next to Elspeth, who I thought appeared quite spinsterish at her father's funeral, you will look positively dewy. Why, the girl's spectacles alone give her the appearance of her own grandmother. I am led to understand she does not so much as rise in the morning without donning them for the rest of the day."

"Exactly! Her clothing would scare away the crows! She was quite dowdy when we attended Uncle's funeral. I don't believe she owns more than two day dresses. I certainly saw no more. I was quite embarrassed for her. And I do not much fancy trumpeting to the *ton* that we have such paltry connections."

"Well, of course, I shall do what I must to make her presentable, Caroline," her mother countered, trying to tamp down her growing annoyance.

"But I need my own wardrobe refurbished, Mama! How much are you planning to spend on my cousin?" Caroline asked, with the maddening illogic that made manipulating the girl so difficult. "As it is, the old biddies are sure to recognize several of last Season's dresses, even remade as they are."

"Indeed, my dear, I was thinking of handing several of them down to Elspeth, You are an inch or two shorter than she—no more than that. Indeed, she is too tall. But you are much the same figure, and I think your old dresses can be recut quite nicely for her. And then, of course, you shall have new."

The magic words spoken, Caroline's mutinous expression turned crafty, then pleased, like a cat who had just stumbled into the dairy and found no one there, just a large bucket of warm, thick cream. . . .

Chapter Two

He was bored. He hadn't yet been in Bath a full forty-eight hours and he had never been so bored in all his life. Unless one counted the last time he put in an appearance at the London Season, some two years ago.

This was a bad idea. Bath in any Season ran a close second to London for bad ideas. Life here was parochial, rigid, choreographed down to the seemingly negligent flick of one's cuff.

Not that he'd been given any choice in the matter, with family responsibilities piling upon him, one atop the other. He had been near to suffocating from the weight before the events of last week.

The final straw had been his father's stroke, which had left the once vital and virile man looking frail, and terribly old, half-paralyzed, and weak, eyes rheumy with the pain and indignity of it all. His father's wavering voice had been barely audible as he had begged his only son to let a pitiful old man die happy. It was the pity that had finally done what hints, sharp words, cajolery and tricks had failed to accomplish in happier times. He was here in Bath so that some demoiselle could make him the happiest of men, or at least marry him.

It had been impossible to say no this one last time, to pull yet one more excuse out of his hat, to make a vague promise that, yes, of course, Father, but next year, when I get this drought problem solved, or when the irrigation trenches are completed, or the stable renovations finished, or this, or that, or another of the unending stream of activities that could immerse a gentleman farmer of substantial estates. Particularly one who found the *ton* and all its trappings far less absorbing than a thumping good experiment as to which particular mix of swill could best fatten up the pigs. . . .

"I say, Julian, are you going to play that card or are you going to stare at it all night?" Wesley Ames asked, eyeing his own hand with obvious annoyance.

"Oh, they all look alike anyway," Julian muttered, snapping the card to the table and hoping it was the right one. He couldn't see a blasted thing in here. The light was too dim, chandeliers blazing away with candles a few hundred feet in the air. How could they expect anyone to see anything? At least the pips on the cards were large enough to count. Not for the world would he bring out his spectacles, lurking temptingly inside an inner pocket of his waistcoat. The few times he'd worn them among the *ton*, his cronies had had great fun at his expense, and "four eyes" had been the kindest of the taunts.

"You have the devil's own luck with cards, Julian, and I'd swear you don't pay the least bit of attention," Wesley said, good-naturedly, when it became apparent that Julian would take the trick.

"Bad luck with the ladies, though," Benjamin Watkins drawled. "Are you sure it's safe to return? I rather thought Lady Helen Sneed would set up a hue and cry after you the last time you graced us with your presence."

Julian ground his teeth and made no reply. It was just this sort of gossip he wished to avoid. Lady Helen's daughter, Honoria, had been a lovely girl in her way, but her prodigious physical charms had palled upon further acquaintance. Actually, his pigs were more intelligent, not to put too fine a point on it.

"I suppose that's why you've chosen Bath, instead of braving the full London Season?" Edgar Randall asked, with his usual feigned disinterest.

One must be quite careful what one said to Edgar. It was always repeated, and not with the greatest of accuracy. "I prefer Bath at this time of year, actually. It's a little less tedious than London," Julian responded. He flicked another card to the table. It made his head ache to fight with the bad lighting, and the room was too close. At home he'd be abed by now, long since, indeed, as he rose with the dawn. The *ton* went to bed with the dawn. It would take some getting used to, and he wasn't sure he wished to be bothered.

"I picked up the most delicious piece of information today," Edgar said, tossing a card to the table. He was an indifferent player, to say the least. His objective seemed never to be the pot, rather, the *on dit*. He let the remark hang in the air, waiting for some fish to snap at the bait.

"Do go on, Edgar. You know you can barely contain yourself," Wesley said with a laugh.

"It seems that Perennial Toast, Caroline Quinn, is importing a country cousin for the Season. Now, can anyone imagine the beautiful but conceited Miss Quinn sharing the spotlight with a lovely demoiselle having her first Season? My suspicions are aroused."

"My word, yes," said Wesley. "Gel must be a positive

Antidote. Else Caroline'd never tolerate the sight of her on the premises. I daresay they've brought in a repellent spinster so as to invite favorable comparison. This promises to be most entertaining."

"One must wonder whether or not Mrs. Quinn's ruse will work, however," said Benjamin Watkins, eyeing his cards dubiously. "My recollection is that the disdainful Caroline can attract multitudes of admirers, but that her waspish temper soon drives them off."

"You had a rather narrow escape there, yourself, Julian, a few years ago, as I recall," put in Edgar, with enough of an amused edge to his voice to indicate that he hoped he'd poked a sore spot.

"Not at all. Lovely girl," replied Julian, keeping his voice nonchalant. "Should have offered for her, indeed. Perhaps this Season I will, at that," he finished, triumphantly trumping Randall's last throw.

"Perhaps your prize pigs will fly, Julian," laughed Benjamin. "Let's see," he went on, fiddling idly with the few cards left in his hand. "You'd insist upon returning to the country to live. Then she'd be bored to tears and would have to take on the steward as her lover, and have you stabbed to death with a pitchfork through the chest. I can see now that it wouldn't work out. Wise choice, my lad."

"Well, yes. That was rather how I thought things would turn out," said Julian, smiling in spite of himself. Benjamin had a way of making him see the humor in any situation.

"Well, I do recall that you and the Perennial Toast were quite the talk of a few Seasons back," said Edgar. "Her first Season, I believe it was, although one does find one's memory fading for ancient history." Edgar threw down a card, paying no obvious attention to his hand whatsoever, now that he had fresh game in his sights. "Refresh my recollection, Julian. Were you the Jilt or the Jilted?"

"There was no question of a jilt, Edgar," replied Julian, trying to hide his annoyance. "Caroline and I are friends, nothing more. We would never suit in a serious relationship."

"Well, that may have been true then. But this is Caroline's . . . what? Fifth Season? Sixth?"

"Oh, not so many as that, Edgar," Wesley broke in, obviously sensing that the jibing had gone too far. "Third or fourth, I'll warrant. And it is Caroline, of course, who is being particular. Though I do believe she liked you best, Julian. She certainly gives the cold shoulder to every new crop of young smitten swains."

"Why don't we pay a call on Mrs. Quinn and her arrogant offspring tomorrow? They've let the late Lord Ewell's place, I understand," said Edgar. "Welcome them to Bath, you know. Perhaps we might catch a glimpse of the sacrificial victim, this cousin from the country."

"It sounds unkind to say the least," Julian snapped. "Do you go to gawk at the country cousin or to annoy Caroline?" His head was pounding like the very devil. He never got headaches at his estate in the country.

"Oh, my, aren't we holier than thou this evening?" put in Edgar, with a wicked gleam in his eye. Julian cursed himself for giving the man the opening to needle him. "But you will come with us on the morrow, of course," continued the relentless Edgar. "To renew your fond friendship with the lovely, not-jilted Caroline."

"Oh, no, I don't think. . . ."

"Nervous, Julian?" needled Edgar. "Frightened of her most formidable mama? I heard a joke recently . . . can't think of the whole thing, but the punch line involved Bettina Quinn being the odds-on favorite at a match at Gentleman Jackson's. Quite amusing, it was. Still," he went on, with the a flick at an imaginary speck on his lace cuff, "I can see why, friends or no, you'd be simply knee-knocking terrified at the thought of facing either of those two dragons again."

Julian did not consider himself a cowardly man by any means, but five minutes alone in a room with Caroline, or her formidable mother, for that matter, might well have him cringing in terror among the divan cushions. Still, what could be worse than failing to rise to Edgar Randall's obvious challenge? If he refused to go, by tomorrow at this time the entire population of Bath would be laughing at his cowardice, and the blood sport would be on.

"What time do we plan to set out?" he made himself ask, playing his last card.

"Oh, latish, to be sure. It would never do to roust Caroline from her repose. No doubt she sleeps till noon." Unexpectedly, Edgar swept up the last trick. Very little money ever changed hands among this particular set. Edgar, often with pockets to let, could not afford high stakes, and Julian would not allow his friend to be put in an awkward position at cards.

"No doubt," replied Julian drily. "Well, I am for bed, myself, gentlemen. I shall not improve my fortunes playing cards with any of you, certainly."

"Julian, you've become a country bore, sir," laughed Wesley. "P'raps you and the country cousin will do well together at that."

"P'raps she weighs as much as one of his prize pigs," added Edgar, wickedly.

"Good night, gentlemen . . . although I use the term loosely," replied Julian.

"Go away!"

"Sha'n't!"

"Please, Harry. I'll only have a few minutes to myself. Then they're sure to want something. Let me have just a little time here and I'll tend to you later."

"Roderick is a pig!"

"Hush, Harry! Someone will hear!" Elspeth said quickly, looking over at the door that Harry had, at least, remembered to close behind him when he'd tracked her to the library. "Remember these are not our servants. Things we say unwisely will be repeated."

" 'Things we say unwisely will be repeated.' I say, Owl Eyes, when did you turn into such a prig? When we crossed the threshold into this fancy house?"

Elspeth rolled the eyes her little brother so maligned. "I'm trying to teach you some manners, but I must say I had better luck with the dog."

"Don't need any manners. Manners are for fops and prissies. I want to go home."

Now he looked a bit as if he might wish to cry, and Elspeth knew he would rather die than show such weakness in front of her. Quickly she climbed down from the rolling ladder where she had perched precipitously, happily picking through the books shelved in this most splendid library. Aunt Bettina carped about all the space the books wasted, and it was quite obvious that during the Quinn tenancy, the books would be ignored by all save Elspeth, who was enthralled by the sight and the endless hours of pleasure they would afford her—if she ever got any hours to herself, which, at the moment, seemed doubtful.

"Actually, Harry, I'd rather like to go home, too," she said softly, pulling him to her. "And so we shall in a few months. But in the meantime, let's enjoy the novelty of it all."

"There's nothing novel about being stuck in this house with my pig of a cousin," Harry muttered, head buried in the folds of her dress, arms wrapped tightly about his sister.

"Yes, but Aunt promises to take us to the Pump Room, as soon as I'm presentable."

"I don't understand all this fuss about your clothing, Elspeth," he pronounced, drawing back and eyeing her seriously. "I think you look fine just the way you are."

"Thank you, Harry," she said simply. From the way Caroline had sneered at her meager wardrobe, Elspeth had been left with the impression that servants in the poorer households were better attired.

"Although," he went on, perhaps unwisely, "I must say you look a sight now, all dusty from these books. You have a large cobweb in your mobcap, but I don't think. . . ." He eyed it carefully. "No, I don't think it has a spider in it," he pronounced with a grin, having achieved the desired effect as his sister blanched at his words. "And you do have the largest smut across the tip of your nose. 'Your appearance is simply unacceptable in polite society, Cousin Elspeth'," he said with a sneer, in perfect imitation of Cousin Caroline.

Elspeth reached up to wipe her nose, but from the delighted expression in Harry's eyes, she was quite sure she had merely succeeded in smearing the smut across the rest of her face. Indeed, the books were exceedingly dusty. She had borrowed the cap and apron from one of the parlour maids. Her day dresses might not be up to Caroline's standards but they were all she had at present.

"Actually," Harry went on, warming to the subject, "if anyone cared for my opinion, and I doubt they do, I'd tell them it's Cousin Caroline who looks absurd. All that cloth, miles and miles of it, and fuss and feathers. And she screams the house down if anyone comes near her, not that anyone cares to."

"Yes, well, see to it that you don't go near her. I won't have you blamed for any more mischief like last night."

"I didn't do it, I tell you! Roderick said I did, but it was him, not me!"

"I believe you, sweetheart, but it doesn't really matter. Just stay out of mischief and before you know it, we'll be home again, safe and sound."

Harry gave her a pitying glance, one full of the wisdom of a nine-year-old-who Knows Better.

"Now take yourself off and read some Latin. It's the one place you can show Roderick a thing or two, if you're keeping a tally sheet," Elspeth said with a laugh. She watched as he carefully shut the door behind him, then scaling the ladder once more, turned her attention with a sigh of pleasure to the splendid wall of books.

He had been mad to come here. And a thousand times a fool for allowing Edgar Randall to goad him into it. Better that *ton* tongues wagged about him all Season than that he should deliberately place himself once again in the direct sights of Miss Caroline Quinn, or, worse, her mother. It had been hard enough extricating himself three years ago, and no doubt Caroline and her mother had honed their skills more finely by now.

"I say, how long has the chit kept us waiting?" asked Wesley Ames, walking once again to the window. "An hour at least, I'll warrant." It was more like a half hour, really, Julian thought, consulting the ormolu clock that graced the mantle. Indeed, time was flying for him. He had no desire to hurry along the process. By custom, these visits lasted no more than the requisite fifteen minutes, once they got under way. For Caroline and Mrs. Quinn to keep them waiting a full half an hour was arrogant, but not unknown in these circles, where one's importance could be gauged by one's tardiness. Of the country cousin there was no sign, but it would be unlikely that she would make an appearance before she could be formally presented by her aunt.

"I know she's the Perennial Toast and all that," Wesley went on, sounding a bit petulant, "but, still, a man's time ought to have some value."

"What else might you be doing with your time today, Wesley?" replied Edgar Randall, his tone indolent as he sprawled across a fussy, brocade-upholstered settee. "Taking a nap?"

"Well, I could always use a good ride," Wesley answered. "My cattle need an outing."

"I could be reading a good book, at least," muttered Julian. "I recall old Lord Ewell was something of a scholar. Kept a good library. Can't think that Caroline or Mrs. Q. will give it much use. Wonder if it's still here?" he asked, hope springing alive with the thought. An idea bloomed. Desperate, even craven, to be sure, but any escape from this iron-jawed trap was a blessing.

"Believe I'll wander across the hall and take a look at the library. Some good books there as I recall," said Julian, ambling with affected nonchalance for the door, half expecting it to blow open and reveal mother and daughter, squatting like gargoyles on the threshold. If he could lose himself in the library until the short visit was well underway, it might lessen the amount of time he would be required to spend with the Quinn ladies. Perhaps they would forget about him altogether, and he could bumble and apologize for his gauche inattention all the way to the front door, making good his escape with a minimum of actual contact.

Once in the hallway, he had to stop himself from tiptoeing like an ill-intending child. Still, he tread rather lightly, considering the sound his heavy boots usually made across a wooden floor. Now where was the library? These Bath townhouses were small by London standards, but no less oppressively opulent for all that. Yes, the last door on the right, he thought, although it had been some time since he had last been in this house,

Lord Ewell having been something of an invalid for whom the restorative powers of the waters of Bath had become less and less effective as time went on.

Lord Ewell's library had been impressive indeed, particularly in Bath where most rooms so designated were fitted out with an ornate desk, several comfortable wing chairs, a few tables holding full brandy decanters and crystal snifters, and, if there was room enough, a book or two, for appearances' sake. Lord Ewell's library, however, had been walled with books, floor to ceiling, marching like stalwart, colorful, well-turned-out soldiers, all in neat, orderly rows, a sight to delight the eyes of the few true bibliophiles among the *ton*. Julian patted his waistcoat pocket and was relieved to feel his spectacles nestled safely within.

He heard no telltale approaching footsteps as he let himself through the door, closing it behind him as quietly and quickly as possible. It was all he could do not to lean against the door and pant, but even a coward had his pride.

Drat! It was no good trying to see anything out of spectacles this dirty. Elspeth had bumped her face right smack into another cobweb and hoped desperately that its eight-legged occupant had been off somewhere else on business at the time. Carefully, she pulled the gold wire-rims from her nose as everything blurred before her eyes. Using what appeared to be a clean corner of the borrowed apron, she wiped the sticky web from the glass, surveying as she did so the books before her nose, now an unfocused wall of color. Ethridge's *Botanical Studies* lay open in her lap, a veritable treasure of precise and intricate drawings that delighted and educated at the same time.

But though she was blind as a bat, there was nothing wrong with her hearing. The sound of the door opening told her she'd been found. Elspeth squinted mightily, hoping to make out the rotund form of the butler, or perhaps, Harry come back to complain loudly of further ill-treatment at the hands of the bully, Roderick.

No such luck. Her distance vision was far better than her sight close up, and the blurred form resolved itself into a gentleman, unknown to her. Trapped like a rat by a terrier, she sat perfectly still. Perhaps he would realize he was in the wrong room and make a hasty departure. Again, no luck. His gaze turned with some apparent fondness toward the shelves and he turned his back to her, fingers tracing along the bindings as if he sought something in particular.

Now what was she to do? Cough delicately? Offer a haughty "ahem"? Aunt Bettina had explained most emphatically that Elspeth was not to be "seen" until she was presentable. No point in making ill first impressions was how her aunt had tactlessly put it. Certainly the apron alone, never mind the smuts and cobwebs, would mark her the Antidote of the Season, not that she cared a whit what these vapid *ton* sorts thought of her. Nevertheless, Elspeth held still, hardly breathing, sitting silent. Her nose itched. Her foot, curled awkwardly around the rung of the ladder, began to cramp. She suppressed a sigh and stared malevolently at the back of this stranger, wishing him in Arabia.

Ah, the library has indeed not been dismantled, Julian thought, as his satisfied eye traveled the comfortable sight of matching row upon row of books. Lord Ewell's taste had run to the scholarly as he recalled, a bit turgid, if the truth were known. The light was poor in the obviously unused room. The titles were a blur in front of his eyes. He carefully took out his spectacles and placed them on his nose, hearing, almost at the edge of his consciousness, a very small intake of breath, not, he was sure, his own. "Who's there?" he called, turning with a frown. Drat! He barely swallowed his expression of annoyance as, peering over the rims of his glasses, he spotted one of the servants, a lower housemaid by the looks of her, perched precariously upon the wooden rolling ladder that Lord Ewell had needed to reach the top shelves. A large book lay open on her lap, and she appeared to have a white cloth in her hand, so she was obviously cleaning the books. She certainly had a large smudge across the bridge of her nose, and unless his vision was worse that he thought, a substantial cobweb was draped rather terrifyingly across her mobcap. At least Mrs. Quinn was seeing to the safekeeping of the library during her tenancy, although Julian thought it unlikely she or Caroline would find entertainment within the leather covers.

Julian gave a pleasant, dismissive nod and turned his attention to the wall of books before him, hoping the girl would scramble down, drop him the obligatory curtsy while mumbling apologies, and go about her business. But as luck would have it, at that moment he heard voices coming from the hallway, Mrs. Quinn and Caroline, unless his memory failed him. This was no time for the servant to be opening the door and drawing attention to the library. A surreptitious look at the girl caused his eyebrows to rise. She had not moved so much as a muscle that he could see, and she looked rather horrified, like a rabbit frozen in the light from a coach lamp. Why would a housemaid be frightened of her employer's mere voice in the hallway? Not that he didn't agree that the piercing tones of Bettina Quinn could turn the knees of the sovereign himself to jelly.

"I take it my browsing will not disturb your cleaning?" he remarked negligently, telling himself he was putting the girl at her ease, but knowing he was really simply stalling his exit. It was likely she was a local girl, hired on since the Quinns had arrived. Perhaps she was new to service and uncertain of her duties.

Oddly enough, the girl made no reply, and Julian turned a questioning stare on her. Not that he cared a fig for the smooth running of Mrs. Quinn's Bath establishment, but this poor girl wouldn't last long in the talons of the Quinn family if she couldn't manage a civil reply to a bland and kindly inquiry from a guest.

Now she stared at him, with a most peculiar expression on her face. "Cleaning?" she stammered finally. "Yes, sir, I mean, no, sir, I mean . . ." She broke off, and Julian had the oddest feeling that she was trying very hard not to laugh,

"Have I said something amusing?" he asked, coolly. He did not consider himself an overly haughty man, by any means; still, he was not used to being the butt of humor for the household staff.

"No, sir, not at all, sir," she stammered again, scrambling down from her perch, and this time, though she averted her gaze and the be-webbed mobcap hid her face, he was quite certain she was nigh to choking to death on stifled laughter.

"Drat!" she muttered as she reached the floor and lurched precariously, grabbing for the ladder before she took a tumble.

Drat? He could not recall ever having heard a servant swear in his presence, unless one counted his father's stable master who had kindly taught Julian, by example, everything the lad would ever need to know about the finer art of shocking language.

"My foot seems to be asleep. Can't quite get it to hold my weight yet," the girl said, grinning at him, mobcap askew, nose black, cobwebs drifting over one eye. It would be interesting to know just how long this impertinent baggage lasted, he thought. A matter of moments, he reckoned, once the punctilious and exacting Mrs.

Quinn caught her first glimpse of the cheeky chit.

He watched, vastly amused, as she tested her foot, wincing, at the pins and needles.

"Are they gone yet?" she asked, dropping her voice to a conspiratorial whisper.

"I believe they are safely ensconced in the drawing room," he replied, choosing not to affect ignorance.

"Good," she replied, hobbling quickly for the door.

"Excuse me." He stopped her, just shy of her goal.

She turned with a questioning look on her face, and not so much as a "yes, sir?" Oh, the girl would be out in the alleyway by midafternoon, no doubt about it. "You forgot to curtsy," he said, but did not manage to keep the smile from his face.

"I did, didn't I?" she retorted, with a matching grin, then slipped from the door with no bend of the knee.

She very kindly closed it and he stared after her, bemused and amused. He had never been one to take off after female servants—considered it unkind to toy with their feelings and all that. But if ever there was one with some spirit to her, and a flash of devilment in her eye, she was it. Too bad he'd never see her again. He was unlikely to darken this doorway any time in the near future and she was likely to be turned off with no reference. Any minute now. Still, this funny housemaid had offered him the best entertainment he was likely to have all day.

He continued his perusal of the library shelves, only half noting the tomes in front of him, the other half of his attention straining to hear approaching voices, not that he'd be able to lose himself further at this point. Coward that he was, he had already noted the room offered no concealment. He paused at the ladder, noting that the book the girl had been cleaning lay open on the top where she had placed it before scrambling down. Curiosity got the better of him and he reached for it. Something tumbled from the volume, hitting him on the toe of his well-polished black boots.

It was a pair of spectacles, obviously dislodged from its perch on the open book. Had Mrs. Quinn actually been reading this . . . what was it? Ah, a botanical treatise, well done by the looks of it, beautifully illustrated. He was about to lay the spectacles on the small table nearest him but as he set them down they seemed to stick rather unpleasantly to his fingers. Careful perusal through his own lenses revealed why. There were cobwebs caught all across one frame. Odd, that. Had the girl been wearing them? He was not sure he'd ever seen a housemaid in spectacles—no real need to go to the expense, after all. For no reason he could think of, he tucked the glasses into his waistcoat pocket with a smile, then turned back to the books.

"So this is where you've gone to ground, sir!" boomed the voice of Bettina Quinn, as the door blew inward, bouncing off the wall beside it. He forced himself not to cringe at the onslaught, instead turning with a great display of sangfroid.

"Mrs. Quinn. How wonderful it is to see you again," he lied, making an exaggerated leg and rising with a vicious smile. Might as well show the lioness his teeth. "Splendid library," he went on, with an affected glance about him. "I am sure you and Caroline will derive a great deal of pleasure from these learned tomes."

"Caroline is far too busy to indulge in such pointless pursuits, sir," she replied with a dismissive glance at the clearly offensive books. "I'm sure we can leave that sort of thing to the bluestockings. We are in the drawing room, sir," she announced, turning her back to him and parading from the room.

So now he was a lapdog, trained to trot at the heels of his mistress? No, worse. A toff of the *ton*, who must, perforce, allow impeccable manners to rule his every movement. Still, like a foot-scuffing, pouting child, he allowed himself a moment's defiance, petty to be sure, but all the sweeter for that, and perused the bookshelves once again. Judging a sufficient amount of time had elapsed that he could not, precisely, be mistaken for a lapdog, he quit the room, throwing a rather longing glance behind him. There had been a treatise on modern agricultural theory that he would have loved to borrow from anyone except Mrs. Quinn. No point in creating further obligation.

In the drawing room, Caroline graced the fussy, brocaded settee that Edgar had apparently ceded to her. Interesting, although perhaps not surprising, that Caroline chose to sit with her back to the windows. Daylight lit her golden hair, but left her face in artful, sculpted shadow. She looked, if anything, more beautiful than she had on her coming out some three years ago, when Julian had fallen, if only briefly, for her splendor. She turned her face just slightly toward him as he entered the room and his breath caught at its perfection, features sleek and elegant, her appraisal cool and distant. As he, himself, had grown older, he had learned to appreciate a somewhat more mature beauty. They seemed less dewy-eyed and silly somehow, or, perhaps, he was merely hoping the ladies felt the same way about him.

Caroline gave him the slightest inclination of the head, less than she might the ostler at an inn, and appeared to barely notice his bow and greeting. Just as well, he was thinking to himself, when he caught the smirk on Edgar's face. Then he forgot them both as he noted the look of calculation that had entered the eyes of Bettina Quinn.

Damned if he couldn't feel the trap closing around him!

"We are so fortunate that our dear Miss Quinn has

chosen to grace us with her presence here in Bath, are we not, Julian?" said Edgar, facing enough away from both the ladies to allow a wicked gleam in his eye. "She has been the toast of any number of London Seasons, as I'm sure you know," he went on cruelly.

Did Julian imagine it or did a brief flash of anger flare in Caroline's eyes? Surely the girl couldn't be upset by such an insignificant little jab. She'd been made of stronger stuff a few years ago. But if Caroline stifled her own reaction, Bettina Quinn did not bother. Her eyes narrowed and two spots of red burned high on her cheeks. Julian knew enough of Edgar to know that the man never minded drawing battle lines, the earlier in the Season, the better, to insure a continuing line of entertainment for himself and his circle.

So Caroline was to be Edgar's victim this year? It hardly seemed fair, particularly since *on dit* had it that Caroline had turned away many a smitten swain. She was hardly a wallflower and couldn't be more than—what? Twenty-one, perhaps? Twenty-two? No spinster surely. Julian should have been able to sit back and watch with amusement, betting on Caroline to best Edgar at his own game. Edgar was a diffident sort of opponent, with no real malice in him, just a bored, small man with not much else to do. Indeed, Julian wouldn't have tolerated him at all, but that they had been friends since school days, when the larger and more popular Julian had taken the boy under his wing and made a place for him in the rigid school hierarchy. But now, seeing that Caroline looked slightly pale, Julian was having second thoughts. Women were rather unpredictable. And so vulnerable, when all was said and done. In the marriage mart, for all that a likely looking, well-heeled girl could afford to be choosy, there was no real equality. She had to wait to be asked, after all. And at a certain point, never visible until one had crossed it, it was simply too late. . . .

"I understand you have broken any number of hearts, Miss Quinn, since you made off with mine. Not that any of us should presume so much . . ." He let the pretty compliment trail off, like the meaningless silliness it was.

"My Caroline can afford to wait for a man worthy of her, Mr. Thorpe, as everyone knows," Mrs. Quinn put in, smiling at Julian in a way to make his flesh crawl. His remark had also earned a smile from Caroline, languid and deep, her full pink lips parting just slightly.

"And where, may I ask, is your lovely cousin-from-the-country?" asked Edgar, clearly unwilling to let things deteriorate into a mere civilized social call.

The smile disappeared from Caroline's lips with the speed of a candle being blown out, and her eyes went cold. It seemed the cousin was already a thorn in the lovely flesh of Miss Quinn.

"Our dear Cousin Elspeth is . . . indisposed at present," Caroline offered, with not even the affect of concern. "It seems the much vaunted country constitution is not all it is made out to be. A journey of short duration and the woman is prostrate." She wafted her hand across her eyes in an affectation of faintness.

"Woman, you say? Is she so very old then?" asked Edgar, catching the scent of fresh prey. Julian shot him a dark look that went unheeded by all save Wesley Ames, who chewed on his lip to keep from grinning.

"Certainly, one would not say 'old,' Mr. Randall," put in Bettina Quinn, but she had taken on that kindly tone, the one used when speaking of the aged and infirm, and she let the remark hang, tempting all to wonder exactly what one would say. "I am sure when the . . . girl"—there was just enough emphasis to make the point—"recovers from her journey she will make for delightful company. She is frightfully well read, you know."

Well, now there was a death sentence pronounced, as effectively as ever heard in the Inns of Court. Even Edgar seemed too taken aback to speak, a condition lasting less than a moment, however.

"I can't tell you how much I look forward to making her acquaintance," he finally remarked, and this time he let everyone see the wicked gleam. Caroline's answering, indolent smile had more of devil than angel in it this time.

The rest of the visit, although short by the clock, seemed interminable to Julian. Caroline continued to bestow that private smile on him. No mistaking the invitation in it. He did find that she still possessed a certain allure, but then, so had the sirens who tried to lure Ulysses' men to their doom. At last, Edgar seemed to feel he had wrung as much fun as he could from the visit, and he rose to begin the adieux. Caroline held Julian's proffered hand just an instant too long, giving him a deep smile straight into his eyes. Mrs. Quinn was less subtle, her look of appraisal similar to those cast at the finer cattle offered at Tattersall's. Julian had rarely felt so relieved to make an exit and vowed to give the Quinn household a wide berth in the future. Except for one small bit of business. He patted his pocket to make sure the saucy maid's spectacles remained tucked discreetly away. He'd send them around with a note to the butler. If the girl got the sack, as he was quite sure she would at any time now, perhaps he could find her employment elsewhere. Impertinent baggage that she was, she should not be thrown into the street.

Chapter Three

"That décolletage is simply indecent on Elspeth, Mama," Caroline snapped loudly, shattering the elegant hush in the private fitting room at the shop of the finest dressmaker on Milsom Street. "She has a long neck and it gives the appearance of entirely too much bosom showing." Caroline stood in the center of her own circle of frantic activity with no fewer than three assistants fussing about her, but couldn't seem to keep her eyes from straying jealously to Elspeth's modest corner of the fitting salon.

Aunt Bettina nodded her vague agreement in the direction of the modiste's assistant who now looked confused, but who set about dutifully repinning the neckline, up several inches. Not that Elspeth minded. She was certainly not comfortable with the latest mode. The remark did seem odd, however, coming from Caroline, whose décolletage left nothing but the tiniest pink detail to the imagination. Satisfied now, at least for the moment, Caroline turned her attention back to her own fitting. She was draped in a beautiful amber confection that, even half-finished, was finer than anything Elspeth ever hoped to own.

"Mama, this color is simply dreadful on me. Makes me look three days dead. I will not wear it!" Caroline declared, in high dudgeon. Actually, Elspeth thought it rather did bring out a sallow cast in Caroline's complexion, but she had learned quickly during her short stay in Bath to keep her opinion to herself.

"The color is all the crack, Caroline," said Aunt Bettina, showing, as usual, a great deal more patience with Caroline than she did with anyone else. "Her Grace wore it last night at the musicale, if you will recall."

"Her Grace is forty years old, Mama . . . more, most like! She already looks three days dead! And anyway, it doesn't fit at all. You call yourself a modiste?" She turned her temper on the hapless dressmaker, who immediately assumed the properly abashed expression.

"It was cut precisely to Miss Quinn's excellent figure," the modiste demurred, "but if Madame would like, I shall refit it myself." She directed her remarks to Aunt Bettina, aware, obviously, that tangling with Caroline was not worth the effort.

"Caroline, the dress fits perfectly, and it's not a ball gown anyway," her mother snapped, her patience obviously wearing thin. "Take it off and put on the rose one."

Elspeth watched as the offending tawny silk confection was slipped over Caroline's blonde head and the magnificent rose gown took its place. This fitting had lasted several hours so far, and didn't appear to be nearly over, to judge from the pile of clothing still left, untried, on the chair nearest Caroline.

Elspeth cast a surreptitious glance over to the chair that held her small pile. Four dresses, two for day, two for evening, modest in fit, modest in quality. They were simple in design, but Elspeth thought them all the more elegant for it, with their clean lines, cut precisely to her figure. And if the colors, a dove gray and dark green for the day dresses, and a deep blue and dark violet for evening, were more favored by the older ladies, well, then they would suit her perfectly. She had no wish to be accused of being "mutton dressed as lamb." Of course, they would last her well into the years to come, and no matter how simple these gowns might be here in the center of the beau monde, they were magnificent compared with what she was used to, or apt to see at home.

"Is this one more to your liking, mademoiselle?" asked the modiste in her questionable French accent. "It's better," Caroline snapped, but her eyes held a haughty approval as she beheld herself in the large cheval glass tilted just so for mademoiselle's pleasure. Elspeth made do with a smaller glass attached to the wall some distance away, but it was good enough for her.

The modiste glanced, wisely, at Bettina, who nodded her approval, then the little dressmaker turned her attention in earnest to the precise measuring of the hem that puddled, unfinished, on the floor. "These shoes, the heels are of the same height as those you will order to match the dress, mademoiselle?" she asked.

"Of course they are," Caroline snapped. "This isn't the first time I've ever come for a fitting." Obviously realizing her own mistake in calling attention to the number of Seasons she'd stood in fitting salons, she flushed a dull, furious crimson. "Here, girl, watch those pins," she hissed, kicking out at the assistant, who couldn't have been more than ten years old, crouching at her feet. Elspeth turned away, mouth thinning, unable to watch further. Her cousin, she had noticed over the last few days, had a nasty streak, and servants, who had no ability to fight back, were frequently her target.

"This needs more lace at the sleeve, Mama," Caroline declared. "I swear this dress will have the entire Assembly Room asleep and snoring within ten minutes of my entrance!"

Elspeth forced herself to stifle a laugh and wound up turning the resulting snort into a vague sort of cough. The dress already looked like a platter of iced cakes, bedecked with more lace than most ladies wore in a lifetime. Indeed, Elspeth's dresses had little lace at all. She hadn't noticed Caroline objecting to the lack there, nor did she. But even as Caroline spoke, one of the assistants unfurled yard after yard of expensive Belgian lace, holding it up here and there against Caroline's dress for her approval. The lace was quite beautiful and Elspeth longed to put on her spectacles and take a closer look. But the dratted things had disappeared just yesterday and she could not for all the world recall when she had had them last. Caroline had sniffed that the loss was negligible, a good thing in fact, if, as she had so tactfully put it, Elspeth cared to make any sort of positive impression at all.

Elspeth longed to order a new pair—she was quite blind without them—but spectacles were not inexpensive and she dared not charge them to her aunt's account, nor could she afford to pay for them herself. Anyway, surely the things would turn up on their own, although if she found that Harry had had anything to do with their mysterious disappearance, he might find himself on the receiving end of the spanking she had so often threatened to give him.

In the center of the room, the modiste and Aunt Bettina conferred in low murmurs, broken by the occasional shrill remark from Caroline, criticizing this, that or the other thing about the dresses. Elspeth stood in her quiet corner, where the little assistant had nearly finished repinning her neckline. The voices stilled and

Aunt Bettina strode purposefully over to Elspeth, eyeing the work in progress carefully. The modiste hurried forward, tape measure flapping behind her. "Would Madame care for lace at the neckline here?" she asked, gesturing at Elspeth's bosom, a distant hope in her tone.

"No. Can't have her looking as if we're disguising her age with schoolgirl fripperies," Aunt Bettina replied. She missed the instantly stifled flare of incredulity in the modiste's eyes, but Elspeth did not. There weren't many months between her birth and Caroline's, and the point was not lost on the modiste, who probably could tell some interesting stories, were she inclined to put an end to her business. It was more likely that Aunt Bettina's decision lay with the price of lace rather than the age of the wearer. Elspeth had learned over the past few days that while her aunt's public demeanor suggested that money was no object, behind the scenes she could pinch a penny till it melted into a lump of copper in her tight fist.

"This gown is quite suitable for you as it is, don't you agree, Elspeth?" asked her aunt coolly.

"Indeed, Aunt. It is splendid. These are quite the finest gowns I've ever worn," Elspeth replied truthfully and with good grace. Not that she was really being asked for her opinion. Elspeth knew well enough not to find anything to criticize. "I am extremely grateful to you, ma'am," she went on, "for your generosity to us." That, too, was the truth.

"Quite so, Elspeth," replied her aunt, accepting her niece's thanks with a condescending equanimity. "Your modesty does you credit. Of course, your dear uncle would have wished that we see to your coming out, since your poor father couldn't provide the means."

Elspeth turned her face toward the mirror that hung on a distant wall, so that her aunt would not see the anger in her eyes. Her father had provided his family with everything necessary to their well-being and good spirits, and had done so with love in his generous heart. Neither her father nor dear Uncle Harry would have approved of Bettina's plan to dress Elspeth like a spinster and stand her next to her be-plumed cousin all Season, for contrast.

"I still do not see why more of my old gowns weren't recut for Elspeth, Mama." Caroline seemed never able to refrain from seizing the attention whenever her mother was engaged with Elspeth. "The gowns were quite suitable, really." Elspeth refrained from reminding Caroline that she, herself, had nixed most of her elegant cast-offs as "too young" for Elspeth. Or the wrong fit. Or too small. Or the wrong color. Or . . . there had been so many reasons her cousin had found to deny Elspeth the glory of her old yet wonderful gowns that Elspeth could not remember them all. One or two of the plainer, over-worn day dresses had been grudgingly approved, but only just.

"Well, done is done, Caroline. Elspeth must, after all . . ." her mother began.

"Mama! This gown won't do at all!" screeched Caroline from the center of the room, obviously loath to give up attention to Elspeth even for a moment.

"What is it, darling?" asked her mother, moving quickly to her side, her niece forgotten for now.

"Shall we try on the blue gown now, miss?" asked the modiste's assistant, in an almost-whisper.

"Yes, thank you," replied Elspeth, in spite of Caroline's haughty reminder of the day before that stooping to thank a servant was a blatant exhibition of one's own lack of stature. In the center of the room, Caroline was finding fault after fault with what looked to Elspeth's admittedly untrained eyes to be the most exquisite gown ever made. Made of a shimmering ice-blue satin, the slim lines of Caroline's evening dress were picked out in tiny seed pearls, iridescent and shimmering, the fabric falling in graceful folds to the floor. Elspeth had seen the slippers that had been ordered for this gown, a perfect match of satin and seed pearl design. Indeed, Caroline had ordered a different pair of slippers for every gown, each in matching material, with higher heels for the evening. Caroline was rather petite in height and was clearly annoyed that Elspeth topped her by several inches. Elspeth's two new pairs of slippers, one for day wear and one for evening, were low in the heels; Caroline insisted that her cousin was not used to higher heels and would likely trip and fall, embarrassing them all to death during the dancing. Elspeth rather thought the decision had more to do with evening out their height, but she held her tongue. Actually, she didn't much fancy tottering about on stilts. It didn't look comfortable.

The little assistant swept the midnight blue satin over Elspeth's head. Filtered sunlight danced through the loosely basted seams and she inhaled the heady, exciting scent of new material, feeling the soft satin slip smooth and cool over her skin.

Her head peeped through the top just in time to see Caroline rip the front off her own gown with a howl of fury. The modiste's lips thinned, but smoothed in an instant to the ever-present accommodating smile.

"Now, darling, we can always make adjustments," Aunt Bettina said, laying a restraining hand on her daughter's fingers. "No need to spoil the fabric," she went on, no doubt calculating the cost of the extra yardage that would now appear on her account.

"It makes me look like a pig!" Caroline spat. "A feed bag would be more attractive!" The modiste snapped her fingers—Elspeth could have sworn even the finger snapping had a sort of Gallic flavor—and a flurry of activity commenced around Caroline, assistants cringing and measuring and fiddling and murmuring soothing compliments.

"Now, miss, what do you think?" Elspeth's own little assistant said close to her ear, this time in a true whisper. Elspeth tore her eyes from her furious cousin and glanced at her reflection in the distant mirror.

"Oooh," she murmured softly, as her eyes drank in the sight of the exquisite blue satin catching the sunlight and reflecting it in a thousand delightful sparkles. The fit was perfect, and the long, elegantly simple lines, sublime. And if the neckline was a trifle too low, a small piece, obviously a scrap, of Belgian lace peeped fetchingly from the décolletage, hiding the swell of Elspeth's white bosom. Never had there been such a dress.

From the center of the room, Elspeth could see Caroline eyeing her cousin jealously, no doubt making sure Elspeth's gown did not eclipse her own. But the sun had broken through the clouds and was now in her eyes, and Elspeth must appear to her in silhouette, dark and uninspiring. No, nothing to worry about there. Elspeth could see the satisfaction register in her cousin's eyes as, with a smug, self-involved sort of smile, she turned her attention back to her own gown, an emerald silk, now being pinned and repinned, ruched and laced by a swarm of busy, terrified seamstresses.

But in her own corner, the satin cool and soft against her skin, Elspeth's smile was one of pure, private pleasure.

Chapter Four

"If you little brats so much as sneeze, I'll have the skin off both of you!" Caroline hissed, sotto voce. The party of varied Quinns drew near to their first entrance of the Season at the much famed Pump Room. Elspeth cast a glance at her brother, telling him with her reassuring smile that he needn't really fear a skinning from his cousin. Or so she fervently hoped. Harry was holding his own so far with Roderick, but perhaps just barely. The older cousin was enough older and enough larger, and certainly enough of a bully, that Harry had to exercise all his wits to stay one step ahead of disaster.

Then the perils of her little brother were forgotten. Elspeth barely suppressed a gasp as they entered through the large double doors. She was quite sure she had never been in such a large room in all of her life. And so magnificent!

"Don't gawk so, Elspeth," hissed Caroline. "People will think you're a perfect fool."

"But it is so remarkable, Caroline!" Elspeth replied, too awed and excited to register her cousin's insult. "I've never seen anything so grand in my entire life!"

"No doubt. But, then you'll never see St. James. This is paltry compared to the palace."

"Oh, I wouldn't think I'd ever need to see anything more wonderful than this," Elspeth declared, determined not to let her cousin's jabs diminish the glory of this afternoon. "I must say," she went on, "I do not know how one would go about constructing a room with a ceiling so high. I cannot see what supports all the weight."

"Why on earth would anyone care about how a ceiling is supported?" asked Caroline, not bothering to hide the irritation in her voice. "Leave that sort of speculation to the architects. That is not what we are here for."

"What *are* we here for?" asked Harry, eying his surroundings with less wonder than his sister, but with more hope, no doubt searching for something to eat.

"Mama, keep the brats away," hissed Caroline, giving Roderick's ear a twist. "You promised they would leave us alone."

"Roderick, Harry, come here to me this instant!"ordered Aunt Bettina. Harry hurried over to her, but Roderick, who had skittered away from his sister's sharp fingers, took his time, eying his surroundings with a slow, deliberate arrogance.

"I explained to you both quite clearly before we left home," Aunt Bettina began in a low but determined hiss, as soon as Roderick ambled over to her. "You are to be seen and not heard, speak only when spoken to, and keep to the rear of the girls at all times. Do not put yourselves forward. You are here only to learn genteel behavior. Neither of you has a father to emulate, so you must pick up the finer points of proper deportment where you can. Now, is that clear?"

"Yes, Aunt," Harry said, while Roderick mumbled something, looking sullen.

Elspeth felt a pang at her aunt's words. Perhaps it had been unwise to allow Harry to learn proper deportment from his ill-behaved cousin and these precious fops who minced now about the room, preening and posturing. As if to underscore the point, two peacocks bore down on Caroline, cooing delight at seeing her again. It was all Elspeth could do not to gape in earnest at their attire. Colors like that should not be placed near one another.

"Ah, Miss Quinn, so you are here in Bath to delight our very souls! What luck for us, eh, Robert? The very toast of London, I declare!" one of the peacocks cooed as he made an exaggerated leg.

"The most beautiful demoiselle of this and every Season, Thomas," lisped Robert, delivering Caroline's delicate white hand to his equally delicate pink lips. Caroline gave a cool smile, but Elspeth saw Aunt Bettina's lips thin at Robert's remark. My, but she was touchy about Caroline's Seasons.

"Do introduce us to the vision at your side, Caroline," said Thomas, turning his simper in Elspeth's direction. "I had heard you'd imported a cousin from the country, but surely there cannot be two such lovely ladies in one family? Wouldn't be fair of nature at all, now would it, considering how short-changed some families can be in that regard."

"Oh, that's naughty, Thomas," tittered Robert. "Darling," he cooed to Caroline, "have you seen Lady Hermione's daughter? A spotted cow, I declare. Quite terrifying to behold. I should lock her away in the country forever were I Lady Hermione."

"Were you Lady Hermione, dear boy, she'd have much better taste in clothes." Thomas and Robert tittered brightly at each other, while Elspeth stood, forgotten in mid-introduction. It was most unfortunate that just as the young fops belatedly turned their attention to the country cousin, Harry, dutifully standing to the rear of the cozy group, chose to express his opinion of the repartee, discreetly to be sure, miming sticking his finger down his throat and making gagging gestures with eyes crossed.

Roderick, equally unfortunately, caught the movement, and chose to make his own comment on Harry's crass behavior. Out of the corner of her eye Elspeth saw the older boy draw back his booted foot and land a hard kick on her brother's shin. A howl of outrage escaped the smaller boy, to be met with shocked silence from what seemed to be the entire assemblage.

The peacocks managed to look appalled and amused all at once, but Caroline's face was suffused with purple rage. As the one closest to Harry, she grabbed his ear and gave it a vicious twist. The boy stifled a cry that turned into a whimper. It was the look of smug satisfaction on Roderick's face that moved Elspeth to action. "You're hurting him, Caroline," she began, raising her voice slightly to compensate for the renewed babble that filled the cavernous room. She rather feared that the conversation now revolved around their own small tableau.

Caroline turned a furious glare on Elspeth, but she did not relinquish her sharp, pinching hold on Harry's poor ear. Harry, bless his stalwart little heart, was biting his lips hard, but Elspeth could see tears of pain and anger standing in his brown eyes. It was enough! "Caroline, please unhand my brother. He cried out when Roderick kicked him in the shin. While we may deplore the conduct of both boys, the one is at least as much to blame as the other."

"I never did! No such thing!" Roderick cried, all outraged innocence.

Caroline's look of haughty incredulity was replaced

by one of triumph. "Elspeth," she cooed, voice dripping malice, "Your brother has clearly been ill-raised. He is not fit to be seen in polite company. I saw no such kick from my brother."

"Well, I must say I did see the kick, my dear Miss Quinn," said a new voice. All turned to see a gentleman bearing down on the little group. Elspeth narrowed her eyes slightly, trying to resolve the blur into a face. There was something quite familiar about the voice.

"I beg your pardon?" replied Caroline, her look of anger replaced quickly by one of embarrassment.

"Delighted to see you again, Miss Quinn," said the gentleman, reaching for a hand not extended to meet his; Caroline's fingers were still twisted around Harry's ear. Belatedly she let go of Harry and offered her hand. The gentleman brought it to his lips, a mechanical gesture, thought Elspeth, noting how his eyes strayed to Harry's ear, even as he bent over Caroline's slender fingers. Forgotten for the moment, Elspeth moved over to Harry, noticing his ear was reddened and already swelling. She placed a protective arm about his shoulder, hoping he'd take some comfort from her presence, or, at least, hold his demeanor.

"Now, Roderick, isn't it?" said the gentleman, turning an appraising stare on the young man. "A gentleman never allows another gentleman to suffer for his own misdeeds. I'm sure you have something to say to this young man?"

Roderick was purple, his hands fisted at his sides. "I'm sorry," came a dark mutter, so low as to be almost indistinguishable.

"Sorry for what, Roderick?" the gentleman went on relentlessly.

"Sorry I kicked him," the boy said through clenched teeth.

Caroline turned a glare on her brother that promised

dire punishment in the immediate future. Roderick, obviously pushed past all endurance, stuck his tongue out at Harry and took to his heels, dodging by the narrowest of margins an elderly lady swaying over her cane. "Oh, dear, please do excuse me!" said Aunt Bettina as she moved quickly after Roderick.

"Well, I was going to mention that a decent handshake is de rigueur after a disagreement between gentlemen, but I suppose that lesson can wait until our next meeting," said the gentleman, turning a smiling face upon the ladies.

Caroline nodded coolly, having regained her composure, but Elspeth, her arm still around the hapless Harry, smiled back. The gentleman still seemed familiar to her, but since she knew no one in Bath save her aunt and cousins, it must be a trick of resemblance.

There was a moment of awkward silence. The peacocks cast their glances rather desperately about the room, no doubt looking for someone with whom to share the amusing little scene just completed.

"My dear Miss Quinn, since your mother has been forced from us, perhaps you could make the introductions?" said the gentleman.

"My elder cousin, Elspeth Quinn, from Shropshire, and her brother, Harry," Caroline offered, a tad too offhand to be considered gracious. "May I present Mr. Julian Thorpe?"

"Delighted, Miss Quinn," responded Mr. Thorpe, extending his hand with a smile that reached deep into his very blue eyes.

For a split second Elspeth's thoughts deserted her utterly; then in confusion she put out her hand to meet his, a gauche, awkward movement. He took her hand with a practiced ease, bringing it smoothly to his lips. But where the kiss he'd bestowed on Caroline's delicate hand had been perfunctory, now he met Elspeth's gaze directly, with a slightly quizzical expression, as if he were trying to puzzle something out.

"And her brother, Harry," Caroline interjected quickly.

"Oh, Caroline, do look!" shrieked one of the peacocks. "It's Miss Jessie Hicks, I declare. How she can show her face after being jilted last year is a wonder to me. We simply must go over and gloat, darling!" With the peacocks on either side of her, arm in arm, Caroline was hustled away, casting one look of veiled annoyance over her shoulder at Elspeth.

"Well, I believe we've been deserted, Miss Quinn. Would you care to take the famed waters of Bath? I have it on good authority that you'll never taste anything quite so ghastly in your life. I recommend the punch myself," Mr. Thorpe finished, offering Elspeth his arm.

Elspeth could feel a flush creeping up her cheeks. At this distance she could make out enough of his face to know that Mr. Thorpe was quite decidedly the handsomest man in the room, far too handsome for the likes of the nearly impoverished Elspeth Quinn from Shropshire. She was acutely aware that she was the "leavings" at this point, with a little brother to boot. What could the gentleman do but politely escort her for punch? And what could she do but politely accept? To decline would leave them standing, staring awkwardly at each other. Well, she would allow him a gracious escape as soon as it was feasible. Her heart pounding in her ears so loudly she feared it might echo throughout the cavernous chamber, she placed her hand as lightly as she could manage on his arm, annoyed with herself when she felt her fingers trembling. He will think me a fool as well as a country bumpkin, she thought to herself, but he smiled at her, a nice sort of smile that reached his eyes, no glittering malice in it. She'd almost forgotten what a real smile looked like, in these last few days with none but cousin and aunt to keep her company.

"Come along, Harry," said Mr. Thorpe, guiding Elspeth away, "and mind, no more gagging gestures at the local fauna. What a gentleman thinks and what he allows the world to know he is thinking are two entirely separate things."

Harry had the grace to look abashed, but Elspeth noticed something else in his eyes when he looked at Mr. Thorpe, something suspiciously like hero worship. Well, the boy could do worse when picking a mentor, thought Elspeth with a glance around the room. Mr. Thorpe, aside from being the handsomest man here, was also the only one, seemingly, who had a sense of dignified restraint when it came to attire. His breeches were a tasteful dun in color, and if they were tight, they were no more so, and possibly a bit less, than those of any other gentleman in the room, including a large number whose silhouettes resembled nothing so much as large, misshapen melons. His waistcoat, of a deep green silk, embroidered with fine and intricate stitching in the same dark color, was worn with a pristine white shirt, and a neckcloth tied with a confounding intricacy. His frock coat was of black superfine, and to Elspeth's admittedly untrained eye, it looked exceedingly well cut, fitting his broad shoulders without so much as a pucker of protest. In short, although his costume was certainly all the crack, an expression she had heard earlier today, he bore none of the signs of a hysterical preoccupation with just how many clashing colors he could drape over his form.

The punch bowl was at quite some distance across the room, in a windowed alcove that gave out over the city and the roof of the Baths terraced below. Elspeth could not quite shake the impression that their trio was collecting quite a few stares along the way, and some downright gawking. It was an effort to keep her expression cool and serene, feeling as she did the heat from her bright pink face. She was keenly aware that she and Mr. Thorpe made an incongruous pair, the spinster from the country and a dashing toff of the *ton*.

She was under no illusions about her own appearance. Her dress was, to her own eyes, quite lovely, a dove gray silk that shifted color when it caught the light. Beautifully cut and stitched, it was quite truly the finest dress she had ever owned. But it was, nonetheless, no match for the riotous colors, flounces, and fussiness, that marked the gowns of the other ladies in the room. Indeed, even many of the older ladies might find themselves all but invisible in a garden of spring flowers. Elspeth cast a surreptitious glance about the room and noted, as she had suspected, that only the most elderly of dowagers, presiding in imperious splendor over their gold-tipped canes, wore subdued dark colors. Now she was quite determined to relieve the kind Mr. Thorpe of his embarrassing burden.

"Your punch, Miss Quinn," he said, proffering a cut-glass cup, brimming with something hideously pink. "And, Harry, I believe you'll find this sweet enough." Julian Thorpe handed a cup to Harry, who took it eagerly. The boy downed it in one gulp, a minor transgression Elspeth noted for later discussion. The pink mustache, however, could not wait. As surreptitiously as possible she fetched a handkerchief from where it perched up a sleeve and gave him a quick wipe. He made quite a face but stood still during the process, thank heaven.

Mr. Thorpe watched her with a faint smile on his face. He hadn't taken a punch cup for himself, Elspeth noted. All the easier to take his leave, she supposed, with no necessity to stand around and make polite conversation while sipping the stuff. Now, how to let him know that his obligation to the Lesser Quinns was mercifully at an end? "My brother and I thank you for your kindness, Mr. Thorpe," Elspeth said, a little tentatively, tucking the much-mended handkerchief back in her sleeve. No doubt he could take that for his cue to bow gallantly and beat a hasty retreat.

"No kindness, surely, Miss Quinn," he returned. He still stared at her with a slightly puzzled expression, as if he were not quite sure who she was.

"You, uh, you needn't . . ." Elspeth began and then tapered off, too embarrassed to continue. In all her upbringing, she had never found it necessary to chase off a handsome man. There was simply no expression in her meager social repertoire that would do for such an occasion.

"I needn't what, Miss Quinn?" he asked, and now she could swear she saw a hint of amusement in his wonderful blue eyes.

"I mean, uh, that is . . ." Drat! Why had she got into this?

"Yes?" he went on. This Mr. Julian Thorpe had a relentless quality to him, she was noticing. Most unbecoming in a true gentleman.

"You needn't stay with us, Mr. Thorpe!" she finally blurted out, then stopped, face red.

"Oh dear. Is my company offensive to you, Miss Quinn?" he asked, and now she would swear he was trying not to laugh.

"No, certainly not, sir!" she stammered, wishing the floor would open up and swallow her whole. It was clear she would simply not be able to hold her own among the *ton*. In one conversation with one gentleman, she had already managed to make a perfect fool of herself, and offend him as well. He continued to gaze at her, waiting, no doubt, for her to finish answering the question. Drat! Drat! Drat! "Your company is most pleasant, sir. I simply thought you might rather talk with more interesting people, than be stuck here with us." There! He insisted on hearing it!

"I see," he said. "So am I to take it that you know yourself to be exceedingly dull company, Miss Quinn, or have you perhaps concluded that I am a shallow sort who must be riotously entertained at all times?"

"Not at all! That is . . . oh, dear—" She forced herself to meet his eye and found he was no longer even pretending not to be amused. "Now you're making sport of me, Mr. Thorpe," she said, her indignation rising. How was she to know how to behave in this confounded society? No one ever said anything directly. Everything was veiled, or dropped by innuendo. Did no one speak his or her mind here?

"I am, am I not," he responded. "And that, Harry," he said, turning to the boy who had been looking, anxious and befuddled, from one to the other, "is something a gentleman should never do to a lady."

"What?" asked Harry, rather desperately, clearly out of his depth here.

"I have entertained myself at your lovely sister's expense. She was obviously trying to spare me the onerous chore of looking after her for a few moments and I have behaved like a churl."

"You have?" squeaked Harry, clearly at a loss.

"You'll figure it out someday, my boy," replied Mr. Thorpe. "And now, Miss Quinn, how may I make amends?"

"Oh, do go away, sir!" she sputtered. "Harry and I have no need of a keeper." Now that really was churlish, she chided herself. Bath no longer seemed like such an exciting adventure. Maybe country girls should just keep to the country and not make spectacles of themselves. Speaking of which, she longed to know where her eyeglasses were. Julian Thorpe's face was clear enough for conversation but she would so love a truly focused image. Now she could almost swear they had met before. There was something about his smile. . . .

"Left alone to the tender mercies of your cousins, I suspect you do need a keeper. May I?" he asked, reaching for her cup before she had a chance to answer. "You're about to spill it on your lovely dress."

"Oh, drat!" she said, then bit her lip in horror, looking around quickly to see who might have overheard her intemperate speech. An elderly lady making her way inexorably toward the refreshments, teetering precariously over her cane, gave Elspeth a thin-lipped scowl. Gauche, awkward, stammering—what a prize fool she was turning out to be. If she ever got safely back to Weston-under-Lizard she vowed never to go so far as the next village. And was he making fun of her plain attire? Elspeth peered carefully into his face, squinting just the least bit. She didn't think so, but so far she wasn't having much luck with figuring out how these toffs entertained themselves.

"Drat?" he said. "Now I'm sure I recently heard . . . Pardon my terribly trite line, but haven't we met before?"

"No, no, it couldn't be, sir," she answered. "I've only been in Bath a few days and today is my first outing. I've met no one, sir."

He peered carefully and now he was squinting at her. "No, I'm quite sure of it. You've been at Mrs. Quinn's, you say?"

"Indeed," was her dismissive response.

"You said you met a toff in the library a few days ago, El," Harry said helpfully.

Two pairs of eyes turned on the boy, then on each other, realization dawning.

"You were cleaning the library."

"I was not! You were hiding from my aunt."

"I was not!"

Their words jumbled together; then they paused, staring at one another. He flashed her a grin and she smiled back. His grin turned into a chuckle and then she started to laugh, too.

"What is so funny?" asked Harry, sounding rather plaintive.

"It was you, though, wasn't it?" she asked, when she could draw breath. "Skulking about, hiding from my aunt in the library?"

"I was *not* hiding from anyone!" Julian expostulated. "I had merely grown weary of being kept waiting and thought to amuse myself among the books. And I take it that was you? Dusting the books, I mean. Promise me your aunt does not require your cleaning services in exchange for your room and board."

"Certainly not!" Elspeth exclaimed. "And I was not cleaning them, for Heaven's sake. I was reading."

"Reading? I wouldn't have thought any of the Quinn tribe cared for such an intellectual pastime."

"Perhaps you should not judge us all based only upon your acquaintance with my aunt and cousin. We are quite a disparate lot."

"I am admirably set down, my lady!" he answered, flashing her a broad smile.

"Julian!" Caroline's imperious tones rang out. Elspeth turned to see her cousin bearing down on them, annoyance flashing in her dark eyes.

"My cousin is quite monopolizing you, I fear," Caroline began, loud enough that several turned to stare. "You must excuse her prattling. I am quite determined to teach her the fine art of conversation while she visits with us. Her sphere is so limited, you know."

Elspeth could feel her face flaming. But Caroline was right—she had made a perfect ass of herself. Not that it mattered, of course. She was here as a foil for Caroline, and was doing a fine job at that.

"To the contrary, Caroline," Mr. Thorpe replied smoothly. "Miss Quinn is quite a spirited conversationalist. I have enjoyed our talk." He made a sharp bow and moved quickly away, no doubt relieved to finally be quit of the awkward country cousin. Oh, how awful this visit would be!

"Well, still waters run deep, I must say, Elspeth," said Caroline. Her voice was low but her tone waspish. "I never expected you to set your sights so high. You'll be wasting your time, I warn you. Julian is much smitten with me. And he is quite the wit. You'd do better to aim at a more realistic target. Ah, yes, I can see Mama has the same thought. Do excuse me, my dear cousin." Caroline abruptly disappeared in a whirl of satin and scent, leaving Elspeth peering befuddled into the blurred distance. The shapes approaching resolved themselves into her aunt, rather literally hauling an elderly gentleman in her wake. It appeared he might just trip over his cane, such haste as they were making.

"My dear Elspeth, here you are. Sir Richard, allow me to present to you my niece, Miss Elspeth Quinn of the Shropshire Quinns. . . ."

"This might be quite amusing, actually," Edgar Randall said, with a wicked chuckle. "Note, if you will, the dramatis personae: Julian has been waylaid by our lovely Perennial Toast, while Mama has decoyed the country cousin with poor old Sir Richard."

"Actually, Sir Richard might be quite a catch for the cousin, if she's as poor as Caroline intimates," said Thomas. "Although I must say the girl is far more presentable that I would have thought. Given the *on dit,* I thought she might be quite the ape leader. She's rather pretty, really."

"Indeed she is," echoed Robert. "Not nearly as old as I'd been led to understand."

"Well, neither Caroline nor her cousin are in the first blush of youth," Edgar said, "but that makes them both so much more interesting. Now, what do you gentlemen say to a little wager? I say Caroline lands Julian before the country cousin lands poor old Sommers."

"Oh, Edgar, you'll be throwing your money away!" exclaimed Thomas. "Julian will not be brought to heel so easily. And Sommers is just too disgusting, even for a poor girl."

"Then I take it we have a wager?"

"How much?" asked Robert.

"One hundred pounds."

"Rather rich for me, Edgar," said Thomas dubiously.

"But you did say I'd be throwing my money away," Edgar coaxed.

"I'll take the wager," said Robert excitedly. "Come on, Thomas. We'll split it!"

"I don't trust you, you know," said Thomas, a little sourly. "No tricks, mind!"

"Tricks? Dear boy, you wound me. Besides, it won't be necessary. See how poor Julian is already caught in the serpent's coils. . . ."

Chapter Five

"I am saying this only for your own good, Elspeth. I know these people. You may think they're all very friendly, but when your back is turned they gleefully pull out the long knives." Aunt Bettina peered carefully at her own reflection in the mirror in front of her. "The left side is a little higher than the right. Perhaps we should start over."

Elspeth sighed. In the dim candlelight, she could barely see to pin up her aunt's hair. The single ladies' maid they all shared was busy, as always, with Caroline. Dutifully, Elspeth plucked the pins from the gray coils, more by feel than sight. Her aunt's hair was thick with goose grease, slightly rancid. Thank God the younger generation had moved away from this particular affectation.

"Now, the other day at the Pump Room, I'm sure it was tempting to throw yourself at Julian Thorpe. He is something of a catch, although I'm given to understand he's quite keen on Caroline, you know. We have it on good authority that he will be asking for her any day now. It will be a perfect match. You, yourself, however, must not be unrealistic. Everyone will have great fun at our expense if you're seen to be making a fool of yourself. I simply cannot allow it."

"Yes, ma'am," said Elspeth. She had heard the same speech too many times from her cousin and her aunt over the past few days to blush any further. Indeed, she had chastised herself a thousand times for her gauche and awkward attempt to converse with the man. Caroline and Aunt Bettina need have no fear that she would go anywhere near him tonight.

"Now, Sir Richard is a good catch, too, my dear," Aunt Bettina went on. "Much more on your level. Quite satisfying accounts, I understand." Aunt Bettina cast a sly look at her niece in the glass. Elspeth schooled her expression into one of bland interest. Poor Sir Richard! Passed every year from one wallflower to the next, and still no one would take the doddering old widower seriously. There were benefits to being single, indeed.

"Mama, this dress will not do at all!" came a shriek from the hallway. Caroline burst into the room, a whirl of shimmering rose satin.

"Why, it's beautiful, darling!" said Aunt Bettina, rising hurriedly from her dressing table, spilling hairpins across the floor. Elspeth bent to pick them up, casting a surreptitious eye on her cousin. Indeed, the dress was stunning, although Caroline was loudly detailing a dozen fatal flaws in its design and execution.

"But she's the best modiste in Bath, Caroline. I declare the seams look straight as an arrow to me. And it's quite the prettiest dress that's finished. It brings out your perfect complexion. I do so want you to make your very best impression tonight. It's the first ball of the Season, after all."

Elspeth rose and placed the pins in their rosewood carved box on the dressing table. In the sudden silence she raised her eyes to the glass, to find her cousin carefully perusing her.

"Will I do?" Elspeth asked, turning so that Caroline could get the full effect. Elspeth had learned over the past few days that Caroline must assure herself on every occasion that her cousin would present no competition. Indeed, Elspeth's dress, the midnight blue satin, while exquisite in her own eyes, was merely passable and spinsterish in the eyes of her cousin. "You'll do nicely." Caroline smiled, not bothering to hide her smug and satisfied expression. "Just see to it that you don't go haring off after Julian Thorpe. You must not make an ass out of yourself tonight. Your conduct reflects on me and Mama, after all."

"Of course," Elspeth murmured. She turned back to the dressing table and busied herself with the pins, keeping her eyes down, so that no one would see the anger smouldering. She'd had about enough of such insults. In a month or two she could take Harry and go home, she consoled herself, the grand experiment over and done with.

"My pearls would look nice with that neckline, Elspeth," mused Aunt Bettina, moving toward the dressing table.

"Mama, whyever does she need pearls with that dress?" Caroline asked.

"Sir Richard has a fine eye, my dear. He'll notice the little elegant touches." Aunt Bettina rummaged through her drawer, pulling out a simple strand of pearls.

"Of course," Caroline purred, looking smug again.

It was all Elspeth could do not to emulate Harry's gagging routine.

* * *

The large room was beastly hot and beastly crowded. Everyone who was Anyone, and some who were Not, was here, the usual great triumph for Lady Dowling, a grand doyenne, who prided herself on giving the first and the most elegant ball of each Bath Season.

"Lovely pearls, Miss Quinn. Very tasteful," murmured Sir Richard, too close for comfort.

"Thank you, sir. My aunt lent them to me," replied Elspeth, grateful that said aunt had taken herself to the punch bowl yet again, and was thus not on hand to hear her ploy savaged by an ungrateful niece.

"I see," said Sir Richard, a trifle more coolly, although he did not, unfortunately, pull away. They stood together and alone against the wall while the others danced. Elspeth could occasionally catch a flash of rose satin as Caroline swirled by. She danced with a nice-looking man, one whom Elspeth had not yet met. The peacocks, Thomas and Robert, were here in full splendor, tittering and mincing about the room, although Elspeth was not yet sure which was which. Neither of them danced, but both had plenty to say regarding the style and grace of those who did. Of Julian Thorpe there was no sign, and Elspeth felt curiously deflated about that, considering that she never intended to exchange a word with him again.

Elspeth glanced rather desperately around the room, but there was no rescue in her blurred sight. It could be no accident that she had been abandoned here with Sir Richard. Those very few people whose acquaintance she had made in the last few days would not approach her now. Sir Richard, Elspeth was fast learning, seemed to be no one's cup of tea.

"I'm quite sure you promised this dance to me, Miss Quinn," came a voice at her elbow.

Turning, she beheld the very object of her thoughts, Julian Thorpe, looking every bit as handsome as she'd pictured him these last few days. "I did?" she managed to say, mortified that her voice sounded like a squeak.

"Indeed, ma'am. I am wounded that you would so easily forget," he said smoothly, but his eyes danced with amusement. He held out his gloved hand. Bemused, Elspeth placed her gloved hand in his, stiffening her fingers to keep them from trembling. "Sir Richard, please excuse us," Julian said, not waiting for Sir Richard's sour-sounding "harrumph" before whisking her away.

"I'm quite sure I did not promise you a dance, Mr. Thorpe," Elspeth began, thoroughly at a loss.

"Indeed, I lied, Miss Quinn. One of my many character flaws. Shall I return you to the devotions of Sir Richard?"

"Heavens no!" she exclaimed, then felt herself blush scarlet. "That is, I know so few people here, and I'm sure he'll appreciate the opportunity to chat with his other acquaintances."

"I'm sure he will not," replied Julian. "In fact, he's still glowering at me," he went on, casting a glance over his shoulder. "I'll bet he's jealous."

"Oh, I do hope not," said Elspeth with a shudder.

"Do you really want to dance?" Julian asked. "We can't talk if we have to parade around and bow to each other."

"Not particularly," she admitted. "I find these steps rather intricate and I fear for your toes. At home, our dances seem simpler, more of a jig than a promenade, really. Not terribly dignified, but we all enjoy them."

"Ah, yes, you're a country lass, aren't you," he replied. "Would you like to take a turn about the library? Lady Dowling has a splendid collection, although *on dit* has it she's never read a word herself."

"Oh, I'm quite sure my aunt said I shouldn't . . . that is, I'm not supposed to . . . oh, dear," she broke off, embarrassed at her foolish stammer. Was there no end to the number of ways she could humiliate herself in front of this man?

"Quite right. You're not to wander off alone with a roué and cad such as myself, particularly not into the shrubbery. Very proper." He kept right on walking, though, leading her toward the wide double doors that led into the grand hallway. "However, the library is quite liberally sprinkled with some of the *ton*'s most formidable dowagers, each trying to bleed the next one dry over a round of cards. Your honor will remain quite intact, I assure you."

Again Elspeth felt eyes upon them, and her aunt's warnings echoed through her thoughts. A furious whirl of pink satin came close to knocking her over and she caught a glimpse of angry eyes before the dance steps carried her cousin off again.

"Caroline is dancing with Ledbetter, I see. Good fellow. Seems quite taken with her."

Elspeth cast a glance up at Julian, trying to read his thoughts. Caroline and Aunt Bettina had taken great pains to assure her that Mr. Thorpe's attentions were entirely engaged in Caroline's favor, but for the life of her, she couldn't find anything but a benign bonhomie in his tone. Either he wasn't jealous at all, or he was very good at hiding it.

They had left the grand ballroom, and the rush of cool air felt wonderful on Elspeth's overheated skin.

"Here we are, one of the finest libraries in Bath, Miss Quinn," Julian said, as he escorted her through the portal. Where the library in Aunt Bettina's leased home was very fine by Elspeth's standards, this one was remarkable by any standard at all. Elspeth turned her enraptured gaze on row upon row of beautiful dark mahogany shelves, up and down the length of a very large, sumptuously appointed room. Someone, mercifully, had opened the French doors at the far end and a refreshing breeze blew through the room. Oh, how she wished for her spectacles, not, of course, that she would dare to don them in front of Mr. Thorpe. She'd certainly made an ass of herself in front of him enough times without that.

"And chaperones to your heart's content, Miss Quinn. There will be no compromise to your virtue this evening." Indeed, small card tables crowded the center of the room, each inhabited by a fierce foursome, dowagers and dukes, cads and ladies. There was little sound but the sharp snap of the cards, and an occasional shout of triumph or cry of angst. Actually, seeing their concentration, Elspeth rather felt Mr. Thorpe could seize her in a passionate embrace right here in the center of the library, to no one's notice. The idea brought a wicked smile to her face, and she dropped his arm precipitously, lest her very touch communicate to him her most unmaidenly thought.

"What sort of reading do you most prefer, Miss Quinn?" Julian asked, steering her to the shelves.

"Oh, I read whatever I can get hold of, sir," she responded, eager eyes on the rich leather spines of the books. "I suppose I like history best of all, although I enjoy poetry and the occasional scientific work."

"Yes, I recall you were perusing a botanical treatise when I first came upon you," he said, reaching for one of the books.

"Oh, yes, Ethridge's. Wonderful illustrations."

"Ah, here we are, Miss Quinn," he said, pulling a book from the shelf, "Ramsey's *History of Troy*. Care to take a look?"

Elspeth reached eagerly for the book. She loved the feel of soft leather in her hands, the smell of it, and the old parchment paper. If only she could see more than a blur this close!

"Let's sit down for a few moments. I'm rather enjoying

the quiet," he said, leading her over to a brocaded settee in a far corner. He sat her down, then sat next to her. The settee was large enough to accommodate them both, and she noted that he made a point not to sit touching her in any way. Chivalrous indeed, but why did she feel a bit disappointed?

"Would you care to read to me from the preface, Miss Quinn? I cannot remember whether I've ever read this one."

Read it to him? She only knew it was a book by the feel of it! "The light isn't very good here, I'm afraid," she said, smiling sweetly.

"Let me fetch a light then," he replied, then rose and made for a table a few feet away, on which perched a perfectly adequate branch of candles.

Drat! She took the opportunity to open the book and peer at it, hoping against hope that the print would be large enough to make out. No such luck. If anything, it was worse than usual, an old book with ink faded to brown, and old-fashioned curlicues that were hard enough to decipher under the best of conditions.

"Now then, Miss Quinn, I think this should be light enough for you," Julian said, placing the candelabrum on a small table right next to her. He sat again and looked at her expectantly.

"I . . . I find I still cannot make out the words, Mr. Thorpe," Elspeth said, looking helplessly at the book.

"Hah! I knew it," he said, laughing. "Never met a Quinn yet who cared a farthing for being anything except decorative. Admit it now, you do watercolors and needlework, but you never could set your mind to reading. Nothing in that pretty little head of yours except what to wear to the next fete, eh?"

"That's not true!" she sputtered. "I most certainly can read! In fact, I'll have you know I read in Greek and Latin as well as English!"

"Shall I fetch you Cicero's *Oration Against Cataline*? I know it's here somewhere."

"No! That is . . . I am not a trained monkey, sir! I do not wish to read to you!"

"Ah," was all he said. He gazed at her with great equanimity. She glared back.

"Perhaps you'd like me to read to you?" he asked, finally, as the frosty silence lengthened. He took the book from her hands.

Elspeth did not deign to reply. Needlework and watercolors, indeed! Actually she was a dreadful watercolorist. Never touched the dratted, runny things.

Julian settled the book on his lap, then reached into his waistcoat pocket, drawing out a pair of spectacles. Elspeth could barely suppress a gasp. They looked for all the world like her lost pair, not that any one pair of spectacles was so very distinctive from any other.

He settled them elaborately on his nose, then made a great show of opening the book to a specific page. "No, no," he muttered to himself, "light's not right." Then he leaned over her and drew the candles an infinitesimal distance toward him. He peered at the book, then brought it closer, peered again, then pushed it a long arm's length away, and peered yet again. "No, that can't be right," he muttered, then made a great display of taking off the spectacles, squinting carefully at them, putting them back into his waistcoat pocket, then pulling another pair from his other pocket. These he settled carefully on his nose, then brought the book up. "Ah," he said, "perfect. Here we are: 'Few mysteries from the dim and distant reaches of time so fascinate our intrepid historian as does the majesty of Troy, so mighty, so glorious, so tantalizingly elusive. . . .' "

"Excuse me. . . ."

"I beg your pardon?"

"That first pair of spectacles you were using. What was wrong with them?"

"What an odd time to introduce a new topic of conversation, Miss Quinn," Julian replied, in an aggrieved tone. "I am trying to better your mind."

"Bother my mind, Mr. Thorpe! Are those your eyeglasses or are they not?"

"Well, actually," he said, taking them again from the pocket, "I suspect they are not mine. Quite the wrong sort of lenses for me. I must have picked them up somewhere." He held one lens up to his eye. "The rightful owner must be walking into walls without them, I must say."

"May I see those, please?" Elspeth held out her hand.

"Well, if you don't appreciate my reading, you might just say so, Miss Quinn," he replied, handing over the spectacles.

She settled them on her nose, then reached for the book. "Ha!" she cried, peering at it, "'. . . so tantalizingly elusive,' indeed! You filched my eyeglasses! I've been blind as a bat for days!"

"I did not filch them."

"Then why had you got them in your pocket?"

"Well, now I seem to remember you dropped them in the library, and I picked them up to return them to you."

"Then why didn't you?"

"Well, it rather slipped my mind." He sat back and regarded her carefully through the lenses of his own spectacles. "You know, you actually are rather pretty when I can see you clearly. A man could drown in those great big green eyes of yours."

"Oh, well, they just look bigger behind the lenses," Elspeth replied, coloring at his remark. "Actually, Harry calls me 'Owl Eyes,'" she finished hurriedly. Now why had she told him that? The man had just paid her a compliment, although, to be sure, he didn't really mean it, and she just had to say something stupid in response!

"Owl Eyes. How utterly enchanting!" he said, smiling at her.

"Elspeth!"

She froze at her aunt's trumpeting tone. Drat! Why couldn't she just have a few more minutes with Mr. Thorpe? He wore spectacles! He said she was pretty, even though he didn't mean it.

"Elspeth, I am very disappointed in you!" said Aunt Bettina, bearing down on her like a ship of the line. "Imagine monopolizing Mr. Thorpe's time like this! Do let me apologize for my niece, Mr. Thorpe. She was raised in the country, you know," her aunt went on, simpering a bit, "and I'm afraid we quite have our hands full teaching her the finer points of deportment."

"It's not Miss Quinn's deportment I find wanting, ma'am," replied Julian, unfolding himself and rising, just a little too slowly. He put out his gloved hand to Elspeth and she took it, rising as well. The forgotten book clattered to the floor as she did so.

"Clumsy gel! Now see what you've done!" snapped Aunt Bettina.

"No harm done, I assure you, ma'am," said Julian, bending over to retrieve the book. "And I must apologize to you, Miss Quinn, for monopolizing your time."

"Oh, of course you did not, sir. . . ."

"That's quite enough, gel," Aunt Bettina interrupted, taking her arm abruptly. "Sir Richard is most provoked that you disappeared." Hard fingers dug into Elspeth's arm and she felt herself being pulled away. "I know Caroline has all her dances promised, Mr. Thorpe," her aunt threw over her shoulder, "she's so very popular, you know—but I'll warrant she'll make room for you if you hurry! Take off those ugly spectacles, gel!" she hissed to

Elspeth. "Don't you understand anything we've tried to teach you?"

Elspeth threw one quick glance over her shoulder as she was fairly dragged to the door. She could see well enough to note that Mr. Thorpe stood staring after them, his mouth a thin slit.

"Why, Julian, I wondered where you'd got off to." Caroline's voice pierced the noise, close to his ear. She had come up behind him. Had he seen her coming, he'd have made a quick getaway.

"Good evening, Miss Quinn," he said, as she floated into his path. "You're looking particularly lovely this evening."

"Liar! You haven't so much as looked at me," Caroline said, pouting. "And I wore this dress because I thought you'd like it."

"Of course I've looked at you. And your dress is lovely," Julian said, scanning the corners of the room for Miss Elspeth Quinn.

"Well, you're just the knight in shining armor I'm looking for to rescue me, Julian," she said, slipping her hand into the crook of his arm.

"How may I be of service, my lady?" he asked absently. Ah, yes! There Elspeth was in the corner, seated between her aunt and poor old Sir Richard Sommers. Hardly any escape for her there. Still, she was safe enough for a few moments. Certainly none of the other young swains would dare approach her in the lion's den, as it were. And when he did ride to the rescue, she was certain to be undyingly grateful.

"I'm supposed to dance the next dance with Mr. Ledbetter. But I've just realized it will be a waltz. I'm quite smitten with him, you know, but I do not wish to appear too eager. Will you dance it with me instead? You must insist you had asked me first; then I'll be mortified to remember it was so. Then he'll be terribly jealous, won't he?" she finished brightly.

On the other side of the room, Bettina Quinn had arisen and was marching off, to the punch bowl no doubt. Surely, Julian thought, she could not be so blind as to Sir Richard's actual intentions, or, indeed, his lack thereof. The old man dallied among the wallflowers every year, terrifying the girls and raising the hopes of their desperate mamas, but he was not such a fool as to marry again. He had married twice for money and had found both arrangements quite to his taste. The good ladies had even been so obliging as to die gracefully as their beauty faded. Now he basked in the attention of the pretty young things, but he seemed to have no wish to make any one of them his very own financial responsibility. Not unless he could find one very rich, and whenever he did, neither she, nor her mama, would have anything to do with him. If Bettina Quinn had expectations of fobbing off the country cousin on old Sommers, she was doomed to failure. Elspeth, he suspected, would bear up under the disappointment.

"Julian! I declare you haven't heard a word I've said!" came Caroline's imperious tones. She had gone so far as to snap her fan at him. He loathed fans.

"Of course I have, Miss Quinn. Although I must confess that my hearing is not at its best when the music is so loud."

"Oh, pish! You can hear perfectly well and you know it. What I said was that you will dance the next dance with me. It will be starting in a few minutes. And now I'd like some punch, please."

"Punch. Ah, yes, of course," he answered lamely, moving her toward the punch bowl, where he could see an encounter with her formidable mother was inevitable. And dance? He did not wish to dance, not with anyone, unless of course Miss Elspeth Quinn might favor him with her attention. Still, it was clear Caroline would brook no dissent on this point. She'd been nattering on about young Ledbetter. Well, maybe she was sweet on him. That would be a fine thing, to put an end to any speculation about himself as the happy suitor. Over in the corner, Sir Richard had bent his head closer to Elspeth and was wheezing with laughter. The girl had a wonderful sense of humor, but he was surprised she bothered to put it to use with Sir Richard. Perhaps the old goat was laughing at one of his own self-alleged witticisms.

"Most interesting, Robert, wouldn't you agree? I do believe I am closer to winning the wager than you are, dear boy." Edgar Randall watched the dancers swirling around, a daring waltz that Lady Dowling had only recently sanctioned at her soiree, several years after it had become fashionable in London. "There, see how he smiles into Caroline's lovely eyes? I do believe it will be a match at last."

"Oh, I don't know, Edgar," tittered Thomas. "Remember there are two couples involved in this wager. And unless I'm much mistaken, the country cousin seems to have utterly captivated old Sommers. He's hardly left her side all evening."

Edgar glared into the corner where, indeed, the delectable little cousin sat, trapped by the doddering old fool for this last half hour. Still, Edgar had it on good authority that the girl was near penniless, and Sommers could not be such a fool as all that. Julian Thorpe, on the other hand, was well on his way. Edgar had not seen fit to mention to the mincing Thomas and Robert, when setting the wager, that he'd had a private talk with Julian a few nights back. Julian was under orders, orders ignored at his soul's peril, to marry and in haste at that. Yes, indeed, he thought, watching avidly as Julian threw back his head and laughed at something the lovely Caroline had just whispered in his ear, Julian was an apple ripe for the plucking, and Caroline just the serpent to pluck him. His own pockets to let, with more creditors than friends these days, Edgar was desperately looking forward to a hundred pounds to pay off the worst of them and fob off the rest.

"I'm terribly warm, Julian. I do believe I might faint from the heat. Perhaps we could take a stroll on the terrace?" Caroline did look flushed from their waltz, which had gone on interminably, Julian thought.

"Of course. Would you care for some punch?"

Caroline cast a quick glance over to the punch bowl and shook her head. "No, thank you. Mama is still there, and I've no wish to be detained."

Blessing her discretion, he steered her to the large French doors that gave out onto the terrace, now crowded with gentlemen and ladies of the same mind and temperature. Glancing over to the corner, Julian noted that Miss Quinn still sat with Sir Richard, ripe now, no doubt, for rescue. He need only shake himself loose of Caroline, who, unfortunately, clung rather tightly to his arm. What was it she'd been going on about earlier? Something about Ledbetter. . . . He peered up and down the terrace, cursing his poor eyesight. While his vision was certainly better than Miss Quinn's—if her spectacles were any measure—it was nevertheless difficult for him to make out much more than forms and colors out here in the dark.

At least it was cooler. A fresh breeze blew across his face.

"Beautiful evening, isn't it, Julian?" Caroline said.

"Indeed," he replied. Now where might Ledbetter be? If he could spot the young man, he might pass Caroline off to him. Tired of being chastised, he had attempted, rather unsuccessfully, he knew, to be responsive to Caroline's conversation, but had found it lacking in depth and interest. Now that he thought of it, it had all been about her. Her country cousin, on the other hand, was most entertaining, indeed.

"Julian, have you listened to a word I've said all evening?"

"Of course I have, Caroline. You know I dote on your every word." No shapes to his left looked promisingly Ledbetterish. He turned to his right.

"Something is preoccupying you this evening," she went on, touching his chin playfully with her fan. God, how he loathed fans.

"I am merely speechless in the face of your beauty, Caroline." There! That had to be Ledbetter, off toward the right, near the end of the terrace. "Let's stroll over this way. It's less crowded."

He saw the very moment Ledbetter spotted them, from the very animation that suffused the young man's face, not, Julian trusted, at the sight of his own. Indeed, as they drew closer, he could see enough to know that the young man only had eyes for Caroline, who was desperately trying to tug him off in another direction. But this was no time to be coy, not with poor Miss Elspeth Quinn languishing in corners under the beady black eye of that old crow, Sommers.

"Julian! Let's go back in!" Caroline hissed in his ear, coming to a dead stop like a mule.

No you don't, my girl, Julian thought. "Oh, let's put the poor man out of his misery, Caroline. I do believe you've made him suffer enough. Mr. Ledbetter!" he called out. "I fear I have inadvertently run afoul of the dance card, leaving poor Miss Quinn stuck with me." The young man virtually sprinted the short distance between them.

"Damn you, Julian!" Caroline snapped, barely audibly.

"Oh, Miss Quinn!" panted the young puppy. "I do hope I can have the next dance."

"Well, I leave you in good hands, Miss Quinn," said Julian, making an elaborate leg. "Thank you so much for our dance." His eyesight was not so poor that he couldn't see her glaring balefully at him as he turned to beat a hasty retreat.

This evening was interminable! Hot, odorous, perfectly foul! Elspeth did not know quite what she had expected of this, her first evening among the *ton*, but certainly it was not to be trapped over in this corner with this poor old gentleman who couldn't hear very well, had little of interest to say, and seemed not the least interested in anything she had to say. Aunt Bettina had deposited her firmly in this chair, hissing firm instructions that she was to keep Sir Richard company and not stir from the spot. No one else even so much as glanced their way. Certainly Caroline was not so restricted. Around and around the floor whirled the pink satin, in the arms of Mr. Thorpe. It was all Elspeth could do not to stare. Actually, she did stare, peering every time they waltzed into her line of vision. There was no mistaking that he cut a dashing figure. Unlike most of the young men here, he eschewed the more violent color combinations. Buff-colored superfine breeches clung like skin to his muscled thighs, and his plain dark maroon jacket, broad at the shoulders and narrow at the waist, suggested a powerful man at ease with himself. Everything else he wore was pristine white, from the stockings covering a well-turned calf, to the neckcloth of impossible twists and foldings.

"Too warm for dancing, wouldn't you say, Miss Quinn?" wheezed Sir Richard, too close to her ear.

"It is warm, yes, sir," replied Elspeth absently. But warm or not, she would love to be whirling round and round in the arms of Mr. Thorpe.

"Don't approve of all this waltzing. It's indecent, that what it is. Don't you agree, Miss Quinn?"

"Well, I suppose if Lady Dowling approves, it isn't for me to gainsay her," said Elspeth, deliberately noncommittal. She now knew better than to contradict Sir Richard on any point whatsoever. He did not take that well, got all prickly and pruney. Best just to be mildly agreeable.

"Quite right. You young gels have entirely too many opinions these days. Most unseemly."

"Yes, sir," Elspeth said with a sigh. Now the music had stopped and the room was abuzz with vivacious voices. Elspeth cast her glance about—the pink satin was hard to miss—there! With a stab of disappointment, Elspeth saw Mr. Thorpe leading her cousin out to the terrace. For a romantic interlude, of course. What on earth was the matter with her? Mooning about over a god of a man, all but declared for her cousin, and far, far above the likes of her even if he were not spoken for. No doubt, he thought Elspeth a gauche curiosity, an interesting oddity, suitable to make sport of, and no more. Well, she had wished for a taste of the *ton*, and perhaps a mildly broken heart was a part of it.

"Tell me, Miss Quinn. Do you play whist?" Sir Richard asked, a trifle avidly.

"Well, I do, sir, but rather badly, and I've no money to wager."

"Ah," was all he said, sounding a bit disappointed. Surely he had not intended to take her money in a game? They sat in silence for a moment, Elspeth willing the orchestra to take up another tune quickly so that she needn't make further conversation. She had learned Sir Richard couldn't hear well with music playing. She glanced longingly at the fan that dangled uselessly from her wrist, wishing she could use it to cool herself. But Aunt Bettina had declared quite firmly that she was not to so much as open it in public, that the use of fans was a delicate and subtle art of communication, and that Elspeth would simply embarrass herself with her awkward handling. And here all these years she'd thought a fan was used to waft a cooling breeze to one's face!

"May I have the pleasure of this next dance, Miss Quinn?" came a voice at her elbow. His voice. Her heart started to beat a little faster.

"But I—" she started, shaking her head.

"I'll teach it to you," he interrupted hurriedly, holding out his gloved hand.

She took it, and turned to excuse herself to the scowling Sir Richard, who barely nodded at her.

"Actually, this will be a quadrille," he remarked, leading her away. "I detest quadrilles. Would you care for a stroll on the terrace? It's quite pleasant outside, and quite crowded, too, if you're still worried about your reputation."

"Oh, yes, that would be lovely. It's stifling inside," she replied, smiling up at him. Her heart was inexplicably beating a little tattoo inside her chest. They made their way to the large open doors. Out of the corner of her eye Elspeth noted the pink satin-clad form of her cousin, standing ready for the opening promenade across from Mr. Ledbetter. She hoped Caroline would not begrudge her a few moments with Mr. Thorpe, as she was dancing with someone else herself.

It was heaven outside, where a cool breeze blew across her cheeks. The air was fresh, scented with roses and lilacs, such a welcome change from the fusty Sir Richard and the crowded, hot ballroom. Mr. Thorpe led her over to the balustrade, away from the long French windows that cast a golden glow across the terrace. A number of couples made their way inside as the orchestra signaled that the quadrille would soon begin. She and Mr. Thorpe stood together in the cool dark, not touching, leaning on the elaborately molded railing, looking out over the small garden that separated Lady Dowling's home from the grand edifice next to it. Elspeth was aware that she was supposed to think of something brilliant to say. Something that would have him laughing and admiring her wit. Nothing came to mind, of course. The man had obviously kindly rescued her from the mouldering Sir Richard, only to find that she and the old goat were a perfect pair!

"It would appear to me that you have been deliberately marooned with Sir Richard, Miss Quinn. Not once, but twice this evening. Why would your aunt abandon such a lovely young woman to the likes of that poor old man?"

"Oh, well, of course, I'm not really lovely, and I'm not at all young, as I am told several times a day." Elspeth knew she was not playing the game, but could not bother to adopt the light and bantering tone so favored by the *ton*. It sounded so artful, somehow. Besides, she had best let him understand that she would brook no empty compliments. Even such a mindless one as calling her lovely made her heart flutter, and she did not really wish to find herself head over heels with this rather elegant gentleman, obviously as far above her as the Prince of Wales himself. Besides, she had better put him off as soon as possible, so that she could not be accused by her aunt of encouraging his attentions, who, after all, reminded her repeatedly that she only had Elspeth's best interests at heart.

"Well, if you are fishing for compliments, Miss Quinn, I shall give you up as quite as unoriginal as all the other demoiselles here this evening," he replied. "And here I thought you might be different."

"I never fish for compliments, sir," she remarked huffily. "Do you not have eyes in your head? All you need do is look around you to see that the 'demoiselles' to whom you refer are all far more suited to this occasion than I am. Why, their attire alone puts them well beyond my sphere."

"As to that, Miss Quinn, I suppose you would slap my face if I were to suggest that the—ah—least—ah—adorned statue by Praxiteles is far more beautiful in its simplicity than any lady ever painted in all her excessive finery by Watteau or Fragonard."

"I must assume, then, that naked Greek statuary is another topic that is out of bounds between a lady and a gentleman, sir?" she retorted with a rueful laugh. She would so love a rousing discussion on the splendors of ancient sculpture.

"How impressive, Miss Quinn," he said, smiling warmly at her. "I should not think there are as many as a half dozen ladies in the room who would recognize the name of the finest Greek sculptor." His smile made her heart skip another beat, and she turned her gaze away. Best not to let him think she was smitten. It would give them all the more to tease her about when the game was done.

"Then that should prove to you that I'm not young," she said, still simmering over the "fishing for compliments" accusation.

"How old are you, then?" he asked baldly. There was a wicked gleam in his eye, as if he knew he tread dangerously here, at least as far as the *ton* would have it. Elspeth knew enough to know that the specifics of a lady's age were never discussed openly.

"Twenty-three," she replied, just as boldly. What was so blessed old about twenty-three, anyway?

"Ah, no wonder you recognized Praxiteles. He was a contemporary of yours, then."

In spite of herself, she giggled. "I suppose I could make a remark along the lines of 'who did you think posed for all those statues,' but I can't risk your repeating it to Thomas and Robert. I should have to leave town."

"And where would you go if you did leave town, Miss Quinn? Everyone tells me you are from the country, but no one seems to know what country that would be."

"Oh, my family lives in Shropshire, sir."

"Well, then, tell me about Shropshire, Miss Quinn. Where is your home?"

Now there was a subject to bore the feathers off a duck! What on earth could she find to say to this worldly, magnificent gentleman about Weston-under-Lizard, a village that only still existed largely because of its proximity to the network of canals in Shropshire and to Market Drayton, a town gaining in popularity as the birthplace of Robert Clive, or Clive of India, as he had come to be known.

"I'm afraid you'll find my recitation about my home exceedingly trifling and dull, Mr. Thorpe."

"Ah, Miss Quinn, again you allow me to understand that I present myself as a shallow, self-absorbed fellow. Indeed, I find nothing the least bit trifling or dull about you."

Did he mock her again? Was she so much the rustic, so out-of-step with the glittering *ton* that she was curiously entertaining? She turned to look at him, only to find that in the dim light she could hardly make out his features. How could she know if he was making sport of her if she couldn't see his face? "Would you mind terribly if I put on my spectacles, sir?" she asked. "I find it difficult to converse with dark blurs."

"As do I, ma'am. You may wear yours if I may wear my own." Without further remark he reached into his waistcoat pocket and settled them on his aquiline nose. She fished hers from her reticule and, her own now similarly situated, they peered carefully at one another.

"You are even more beautiful than I realized," he said softly.

Her heart knocked about a bit in her chest. Then someone's laughter rang out, reminding her of the game that was played among the 'Quality.' "You flatter me, sir," she said simply, looking away. "It's not a good idea, really. I am woefully ill-used to such remarks and quite apt to take you far too seriously."

Her white-gloved hand lay on the railing of the balustrade. She started when his hand, discreetly gloved, of course, covered her own, but she did not draw it away. "I am guilty of the foolish repartee of the Beau Monde, Miss Quinn. But not with you. There is something about you that calls out the better in me—such as it is, of course," he added.

"Weston-under-Lizard," she said, in a shaky voice.

"I beg your pardon?"

"I live in a little town called Weston-under-Lizard, not far from Market Drayton. I am the eldest of five in my family. Papa died a little less than a year ago, and we are rather modest in our demeanor and society. Not at all interesting, you see." She finished near breathless.

"Modest in your demeanor, and yet you read Latin and Greek?"

"I should not have boasted, sir," she said, feeling her face flush. "Indeed, my Latin is only acceptable and my Greek barely passable. Papa was teaching me, you see, and we only got so far with it. It's heavy going alone, so I'm afraid I neglect it terribly, now."

"Dreadful of you."

She stole a glance at him and found he was staring at her. Although she would not tell him so, he was extraordinarily handsome, now that she got a good look at him through her lenses. He had not moved his hand. It lay lightly on her own.

"And how do you find the contrast, Miss Quinn? Surely there is a world of difference between Weston-under-Lizard and Bath."

"Oh, indeed, sir! Too much so, I must say. In fact, without meaning to sound ungracious, I am so sorry we ever came here. It has been worse even than I imagined, and I thought I was being fanciful at the time."

"Well, why did you come then?" He stared at her. Behind his lenses his eyes were a deep and beautiful blue.

"I thought it would aid my mother to have the two of us away for a while," she said, unwilling to say that it gave her mother two fewer mouths to feed. "And also because I thought Harry might benefit from seeing a bit of polite society. He has so little opportunity at home. We are quite rustic at Weston-under-Lizard."

"And not to find a husband for yourself?" Now his deep blue eyes were amused.

"Hah! I wouldn't marry any of these puffed-up popinjays if any of them did ask me!" she declared.

"Oh, dear. I believe I am wounded, Miss Quinn."

"Well, naturally I didn't mean to include you, sir," she answered in some confusion.

"Naturally."

"Although you are no kinder than any of them," she said.

"How so?"

"You flirt with me just to put Caroline into a pique."

"Why would you think that?" he asked, looking at her. He still had not moved his hand.

"Ask anyone in the Assembly Rooms what they think," she replied smartly.

"And do you always draw your opinion from what everyone else thinks, Miss Quinn?"

"Certainly not. I don't give a . . . a . . . I don't care at all what these . . ." She broke off, embarrassed, aware that she was insulting his set.

"Puffed-up popinjays?"

"Well, perhaps I shouldn't have said that. Papa always said my tongue would be the ruin of me."

"A wise man, your papa."

"Still, Harry will be no better for having spent the Season watching these . . . gentlemen of the *ton* mince about," she declared.

"Now I must take exception, Miss Quinn. I spent a great deal of my youth teaching myself not to mince. It was quite a point of honor with me. In fact, I took to practicing striding about looking purposeful, and now you tell me I mince."

"Well, to be fair, I can't say I've ever seen you mince, sir," she said laughing.

"I can't tell you how deeply relieved I am to hear you say that. Thank you for putting my mind to rest on that point. Although, I do not believe I shall ever be able to put one foot in front of the other in your presence again. I shall be so paralyzed at the thought of inadvertently mincing, I'll fall flat on my face. Would that be worse than mincing, by the way? Falling down, I mean?"

"You are impossible, sir!"

"Please don't tap me with your fan. I am quite tired of being tapped by lady's fans."

"Oh, I'm not allowed to use my fan. My aunt says I hold it like a cow would. Most unacceptable, she says."

"I have my strong suspicions that your aunt has never seen a cow hold a fan. Still if you don't care to use it, that's fine with me. Dreadful invention, ladies' fans. The very plague of gentlemen."

Now he did move his hand, and turned, leaning his back against the balustrade. She could see his eyes even better now, in the warm light cast by the long French windows. Big beautiful blue eyes, made larger by his lenses.

"And what shall you do if one of the puffed-up popinjays begs for your hand in marriage, Miss Quinn?" he asked her, smiling.

"I shall decline with feigned regret, sir," she said, with a loud dismissive sniff.

"To what end, may I ask?"

"Not that it is any of your business, but I prefer to go home, sir, to live out my life in quiet amiability with my family in the country."

"That does sound rather enviable, at that."

"Now you mock me, sir."

"Indeed, I do not. I should above all like to return to the country, to live out my life in amiable pursuits."

"But I thought. . . ." She stopped, confused by the turn of conversation.

"What did you think?"

"Caroline said . . ."

"What did Caroline say?"

"Why nothing at all, actually. I can't think why her name popped into my head," Elspeth said, reddening. It was ill done of her to tell tales on her cousin, however well deserved.

"Elspeth!"

Elspeth jumped at the sound of her aunt's strident tone. Her heart sank as she turned her head to find Aunt Bettina bearing down on them like a ship rigged for battle.

"I've been looking high and low for you, gel. And here I find you skulking about out here, quite monopolizing poor Mr. Thorpe. My apologies again, sir, for my niece's forward behavior."

He made a slight bow to Mrs. Quinn. "I can assure you, madame, Miss Quinn's deportment has been decorum itself," he said coolly. "And, again, it is I who have been monopolizing her, not the other way around."

"You are kindness itself, sir, to say so. Just what I would expect from a gentleman such as yourself. Still, I know what I see. Come along, gel. We're going home."

Elspeth's heart gave another lurch. "Is the ball at an end already?" she asked.

"Not for a good number of hours yet, you silly gel. But I find I have the headache, and I need you to see to it at home." Her hand closed on Elspeth's arm like a vise and she felt herself good and trapped. "Mr. Thorpe," Aunt Bettina went on, turning her attention to him, "I have convinced Caroline she must stay so that we do not offend Lady Dowling with a too-hasty departure. Caroline, of course, is frantic to come home and minster to my pain, but I'll hear none of it. Mrs. Hastings has kindly agreed to see her home in her carriage, but I'm sure I can count on you to keep an eye on her for me, can't I?"

If it was all Elspeth could do to keep from rolling her eyes at this speech, Mr. Thorpe was not quite so circumspect. Eyebrow cocked, expression dubious, he made no reply, merely sketching a bow so slight as to be nearly an insult.

Squeezing her niece's arm, Aunt Bettina nearly yanked Elspeth forward, propelling her to the doors that led into the ballroom. Just inside the doors stood Caroline, face bright red, eyes snapping with anger. She said nothing, merely watching as her mother and cousin went flying by. Elspeth turned her head and saw Caroline slip out of the French doors, onto the terrace, where Julian stood.

If Aunt Bettina had pulled her unceremoniously from the library, now she barely allowed her niece to put one foot ahead of the other as they made their way straight for the doors that led into the grand hall, and thence to the broad doors and the stairs that swept with staid elegance down to Duke Street, where the groom whistled up their carriage, which had waited down the street.

Behind her Elspeth could hear the orchestra strike up another waltz, and it was all she could do not to weep.

Chapter Six

"I have never been so humiliated in all my life, Elspeth! What can you have been thinking? Once was bad enough, but twice? Why, never mind what the man thinks of you—that's lost already—but you've made a laughingstock of this family. Throwing yourself at the likes of Julian Thorpe! Why, do you know his second cousin once removed is an earl? Julian has a townhouse in the finest part of London, and magnificent estates in Suffolk. He is welcome in the very best of homes in all of England. How dare you debase me, not to mention your cousin, in front of the entire *ton* of Bath by making such a fool of yourself?"

As this tirade had been going on without variation for the better part of the last hour, Elspeth made no reply. In the carriage she had attempted to defend herself by suggesting, ever so gently, that Mr. Thorpe had actually sought out her company, but she had given up that tack as ineffective. Now that they were home, Mrs.

Quinn seemed to have undergone a miraculous cure. Of her headache there was not a sign. On the other hand, she had passed it on to Elspeth, who suffered in silence.

"Now I am going to bed. I have half a mind to send you and your brother home in disgrace, indeed I do. The very idea! The *very* idea." Aunt Bettina was fairly humphing as she spoke.

"Good night then, Aunt," said Elspeth. "I'll retire now as well."

"Do not think to show yourself anywhere tomorrow, miss. I'll speak with Caroline and see how the tongues have wagged about you this evening. She'll hear whatever is being said, I'm sure."

And a great deal of the worst will be said by her, mused Elspeth, who wisely did not voice her thoughts.

"Good night, Aunt," Elspeth said again firmly, then turned and left the room, not willing to hear any more. But outside her aunt's room, her step lightened and a smile lit her face in the dark hallway. She should be devastated at her aunt's words, but she knew in her heart they were spiteful nonsense. Julian had sought her out, not once but twice! And he had held her hand. Oh, she knew not to lay too much importance on that. Hands were offered and accepted quite casually among the *ton*. But this had been different, hadn't it? A quiet, private touch.

Or was she a rather pathetic country girl—woman, actually—just another foolish spinster fast on her way to a broken heart? Her spirits plummeted. It felt as if her feet had landed with a thud on the carpet. She stopped in her tracks and stared at nothing in the dark. Didn't she know enough about the idle flirtations of this society not to fall wildly in love with the very first (and only) man who paid her a light compliment? Was the entire *ton* laughing at her? Was Julian laughing at her with Caroline at this very moment, his arms locked around her pink-satined form as he waltzed her around the room, eyes only for her?

It took an effort to walk the last few steps to her room. And the chilly water that she poured into the basin on the washstand was warmed by her tears.

"A picnic, my dear Miss Quinn. The weather will be perfect! We can ride out to the vineyards at Claverton. Do say yes!" Edgar Randall implored.

"Whom shall we invite to join us?" asked Caroline. Her eyes scanned the room, but he sensed she was having no luck in spotting her quarry, whoever he might be. She had danced a good bit with young Ledbetter all evening, something he must nip in the bud.

"Oh, I suppose I can round up our usual crowd, Benjamin Watkins, Wesley Ames, Thomas and Robert, although to be sure I can never quite tell those two apart. . . ." This did not receive the expected wicked laugh from Caroline. The chit was preoccupied, indeed. The question was, with what—or whom? "And Julian, of course." Now that got her attention, he noted with approval. Good. So Julian had caught her eye again. The hundred-pound winnings almost made a weight in his pocket.

"Well, I suppose it might be pleasant at that," she responded, turning her attention to him at last.

"You must invite some of the ladies to join us. Say an hour or two after noon? Won't do to try to start too early. We shall barely get enough sleep as it is. Well, I shall pop off and speak to the gentlemen. We'll call for you and your cousin at the appointed hour." Now that brought a scowl to her lovely face. Interesting. So the cousin from the country was proving something of a thorn in the flesh. It might prove an entertaining sidelight to watch that byplay at tomorrow's picnic. Perhaps he could throw a little oil on the fire. This Season was shaping up nicely, indeed. . . .

"Julian, you simply must join us," Edgar importuned, having run his friend to ground in the card room, where Julian had sought refuge from the relentless Caroline Quinn.

"I've got business and correspondence to tend to, Edgar," Julian replied, absently throwing down a card from his whist hand. "I don't have time to cavort about on ant hills."

"Actually, dear boy, we need your carriage. Fine pair of bays, you have there. Don't you wish to give them a bit of a run?"

Julian sighed. Edgar had been pleading with him for at least the last ten minutes and showed no sign of weakening. "Can't you hire a carriage? I really have no wish to spend tomorrow afternoon exchanging idle remarks with the same people I'm exchanging idle remarks with tonight and the same people I'll be exchanging idle remarks with tomorrow night at Mrs. Danbury's musicale. Actually, I'm sick of this nonsense already, and I've only been here a bare fortnight. How do you stand all this banality year in and year out?"

Across the whist table, Wesley rolled his eyes. Mr. Middleton, a newcomer, looked vaguely offended, and Sir Henry snored into his prodigious mustache. He had to be awakened each time it was his turn to play a card.

"I'd take offense, dear boy, but I'm sure you're just annoyed because you have such a bad hand." He paused to allow Julian to throw him an exasperated look over his shoulder. "Look here, Caroline Quinn is gathering up the demoiselles to grace our picnic. And if their conversation bores you silly, why you can entertain yourself watching Caroline make the country cousin's life miserable. I do believe things are fraying there quite satisfactorily."

"The cousin will come as well?" Julian asked, very deliberately keeping his tone disinterested. Edgar was like a rat terrier when it came to sniffing around other people's business.

"Why, of course she will. P'raps we could ferret out what happened this evening. Mama Quinn bounced the cousin out of here several hours ago, most unceremoniously. Quite the delicious mystery, eh?" Edgar smirked.

"Not at all. I happened to be there when Mrs. Q. made her excuses. The Headache, Quite Severe. Miss Quinn kindly offered to see to her comfort, that's all."

"Ah, quite the little spinster-companion she's turning out to be. No competition for our Perennial Toast, is she?"

Julian made no reply, merely threw down another card, barely noticing which one. The hand really was an abomination.

"You'll come then, Julian? We'll have no fun at all without you."

"Oh, I suppose I must. You're not going to leave me alone until I agree, are you?"

"Not for a moment."

Julian kept the look of exasperation on his face until Edgar had wandered off to bedevil someone else. Then he allowed a small smile to grace his features. An idyllic afternoon in the country with Miss Quinn. Miss Elspeth Quinn, of the large green eyes behind bewitching spectacles.

The early afternoon sun tried its best to get through the heavy brocade curtains in the Quinn drawing room, but the effort was not terribly successful. The room was dark and close and Julian could hardly make out the words on the page of the book he had filched from the library to while away the time. He was tired of waiting already, although it had only been a quarter of an hour, nothing at all to a demoiselle of the *ton*. He heard the slightest squeak of the door and looked up, hoping against all hope that the ladies would defy convention and actually make an appearance before the obligatory half hour had elapsed.

A small face barely peeped around the edge of the door. Julian couldn't quite make out the features in the gloom, but he could hazard a good guess. "Harry, is that you, sir?" he asked.

The small figure stepped furtively into the room and shut the door hurriedly. "Good afternoon, Mr. Thorpe, sir," came the small voice.

"And to you, sir. Are you well today?"

"Not terribly, no."

"Ah. I see. Well, Harry, my boy, generally when one gentleman asks another in passing if he is well, the expected answer is 'Very well, sir, and you?' no matter what his actual state of well being. Nevertheless, when the gentlemen are friends, it is occasionally accepted for the one to unburden himself of his troubles. What seems to be wrong today?"

"Everything!" Harry announced dramatically, flinging himself down on one of the several brocaded occasional chairs placed around the room in strategic, if irritating, angles. It was remarkable how children could screw themselves up like that, into such remarkable shapes. Julian was quite sure that if he were to adopt such a posture, he might well remain that way forever. "Everyone is at sixes and sevens," the child went on, darkly. "Caroline is screaming like a banshee, Aunt Bettina is threatening to send us home, and my sister has been closed away in her room crying all morning. I'd like to go home myself, but Elspeth thinks we'll be disgraced.

I've been disgraced a great many times. I don't see what's so awful about that."

"Well, gentlemen seem to bear up better under disgrace than ladies do. They're very delicate, you know."

"Caroline is not delicate," Harry pronounced.

"Well, no, I would not call Caroline 'delicate.' Actually, now that I think of it, none of the ladies of my acquaintance could be called 'delicate.' It must be just a figure of speech. What is everyone so upset about?"

"I'm sure I shouldn't tell you," Harry began, but he didn't sound sure.

"Well, tell me and then we'll decide whether you should have told me or not." Normally Julian would consider it caddish to pressure a mere child like this, but last night had been infuriating and baffling and he damned well felt like getting to the bottom of it all.

"Well . . ." Harry began again, then tapered off.

"Yes?"

"Caroline says Elspeth made a fool of herself last night and that the entire *ton* is laughing at her. She made my sister cry. And why do we have to call all these English society people '*ton*' anyway? Why can't we just speak English?"

"Well, as to the French, Harry, I suppose that all has to do with 1066 and the Norman Conquest and all that, but I must say I was at the same ball last night, and I didn't hear a single soul laughing about your sister."

"Well, of course not! Elspeth's not funny. She's a good egg, really, but she's rather a bore for all that. Reads all the time. Nothing to laugh at there."

"Why does Caroline think people are laughing at your sister?" Julian asked. Interrogating a nine-year-old was difficult to say the least.

"Don't know," came Harry's answer, rather muffled. He wouldn't look at Julian.

"I think you do, Harry. Tell me, were you listening

at doors or did they have these conversations in front of you?"

"Well. . . ."

"At doors, then. So be it. Naturally, a gentleman does not do such a thing except when it is absolutely necessary, and this does sound like one of those times." He watched while Harry worked that out, then brightened considerably. "What did you hear?"

"Well, I didn't understand it really. I couldn't hear very well. But Caroline screamed the place down about Elspeth running around after some man."

"I did not see your sister running around after any man at all, Harry. Did she say who the gentleman was?"

"Just a man named Julian. Do you know anyone named Julian, Mr. Thorpe?"

He took a deep breath, shocked at the flare of anger that shot through him. "Well, I suppose she must mean me, Harry. I'm the only Julian in our set, at least here in Bath. Unless, of course, they mean old Julian Forbish. I expect they can't mean him, though. He's well into his eighties and he doesn't run at all. No need running after him all night." It was a small joke and treated accordingly. Harry looked chagrined. "See here, Harry. I can promise you your sister most decidedly did not run around after me at all, not even a little. And no one else thinks so, either. I don't know what this is all about, but I'll be happy to straighten it out. When will your sister be ready for the picnic?"

"Oh, she isn't to go on the picnic, sir. Aunt Bettina told her she couldn't stir from the house today at all. Caroline will go, though."

"I see." And he did. A nasty little bit of jealousy. Caroline couldn't stand to share the attention, not with anyone. "How soon do you suppose Caroline will be ready to leave?"

"Oh, hours yet. She's running around upstairs in her

dressing gown, shrieking about how she hates all her dresses. Actually, I think they look awful, too. All that fuss and stuff. Elspeth's dresses are much better. She doesn't look like a ninny."

The boy was shaping up at that. "Harry, I need to talk to your sister, but you say she's been crying all morning?"

"All morning. She wouldn't even let me in her room."

"Where is your Aunt Bettina?"

"In her room, lying down. She told us to be very quiet and leave her be."

"All right. I have a favor to ask of you. Go to your sister's room, very quietly. Tell her you really, really need her to get you a book from the library. Say, uh, Homer's *Odyssey*. Tell her you need to settle a score with Roderick."

"What score? She's bound to ask."

Elspeth would ask, too. Even distraught, her curiosity would get the better of her. "Uh, say Roderick is arguing about Scylla and Charybdis. About which is the whirlpool and which is the rock."

"Oh, she'll know the answer to that. She knows all that stuff without a book."

"Yes, but Roderick wouldn't believe it unless you showed it to him, would he?"

"That's true. He won't even believe it sometimes when you do show it to him."

"I'm not surprised. Still, you get her down to the library, then make yourself scarce."

"I say, I'll be lying, won't I? Everyone always gets into such a pother when I lie the least little bit."

Ah, children were taught to be such absolutists. "Well, yes, you'll be lying, and this is, again, one of those things where it's hardly ever right, except only under very rare circumstances, such as these. Your sister has been upset unfairly, and I mean to set it right."

"You'll vouch for me, then? She'll be awfully annoyed." Harry sounded dubious about the strength of character of his accomplice. Didn't want to be left holding the bag, as it were. Julian didn't much blame him.

"Harry, I'd be an awful coward to put you up to something, then desert you under fire, wouldn't I?"

"Roderick would."

"I won't."

For a moment they stared at one another. Julian could see Harry working it out in his head. Things were so simple to a child. Things were right or they were wrong. Something was a lie, or it was the truth. When did one learn to shade and color and make excuses, Julian wondered. Still, he couldn't very well send up his card and ask to see her. He could just imagine the "pother," as Harry would put it, that would cause.

"I'll do it, sir. I can trust you," Harry said drawing himself up straighter.

"Good lad. Hurry on now. I'd like to speak with your sister before Caroline is ready to go."

"Well, not to worry. You'll have all day, then," Harry said drily and took himself off.

Julian waited a moment, then slipped from the drawing room across the hallway to the library, closing the door behind him. He didn't have too long to wait. He heard the door open quietly, and watched a bedraggled figure creep in. Perhaps ladies moved more quickly when no one waited for them, an odd, ironic little thought.

He did know a moment of guilt. No lady of any social stratum whatsoever appreciated an ambush, particularly if she'd been crying all day. He stood in a corner, away from the light. She hadn't seen him yet. Of course, she wasn't expecting anyone to be there. She wore her spectacles and a simple day dress, gray, possibly, although in this light it was difficult to tell. It was a soft color. Caroline wouldn't be caught at a cock fight in any color so quiet. Pity. It might have lent her some grace.

Elspeth moved to the bookcase nearest her and peered somewhat myopically at the titles, her back to where he stood in the shadows. Her shoulders were slumped and he could feel the misery emanating from her slight form. Surely he ought to make himself known, but he found himself disinclined to move. She would be so upset to find him here. He heard a great sniff and it gave him a pang. He watched as her hand lifted and fell on a book. She pulled it out, thumbed it open, then gave a great sob and let it slip to the floor. Fumbling in a skirt pocket for a handkerchief, she must not have heard him as he crossed over to her.

"Elspeth," he said softly, just behind her.

She gave a squeak and jumped, turning quickly. Shock, followed by anger, chased across her face. "Oh, no! Not you! How could this day get any worse?" she cried, and buried her face in her handkerchief.

"I suppose I deserve that," he whispered, stepping closer and reaching for her.

"Not another step," she said, stepping back so quickly that she bumped up against the shelves. She glared up at him. "Things are bad enough without my being caught in flagrante delicto in the library with you! Now they'll accuse me of conniving an assignation."

"Please tell me what on earth is going on. What is this all about?" he asked.

"As I am the laughingstock of the *ton*, I suppose you already know what it's about," she said, glaring all the more. "Did you entertain everyone with tales of my pathetic and gauche behavior?"

"Elspeth, I played cards in Lady Dowling's library until the wee hours. Your name was mentioned only once, by my friend Wesley Ames, who made a flattering remark about your demeanor, with which we all agreed. I was careful not to say more to avert the very gossip Caroline claims to have heard. If you were the laughingstock of the *ton*, I would have heard it." She continued to glare, but she looked a bit less mutinous. Emboldened, he went on. "I suspect you have been treated unkindly by your cousin. Tell me what she said to you."

Elspeth blew her nose. Her eyes were all puffy and red-rimmed, large as saucers behind the rims of her spectacles. Beautiful, luminous green saucers. He longed to take her in his arms, but he rather feared getting brained with a book should he make the attempt.

"She said that after I left, my name was on everyone's lips, that I had made an ass of myself chasing after you, and that she could barely hold her head up the rest of the evening. So help me, I don't understand how anything that I did could be so interpreted, but if this is what passes for fun among the 'Quality,' then I want no part of it."

"I cannot defend the *ton* on the subject of malicious gossip, Elspeth. God knows they are guilty of much worse on any given day. But this time, I think not. It may be ungentlemanly of me to say it, but I think your cousin is just plain jealous of you."

"Jealous of me?" Elspeth asked, incredulity plain in her tone. "What on earth would she find to be jealous of? She is beautiful, I am plain. She is witty, I am dull. She has money, I am poor. I cannot believe it."

"Were you any other demoiselle in Bath, I would assume you were fishing rather desperately for compliments. But I believe we have established to my satisfaction that you do not stoop to such. As it is, I think you have no idea of the truth." He smiled into her great, green eyes.

"Please don't bother with idle flattery, sir," she said

with a snuffle. "I have explained to you that I do not require it."

"You are very beautiful," he said softly. She refused to meet his eye. "You have more wit in your hat that Caroline can muster in any given year." She still would not look at him. "Money doesn't matter," he finished, rather lamely, he thought.

Now she gave him a look that could blister the paint off the walls.

"I mean, it does not matter to me." He stepped forward slowly. She shrank back, but there was no place for her to go. She gazed up at him, eyes impossibly large, impossibly beautiful. He placed his hands on the bookshelf, one to either side of her face. He lowered his head to hers, slowly, slowly. As gently as a whisper, his lips touched hers. Her lips were soft and delicious. He longed to deepen the kiss, to stir a passion he knew swam just beneath her cool surface. Instead, he lowered his hands and slipped them softly around her shoulders.

"Unhand my sister, sir!" came a shout from behind.

Unfortunately, Julian and Elspeth both started at the same time, butting their heads together.

"Harry, my boy! It is customary to knock before entering a room," Julian said, wincing, as he turned to face his accuser.

"You—you are a cad, sir!" the boy declared, standing his ground. "I—I challenge you to a duel!" he announced, his young voice ringing with righteous indignation.

"Uh, no, actually, Harry, that's not quite the right thing to do here," Julian said, stepping prudently away from Elspeth. He cast a look at her and noted that she was still pressed against the bookshelf, her face flaming scarlet.

"It isn't?" Harry responded, looking less sure of himself.

"Well, no. You see, a gentleman and a lady might have a few moments together to—that is, it is not inappropriate for a gentleman and a lady to—Elspeth, help me!" Julian cried in sheer desperation.

"Harry, go away and hold your tongue!" Elspeth snapped.

"Shan't! I will not leave you alone with this—this rake!"

"Oh, hush! Do you want the whole house to hear you!" she hissed, stepping forward menacingly.

"I'm only trying to protect you, Owl Eyes," he said, pouting a bit and looking hurt.

"Yes, thank you," she said, obviously trying to sound calmer. "But I do not need protecting from Mr. Thorpe. He is a gentleman, and I trust him to behave like one at all times." The glare she threw at him suggested quite the opposite. Julian gave her a large, abashed grin. It didn't seem to help.

"He wasn't acting like one just now, El. He was kissing you," Harry muttered darkly.

"Hush, dear. Mr. Thorpe was just—just expressing a—a kindly affection. Don't speak of it again, please," she continued, hurriedly, noting her brother's skeptical look. "Now, what did you want, dear?"

"I came to tell you that Caroline is . . ."

"Caroline is what?" came a waspish voice from the door. "How dare you come in here and bother Mr. Thorpe? Get out of here! You're not even allowed in these rooms, you dirty little brat!" Caroline sailed into the room, glaring about, her baleful gaze coming to rest on Elspeth. Harry took two steps to the rear of her, but otherwise stood his ground. "And you, cousin," she continued, her tone dangerous. "I think you must be very thick-witted. I think you have not heard a word I've said all morning."

"Actually, Caroline—and good afternoon to you, too,

by the way"—Julian said, stepping forward and making a perfunctory leg in her general direction—"Miss Quinn seems to have heard a good many words, all of them sheer nonsense. She's been quite upset by something that simply has no truth to it whatsoever. Silly stuff, wouldn't you agree?"

Caroline said nothing, meeting his eye, her look furious. Finally, she turned away disdainfully. "Well, far be it from me to care if she wishes to make a complete fool of herself," she said dismissively. "I'm sure that's what I get for trying to help a penniless distant cousin. I'm ready to go now, Julian," she announced regally.

"Are you ready, Miss Quinn?" Julian asked pointedly of Elspeth.

Caroline whirled around furiously. "Elspeth is not going! She has—the headache!" Caroline declared triumphantly.

"Well, some fresh air will be quite the thing then," Julian said amiably. "You'll need a wrap, Miss Quinn. It's breezy today."

"Oh, I don't think. . . ." Elspeth began.

"Elspeth, remember what I've told you!" Caroline said at the same time.

Julian watched them both. Caroline stared imperiously at Elspeth, who stared back in appraisal.

"I'll just get my wrap, then, Mr. Thorpe," Elspeth said finally, turning a grim smile on him, and moving toward the door.

"I'm going too. I'll be the chaperone," Harry announced with a certain manly pride in his voice.

"You'll do no such thing, you awful little beast!" Caroline cried, turning to vent her wrath on the boy. "I told you to leave the room, didn't I?"

"Actually, that's an excellent idea, Harry. With you along, no one can raise an eyebrow, as your cousin seems to so fear for your sister. Get your cloak, my boy, and meet us in the street. You'll see my carriage right outside. Wake up my coachman, will you, sir?"

Harry just grinned as he quit the room.

"Julian, I have no idea what you think you're up to, but I swear. . . ."

"I'm 'up to' nothing at all, Caroline," he interrupted. "If you'd just relax, we could all have a pleasant outing. Now, why don't you get a cloak and we'll be off? Half the day is gone already. In the country I'd've done a day's work by now."

She just stared at him, expression incredulous, then turned on her heel and left the room. Idly, Julian walked over and picked up the slim book Elspeth had dropped. He scanned the spine. It was Cicero's *Oration Against Cataline*.

Chapter Seven

Edgar was not happy. The weight of one hundred pounds felt as if it were evaporating from his pocket, farthing by farthing. The small party strolled among the grape arbors of the new vineyard at Claverton, seemingly happy, unless one got close enough to observe the tense postures and tight lips. Whatever perversity of spirit had possessed Julian to attach himself like a limpet to the country cousin, and, worse, to let the little brother tag along like a wart on the heel of one's foot? Caroline's fingers dug like claws into his own arm. The chit was livid, there was no doubt about that, but after one or two vague rebuffs, she made no further effort to cut Julian from the herd, instead trailing along behind, glaring daggers into his back.

Wesley Ames had elected to stay behind with his wife, and was snoring on the blanket before the rest of them had strolled beyond earshot.

"That was quite a delicious repast, wasn't it, Miss

Quinn?" Edgar ventured finally, abhorring silence.

"Indeed," was her terse reply. Well, the chit could at least make some effort! Why, he had put together the entire outing with her own best interests at heart. Actually, his own interests stood to gain as well, if only Julian had not decided to play such silly games. Was the man trying to make Caroline jealous? If so, he might well be succeeding admirably, if her angry demeanor was any measure. Surely the man could not be seriously interested in the country cousin? The girl was pretty enough, of course, but a man did not choose a wife on looks alone, and *on dit* had it that the girl was near penniless, of the Lesser Quinns, as Caroline had put it. Nor was the country cousin a particular wit. She seemed oblivious to the latest gossip, and, worse, she and Julian had had the most stultifying conversation over the picnic luncheon, nattering on and on about canals, apparently terribly important to trade in the cousin's corner of England, although why anyone but merchants themselves would care to know anything at all on the subject was beyond his own comprehension.

Julian must be humoring the girl in order to secure Caroline's attention. There could be no other explanation. Still, Julian had made no effort to seek out Caroline today, and had, indeed, spent more time talking to the tiresome boy than to anyone else of the party except the country cousin herself.

Edgar picked up the pace a bit, curious as to what the two could be discussing so assiduously. "The vineyard shows signs of producing a good wine. The recent yields have been quite promising, I understand," Julian was saying. Good God, did these people have no idea how boring they were? Now Edgar glared at Julian's back as well. Here was a man who had everything one could want in life—social position, plenty of scratch and a fine-looking face and form to go with it. Not to mention the wit to carry it all off. Julian Thorpe lacked nothing God or family could provide. There were times, particularly when the creditors became more wolverine than human, when Edgar felt he could hate Julian for all that he had, all that Edgar himself lacked. Well, there was one thing Julian needed and that was a wife. Something pitiful, ne'er-do-well Edgar could help him with. Julian needed a wife and had lots of money. Caroline needed a husband and could spend lots of money. It was a match made in heaven. But creditors being the howling, craven curs that they were, Edgar would have to find a way to move things along, and right quickly, too.

As if reading his mind, Caroline gave a little cry and went tumbling down, pretty little feet flying among lacy petticoats. "Julian!" she cried faintly, but she needn't have bothered. Ever the gentleman, Thorpe was already on his way back to her. On a suspicious impulse, Edgar checked the path where Caroline had taken her fall. As he had guessed, it was as smooth and level as glass. The clever little minx. While Julian busied himself over Caroline's prostrate, moaning form, Edgar bent down, finding immediately what he sought, beside the path. Quickly he pried the rock loose, then shifted to stand over the hole it left. It was clear this rock had lodged on that spot since the Romans, but no one else need know that.

"Oh, Julian, I tripped on a beastly rock. I believe it's my ankle," Caroline said, pouting prettily. "I don't believe I'll be able to walk on it at all."

"Well, I'll have to carry you then," obliged Julian.

"Oh, I say, look here!" Edgar called, holding up the rock. "Caroline, you must have slipped on this. Nasty, sharp thing. It was right in the middle of the path. I'm sorry I didn't fall over it first and save you the discomfort." He stole a glance at the country cousin and was amused to note her giving him an appraising look. She was a quick-witted little thing—he had to give her credit for that—for all the good it would do her. Which was none at all.

The frosty silence had endured so long, Elspeth hardly noticed it now. For the past two days, she might as well have been on another continent as living in this ice-cold household. Even Harry tiptoed about, eyes large and bewildered. He had taken to hiding out in the kitchen, where the two kitchen maids were young enough to recognize a fellow playmate and tolerated his presence with a good-natured cheer.

No one had said she was to attend tonight's assembly, but then no one had said she was not to attend, so Elspeth dressed now in the dark silence of her room, the single candle casting barely enough light to see by. She pulled on the deep burgundy moiré silk gown, enjoying the cool, smooth touch as it slipped over her shoulders. A lace fichu was artfully sewn into the décolletage, modest even by country standards. She had only a small mirror at her dressing table, but there was a large pier glass in the hallway, so she stepped out to check her appearance. The hallway was no better lit—Aunt Bettina was nothing if not frugal where the *ton* couldn't see—but there was enough light to make out her reflection. Elspeth settled her spectacles on her nose and peered closely. She had pinned her dark brown hair up higher than usual and would have been pleased with the effect, had a few errant tendrils not asserted their independence. She attempted to fiddle the stuff up again, but gave up in defeat. Perhaps the one lady's maid they all shared might be along to help her in a few minutes, but Elspeth had the sneaking suspicion that she might wait a long time for that to happen.

She touched the lace fichu lightly, smiling at its delicate intricacy. The deep burgundy color suited her, she thought—not too drab, but not so vibrant as to draw too much attention to herself, something she wished to avoid at all costs. Julian had promised her that virtually no one in the *ton* was gossiping about her, other than perhaps an amused speculation as to how soon she might forfeit Sir Richard's rheumy eye—but, still, she felt more comfortable in modest, quiet attire. She had no wish to compete with her spiteful cousin.

She heard a gasp behind and turned quickly, in time to hear Caroline, her face mottled red, scream, "Mama! You promised!" Before Elspeth could react, Caroline had turned on her heel and flounced off in the direction of her mother's room. Entering, she slammed the door behind her, and from within, Elspeth could hear raised, angry voices.

"What's wrong, Owl Eyes?" hissed a small voice behind her. Harry had crept from his room and now stood behind her skirts, ready, no doubt, to bolt for safety should the need arise.

"I don't know, Harry," Elspeth sighed, turning to place her arms around the boy. She regretted having insisted that Harry accompany her on this blighted visit. She had thought to expose him to the gentry and improve his manners to some small extent, but between Caroline and cousin Roderick, she feared he was learning the very worst about human nature. Of course, there was Julian. . . .

Aunt Bettina's door opened and Caroline issued forth, pausing only to bestow a triumphant smile on Elspeth, before hastening back to her own room and again slamming the door.

"Where are you going tonight, Elspeth?" Harry asked, stepping out from behind her and casting a dubious eye at her gown.

"To bed, I fear, dear. Just where you should be," she replied, bending to give him a kiss.

"But you're all dressed up," he answered, looking confused.

"I was just trying it on to see how it looked. Now run along to bed, darling." She heard Aunt Bettina's door open behind her. "Hurry," she said, giving him a playful swat. Harry was apparently of like mind with regard to confronting his aunt, and he beat a hasty retreat.

"Good evening, Aunt," said Elspeth. "I hope you are well this evening?"

"Well, yes, thank you, Elspeth. But I fear there has been some misunderstanding. You see, under the circumstances, what with all the tongues wagging, and you know how awkward that is for poor Caroline. . . ."

"You'd prefer that I not go to the assembly this evening, I presume?"

"Oh, no, no, my dear," Aunt Bettina said hurriedly. "I do so wish you could. Sir Richard, you know. There are any number of ladies vying for his attention, but he seems quite taken with you. You could do worse, you know . . ." she trailed off, aware that she was digressing. "It's just that I feel it would do more good for you to go to ground for a bit, as it were. Out of sight, out of mind. . . ." She broke off again, reddening, as if she'd just realized her words could have more than one interpretation. "That is to say," she went on, collecting her authority about her, "the tongues will stop as soon as they have other things to wag about. And when you are not present, there can be no gossip about you. Caroline feels so dreadfully for your reputation, you know," she added, rather lamely.

"Yes, I know just how she feels," replied Elspeth.

"As it is, I expect Mr. Thorpe to offer for Caroline, possibly this evening," Aunt Bettina said, with a proud smile. "Such a fine match it will be, don't you think?"

It was as if time had stopped. Elspeth could hardly breathe for the sound of her heart pounding in her chest. She made herself take a deep breath. "Indeed. My congratulations, Aunt," she finally replied. She was surprised that the words came out at all, so constricted was her throat. "Well, I'll say goodnight, then," she said quickly. Without waiting for a reply, she turned away from her aunt and sought the sanctity of her own room, closing the door quietly behind her.

She sank into the chair at her dressing table, and peered into the very small glass that sat in front of her. Large eyes, magnified, stared back at her. Julian had said her eyes were beautiful. But, of course, all the gentlemen in Bath said such silly things. It meant nothing. A toff might well tell a lady she was beautiful, and an hour later, propose marriage to another. She was confused by the dark pain in her chest. It wasn't because she was not going to tonight's assembly. There was nothing about the evening's entertainment itself that had engaged her anticipation. It was Julian Thorpe, and Julian Thorpe alone who had kept her here in Bath, in a cold and angry house where even her small brother suffered from a surfeit of disdain. It was preposterous to stay. Now he would be engaged to Caroline, and all the tongues would find amusement in the fact that the foolish country cousin had dared to presume so much. Had dared to set her sights on Mr. Thorpe, he as far above her meager circumstances as any of Queen Charlotte's eight living sons. And then the *ton* would indeed laugh at the foolish Miss Quinn, Julian laughing longest and loudest at her naive temerity.

She would take Harry and go home to Weston-under-Lizard, and Julian Thorpe would never give Miss Elspeth Quinn another thought again as long as he lived on this earth. She raised her hands to her hair and began removing the pins slowly, one by one. It was hard to see by the one candle, harder still with her eyes swimming in tears. She would go home, and think about Mr. Julian Thorpe for all the rest of her lonely days.

Julian scanned the Assembly Room but there was no sign of Elspeth. Caroline, however, was much in evidence. It seemed she managed to be everywhere he looked, smiling invitingly at him. There was no doubt she was the loveliest of all the demoiselles in attendance this evening. But hers was not the face he sought. For some reason he found he had a strong preference for soft brown hair rather than blonde, and large green eyes, rather than hard blue ones.

"Caroline is at her lovely best tonight, wouldn't you say, Julian?" came Edgar's voice at his elbow. "Of course that puppy Ledbetter seems to have staked out his territory. I can't believe you'd let him poach on your grounds like that. You'd best be careful or you'll lose her to him. And what will the Pater Familias have to say if you arrive home without a bride?"

"Good evening to you, Edgar. And don't worry about me, thank you." No point in taking any of that prodigious amount of bait. Edgar would like nothing better than to run through the Assembly Rooms this evening scattering new tidbits about Julian Thorpe and Caroline Quinn.

"Good evening, Mr. Thorpe," came a voice at his other elbow. That voice. So far this was not shaping up to be much of an evening.

"And good evening to you, Mrs. Quinn," he replied smoothly, bending over the hand he was offered. "I'm pleased to see that your daughter suffers no lingering effects from twisting her ankle the other day."

"Oh, she suffered dreadfully, Mr. Thorpe," gushed Bettina Quinn. "But you know my dear Caroline. Not a word of complaint. Not a word. I've put warm compresses on her ankle and it has reduced the swelling.

Nothing would do but that she come this evening. She did so wish to get out a bit after being confined for the last few days. But I know she is in great pain. Not that she will ever say a word. Not a word."

Julian refrained from mentioning that he had caught a glimpse of Caroline in High Street two days ago, strolling along with no hint of a limp, or any sort of discomfort whatsoever. Indeed, when he had examined the ankle himself shortly after the mishap, there had been no sign of swelling or bruising.

"And where is Miss Elspeth Quinn, ma'am?" he asked, again looking about. "I've not seen her this evening."

The woman's lips tightened visibly. "Elspeth is home with the headache. She is a sickly gel. Quite a lot of constant fuss about her health, really. Very demanding."

"Sir Richard must be *trés distrait*," put in Edgar.

"Oh, indeed. He asked after her first thing," replied Bettina Quinn, sounding a bit smug. "You must dance with Caroline, Mr. Thorpe. I must tell you," she added, with an exaggerated look over her shoulder at no one, "I do believe Mr. Ledbetter will ask for her any day now. You'd best be on your toes, young man," she advised, simpering.

"Ah, indeed," was all Julian could muster, making a leg in preparation for a quick retreat.

"Mustn't waste any time, then, Julian," said Edgar, taking Julian's arm, as if sensing his intention to flee. "Good evening to you, Mrs. Quinn," Edgar murmured, then propelled Julian directly into the path of Caroline, who, as a matter of great coincidence, happened at that moment to be sauntering by.

"Why, good evening, Mr. Thorpe," Caroline said with a sweet smile. Recognizing defeat when he stared it in the face, Julian offered a bow. . . .

* * *

It had taken a good deal of maneuvering, but Julian had at last freed himself of the determined Miss Caroline Quinn. Now his carriage approached the Quinn residence. He had slipped away from the Assembly Rooms, hoping he would not be missed, although Edgar had seemed harder to shake than Caroline. The carriage slowed and Julian peered out. The street and house were dark. He had been an idiot to come, but now that he was here, he could not make himself rap on the front of the carriage to tell his coachman to drive on.

What if she really did have the headache? He dismissed the idea immediately. Despite Bettina Quinn's protestations, Elspeth Quinn was a sturdy young woman, not at all given to the vapors. But headache or none, how was he to knock on the door at this hour, just shy of midnight, and say he'd come calling? With her aunt at the Assembly Rooms, it would be most improper. Still, he sat inside the coach, exhorting himself not to act like a perfect fool.

He looked again, but not a flicker of light appeared at any of the windows. Wait. Was it a trick of the light, or perhaps just wishful thinking? He peered up at a window on the second floor. Indeed, what had been the faintest suggestion of light now became, very decidedly, a candle flickering against the window pane.

But who was it? That didn't matter, he decided, springing from the carriage, since it couldn't be Bettina or her spawn, and those were the only residents of this establishment he'd prefer not to meet up with again this evening. He stood near a street lamp and waved his arms at the candle bearer, feeling like a fool. The candle lit the window for a minute, then retreated, its light growing dimmer and dimmer until it faded altogether. Telling his coachman to take the carriage around the corner if he gained admittance, and hoping for the best, Julian climbed the steps and stood expectantly at the front door. If no one came in a moment, he decided he would ring the bell. But less than a moment later he heard the creaks and groans of the lock being thrown. His heart was beating a tattoo in his chest. Must be drinking too much coffee these days.

The door opened just a crack and a small white face peeped out. "It *is* you, Mr. Thorpe!" Harry exclaimed. "Have you brought my aunt and cousin with you?" He peered with some apprehension at the carriage, which had just started off.

"Well, no, Harry. Actually, they're still at the Assembly Rooms. May I come in?" Harry stepped aside. Blessing the lack of sophistication in a nine-year-old, Julian stepped in quickly, closing the door behind him. His carriage was unmarked, and he might not have been spotted at this hour by nosy neighbors anxious to pry into the affairs of others.

"Does Elspeth really have the headache, Harry?" Julian asked, taking the candle from the boy and heading for the library. The boy wore an old, faded dressing gown, much too large and a bit old fashioned. Julian was certain it was a hand-me-down from the boy's dead father, and the thought gave him a pang.

"Headache? Elspeth never gets headaches," replied Harry, trailing behind. "What do you want, anyway? Isn't it rather late to call?"

"Well, yes and no, my boy," Julian said, lighting a branch of candles in the library from the one he carried. "We do tend to crawl about at all hours of the night. Now, nine in the morning—that's an ungodly hour to call. Now, then," he said, handing the candle back to Harry. "Run and fetch Elspeth for me. Tell her I must see her."

"Is this entirely proper?" Harry asked, dubiously. "I don't want to have to call you out for a duel, sir. I'm not much good with pistols yet, actually."

"No matter. We can fence, then," Julian said. "Swords, it will be. That will give you quite an advantage, by the way. I'm dreadful with a sword. Trips me up every time." Harry giggled. "Actually, it will be quite proper for me to speak to your sister. You're here, after all, and surely there's a house full of servants."

"The servants can't hear anything," Harry said, frowning. "They're all way up on the top floor."

All the better, my little man, Julian thought, making sure his face did not betray his thinking. "Well, you're here, anyway. That's good enough. Go on. Get her." Julian made shooing motions. His nocturnal visit wasn't at all proper, really, but as his intentions were pure, and no one would know anyway, he didn't feel any significant qualms about the dangers of compromising Elspeth's honor.

The boy paused at the door, turning back to look at Julian.

"Yes?" Julian queried, hoping the child wouldn't balk now.

"No kissing, sir," came the small but firm voice.

"None?"

"Not even one, sir. Those are my terms."

"Very well, Harry. You drive a hard bargain."

The boy left the room and Julian paced back and forth, waiting. Now that the die was cast, he wondered what on earth he could have been thinking of. There was no use blaming it all on demon liquor. He had had nothing to drink this evening. Not yet, anyway, he thought to himself, spying the brandy decanter that sat invitingly on a small table. He crossed the room in several long strides and poured a hefty tot into one of the cut-glass snifters that sat on the silver tray with the decanter. He took a long and satisfying draught. The brandy wasn't bad. Probably from the late Lord Ewell's cellar. He had kept a decent cellar, Julian recalled fondly. That and a good library. Excellent gentleman.

"Mr. Thorpe, what on earth are you doing here at this hour? What is wrong?"

He started at her voice, but fortunately the deep-sided snifter did not slop the brandy all over his cuff. Just as well. He had behaved enough like a fool already. He turned. Elspeth stood in the doorway, looking alarmed, Harry's little face peeping out from behind her skirts. She had obviously donned her gown in a hurry. The buttons were done up crookedly. Her dark brown hair fell about her shoulders. She was beautiful. That was when he realized why he had come this evening.

"I'm sorry to have unduly alarmed you," he said, setting down the snifter and crossing over to her. He took her hand in his. "There's really nothing wrong, other than that I missed you at the assembly this evening. Why didn't you come?"

Elspeth just stared at him, making no answer.

"Harry, my boy, I need you to be my lookout. Can you wait in the hallway and tell us if anyone comes?"

Harry was learning. He cocked an eye at his mentor. "I'm not supposed to leave you alone with my sister, am I?" he asked.

"Well, to be painfully precise, no," Julian answered. "But under the circumstances, with us right here in this room, and you right outside in the hallway, we are within the bounds of decency." *Only just*, he added mentally. Fortunately the boy accepted this quibble without fuss and turned to go. Yet, once again, he stopped in the doorway.

"Remember your promise," he warned.

"What promise?" asked Julian.

"No kissing," announced Harry.

"Harry! Out!" cried Elspeth. The door slammed behind the boy.

Elspeth stood at some distance, her expression wary.

She was beautiful in the candlelight. But then she was beautiful in the daylight, and full dark as well. She said nothing. There was a stiffness to her, a distance that he could not fathom. Unless the harpies had been sowing their poison again. He crossed the room toward her. She watched him come, but did not move. Reaching her, he took her elbow. Her expression did not change.

"Come and sit down, Elspeth," he said gently. He led her over to the settee and sat her down. He seated himself next to her, finally letting go of her arm. It was a small settee, with barely enough room for the two of them. Through the silk of her gown he could feel the warmth of her thigh pressed against his. He had bedded more than his fair share of lovely ladies, but this woman excited him like no other.

"It's not really true, of course. I'm aware of that, you know," Elspeth said finally, her voice distant and cool. She had not put on her spectacles, and her green eyes stared large and unfocused at him.

"What isn't true, Elspeth?" he asked, although he thought he knew what she was talking about.

"It *is* most dreadfully improper for me to be alone with you like this," she said gravely. "Harry manning the hallway doesn't do much as far as observing the proprieties."

"Well, I certainly don't plan on mentioning it to anyone," he responded, laughing. "I trust you will not?"

Her humor did not match his. She just looked at him. "Why are you here, Julian?" she asked.

He took her hand. He had long since removed his gloves, and she, of course, wore none at this hour. Her hand was soft and delicate. His own fingers, hard and callused from laboring at his estate, felt large and clumsy against hers.

"Why didn't you come to the assembly tonight?"

"I think you must know why, Julian," she said softly. She withdrew her hand from his.

"Caroline would have none of it?" he asked.

"I think that's not for me to say," she replied, standing and moving away from him. She stopped in front of one of the tall bookcases and stood ostensibly perusing the titles. As she was not wearing her spectacles, Julian knew she saw nothing of the books. He stared at her back, wondering what to say. She seemed so distant, so cool, not like her usual jovial self.

"Am I to wish you joy, then?" she asked, finally, keeping her back to him. "Have you come to express your happiness to me in person?"

"For what?" he responded, perplexed.

"I was led to understand that this evening you would ask my aunt for my cousin's hand in marriage," she said. He had to strain to hear her, but her meaning was clear enough. He was on his feet instantly, crossing the distance between them in two long strides.

"Who told that?" he asked, placing his hands on her shoulders. She flinched and twisted away, keeping her back to him. He lowered his arms slowly, waiting for her answer.

"Elspeth, please turn around," he said softly, when it became clear she would not speak.

She shook her head, but by the hunching of her shoulders, he feared she might be crying.

"Elspeth, I have no intention of asking your cousin to marry me," he said. Her back stiffened, but she said nothing. "I don't know who could have told you such a thing. I know silly gossip is rampant among the *ton*, but I swear I've said nothing to anyone to leave the impression that my feelings for Caroline are anything but distantly cordial. Actually, they are not even that. To be candid, I do not much care for your cousin at all." Still, she said nothing, but she raised her head. She had a sweet scent, lavender, he thought, light and lovely, just like herself.

"Actually, I had rather thought to ask if you might consider marrying me, yourself," he finished. The words surprised him as they came out. He had not really been aware that he wanted to marry her, but now that he had said so, he realized that he had known it from the first day they had met. How could he not have known?

"How dare you!" she cried, turning to face him.

"What?" he asked, stunned. He had been about to embrace her, and her words caught him with his hands in midair.

She moved quickly away from him, stopping so that there was a little table between them.

"How dare you play with me like that," she went on. There were tears on her cheeks and he longed to kiss them away, but for now he held still. "I have explained to you—I thought you, at least, understood. I am a simple country woman. I am not used to your silly flirtations and idle remarks. I take you seriously. When you say things like that, I believe you. Please don't hurt me like that again," she finished, choking out the words.

"I love you so much," he said almost in a whisper.

"Please stop, I beg of you," she said, lowering her head into her hands, with a sob.

"What can I do to make you believe me?" he asked, crossing the distance to her. She raised her head and just stared at him, green eyes large and swimming in pain. He reached the little table that separated them. "Will you marry me?" he asked simply.

She drew a shaky breath, then slowly shook her head in the negative.

She meant it. She was not one of those demoiselles who would refuse a man a dozen times just for the sport of it. The knowledge cut through him like a knife. "Why not?" he asked, in pain. Did she not love him then? Was he so blinded by his own sense of magnificence that he had taken it for granted any young woman would leap at the chance to be Mrs. Thorpe?

She took a deep breath. "I am not fit to be your wife, Mr. Thorpe," she said, simply. "I think you ask me now because you feel trapped into it. . . ."

"I am trapped by nothing, Elspeth, except by my love for you!" he interrupted.

For a moment she just stared at him. "You see, already I forget the rules, Mr. Thorpe," she said, finally, pain in her voice. "I find myself believing you, and I know I should not. But," she went on, "even if you think you have a certain fondness for my company, you should know that my circumstances are far beneath your own, sir."

"You are the daughter of a gentleman, Elspeth," he exclaimed. He longed to kick over the nasty little table that separated them, but he thought better of frightening the life out of her. He made a mental note to banish all such meaningless furnishings from his home. "More to the point," he went on, "you are witty and wonderful, and I love you! What other circumstances need we consider?"

"I think I've failed to tell you the truth, sir," she said, sadly. "My father was a gentleman, yes, but I should have made certain you understood that we are quite poor, virtually penniless, in fact."

"Well, I am very rich! What do the state of your finances have to do with anything at all? And if you think I was unaware of your 'penniless' state, let me assure you that your cousin and your aunt have mentioned it repeatedly. Ad nauseam, in fact."

"You would be the laughingstock of the *ton* if you were forced to settle for the likes of me, sir."

"Do you not care for me at all then, Elspeth?" he asked softly. He felt a sinking feeling in the pit of his stomach. If she said no, however gently, he would slink away to the country and never be happy again.

"I care for you above all others on this earth, Julian!" she cried. "You must know that. I know I'm never supposed to say such things to a man, but that doesn't matter now. I love you. I love you too much to accept this gentlemanly offer, to see you one day come to believe that you were maneuvered into marrying me, to watch you grow more and more bitter and embarrassed year after year at what a poor little bargain you have made." She choked on these last words and buried her head in her hands again, sobbing.

It was too much! In an instant he had moved around the beastly little table. This time she did not pull away as he put his arms around her and pulled her to him. He buried his face in her soft hair. She smelled of lavender, clean and fresh, with no hint of the cloying scent so popular among the ladies of his set. His arms went around her, the satin of her dress soft and cool against his callused fingers. He could feel her arms slip around him, pressing against his back. It set off fireworks in his brain. He moved his lips across her hair, drinking in the clean scent of her, not stopping until he reached her cheek. Her skin was warm and soft. His mouth slid down, barely touching her until his lips reached hers. There, he stopped, brushing his lips softly against her own.

She did not pull away. He drank in the taste of her, sweet and soft. Gently he let his tongue push against her lips, opening them slightly. He caught her lower lip gently between his teeth and brushed it lightly with his tongue. Her lips parted beneath his and he slipped his tongue between them, just slightly. He could feel her heart pounding against his chest, in rhythm with his own. She was delicious, soft and yielding. He felt that he could drown in the feel of her. He moved his hands down her back, down, down . . . and then stopped. He would not drink of this nectar until he knew that she would be his wife.

Quickly he pulled back, staring at her beautiful face. Her green eyes were wide and fathomless, gazing on him with the passion he knew lay hidden in their depths. "Marry me, Elspeth," he whispered raggedly. "I love you and no other. I need you. Please say you'll marry me."

"I will marry you, Julian," she answered softly.

With a cry, he crushed her to him. "Shall I speak with your aunt tomorrow, my darling?" he whispered against her ear.

"Oh, heavens, no!" she exclaimed, starting back. "Please let's not say anything at all to anyone. It's my mother we must speak with first, but not my aunt, never my aunt," she finished with a shudder.

"You'll have to give me directions to Weston-under-Lizard, then," he murmured, through lips that were busy again tracing a path from her ear to her mouth. She giggled and turned her face to his, her lips now seeking out his own. With a groan he pulled her to him, reveling in the heat of her, pressed up and down the length of his body. Her hands now roamed his back, insistent and sweet. He deepened the kiss, probing now with his tongue, finding hers. She gasped, then pressed herself harder to him, her tongue answering his.

"Mr. Thorpe! You promised!" cried a sharp little voice from the doorway.

They sprang apart and turned guilty eyes upon an outraged little brother.

"I shall have to challenge you now, sir," said Harry solemnly. "You have sullied my sister. Elspeth, I am ashamed of you. Mama would be shocked at your behavior."

He sounded so like a little man, Julian was hard pressed not to laugh, but he dared not make fun of this dear boy who, after all, was behaving far more properly than he and his beloved at this moment.

"Actually, Harry, your sister has not shamed the family at all. Nor have I sullied her. I'll tell you the truth, but it must be kept a secret for now. Your sister has accepted my proposal of marriage. Therefore, it is permitted that I kiss her."

"Like that?" Harry asked, dripping disgust. "That wasn't a kiss. I thought you were eating her up."

"Well, er . . . perhaps you'll, er . . ." He broke off, at a loss. Next to him, Elspeth giggled. She had taken his hand and was holding it tightly. "That is, perhaps some day, when you are my age, you'll see it somewhat differently, my boy." Harry's expression suggested he would never, so there.

"What did you want, brother?" asked Elspeth, gently.

"They're coming. I heard the carriage a minute ago."

"Good God! Why didn't you say so! Elspeth, will they come in through the front or from the mews?" he asked.

"They'll come in through the front; then the coachman will take the carriage round back," she answered, breathless. "We have only a minute then. Where is your carriage?"

"I sent him around the corner. They won't see it. The coachman will pass it but as it isn't marked, he'll not take particular notice. Harry, get in here and shut that door." The boy did so. "Is either your aunt or Caroline likely to come into the library before going upstairs?"

"Not terribly likely, no," was Elspeth's dry reply.

"Blow out the candles, Elspeth, and everyone be very quiet."

Elspeth leaned over and did so. Julian hoped the smell of just-snuffed candles would not carry under the door to the hall. In the dark now, he reached for her and pulled her close. He felt a small body snuggle against him on the other side, and he put a comforting arm around the boy's shoulders.

In the space of a heartbeat they heard the sound of the front door opening, then voices raised in anger, Bettina and Caroline.

"I tell you I don't know, Mama. He just left, that's all. One moment he was there and then the next he was gone. I don't know why!"

"Well, something needs to be settled here, Caroline! This has gone on too long. . . ." Her strident tones faded, and their footsteps could be heard on the stairs.

Julian could feel Harry fidget under his hand. "Shhh. Hold steady, boy," he whispered. "We're not out of the woods yet. What will they do now, Elspeth?"

"Argue some more," she whispered. "Or go to bed, probably. But they'll retreat to one or the other's bedroom. If we hear doors close and wait a bit, we should be safe."

They stood quietly in the dark. Julian felt a bit foolish until he felt Elspeth's fingers tracing up his chest. Abandoning Harry, he slid his arms around Elspeth and pulled her close, finding her lips in the dark with unerring instinct. The kiss was long and deep, and would have been utterly delicious, had not the boy decided to tug on Julian's coattail in the middle of things.

"I heard two doors close, sir," Harry whispered. "I think it will be safe for you to go now."

"Don't think I want to," Julian murmured softly into Elspeth's hair.

"You'd best get out while you can, Mr. Thorpe," she said, giggling and pushing him away.

"How will you get upstairs after I leave?" he asked, sliding his hands down her arms to take her hands in his own.

"We'll take a book, and slip upstairs, Harry and I. If

we're spotted, I'll say Harry had a nightmare and I'm planning to read him to sleep."

Julian nodded. Elspeth was clever. He liked the way she could turn her mind to practical solutions. Few woman of his acquaintance claimed to be able to think at all, except to plot matrimony.

"Harry, open the door just a crack, and see if there's any light in the hallway," Julian said. His callused fingers rubbed her soft hands.

He heard a small squeak and as the door was opened, he could make out the slightest line of light, probably from street lamps outside the windows of the drawing room across the hallway. "All clear, sir," came Harry's excited little whisper in the dark. No doubt this would become a tale for him to tell his grandchildren some day. *The Unusual Marriage Proposal to My Sister*.

Clutching Elspeth to him, Julian gave her one more kiss, hard and brief. "I'll see you tomorrow, my darling," he whispered, then slipped away from her. He paused at the doorway, giving Harry's head an affectionate pat. The boy meant well. He just had a bad habit of showing up at the most inconvenient times.

The hallway was dark, both on this floor and the one above, with no faint light spilling around any of the corners. Praying that the front door would not squeak, Julian made his way to it, only to be confronted with an elaborate set of locks, which Bettina had obviously thrown before going upstairs. "Harry, come help," Julian whispered, figuring any nine-year-old boy worth his salt knew how to open a lock in the dark. Little hands pushed his away and he heard bolts slide and tumblers fall. Bless the well-oiled machinery, Julian thought. The door opened and a cool breeze hit his face. "Lock it behind me, son," Julian whispered, then he was through, Harry shutting the door behind him.

Outside, Julian waited on the steps while he heard

the locks slide into place. He took a deep breath. His heart was singing as he descended the steps. It was not until he turned the corner and spied his carriage that he allowed himself a great triumphant shout.

Chapter Eight

"Your sister is the ape leader this year," Roderick said, in a singsong voice over porridge in the breakfast room, reserved these days as the children's exclusive domain.

"She is not!" Harry fumed. He grew tired of the incessant teasing and somewhere along the line, Roderick had apparently figured out that the surest way to get Harry's goat was to malign his older sister, a goddess in Harry's young eyes. Roderick was obviously not so enamored of his own sister, although considering the slaps and pinches he endured at the end of her sharp fingers, that was perhaps understandable. Elspeth had never slapped or pinched Harry, not as far back as he could remember.

"Caroline says so. She says Elspeth will be lucky to marry old man Sommers. He smells bad and he's nasty. That's the best your sister will do," Roderick announced, dipping his spoon into his hot porridge and blowing noisily on it. He slanted his eyes at his target, waiting for a reaction.

Harry was used to this drill by now and was quite determined not to rise to the bait, although he wrestled with the pain of allowing this outrageous slur on his sister's honor to pass without remark, particularly since he had a delicious secret that fairly burst to be set free. Mr. Thorpe was to be his brother-in-law! Julian Thorpe would teach Harry all sorts of wonderful things about being a man, maybe even how to duel with pistols. Harry was quite sure Mr. Thorpe had killed any number of other gentlemen in duels, scurrilous cads that they must have been. And when he grew up, he himself would have a valet who would tie his neckcloth just so, and all the ladies would swoon at the very sight of him. It was all too wonderful! Old Man Sommers, indeed!

"Caroline is going to marry the most eligible bachelor in Bath this Season," Roderick announced, splatting his spoon into the porridge to satisfactory effect. "Do you want to guess who?"

"I don't care whom your sister marries," said Harry, quite sullenly. Some of Roderick's porridge had slopped over to his side of the table and he was bound to get scolded for it. Julian had said he must let the little things pass, but Harry was finding it a rough go to take the blame for misdeeds that positively were not his fault.

"Yes, you do," said Roderick in his singsong voice, always a sign that he was about to say something that would make Harry mad. "You won't like it one bit when your hero marries my sister. He'll never have time for you again, only me."

"You're never meaning Mr. Thorpe," said Harry darkly, spoon still.

"Yes, I do. Mr. Thorpe is mad about Caroline. He's

going to ask her to marry him, may have last night already!"

"He did not. And he isn't going to," Harry cried. Some insults were just too much to take. "Mr. Thorpe is going to marry Elspeth!" He regretted the words the minute they were out of his mouth, but he did take some satisfaction in the red anger that suffused Roderick's face.

"He'll never marry your cow of a sister, and you're a bigger fool than she is if you think he will!" Roderick cried, porridge forgotten. "He's just making fun of her, that's all. They're all laughing behind Elspeth's back about how gullible she is—everyone in the *ton!*"

That did it. Knowing even as he acted that he would live to regret it, Harry leaped from his chair and pulled Roderick from his. He had Roderick on the ground and was straddling him before his older cousin even knew what had hit him. It was, Harry had found, the only way to hold his own with Roderick, to get on top and stay on top. "Take it back, you pig!" Harry cried.

"I'll not!" Roderick shouted back, trying to buck his cousin off. "Julian is going to marry Caroline, and he thinks your sister is an ugly, stupid old cow!"

"He's going to marry Elspeth! He asked her last night! He told me so himself, so there!" Harry was goaded into saying. His words produced the desired effect. Roderick could be as dull as a clodpoll when he wanted to be, but now Harry had his attention. His older cousin went very still, looking up at Harry with narrowed eyes.

"Master Harry, you get up off him at once, do you hear me?" cried Bessie, always one to interfere in Harry's rare moments of triumph. Strong, reddened hands helped him ungently to his feet. "Are you hurt, Master Roderick?" asked Bessie, but to be fair, she didn't sound all that sympathetic to him either. She thought both of them were a great trial laid upon her.

"Yes, and I'm going up to see my mother!" announced Roderick, as he scrambled to his feet. "She'll beat you, Harry, she will, and then send you home in disgrace, you and your stupid cow of a sister!"

Roderick stormed off and Harry knew a moment of fear, not that he was really scared of a beating—Aunt Bettina would not trouble herself—but because he had broken his promise to Mr. Thorpe, and told Roderick about the engagement. Still, no man should have to put up with his sister being insulted like that. Any man, Mr. Thorpe included, would understand why he had done what he did. And surely no harm would come of it. Why, they'd have to tell people anyway, if they were going to plan a wedding. And he'd really gotten his own back on Roderick with that one. It was one of his rare triumphs, and it tasted better than porridge.

"What did you say?" Caroline turned angry eyes on her little brother. "You expect me to believe that, you little brat? I should throttle you for coming in here with that silly nonsense just to upset me."

Whenever Roderick entered her room, it was to make mischief. Now that he had something serious to tell her, he was irritated to find that she seemed disinclined to take him seriously. "No, it's true, Caroline, I swear it! He said Mr. Thorpe asked Elspeth to marry him last night and told Harry so himself."

"Elspeth didn't see Mr. Thorpe last night, you little beast. She was home here alone all night."

"Where was Mr. Thorpe?" asked Roderick sullenly. He knew he was right about this and he wasn't getting the proper credit for telling the tale.

"He was at the assembly with me, of course!" Caroline cried, but there was just that something in her voice that indicated she was thinking about it.

Roderick pressed. "All night? Was he with you all night?" he asked.

"Most of it," Caroline said, but she stared off at nothing, as if she were doing sums in her head.

"I heard voices here last night—downstairs," Roderick said. He was lying, but if that was what it took to get her to believe him, so be it.

"Whose voices?" his sister asked sharply.

"Well, Elspeth's, of course, and a man's. I was sleepy at the time. I meant to go down and see who it was, but I guess I fell asleep." That should do it.

Caroline said nothing for a long time. "Yes, I see," she finally said, very quietly, to herself. She seemed to recollect herself. "Thank you, Roderick," she said, uncharacteristically giving him a pat on the head. "You're a good boy sometimes. I shall buy you a treat next time I'm out. Now run along, please."

Roderick gave her a big grin, content with his day's work. He had managed to throw a spanner into his cousin's works with this one, no doubt about that. Now he'd see who had the last laugh. He took off, feeling exceedingly proud of himself. That nasty little Harry would go home in disgrace and stupid old Elspeth with him.

Caroline sat for a long time, staring with unseeing eyes at the large looking glass before her. How could she have been so stupid? She had assumed Julian Thorpe was taunting her, playing little games with her by seeking out Elspeth. How could it be otherwise? Aside from having no money whatsoever, and little enough standing among the *ton*, the chit was nothing if not insipid. What could he find the least bit interesting about Elspeth? She was several years older than Caroline herself, and had no conversation at all, unless one allowed stultifying remarks about the proper fertilization of grape arbors to pass for scintillating repartee, which Caroline certainly did not. Obviously, still waters ran deep, or, more to the point, Elspeth was much more of a contriving minx than Caroline had given her credit for. The little hussy!

Perhaps Elspeth had trapped Julian into a compromising position. Yes, Caroline mused, seeing her own reflection now, that must be it. She examined her face carefully. No sign of the lines that would come later, no hint of a sag, or an extra chin or two. Beautiful blue eyes looked back at her, surrounded by cascades of luscious blonde hair, all her own, no chignons or hairpieces hidden among the golden depths. No one who saw the two cousins together could ever prefer Elspeth's dark plainness to Caroline's own glittering beauty and wit. The scheming little witch must have trapped him, must have used what paltry wiles she could muster to maneuver the gentlemanly Julian into an unlooked-for marriage proposal.

Well, two could play at that game. All Caroline needed to do was act before Julian and Elspeth made their announcement, something they couldn't very well do before receiving Elspeth's mother's blessing. And if Elspeth had some small skill at scheming, Caroline was a veritable master. She would need a confederate—someone, perhaps, whose pockets were perennially to let, and who had an appetite for delicious mischief, particularly if the price were right. Caroline had a bit put away for a rainy day, enough to interest one particular gentleman she had in mind, a gentleman who had already shown an interest in the situation over the matter of a small rock. . . .

Edgar stared thin-lipped at the couple promenading through the Pump Room ahead of him. Julian had bent his head to that of the lesser Quinn girl and now laughed uproariously at something the chit said. Edgar was beginning to think there was more to this literal little tête-à-tête than a case of Julian's trying to engage Caroline's jealousy. His pockets were feeling particularly vacant this morning. He had had quite a contretemps with a tradesman in Milsom Street; the oaf had refused to allow Edgar to pick up his new pair of shoes unless he paid for them with filthy lucre right then and there, most unheard of. It meant that his reputation among the trading set was quickly running to ruin, never a good thing when one lived, as Edgar did, entirely on the come. Oh, he could pick up a pound or two at cards, but never enough to get ahead and stay there. And the rent, soon due, on his pitiful lodgings in Westgate Buildings in the lower part of town, while modest by Bath standards, was still more money than he had available at this moment. Far more. He would not be able to go to the King's Bath today, nor, indeed, until he could get the new pair of shoes. The ones he wore now were literally worn through the soles to his stockings, which were fast shredding to tatters. The valets in the dressing rooms at the Baths would gossip to each other, and from thence the story of his soleless shoes would make the rounds as a most delectable tidbit of *on dit*. And while Edgar never minded spreading a new bit of dirt, he loathed being the dirt itself. He scowled at Julian Thorpe's back. Here was a man who could buy ten pairs of leather riding boots at one sitting and pay for them out of the small change in his pocket. His scowl deepened as Julian placed his hand over Elspeth's Quinn's hand, the one she already had wrapped around his arm. He could feel the hundred-pound wager loom as a liability rather than as an asset, and at this time, he could afford no more liabilities.

"Good morning, Mr. Randall," came a soft voice at his elbow. Schooling his features into a pleasant expression, he turned without enthusiasm. Right now his quest was not for conversation but for funds, and one could rarely cadge any significant sums off of demoiselles, who, however well off they might be, could never actually get their hands on the stuff to lose it to an importuning friend.

His black mood lifted when he saw that this demoiselle was the one much in his thoughts. Caroline Quinn stood before him. "Ah, Miss Quinn, you're looking too, too lovely this morning," he trilled. In truth she was not. She looked peevish and provoked, thin-lipped and sour, as well she might. This was not a woman who would age with a pleasing grace.

"I wish to speak with you," snapped Caroline, utterly ignoring all the rules regarding empty morning repartee. He was instantly intrigued. Promenades in the Pump Room were strictly for show. No one expected any business to be conducted. It was strictly a "see and be seen" occasion. Indeed, most strollers didn't feel terribly well at this hour, shortly before noon, and could be found later at the King's and Queen's Baths, taking the waters. Edgar loathed "the waters," hot and sulphurous as they were. But he did conduct some of his most profitable business while in hot water up to his chin.

"At your service, as always, my dear Miss Quinn," he said smoothly, tucking her arm through his. "What may I do to bring a smile to your exquisite lips?"

"Stop blathering nonsense for one thing," she snapped. Oh, the chit must be in quite a pother, indeed!

"Done," he replied. Straight to business, then. Nevertheless he kept a vacuous smile on his face as they strolled together. No point in appearing unconventional.

"You were very clever about the stone in the path the other day," she said baldly.

He raised an eyebrow. Boxing without gloves this morning, she was.

"I undertook to make it my business to find out just why you were so interested in helping me in that little matter. It seemed more than your usual propensity for idle mischief. I managed to get the truth out of Thomas and Robert last night. About your little wager."

"Blast them for the chattering hens that they are," replied Edgar, but he was not disturbed that the chit knew. Provided that she kept her mouth shut about it. She would, of course. It would do her reputation no good were gossip about the wager to get about, particularly if Julian could not be brought to heel.

"You have a financial interest in who marries whom then, I understand," Caroline said, softly enough not to be overheard. She did, however, shoot a venomous look in the direction of Julian Thorpe and her cousin. Edgar inclined his head in a nod. "I have an interest as well, as you might imagine, Mr. Randall," she went on. "I thought perhaps our interests might dovetail."

Now she definitely had his attention. Interests that marched together were often profitable together. "What are you proposing, Miss Quinn?" he asked.

"I understand you get a hundred pounds from Thomas and Robert if I marry Julian Thorpe. I'll give you another hundred if you'll help me to the same goal."

"An interesting proposition, Miss Quinn," Edger said, his idle drawl belying his furious thinking. He saw no sign that the chit was pining with love for Julian. He rather thought she burned with a different passion, the green-eyed monster jealousy. And while two hundred pounds was good . . .

"As Mrs. Thorpe, you'll have access to Julian's prodigious accounts, won't you, Miss Quinn?" he asked mildly, smiling and nodding to several old biddies who promenaded past.

"I have no idea how prodigious his accounts are, Mr. Randall, and I have no expectation of actually having access," she snapped. The woman was quick, no doubt about it. She would make an admirable sparring partner.

"Nevertheless, what you propose, I think, requires some delicacy of effort, and there is some risk of being found out. I, for one, would find life not worth living were Julian to cut off our friendship because of some perceived interference on my part."

"You'd miss his largess, I think," she replied dryly.

Edgar did not deign to reply. She was right, of course. Many the meal Edgar ate off of Julian's accounts.

"You want something more. What is it?" Caroline snapped. No doubt she had noted that Julian and Elspeth continued their cozy promenade, tête-à-tête, arm in arm, drawing amused and knowing glances. Good. She must recognize that as the level of difficulty increased, so did the price.

"I am not greedy, my dear Caroline, surely you must appreciate that. Still, a fellow must watch his pockets and I think it no secret that I am not terribly well-endowed in that regard." He ignored her derisive snort. The chit could be very irritating when she set out to be. "I think it only equitable that you pay me the hundred pounds when you get engaged, but I would expect no less than a hundred pounds a year, discreetly paid, of course. Julian would give you that for pin money and not notice it . . ."

"You're mad!" she cried, then smiled quickly as several curious stares turned their way. "You're mad," she hissed. "I cannot promise such a thing! I have no idea how the man keeps his accounts. Many men give their wives no money at all."

"Oh, my dear Caroline, women who want funds know how to get them. I do have an alternative suggestion, however. You could pay me the hundred pounds upon your engagement, and then five hundred in one lump sum after the marriage. That will be all. We could call it an old gambling debt, if you like. I could say I'd held off so as not to distress your mother. Julian's too much the gentleman to ignore a debt of honor."

"And then I'd owe you no more, is that correct?" Caroline asked sharply. He could see the wheels spinning in her head. This had been his original plan, of course, but she never would have considered it had he not first made the extortionate demand for a lifelong annuity.

"Not a farthing. You can give me your vowels for the five hundred and I'll just hold it until after the wedding."

"I'll give you the vowels after the wedding," she said shrewdly.

"My dear Miss Quinn, you wound my vanity by thinking me such a fool as that. There won't be time after the wedding. He'll whisk you straight off to the country. Surely you can trust me. Besides, if the scheme unravels, I can't very well present the vowels to you for payment, can I?"

She looked at him narrowly, considering. At that moment she must have heard the deep laugh that resonated from Julian at something the little country cousin said. That seemed to settle her resolve. "Very well," she said in clipped tones. "It shall be as you say. But I must warn you we have very little time. I expect him to announce his engagement to my cousin at any moment. The little witch has trapped him into a proposal."

Her words had the sting of an adder's tongue. Trapped, indeed. If Elspeth Quinn had Julian Thorpe in a trap, it was one the man wouldn't ever wish to be free of. In love, more like. Edgar felt a pang. If his friend really did love the country gel, it would be cruelty itself to force a marriage with Caroline upon him. At that very moment, he stepped on a sharp piece of broken glass, no doubt from a carelessly shattered cup of Bath's disgusting effluvia. He could feel the shard slash though what was left of his stocking, a deep, sharp pain. Now he would leave a bloody footprint wherever he walked. That did it. Julian would have to take what fate dished up for him just as Edgar did. But if Edgar helped fate along now and then, it was no less than Julian could do for himself.

"I'll need ten pounds now, Caroline," Edgar said, the pain making his tone sharp.

"But you said after. . . ."

"If we are to act immediately, which, by the way, you did not mention before we came to terms, I shall need ten pounds to set things in motion. Confederates need to be compensated, you know."

"Confederates?" asked Caroline, with obvious alarm. "The fewer who are involved here the better, Edgar. I don't mean to be blackmailed for the rest of my life by anyone else."

"I am not such a complete fool as all that, my dear," he replied, ignoring the barb. "Naturally, I mean to tip a messenger or errand boy here and there. No one will know anything in particular except you and me."

"Very well," she replied, seeming satisfied. "I'll send the ten pounds round to your rooms this afternoon."

"Never mind that," Edgar said quickly. He made a point of never giving anyone his actual address. Too humble by half. "I'll come to you in an hour or so. Will you be home by then?"

"Yes," she answered, voice sullen, eyes still riveted on Julian and the cousin.

"Good. Are you going to the concert in Sydney Gardens this evening?"

"Isn't everyone?" she answered again, now looking at him with interest.

"Wonderful. I shall see you in an hour or so. I'll devise something between now and then. A *bíentôt*, my dear Caroline." He bent elaborately over her hand but managed to miss it with his lips, so intent was he on the sight of Julian's face as he gazed upon Elspeth Quinn. Julian was a man in love, no doubt about that. Oh, well, he'd get over it. Everyone did.

Edgar Randall left the Pump Room, hoping no one would notice the trail of blood.

His meeting with Caroline in her drawing room, brief and elliptical that it had necessarily been, had left him the richer by ten pounds. Not much above an hour later, he left the shoemaker, wearing his new soft leather pumps, and new stockings, as well. The shopkeeper had been all too happy to sell him a pair of stockings. The old ones he had stripped off in bloody tatters in a nearby alleyway, where he effected a quick change in footwear.

Now, how to solve Caroline's problem, incidentally breaking two hearts? An idea had been taking shape over these last two hours. As if fate approved, who should loom into view on Milsom Street, but Lady Haverford, herself, a grande dame of the *ton*, perennial fixture in Bath every summer, indeed, one of the old biddies who kept Bath from falling into utter oblivion now that that scion of society, Beau Nash, had seen fit to shuffle off this mortal coil, incidentally leaving behind scads of vowels worth no more than the paper that held their shaky scrawl. A rancid old gossip was Lady Haverford, just the very sort that Edgar needed at hand tonight if the foul deed was to be done.

"Good afternoon, Lady Haverford," he said, after she had acknowledged him. "I am most delighted to see that you have graced us with your presence this Season. Bath has seemed dull without you."

She smiled—simpered, really. Good. He'd need lots

of oil to make this one work. She was a wily old thing and could easily get the wind up. He turned to walk in the direction she had been headed. "We've had the most interesting little situation developing over the past few weeks," he said in a conspiratorial sort of low tone. As he hoped, she was all ears. "You would remember the Quinn family, I'm sure, Bettina and her daughter, Caroline. . . ."

"The gardens are beautiful," Elspeth exclaimed as their party entered the gates at Sydney Gardens that evening. "Far more extensive than I had thought they would be."

"That's because anything outside of your little country lanes looks exquisite to you," Caroline snapped. "You should learn to keep your opinions to yourself if you're going to sound so ill-informed." They walked slowly along the paths, where colorful lanterns hung in the branches of the trees that lined the narrow walkways.

Elspeth ignored her, determined not to let her cousin's waspish temper spoil a lovely evening. She was happy to be out at all, having earlier been afraid that her aunt and Caroline would trot out the same excuse they had used to keep her from last night's soiree. But although Elspeth had dressed and presented herself downstairs, half-expecting to be sent upstairs again, nothing had been said, so here she was, gawking like the country "gel" she was. Julian would be here a little later, in time for the fireworks. She had refrained from telling Caroline that she had never seen actual fireworks before. No point in leaving herself open for another attack. In the meanwhile, there would be a concert, possibly indifferent, but it could be played by Haydn himself and Elspeth probably would not notice, so delicious was the secret she carried with her everywhere she went.

Julian loved her! He really did. She was sure of that

now. He had promised to leave in the next day or so for a quick visit to Weston-under-Lizard, to seek her mother's permission for their marriage. It was too bad they had to keep their engagement secret until then, but the formalities must be observed, particularly in a place like Bath, largely populated by the older generation, rigid and unyielding about The Rules of Society.

In the meanwhile, he had stolen no more than a kiss or two, and had been lucky at that, considering how impossible it was to find five minutes to be alone, even in the library. Caroline did not suspect the truth—she could not, after all—but she had been even more waspish than usual. Of course, Julian and Elspeth had not been able to hide completely their fondness for one another, but Julian had assured Elspeth that he had never had any sort of "understanding" with Caroline, so she shouldn't feel that Elspeth had trod on her territory.

"Quite a crowd this evening," remarked Aunt Bettina, quite likely trying to smooth over the awkward conversation. "There's Lady Haverford. I'd heard she'd come to Bath but I've not seen her till tonight. We must call and leave our cards tomorrow, Caroline."

Caroline ignored her mother utterly, her gaze roaming the gardens ceaselessly. She must be looking for young Mr. Ledbetter, thought Elspeth. The young man had shown Caroline a great deal of attention, although, to be sure, Caroline acted as if she barely knew he existed.

"Ah, Mrs. Quinn! And the two lovely Miss Quinns," came Edgar Randall's lilting tones close by. Caroline turned eagerly to him—odd, that, thought Elspeth, as he certainly could not be the one whom she sought so avidly. Mr. Randall looped his arm casually through Caroline's and bent his head to whisper something he obviously thought delicious into her shell-like ear. She smiled broadly at him when he finished, but they did not share the bon mot. "Now, Mrs. Quinn, tell me how you enjoyed the waters at Queen's Bath this morning. I regret I could not attend the King's Bath, but I had pressing business."

Pleased to have an audience, Bettina Quinn nattered on about how over-hot the water had been, and over-sulphurous. And over-crowded. Bath wasn't what it used to be, they agreed quite firmly with each other, what with all these New People no one knew or cared to know. Former tradesmen, no doubt, who'd made a bit and wanted to move up the social ladder. Not likely.

"Ah, my dear Caroline," Edgar exclaimed, when he could get a word in edgewise. "I quite forgot. Hester and Fanny have a lovely piece of gossip they wish to share with you. They made me promise to bring you right over. Mrs. Quinn, may I spirit off your daughter for a few moments? I promise we shall remain quite in the thick of things. Most proper, I can assure you."

Aunt Bettina fairly simpered her acquiescence, and Edgar took Caroline's arm and they wandered off. It was rude, of course, but Elspeth could not have cared less about some silly tidbit of *on dit*, not even if it concerned herself. Julian loved her. They would be married and retire to a pleasant country society. All the gossip in Bath could not touch her now. Elspeth watched Edgar Randall bend his head to whisper something to Caroline. It must have been complicated because Caroline listened carefully. Elspeth waited for the flash of derisive laughter at some hapless soul's expense, but it never came.

Julian was late, but he had known he would be. He'd been taking care of correspondence and dealing with his man here in town so that he could get away to Weston-under-Lizard tomorrow, or the next day at the latest. Now he scanned the crowd, but could see no sign of Elspeth, nor of the rest of the Quinn family.

"Evening, Julian, lovely night for fireworks, don't you think?" came Wesley Ames's amiable tones.

"Indeed it is," said Julian, affably, turning and making a leg for Ames's wife, Helen, a lovely woman, although rather quiet, something Julian thought Ames didn't much mind, in truth. "Have you seen the Quinns this evening, by the way?"

"Saw the ladies wandering about with Edgar not too long ago," replied Wesley. Julian ignored the eyebrow cocked his way. Wesley wasn't much of a gossip, really, at least by comparison with most.

"Excuse me, Mr. Thorpe?" came the butchered accent of a messenger boy who had materialized at Julian's elbow.

"I am he. Do you have a message for me?" Julian replied.

"From Miss Quinn, sir," the boy handed Julian a folded-up note and stood expectantly while Julian fished around for the expected emolument. Pocketing the coin, the boy vanished.

"Everything all right?" asked Wesley.

"Mmm," Julian assented, stowing the note away with a smile. Elspeth was getting quite good at arranging the rare assignation. "Meet me in the labyrinth," the note said bluntly in feminine handwriting. "Three right turns, two left, and one right." His affianced was turning into quite a minx, and Julian felt his loins tightening at the thought of a stolen kiss or two. "Well, you must excuse me," he said, his mind already on the taste of Elspeth's soft lips. "I've someone I must meet." He gave an absent bow to Mrs. Ames and took himself off with a smile.

"Well, I must say I didn't think Caroline was the woman for Julian Thorpe," said Helen Ames, thoughtfully, observing Julian's back disappearing into the crowd.

"I'd say you'd be right at that, my dear," replied Wesley. "I do not think it's Caroline who has Julian's attention."

"But the boy said 'Miss Quinn' . . . oh, I declare, Wesley, you don't mean he's sweet on the quiet little cousin, do you? I understood from Caroline that her family is quite impoverished."

"So I understand, but Julian's accounts are prodigious and I don't think he much cares what she has."

"My word, how extraordinarily refreshing," said Helen, tucking her arm into the crook of her husband's. He gave her hand a squeeze and she answered with a little smile meant just for him. "Julian Thorpe has gone up considerably in my estimation, Wesley," she added. "I do believe I might allow you to remain friends with him after all."

Wesley answered with a hoot of laughter and they wandered off, arm in arm, in search of refreshment.

Julian moved as quickly as he could through the throng, stopping for no more than a cursory greeting whenever he absolutely must. Elspeth could not be off on her own for long without exciting comment. The labyrinth was well away from the site of the musicale, a good thing, considering that the quality of the music was not what drew the *ton* to the gardens. As he drew near the labyrinth he could see that two men in Sydney Gardens livery lounged at the entrance, but no one else seemed to be about.

"Evening, sir. Mr. Thorpe, i'n't?" said one of the men, touching his cap. Julian gave him a nod, annoyed and surprised that he could be so well known among the public staff. The man stepped aside, letting him through, while the other man took off at a trot without so much as a nod. "The lady is waitin'," the first man said, his eyes flat. Julian looked about quickly. Seeing no one close enough by to recognize him, he ducked in, then hurried through the turns as directed, marveling that Elspeth had made such a quick study. He was quite sure she had said she'd never been to Sydney Gardens before. Still, he blessed her resourcefulness. A few moments alone with her would be worth the painful warbling still to come on the evening's programme.

He was drawing near to the center of the labyrinth and he had not seen a soul, which was rather unusual. Dismissing his misgivings with a shrug, he turned the last corner, and beheld—blond hair, not the dark brown of his beloved; a brightly colored, befrilled gown, not the quiet elegance of Elspeth's attire. Caroline! Not Elspeth at all, but Caroline! What malevolent nonsense was this?

The figure stood with her back to him but she turned and, with a cry, rushed forward. As she approached, his eyes resolved the details. She was greatly disheveled, her hair tumbling from its pins, and her neckline was pulled askew, one shoulder exposed. Only luck held the rest of it in place.

"Julian! Thank God you've come!" she cried, launching herself at him with a sob.

"Caroline, what on earth has happened?" he asked. She sagged against him and his arms went around her to hold her up.

"Just hold me, Julian, help me!" she sobbed into his chest. Helpless and horrified, he patted her back while she shuddered in his arms. Someone had attacked her, and now he was duty bound to find out the cad and set things to rights. But why now? Why him?

"Who has hurt you, Caroline?" he murmured soothingly into her hair. "We'll find him and settle the score. But in the meantime, let's get you all straightened up. No one needs to know a thing about this. He tried to disentangle himself gently, but Caroline clung tenaciously, her arms wrapped tightly about his neck.

"Caroline, listen to me," he began again. "Someone might come and that would make things worse. Let's try to get you looking presentable." With his hands at her waist, he tried to push her gently free, but she wouldn't budge.

"Believe me, I'll see to it that this cad wishes he'd never laid eyes on you," he tried again lamely. "Let's sit down on the bench. . . ." He could get no more words out as Caroline suddenly raised her face and planted her lips squarely on his mouth. At the same instant he became aware of voices close behind him. "Mmmphh," was all he managed to grunt, trying to pull his head back, but Caroline had reached up and clasped her hands around the back of his neck in a viselike grip.

"Well, Bettina, I see felicitations are in order. When will the wedding be? Soon, I fervently hope."

Oh, God, please let that not be Lady Haverford's voice. The old biddy was one of the most voluble-tongued of the *ton*.

Suddenly Caroline let go and Julian stumbled back.

"Caroline!" came Bettina Quinn's horrified tones, as her daughter's disheveled appearance was revealed in all its shocking detail. But Caroline just stood there with a sly little smile on her face, slowly—too slowly—pulling up the shoulder of her gown.

"Well, old man," Edgar's voice intruded, with something of a harrumph. "No point in keeping this engagement a secret any longer."

Burning with rage and shame, Julian drew himself up and turned to confront this outrageous circus act. And stared right into Elspeth's eyes. He started forward, an explanation on his lips, but even as he moved, her face drained of color and his beloved slipped slowly to the ground, insensible.

He started forward to her. "Elspeth, no! This isn't what it seems!" he murmured, as he went down on one knee and gathered her in his arms. "Caroline, for the love of God, tell her!" he cried, but as he looked up at Caroline, waiting for her to step forward and clear up this abominable mess, he saw the truth in her eyes. She smiled at him, a slow and malicious smile.

"Why don't you see to my cousin, Mr. Randall?" she asked, almost purring at Edgar. "I'm sure my affianced would prefer to be relieved of his burden."

"Caroline, don't do this!" Julian raged through clenched teeth. Elspeth lay limp in his arms. He dared not let her go.

"I believe we've all had quite a shock, Mr. Thorpe," Bettina Quinn broke in hastily. "Your . . . ah, engagement"—she emphasized the word slightly—"was supposed to be a secret for now. Still," she prattled on hurriedly, "I'm sure Lady Haverford is relieved to know that a wedding has been in the works for some time. Nevertheless," she went on, her voice gaining in strength and purpose, "Caroline, I'm ashamed of your immodesty, and, Mr. Thorpe, your haste bespeaks your love for my daughter, but not your judgment. Mr. Randall, if you'd be so kind as to see to my niece . . . ? I can't think why the gel has to make more trouble by swooning. No purpose to be served in that."

Julian watched as Edgar Randall stepped forward, noticing in an oddly incongruous thought that his friend's shoes were almost certainly brand new, something unusual for Edgar, who was known to be short of funds for even the barest of necessities.

"If you don't mind, old man," Edgar said softly, bending down. "I think you'd best go with Mrs. Quinn and Caroline. I'll see to Miss Quinn."

Julian looked up at him, rage at war with despair in his heart. Trapped! Trapped like a rat by a scheming minx, and, no doubt, her equally culpable mother. He felt Elspeth stir in his arms and all else was forgotten.

He looked down into the swimming green depths of her eyes and beheld utter contempt. "Elspeth . . ." he murmured.

"Let me up," she spat out at him in a barely audible whisper. "Let go of me and never come near me again."

For a moment he just stared at her, saw in her eyes that all was lost.

"Miss Quinn, allow me to help you," said Edgar gently. She reached up and grasped his extended hands. He pulled her away from Julian and set her on her feet.

"Julian, let's go!" barked Caroline imperiously, her hair and gown now miraculously in order. But Julian stood his ground watching as Elspeth moved resolutely forward, on Edgar's arm, never glancing back. Lady Haverford cast one amused and knowing glance about her, then hurried to catch up with the pair as they disappeared around the first turn in the shrubbery. Alone now with the scheming harpies, Julian turned slowly to face them. He did not think Caroline cared for the look on his face.

Chapter Nine

"Excellent sensibilities, my dear child," Lady Haverford murmured in Elspeth's ear, tucking her clawlike hand under Elspeth's arm as they departed the labyrinth. "I, too, would have been shocked senseless at such a sight at your age. You must convey my respects to your mother. I am most impressed with your upbringing. Too few young ladies these days have the sensitive breeding so necessary to a mannerly society. . . ." Elspeth could no longer be bothered to follow the thread of this inane conversation. It was all she could do to put one foot in front of the other. Edgar held her arm as if she were about to slip under the waves for the third time, patting her hand as if she were an imbecile in need of sedation. The Chinese lanterns danced madly in the trees; the hideous warble of the musicale assaulted her ears. They strolled through a nightmare, some kind of monstrous, genteel hell. All about her, ladies and gentlemen nodded and smiled politely, as if the world had not stopped spinning on its axis.

Elspeth bit her lip to stop its infuriating trembling. She blinked back the tears that threatened to spill out and bring her to one final humiliation this hateful evening.

What in the name of all heaven had she expected? That a gentleman the likes of Julian Thorpe, a great toff of the *ton*, wealthy and urbane, had actually stooped to love an impoverished Miss Nobody Much from Weston-under-Lizard? That all his talk of love and marriage had been anything more than the prattle and gamesmanship of a bored and callow rake, self-amusement his only goal in life? She was a fool! An idiot! And now a broken-hearted fool and idiot. She closed her eyes, biting back a sob. Perhaps Julian and Caroline were laughing at her even now, strolling back this way, nodding and smiling, arm-in-arm, Caroline prattling of wedding finery, Julian regretting only that the country fool had caught him out before surrendering her virtue at last. And how close she had come! Just last night she had allowed his hands to roam, gasping with the unexpected pleasure of his touch. Her face flamed at the thought.

"Hester, dear! I've the most exciting news!" hallooed Lady Haverford, dropping Elspeth's arm as if it were on fire, and making off in the direction of a lady who looked, if anything, more formidable than she. Now the cat was out of the bag.

"Would you like to sit down, Miss Quinn?" came a gentle question from Edgar Randall, who continued to pat her hand.

"I should like to return to my aunt's house immediately," Elspeth forced out the words through teeth clenched to keep them from chattering. She held herself as stiff as she could, but a shudder ran through her just the same.

"If you'll pardon the liberty, Miss Quinn, I don't think that would be wise just now. Do you think you could manage to act as if nothing at all is amiss? You don't really know these people. They thrive on any hint of scandal—or another's pain, for that matter." Edgar sounded almost as bitter as she felt. But his voice was kind. Resisting the urge to sink to the ground with a wail, Elspeth allowed Edgar to lead her over to a bench, far enough from the music that it was a distant cacophony. "May I get you some refreshment?" he asked, seating her.

"No, thank you, sir," she replied by rote. Her mind was chasing around in circles, spiraling ever downward. Julian did not love her. He had never loved her. It had all been a game, nothing more than that. A demoiselle of the *ton* would have known that much and played a winning hand. Country fools were the losers. She wanted to scream. She would go home. Take Harry and quit this awful place where no one meant a word uttered, and to cause someone pain was to entertain all.

"Ah, there you are," her aunt's voice added to the already unpleasant din. "Mr. Randall, may I have a word with you?"

"Certainly, madam," answered Edgar, but his tone was frosty and aloof.

Aunt Bettina cast an anxious eye at her niece, but plunged on. "I'm sure I do not need to tell you how awkward and precarious this situation is. I know I can rely on your discretion as a gentleman. Caroline and dear Julian have been engaged secretly for some time, of course, and I'm afraid their impatience got the better of their judgment. . . ." She trailed off, obviously noting that Edgar did not appear to be thawing toward her.

"I rather thought Julian's affections were engaged

elsewhere," Edgar put in, flicking his cuff with bored affectation.

"Yes, well, I'm sure that was an easy mistake to make," Aunt Bettina answered hurriedly, casting an angry glance at Elspeth. "They were so anxious to keep the engagement a secret. It was to be announced at the Viscountess Alderson's ball tomorrow night, you know," she offered, breathless. "We are just a bit beforehand here," she went on, with a nervous chuckle, as if she were making a small joke. Very small.

"Indeed," was all Edgar replied, one eyebrow cocked, a smile closer to a sneer on his lips.

"Perhaps you might call on me privately tomorrow so we may discuss this further—come to some mutual—ah, agreement on the matter that would suit us all," Aunt Bettina offered. The innuendo was deafening. She was offering a bribe. Had Elspeth been capable of any further feeling, she would have been shocked.

"I'm afraid I have engagements tomorrow, Mrs. Quinn," he responded coolly.

"I see," Aunt Bettina replied, considering. Elspeth was saved from wondering what her aunt would next pull out of her hat by the appearance of her cousin Caroline. Julian was nowhere to be seen, thank goodness.

"Where is Mr. Thorpe?" asked her mother.

"He's run off to talk with friends," Caroline answered, but her cheeks were mottled red and her eyes snapped with anger. She turned to her cousin. "I trust you're enjoying your first visit to Sydney Gardens, Elspeth? It's a glorious evening, isn't it?" Caroline asked, her tone singing with malicious enjoyment. Elspeth turned away from her cousin's smug smile, in time to see a look of incredulity and anger cross Edgar Randall's features.

Edgar could not sleep to save his soul. The room was too hot, he had decided, so he'd opened the window, only to find that the breeze was too chilling across his limbs. His bedclothes were in disarray from his tossings and turnings, but he'd already straightened everything out once and had no wish to spend the night making and remaking his bed. Again and again he replayed his role in tonight's nasty little fiasco, but no matter how many times he rehashed it, his part had been that of the villain, evil and unforgivable through and through. It had seemed so simple at first, a quick ten pounds to stanch his bleeding foot, a bet won from Thomas and Robert, and a tidy sum to see him through several more years of the beau monde.

Why had he not seen his role for what it was: treachery to a good friend, punishing pain to a young lady who had done him no ill, and an ugly, ill-deserved conquest for another young lady who had done nothing to merit such victory? Julian's rage, Caroline's smug viciousness, these were bad enough, but if he lived to be a hundred years old, he would never forget the white shock of betrayal on Elspeth Quinn's face, nor the trembling in her hands that she tried so hard to still, nor the sheen of misery that filled her sad eyes as she had tried to get herself through this vile evening. He had done wrong and now he must live with it, although he'd throw his new shoes into the dustbin and go about bleeding and bare-footed if that would set things to rights again.

Julian sat in the brocaded wing chair of his sitting room. He had drunk enough brandy to float the Spanish Armada, but it had not dulled the pain. How could he have been so stupid? How could Caroline have been so evil? The trap was sprung, iron teeth tearing at his flesh. Any number of well-meaning friends had sidled up to him this evening at Sydney Gardens offering whispered congratulations. He had not bothered to acknowledge them. Lady Haverford had certainly lost no time in spreading the gossip. Her presence in the labyrinth this evening had been no accident, of that he was sure. But who else had played a part in this villainy? And how could he ever expect Elspeth to believe, fool that he might be, that he was no philandering jilt? He rose to refill his snifter, and was disgusted to find that he could barely stand, having to clutch at the armrest to hold his balance. With a snarl of rage he flung the snifter across the room, taking pleasure in the sound of it shattering into a thousand glittering shards against the stone of the fireplace. A wave of sodden dizziness overcame him, and he sank back into the chair, head in his hands. When he closed his eyes all he could see was Elspeth's face as she had looked when he last beheld her, her eyes filled with shock and betrayal, and the death of trust.

It had been a long night of waking nightmare. Having cried herself to sleep by dawn this morning, Elspeth had kept to her room all day. Harry, bless his dear heart, had crept in several times, white-faced and frightened. He hadn't even complained to her of how Roderick was tormenting him downstairs, but she knew. At last, she had allowed an awkward and solicitous Bessie in with a tea tray, surprised to find that she had something of an appetite after all. She had munched the tea cakes and toast, and wiped the tears away so that they wouldn't salt her tea.

Now she had no more tears left, just anger.

In the dark of the evening, she stood in the downstairs hallway, dressed and ready for the ball. Only she would know what it had cost her to drag herself through the preparations, one step at a time. She heard her aunt's door open, then the woman's heavy footsteps descending the stairs. She watched as her aunt caught sight of her, the startlement evident in the older woman's eyes.

"I thought, ah, that you might prefer to stay home this evening, Elspeth," Aunt Bettina said, obviously taking in her niece's finery.

"Would you prefer that I not go, Aunt?" Elspeth queried coolly. After all this effort, she would go indeed. She would show the entire *ton* just how little she cared about Julian Thorpe's coming nuptials. Cool damp cloth compresses these last few hours had brought down the puffy redness around her eyes, and she had made herself presentable. She wore her dark green satin gown but had deliberately ripped out the lace fichu that Caroline had insisted upon to hide her décolletage. Not that she intended to behave like a hoyden this evening, but she planned to make the point that she was not the heartbroken, jilted old maid.

"No, certainly you may do as you please, my dear," murmured her aunt, looking up the stairs toward Caroline's door. "It's just that, under the circumstances . . . well . . ."

"I am quite looking forward to the evening, Aunt. I've promised several dances as I recall," Elspeth lied boldly.

"To whom?" asked her aunt, with unflattering surprise in her voice.

Elspeth was saved from having to come up with names that would prove her a liar later on by the sound of Caroline's door opening, then slamming, her footsteps slapping hard on the carpeted hallway floor. Aunt Bettina cast an apprehensive eye on her daughter as she descended the stairs.

"Well, I see you've decided to rejoin the living, Elspeth," Caroline said as she reached the last step. She ran her eyes up and down Elspeth's dress, stopping at the décolletage. She started to say something, then obviously thought better of it, shrugging and continuing on, leaving her mother and cousin to follow in her wake. The footman scrambled to open the door quickly, and the trio made their exit. The carriage waited at the front curb.

"Did you hear from dear Julian this afternoon, Caroline?" Aunt Bettina asked after they had settled themselves in the cramped, dark interior.

"No, but I did not expect to," Caroline answered. "He has business to tend to."

"Well, I do think a wedding is business enough," sniffed her mother.

"I'll discuss it with him this evening," Caroline snapped, closing the subject.

The badly sprung carriage rattled through the badly paved streets of Bath. Elspeth's heart pounded faster and faster. Of course he would be there. She had known that. She was prepared to give him a haughty, careless greeting, then ignore him for the rest of the evening.

It seemed to take forever to get to the Viscountess Alderson's grand establishment in the Crescent. But then all too soon they were there. Elspeth alighted from the Quinn carriage, and found herself scanning the line of black conveyances along the street for the one she most did not want to see. It was not there.

"Julian, you must go to the Alderson ball. Everyone is expecting you to be there. The announcement of your betrothal will be made. It will look dreadful if you are not there." Edgar was exasperated beyond measure. Julian was foxed. Foxed and angry, disheveled and cantankerous. He'd spent the afternoon downing one brandy after another at their club, refusing to stop even when Wesley Ames had tried to put a flea in his ear.

"Don't speak to me of my betrothal," Julian growled deep in his throat. "And I tire of doing what 'I must do.' I want to do what I want to do for a change."

Wesley and Edgar exchanged glances over their drunken friend's head.

"I'm leaving now to go home and dress for the ball," Wesley said, rather tentatively. "Why don't I see you home? You've several hours yet before you need to put in an appearance." Edgar rolled his eyes. Several hours wouldn't be nearly enough time to sober Julian up.

"Leave me be!" Julian roared, attempting to rear himself to his feet. "I'll get myself home, thank you very much." The effort failed. He sank back down, unfortunately missing the actual seat and hanging up on the arm of the wing chair, where he teetered precariously, until Edgar shoved him toward center. He landed with a whoosh of upholstery.

"Well, I'll be off then," Wesley said, lifting his eyebrows to Edgar in a gesture of defeat.

"A word, please, Wesley," Edgar murmured over Julian's head. He took Wesley's arm and pulled him away. "Let's see if Julian's footman is here," he said, voice low. "We can have him hauled out if necessary. It doesn't matter how much of a scene we make. There aren't enough gentlemen here to notice."

"Do you think that'll work?" Wesley asked, casting a dubious eye back toward Julian, now a sodden lump listing to port in the wing chair.

"We haven't any other plan, have we?" asked Edgar, trying to hide his exasperation. "I'll go home with him in the carriage. Surely he has enough manservants that we can get him into a hip bath of cold water. That will sober him up."

"I'm glad it'll be you and not me trying to get him into a bath," said Wesley. "The mood he's in, I'd watch my teeth if I were you. What's wrong with him anyway? Every time I mentioned Caroline this afternoon, I thought he'd have my head off. I'll warrant there's something odd about this betrothal. I've never seen a groom so glum."

"Glum" wasn't the word Edgar would have chosen. "Homicidal," perhaps. "Well, as to that, I couldn't say," he put in distractedly. Watching Julian drink himself insensible this afternoon had been excruciating. His friend was a man in torment, and Edgar knew just where to place the blame.

Edgar signaled the steward and passed the word that Mr. Thorpe was ready for his carriage. The steward cast an anxious glance into the room. No doubt Julian's immoderate consumption was the talk of the back rooms and below stairs. And, of course, there remained the matter of actually getting Julian into the carriage, much less a cold bath. . . .

Coming here this evening had been a mistake, a terrible mistake. Elspeth stood alone in a corner of the Viscountess Alderson's ballroom, willing the floor to collapse beneath her feet so that she could have an excuse to leave. She had convinced herself that making an appearance would show anyone who was interested—and apparently they all were—that she could take a joke as well as the next young lady; that her flirtation with Julian Thorpe had been nothing more that an idle and amusing way to pass the time. Whether the ploy was working or not, she could not tell. And did not care.

Caroline had thus far spent the evening standing in the middle of this colorful clot and then that one, reveling in the attention, accepting felicitations with a haughty grace and satisfied smile. Once in a while she turned the smile Elspeth's way, probably making sure that her cousin had not snagged the attention of any eligible young men. As if there were any chance of that! Elspeth had spent much of the evening alone, or in the company of dowagers and elderly maiden ladies who seemed to accept her now as one of their own. So much for her plan of showing the *ton* that she was not an old maid.

Of Julian Thorpe there was no sign. Elspeth did not know whether that was a blessing or a curse. On the one hand, she hadn't yet had to face him. On the other, her heart would not stop pounding with apprehension. Perhaps it would be better to get it over with, but Elspeth was quite sure that the entire room waited with bated breath to see how she would react to the sight of him. Of course, that thought was self-centered in the worst way. It was more likely that most in the room cared nothing at all about the little Quinn spinster from the country, except to think she was a blithering idiot.

With a sinking feeling, she noticed poor old Sir Richard tottering her way. He was still a good distance from her. Perhaps she might have an opportunity to escape before he reached her. At least she could still outrun him. Turning on her heel, she moved quickly toward the large mahogany doors that gave onto the magnificent hallway. There were a few ladies coming down the grand staircase, so Elspeth assumed that the retiring room was upstairs, and made her way up. She cast a glance behind her, and saw through the great doors that poor old Sir Richard now stood alone, looking doddering and confused. Feeling guilty and ashamed, she nevertheless continued her climb. There was only so much she could bear this evening, and Sir Richard was not on that list.

There was no one in the hallway as she slipped into the ladies' retiring room. Perhaps if she wasted enough time out of sight, Sir Richard would fasten upon some other hapless soul. She slipped behind the modesty screen, hoping no one would come in.

She heard the door open and a burst of giggles with it. Sighing at her bad luck, she made a bit of noise with her skirts to keep them on the other side of the screen. It was bad form to tie up the facilities unduly, but with any luck they were just here to tidy hair and clothing and would move on before she had to give up and show herself.

"Oh, my dear, it is quite the scandal of the Season!" A voice floated over the screen. As every day produced a new scandal of the Season, Elspeth's ears did not perk up.

"It's quite the match of the Season, actually. Although I must say I thought he'd escaped her coils," said another voice.

"Yes, several Seasons ago, as I recall," said a third.

"*On dit* has it that he was making her jealous by playing up to the cousin. I can't remember her name. . . ."

Elspeth froze, her breath catching in her throat.

"Nor I. She's from somewhere in the country, I believe."

"Still, it's not very nice of him. The cousin looks quite pale this evening. Poor thing . . ."

"Cecilia, you are such a bore, really. It's all part of the game. If the cousin doesn't know the rules, she should not play. She's brought it on herself."

"He's a cad, nonetheless. They deserve each other. I never liked her, really. Terribly arrogant," came another breathless voice.

"The cousin seemed quite taken with him. You don't suppose she let him . . . ?" put in another. They giggled.

"Oh, Lenore, you are so naughty! She cannot be such a fool as all that! Still, her reputation will suffer. Pity, isn't it?" They laughed uproariously, and no one seemed to think it was a pity at all.

Elspeth heard the door open and close again, and then all was silent. Lenore Watkins, of all people! Tittle-tattle, the more spiteful, the better. Elspeth peeked out from behind the screen. She was alone. Her knees would not hold her up. She sank to the chaise longue and willed her heart to stop pounding. She must find her aunt right away, and tell her she needed to go home. She had had enough of this vicious nonsense. She wanted her mama and her little house in the country. And if she never saw any of these vile people again as long as she lived, it would be too soon.

Elspeth put her ear against the door and could hear no giggling voices. Hoping that the ladies were well on their way ahead of her, she crept out and down the stairs.

There was something of a commotion at the front door. Raised voices could be heard over the strains of music that floated from the ballroom. Some gate-crasher, thought Elspeth as she hurried down, glad of the diversion. She hoped to slip into the ballroom and find her aunt before anyone spotted her. Her face must still be scarlet with shame. At least no one would think her pale now.

"Elspeth!" Julian's voice rang out in the hallway, loud and uncontrolled.

Elspeth froze near the foot of the stairs. This was not how she'd planned it! Their meeting must be cool and proper, not wild and ranting, all the more so after her unfortunate eavesdropping upstairs.

"Elspeth, for God's sake you must let me speak with you!" Julian cried. He lurched forward, breaking the grip of an outraged footman and two horrified gentlemen. Elspeth could not move, watching him come toward her. His appearance was astonishing. He was disheveled, a mess really, wearing day clothes he might have been riding in. His neckcloth was askew, nearly untied, and his waistcoat was unbuttoned. No wonder the footman had not wished to admit him. What in the name of heaven was he up to? The Viscountess Alderson would be outraged.

Julian came to a stop in front of her. Elspeth was shocked at how he looked. As if he had not slept in days. As if he had been to hell and back. As had she.

"I'm begging you, Elspeth. Please let me talk to you," he said, quieter now, just for her ears. He reached out, but she stepped back. He did not withdraw his hand.

Even at the distance of a few feet, she could smell the brandy. He had been drinking, and by the looks of him, quite a lot. Over the top of his head, she glanced at the two gentlemen who stood in the hallway, nearly open-mouthed, but soaking it all in. She could not bear to be the subject of any more tittering malice!

"Go away!" she hissed. "We can't talk now! Things are bad enough!"

At that moment the door across the hallway opened. Lenore Watkins and several young ladies wandered out. Their eyes widened at the sight of the tableau.

"Why . . . Mr. Thorpe, how lovely to see you," Elspeth said, a little too loudly, smiling broadly despite gritted teeth. "Caroline is in the ballroom, and we've been planning a wonderful wedding!" She stepped down and took his arm, and firmly turned him away from the gaping ladies. "I'm going to be an attendant. Won't that be fun? We'll have such a time picking out our gowns." She simpered up at him. Julian stared at her stupidly, as if he were trying to piece together her words. Small wonder he couldn't make sense of what she said. The brandy smell nearly knocked her over. She was surprised he could put one foot in front of the other. He leaned heavily on her arm, and she was aware that if she withdrew her support, he'd fall right over. She smiled at the thought. But, no, it wouldn't do in front of all these wagging tongues.

Steering him firmly into the ballroom, Elspeth braced herself for the shocked murmurs that would greet their entrance. She was not disappointed. Every head turned as they passed. Every single one, lips parted and eyes bright with anticipated entertainment. Elspeth murmured inanities at an increasingly befuddled Julian, while she concentrated on smiling benignly, nodding at those who stared most bluntly, and, above all, keeping Julian from falling over in a sodden heap. The excited murmurs flowed throughout the room like waves on the shore. It was Elspeth's bad luck that the musicians happened to be in between dances at this moment. She headed for the long French doors at the far end of the room that led onto the balustraded terrace. It seemed an awfully long way at this moment. Just then, the orchestra struck up the lilting strains of a waltz, and Elspeth felt encouraged. The waltz, having been banned as scandalous for so long, had become so popular that most would now flock to the business of dancing, perhaps leaving her to escort this rogue outside, possibly to boot him over the balcony.

"Will you give me the pleasure of this dance?" Julian murmured in her ear.

"Are you mad?" she hissed back, smiling for the benefit of all who still gawked. "Not only would it be most improper, but you'd fall over if you tried."

"We'll see about that," he growled, and with surprising strength, swept her up into an embrace, flowing smoothly into the dance steps. It was all Elspeth could do not to stumble over her own feet to catch up with him.

"Stop this instant, sir!" she hissed, her expression more grimace than smile. "I've no wish to dance with you. Your engagement to my cousin is to be announced shortly. You've made a big enough fool of me as it is."

"The engagement is a farce, Elspeth. You must believe me. I've never cared for your cousin." He was surprisingly coherent. And steady on his feet. Of course, he might fall over at any moment.

"My eyes have told me otherwise, sir. Did you plan on trying my virtue as well or were you content to have my fool's declaration of love?"

"I love you," he said simply.

"You will not say that to me again. I will not listen to your lies. If I was a fool, then you were a villain, sir, but while I am no longer a fool, you are still a villain." It was hard to say these things through smiling lips, but Elspeth was aware that interested gazes still followed them across the floor. Added to that, she wanted very badly to cry. His arms were strong and hard around her. And beneath the brandy, she could smell the clean cotton of his neckcloth, and the light scent of his soap.

"What is the meaning of this, Mr. Thorpe?" rang out the hushed, shocked tones of Aunt Bettina. Elspeth did trip over her feet as she came face to face with her aunt, who looked angry enough to spit out nails. "Your engagement is to be announced shortly, and here you are, looking like a bumpkin, and not only have you not said hello to your affianced, you are dancing the waltz with another woman!"

"Take yourself off, madame," Julian growled, "or so help me God, I will denounce your scheming daughter to the assembled multitude right here and now."

Aunt Bettina's eyes fairly goggled. She swayed, mesmerized for a moment, then she lifted her fan and began using it in earnest. She turned, still swaying, and tottered off, still fanning herself. Elspeth was quite sure it was the first time she had seen a fan used merely as a fan since she'd arrived in Bath.

"She is right, you know, sir," Elspeth said. "Your behavior is abominable. I will return to the country soon enough, and I care not what anyone here thinks of me, but my cousin must make her way in this society. It does you no credit to demean her like this."

"Demean Caroline?" he asked, incredulity dripping

from his voice. He seemed to be sobering up more and more each minute, although for the life of her, Elspeth couldn't see how whirling about on a dance floor could be doing his head any good. "Is it possible to demean a woman who has already lowered herself to this degree?"

"If you mean to cast aspersion on my cousin for falling for your wiles in the labyrinth, Mr. Thorpe, allow me to assure you that I hold you responsible for corrupting an innocent woman."

"Innocent?" he asked, staring down at her. "Do you really believe I would stoop so low as to ask you to marry me, then ravish your cousin the first chance I got?"

"I know what I saw, sir," Elspeth answered, voice small. She did not wish to discuss this at all, ever.

"You know what you think you saw, Elspeth."

They danced now in silence, Elspeth could think of nothing to say that would not bring on her tears. She did not know what Julian thought, but whenever she glanced at his face, he looked grim and gray. At last the music came to a halt. Of necessity their feet stopped moving. Elspeth made to pull away, but he held her fast.

"Unhand me this instant, sir!" she hissed. "Everyone will be staring."

"Let them stare," he muttered.

"Julian, if you do not wish to be hauled before the magistrate and charged with my attempted rape, I suggest you let go of my desperate little cousin this minute," Caroline's voice hissed like a snake, low and deadly over Elspeth's shoulder.

Julian smiled a slow, vicious smile. "I would welcome such an opportunity to set the record straight, Caroline. Go ahead, I dare you." His grip lightened on Elspeth's hand and around her waist, and she took that opportunity to step away from him.

"On second thought, I do not care to sully my own name," Caroline said. "However, I do think the *ton* would be more than willing to believe that my cousin is so lost to all propriety that she throws herself at you even now, when you are affianced. Have you heard the *on dit* about you this evening, Elspeth?"

Elspeth could feel the hot flush creeping up her throat. Indeed, she had heard. Every nasty word.

"I can see that you have. If you know what is good for you, you will smile your insipid little smile and remove yourself from our presence immediately. My fiancé and I have nuptial matters to discuss."

"You are a vicious woman, Caroline. I despise you," Julian said. Elspeth heard Caroline's shocked intake of breath. She was aware that Julian had not taken his eyes off of her. Confused and angry, she dared not raise her gaze to the rest of the room, but from the corner of her eyes she sensed couples edging closer, obviously hoping to hear the contretemps.

"Ah, Miss Elspeth Quinn, you are looking divine as always, this evening. Might you honor me with the next dance?" Before she had time to place the voice, Elspeth found herself seized from behind and swept away on the arm of Edgar Randall, who was moving just as fast as propriety would allow.

"I must warn you, I'm a dreadful dancer. Worse than most, really. Actually, I cannot abide dancing. Perhaps you'd care to sit this one out with me? It's terribly stuffy in here, don't you think?" Mr. Randall nattered on and on, not pausing for breath, moving inexorably toward the terrace. "Do smile at me please, Miss Quinn. It does not do for you to look as if I'd taken a poleax to you. Now, perhaps we can relax away from the prying of the gentry." He finished with a flourish, depositing her on a bench on the terrace, far enough from the French doors to be out of earshot, but not so far that anyone could think mischief was afoot.

"There," he said, seating himself next to her. "I suppose you do not wish to talk about it. Quite so. We can discuss the weather, or the viscountess's increasingly appalling guest list, Fanny Leicester's shocking gown—you choose the topic. You'll find me conversant on the subject of most inanities."

"I . . ." Elspeth ventured, then trailed off, nonplussed.

"Exactly!" Edgar. "Couldn't have put it better myself."

Despite herself, Elspeth laughed. From the long French doors came the lilting strains of a quadrille. She wondered if Julian and Caroline now traced the intricate steps. Perhaps he would fall over with no one to hold him up. It would serve him right. With dismay, she noticed two gentlemen hurrying toward them. With the light from the doors behind them, she could not make out their features, but as they drew closer, their glorious raiment gave them away. Thomas and Robert. Or was it Robert and Thomas?

"Edgar, you must come!" sang out one of the peacocks. "Julian is causing the most dreadful scene! He's refusing to leave, although Viscountess Alderson has asked him to herself."

"Oh, dear me, this won't do at all," Edgar muttered next to her. "You must excuse me, Miss Quinn. No, on second thought," he said, rising and holding out his hand, "you must come inside with me. I cannot very well leave you here alone in the dark."

Elspeth took his hand and stood, not that she cared a fig whether or not she sat alone. She did, however, wish to see what was happening in the ballroom. She had a morbid curiosity, much the way one paused at the scene of a carriage accident. They hastened into the ballroom, Elspeth scanning the room. Her blurred vision spotted a tight group of people near the center of the room. Edgar made for the spot, with Elspeth, possibly forgotten, on his arm.

"Lady Alderson, you must excuse dear Mr. Thorpe."

Elspeth heard her Aunt Bettina's pleading tones before the figures resolved themselves into individual identities. "I'm sure there is some explanation."

"There is, madam," said Julian. "I am exceedingly drunk," he went on, making an exaggerated, unbalanced bow. Elspeth was quite sure the excessive slurring was put on for effect. He had spoken much more clearly a few moments ago.

"Well!" replied the viscountess in frosty tones. "I daresay your poor mother would be mortified at your performance this evening, Julian. As it is, you will kindly remove yourself from the premises at once. I will expect a fulsome and abject apology from you when you are capable of it, tomorrow at the very latest. I'm sorry, Bettina," she said, turning to Mrs. Quinn, "but under the circumstances, I think the announcement had best be put off until a more auspicious occasion. I'll not have my ball turned into any more of a carnival than it is already. If you gentlemen will assist Mr. Thorpe . . ." she said, turning to Thomas and Robert, who had insinuated themselves into the group.

"Thank you, Lady Alderson, but I require no assistance," said Julian. This time he made a formal, and perfectly executed bow. He rose, and with a slow and deliberate smile, turned and made a surprisingly dignified exit. All heads turned to watch his progression and a buzz of whispering swelled throughout the room. At a haughty signal from the hostess, the orchestra struck up a lively tune.

"We shall be taking our leave as well, Lady Alderson," said Aunt Bettina, her eyes darting about, trying to assess the damage.

"Oh, I hardly think that wise, Bettina," the lady said coolly. "Thomas? Or are you Robert? I can never tell you apart. One of you will dance with Miss Caroline Quinn. And you there"—she gestured imperiously at

Edgar, who had maintained his grip on Elspeth's arm—"Dance with the other gel—the cousin." Thomas—or was it Robert?—simpered and bent over Caroline's hand, murmuring nonsense. Caroline looked ready to commit murder. "Smile, gel," ordered the viscountess. Caroline managed a rictus as she was whisked away.

"I believe we'd better have that dance now, Miss Quinn," Edgar Randall murmured in Elspeth's ear. "Go on as if all were well, don't you know."

"I agree with you, Mr. Randall. I accept."

"You'll be sorry, of course," he answered. "Mind your toes."

He swept her away to the beat of the music that swelled around them. Colors in silks and satins swirled by, a kaleidoscope of madness. Elspeth's feet kept the rhythm, but her mind reeled in pain and confusion. To the side she saw the viscountess standing in a clot of rapt ladies, her aunt in the middle, gesturing with a weary drama. Caroline swept past, the smile chiseled into her stony face.

"You're doing beautifully, my dear," Edgar murmured in her ear. "Now if you could just manage to look rapturously amused at my repartee, we may yet pull this off."

She stared up at him, hardly registering his remark. He wanted her to smile, that was it. But she did not think she would ever smile again. Nevertheless, she made the effort.

"That's better, if only barely," he said smiling. "Now, I want you to titter uproariously, please. A thin little smile like that will ruin my reputation as a wit." She managed a small laugh, turning her eyes on him. His face was a blur as she blinked back tears. "Oh, no, no, no, my dear, absolutely no crying. Not a single tear. Why, that would set the tongues awag all over this ballroom. Another titter, if you please."

Another titter. She complied, but it ended in something of a gurgle and a hiccough.

Now he laughed, a genuine guffaw. She couldn't help laughing with him, fool that she was; she was not sure whether to laugh or cry.

"Excellent, positively excellent, Miss Quinn. I declare I shall make a dreadful flirt of you yet."

Caroline whirled by, casting a look of such malevolence at Elspeth that it almost hurt. Such a long evening it would be, smiling and tittering at empty nonsense. She would collect Harry and head back to Weston-under-Lizard. At least there she could grieve in peace.

Chapter Ten

The sound of rhythmic explosions threatened Julian's very existence. Muskets were going off in close proximity; the enemy was closing in for the kill. He grabbed the nearest thing to hand and pulled it over his face for protection. It was his pillow, apparently. The explosions continued, now accompanied by some sort of shouting. He pulled the pillow closer around his ears, but the shouting and explosions continued. Ah, he must have been hit already. No way to explain the searing pain in his head other than a bullet through the brain. Too bad. Now he'd never get to set things right with Elspeth—never feel the touch of her soft lips against his own. On the other hand, death would be a welcome relief from the pounding and shouting.

And then, mercifully, came silence. No more explosions. He thought about putting a hand to his head to see how bloody the wound was, then decided to just lie there instead, savoring the exquisite pain. Surely no man had ever suffered so. . . .

"Excuse me, Mr. Thorpe, I had to take the liberty of entering since you did not respond to my rapping. . . ."

Ah, and now he was taken by the enemy. Well, small good it would do them. He'd reveal nothing, and all they'd have was his bloody corpse to bury. . . .

"Sir? Are you awake, sir?"

Torture. He'd heard that the French were not above torturing prisoners of war. Well, he would die long before they made him crack. Couldn't remember what the devil he wasn't supposed to tell them anyway.

"I am so sorry, sir, but you simply must rise. The Viscountess Alderson is downstairs. She is most insistent, sir. Gave me exactly five minutes by the clock to get you downstairs, or said she would be up to roust you herself. I do believe she means it, sir."

Ah, yes, the Viscountess Alderson. Secret head of the French torture unit. He should have known it would come to this.

"I've brought coffee, sir," came the insistent voice. Trying to trick him into opening his eyes, they were, but he was nobody's fool. Hands pulled at him, and he tried to wrench himself away. Got caught up in some sort of net, or perhaps it was a feather comforter. Oh, they'd stoop to nothing. Gad, how his head pounded. He'd be dead in minutes, no doubt.

"Julian! Get up this minute. I haven't got all day!" The strident tones of The Alderson Horror, rang out. Now he knew he would die a hero's death. Ungentle hands pulled him up. Against all his will power, his eyes opened. Ahhh, there she was, snake-headed Medusa, the Gorgon, *sans merci*. The pain in his head was unbearable. Death could not come too quickly.

"I've had enough of this nonsense, Julian. Come alive, boy, now!"

He shook his head. That was a big mistake. From the fireworks exploding inside his brain, he might almost think the enemy was still shooting at him. Except he had a sinking feeling that things were much worse than that. Infinitely worse.

"Lady Alderson?" he heard himself croak, his voice muffled by pillows and bedclothes.

"Exactly," came her redoubtable tones.

"Er—I—er—I don't believe I'm dressed to receive you, ma'am," he muttered, trying frantically to recall his attire of the evening before. No doubt he'd been divested of a good bit of it before falling into bed.

"I've buried three husbands, young man. If you think I do not know what gentlemen's small clothes look like, you are sadly mistaken." Just then the door opened timidly, and one of the kitchen maids pushed through, eyes popping. She carried a large silver tray bearing Julian's grandmother's best coffee service. She placed it on a small table between the two wing chairs and with a hasty, terrified bob, scurried away.

"Er—well, I'm not sure I'm even wearing . . ." And he wasn't entirely sure. Things were feeling awfully bare under these sheets.

"Well!" she said, her tone, if possible, even more frosty. "I certainly do not care to see what you consider appropriate attire for sleeping. Particularly considering the shape you were in last night. I shall busy myself with the coffee while your man here remedies your sartorial inadequacies."

"Lady Alderson, I'm really not feeling very well at the moment. . . ."

"I do not care how you're feeling, boy," she snapped. "Indeed, in view of your behavior last night, I trust and fervently hope you're feeling quite poorly. You deserve that. Nevertheless, I require your undivided attention this morning, and I shall have it." She turned and snapped her fingers at Forbush, who stood goggle-eyed by the coffeepot. "You, there," she announced. "See to your sorry sot of a gentleman. I shall observe the proprieties by pouring myself a cup of coffee. Not," she added acerbically, "that I've been offered one." She turned toward the silver coffee service.

"Oh, by all means, madam," Julian mumbled, "do have some coffee." He eyed her rigid back with some alarm as he slipped out of bed. Naked he was, indeed. As the day he was born. He'd never seen old Forbush move quite so fast. The handsome burgundy silk robe was around him and tied up tight in seconds flat. A neckcloth, too, appeared around his neck, fast enough to near strangle him, had Forbush not had such a practiced hand, although that hand was certainly shaking now. Forbush stepped back and eyed his work with concern. If Julian hadn't known the man since his own birth, he'd have sworn the fellow was near to swooning like a lady overset. Perhaps he might at that. Julian gave him a weak grin and stepped away, ready to beard the lioness in his own den. Well, if she wished to so flaunt proprieties, who was he to quibble? Besides, his head hurt like the devil himself was marching up and down in his brain with hobnailed boots on. Coffee was required.

"Now then, Lady Alderson," Julian murmured, moving with purpose toward the silver coffeepot. "To what do I owe the pleasure of your delightful company this morning?"

"Well, to begin with, Julian, it is afternoon. Well into the afternoon, to be precise. You young people today think nothing of wasting the day entirely. You may go," she announced to Forbush. Not certain whether or not to be scandalized, Forbush glanced questioningly at Julian, who shrugged and nodded. He doubted seriously that the viscountess's honor and reputation were at stake here. As Forbush quit the room, the viscountess seated herself with a flourish in a wing chair near the fireplace, giving Julian an icy stare, as if to rebuke him for failing in the most basic courtesies of seating a lady. He sighed and sank heavily into the chair next to her. At least the porcelain coffee cup sent a pleasant warmth through his hands. He took a small sip. It was heaven-sent.

"I wish to know the meaning of your conduct at my ball last night, Julian. I've known you since you were in leading strings, and your dear mother before you, and that was not an exhibition I would care to witness again."

Now, here was a minor problem. Julian had no idea what she was going on about. Didn't remember attending her cursed ball, in fact. Last thing he remembered, and that not so clearly, was sitting in his club offering to fight anyone who cared to take him up on it. Come to think of it, they must have been a cowardly lot. No one had felt up to the challenge. Now, should he admit his lack of memory, which would be an indictment in and of itself, or bluff it out?

"Well, what have you to say for yourself, Julian?" she demanded.

"I must offer you my abject apologies for my deplorable conduct, Lady Alderson." There. That should do it. Ladies always liked a handsome apology. Take full responsibility and all that. Never mattered whether a man was guilty or not. Just confess and move on. And then she would move on and leave him to his misery. The coffee was good but it was not magic. His head still pounded like the very devil. Perhaps he had had a drop too much last night, at that.

"You have no idea what I'm talking about, do you, Julian?"

"Er—well, I'm sure you are referring to my somewhat inebriated state," he floundered. If she wanted details, he was lost. "I'm sure I said something to offend. I was a bit foxed, I admit. . . ." He let it trail off. That had to be enough of an admission.

"Foxed?" The viscountess drew herself up in apparent outrage. "You call that merely foxed? You were an absolute disgrace. I've seen bounders passed out in the gutter in better shape than you were. And what, do you mind telling me, do you think you are playing at by deviling that poor gel—the Quinn cousin, what's her name?" The viscountess paused peremptorily.

"Miss Elspeth Quinn?" Julian filled in, horror growing in him. What had he done to Elspeth?

"I thought so!" the viscountess exclaimed triumphantly.

"Thought what, ma'am?" asked Julian, voice faint. Why couldn't he just die and have done with it all?

"It's the Elspeth chit you're after now, isn't it? And here you are, engaged to her cousin Caroline. Why, it's an absolute disgrace the way you young men set about ruining these girls' reputations. Not a care in the world for what becomes of them when you've finished your dalliance. Have a care, boy, or I shall give you the Cut Direct in the Assembly Rooms and you'll dare not show your face in Bath or London. You mark my words."

"I don't care about that," Julian mumbled into his coffee cup. Dowager she might be, but he'd had about enough of the proprieties.

"I beg your pardon?" came her frosty tones.

"Lady Alderson," he said, wearily, putting down his sadly empty cup. "I begin to understand I behaved like a clodpoll at your ball last night. For that I am truly sorry. It is not my habit to act the pickled fool. Nevertheless, I beg you to understand that I was most provoked, and leave it at that. I can offer you no other explanation as a gentleman."

"I rather think your credentials as a gentleman are sorely tarnished at this point, Julian. I begin to suspect rather strongly that you are not over the moon about this engagement of yours. You've got yourself into some fool of a situation and cannot extricate yourself. Am I correct?"

"I have nothing to say on that point, madam," he said, but it came out sounding more like a growl than polite conversation.

"Your silence speaks volumes, boy. On the whole, I have found you to be a cut above your peers as a rule. Has Miss Caroline Quinn got you trapped, or have you simply made an ass of yourself chasing after both gels, and got yourself in a stew of your own making?"

"I—I—Lady Alderson, I beg of you," Julian said in a near whisper, "leave me to my slow death. I am not up to your withering cross-examination."

"Well, based on what I saw of your performance last night, Julian, I'd hazard a guess that your heart is engaged by the country cousin, but you have somehow got yourself entangled with Bettina's viper instead." The viscountess raised an eyebrow, as if she were expecting a response. Julian reached for his coffee cup, peered into its empty, beflowered depths, then put it down with a sigh.

"Oh, for heaven's sake, boy, give it here," she said, holding out her hand imperiously. He put the delicate porcelain cup and saucer in it. Dratted little thin things. Forbush knew to serve his usual morning coffee in the sturdy, good-sized china mugs the staff used in the kitchen, but obviously the man did not dare place such offending vessels before the grande dame of Bath. She poured a jot into the little cup. A thimble would hold as much, he thought sourly, but he reached for it like a drowning man, nonetheless.

"Now, then, Julian. You are in a pretty mess, I'd say. I can't think how you'll get out of it. I suppose I have to assume you have engaged the country cousin's heart?"

Julian just stared at her over the rim of the nasty little cup.

"Yes, I could tell by the look of her last night. Although she's a plucky little thing, I have to give her credit for that. Held up rather well for all that the tongues were wagging. Deserves better of you, I'd say." She cast an accusatory glance at him. "Well, I can't mend what's broken, boy," she went on briskly, "but if I can aid you in setting it right, I will. Otherwise, you are in for a long and unpleasant married life. Never could abide Bettina Quinn, and her spawn takes after her. I couldn't for the life of me think what had possessed you to ask for Caroline's hand. You're not at all suited, unless I miss my guess, and I never do."

Julian said nothing. What could he say? The very idea of spending long years of marital acrimony made him wish he hadn't put all that coffee into his querulous stomach.

"I suggest you set about putting your house in order, Julian, for everyone's sake," she announced imperiously, standing and moving toward the door. "I believe I'll pay a call on Bettina. An explanation is owed me from that quarter as well."

As she reached for the door handle, it turned and the door swung open, nearly knocking her down.

"Oh, I do beg your par—good heavens! Lady Alderson! What in heaven's name—?" Edgar Randall stammered to a close. His gaze took in Julian's dishabille, then halted abruptly at the viscountess's magnificently arched eyebrow. "T—that is to say, good morning, Lady Alderson. How lovely to see you looking so well this morning. We had such a splendid time at your ball last evening, I do declare it was the most—"

"Oh, do hold your tongue, Mr. Randall. I heard enough inanities last night to last me a lifetime. Julian, you should discharge that man of yours. Entirely too much unannounced traffic in your boudoir. I suppose you're expecting the Prince of Wales himself at any moment."

Julian fairly goggled at her, then reached for the coffeepot.

"I trust, Mr. Randall, you will be at some pains to help your friend sort out his difficulties?" she said.

"C—certainly, Lady Alderson. I live but to serve," Edgar replied, although somewhat faintly.

"Then I bid a good day to you both," she stated. "Don't bother to ring; I'll see myself out," she announced, and took herself off with a stamp of her gold-tipped walking stick.

By tacit agreement Julian and Edgar held their peace as the rhythmic tapping of her cane and the sound of footsteps receded down the hall.

"Dare I ask . . . ?" Edgar ventured when nothing more could be heard of the retreating Personage.

"No," growled Julian.

"Ah, well then, I simply must assume that you've gone and compromised the Viscountess Alderson. Good heavens, man, the woman must be past seventy! I should think there's many an ample kitchen maid who would cheerfully oblige. I shall, of course, have to spread this little tidbit all over Bath by evening. I cannot for the life of me, though, see how I am to make people believe it."

"I must assume you're joking, Edgar. I am not in the mood, to tell you the truth."

"Headache?" Edgar asked, with a somewhat wicked grin.

"A slight one," Julian acknowledged with a shrug.

"I should rather think, based on your conduct last night, that this headache is—how shall I put it—one of the great headaches of all time, a headache of Olympian proportions. Indeed," Edgar trilled, "I rather expected you to be dead this morning."

The door opened and Forbush entered with a large tray. Julian was gratified to see a substantial coffeepot on it, and two kitchen mugs. The man glanced around the room with some apprehension. "I did hear her ladyship leave, did I not?" he asked in a whisper. The cups rattled on the tray.

"You did," Julian replied, inhaling the restoring scent of freshly brewed coffee.

They were silent while Forbush served them. Julian felt the weight of the large, hot china mug with great satisfaction.

"Edgar," he began, as Forbush quit the room, "I hate to ask, but what, exactly, did I do last night? Must have been rather amazing to bring the Viscountess Alderson to the very foot of my bed. Like some goddess of vengeance out of myth, she was."

"Well, I'd laugh about it, if it were funny, dear boy, but I fear it really is not."

"I was afraid of that. Go ahead."

Julian sipped his coffee in growing horror as the evening's atrocities were laid out before him. As for offending Caroline, he cared not a whit. Making a drunken spectacle of himself in his club and at the viscountess's ball, was merely an outrageous bit of folly they could all, he hoped, laugh about in years to come. Humiliating Elspeth, however, was unforgivable. Julian had dropped his head into his hands by the end of Edgar's recital, the coffee worthless and forgotten.

They were silent for a moment. Edgar seemed edgy, perturbed, unlike his usual bon vivant self. "What shall

I do?" Julian finally asked. He could see no solution to his dilemma, nothing but a lifetime of misery for them all. But he was damned if he could figure out how he had deserved this.

"Well, I suppose you owe Caroline and her awful mother an apology," Edgar ventured.

"Caroline? What the deuce do I care what she or her mother, think about my conduct? It's Elspeth I'm worried about. What has this done to Elspeth?" He slammed the mug down on the small table next to his chair. The table teetered precipitously.

"You do love her, don't you?" Edgar asked quietly.

"More than my life," Julian replied, dropping his face into his hands again. He rubbed at his temples, but the pain would not go away. He thought it had nothing to do with brandy. This was a pain he would feel for the rest of his life. The dull ache of a long and lonely defeat.

"You—you don't much care for Caroline, I suppose?" came Edgar's response.

"I loathe the woman. What she did to me—" he stopped and looked at Edgar sharply. "I suppose there's no reason for you to believe me—no one else does—but I did not lay an improper hand on Caroline the other night in the maze. She had been roughed up before I got there—" he stopped, aware how lame an excuse that sounded.

"I have reason to believe you," Edgar said, his voice almost a whisper. "Actually, I do believe you, Julian. I've known you for most of my life, and it would not be like you to despoil anyone, much less Caroline Quinn."

"Would that Elspeth could believe in me as you do, Edgar," Julian replied, his voice nearly breaking. "She's the one who matters. She thinks I'm a rutting, faithless pig, and I cannot convince her of the truth. How can I? As she said, she saw with her own two eyes. . . ." His voice broke.

"Well," said Edgar. Then he stopped. Julian looked up at him. "It would seem you have been much abused, Julian. Elspeth, as well. You have been a good friend to me, all these years. A better friend to me than I have been to you, to my shame. I think we must devise some sort of plan to extricate you from this marriage trap."

"But all will be for naught if Elspeth does not believe in me."

"We shall have to work on that, as well. The first thing we must do is convince Bettina Quinn that it is not in Caroline's best interests to announce this engagement so precipitously. Then, perhaps, we might approach Lady Haverford. She's the one who matters most, after all. If she can be convinced all was not as it seemed in the labyrinth, you might stand a chance."

"Lady Haverford is the biggest gossip in Bath, Edgar," Julian said wearily. "I don't think she cares as much for the truth as for the fun of the *on dit*."

"Indeed. But think how much fun the truth might be."

"What is the truth, Edgar? What could it be other than that Caroline set up that evil scenario to do exactly as she did—trap me into marriage. How do I go about convincing Lady Haverford of that without appearing to be precisely the sort of cad she thinks me already?"

"I shall make it my business to set this right, Julian. I owe you that and more," said Edgar quietly.

"You owe me nothing, Edgar. Just your friendship."

"I wish that were so, dear boy," Edgar said. "More than ever, I wish that were so. Now, I have the glimmering of an idea. . . ."

"Your ape leader sister made a fool of herself in front of all of Bath at the ball last night!" came Rodney's singsong taunt. Harry swallowed hard, his barley soup sticking in his throat. Elspeth had begged him not to rise to Roderick's jeering but it was a hard task she set him. "Caroline says everyone in Bath is laughing at Elspeth," Rodney went on, his own soup forgotten in the joy of the moment. Harry continued manfully to spoon the stuff down, eyes on his bowl, face reddening. "You're just a coward anyway, Harry. You don't know how to fight like a man. Julian Thorpe says he'll teach me how to fence, but you're too stupid. He thinks you're a fool just like your sister."

That did it. Harry was out of his chair in a flash, and pulling Roderick out of his by his shirt front. The stout cotton held up under the onslaught, but the buttons, unfortunately, did not, yielding with a great ripping sound. Roderick howled in outrage as his feet scrambled to find the floor. He drew back his fist and was about to land a good one, when Harry pinned his cousin's arms back and fell against him, tumbling them both to the floor.

"Master Roderick! Master Harry! You will stop this at once!" came Bessie's outraged tones. She bravely waded into the fray and fished them out by the collars, one in each hand.

"He attacked me for no reason at all!" wailed Roderick. "He tore all my buttons. I want him to have to sit like a girl and sew them back on!"

"He insulted my sister!" countered Harry, trying to take aim again, but thwarted by the distance at which Bessie held him apart from Roderick. He swung his foot but that missed, too.

"I'm going to march you up to your aunt this minute, young man," said Bessie, giving Harry a shake and a dark look.

"She'll make you sew my buttons back on!" Roderick screamed with glee. "You can just sit there all prim and proper in a mobcap and do our mending!"

With a great heave, Harry twisted himself loose and was out of the breakfast room like a shot. He needed to get himself good and lost, at least until Elspeth finally came out of her room and could stick up for him. He could hear Roderick whining loudly for Bessie to let him go, but there were no footsteps following behind him. Harry pounded loudly up the rear stairs, then tiptoed as lightly as he could down the main hallway. All of the bedroom doors were closed. He supposed the ladies were having a lie-in after the ball last night. He paused and still heard no sounds of pursuit. So far so good. He crept down the main staircase to the front hall, pausing on the last stair to listen. All was heavy afternoon silence. Either Roderick had left off with his wailing, or Bessie had pulled him into the kitchen to quiet him down.

Suddenly the doorbell pealed, startling Harry into an undignified jump. He heard a rear door open, and knew he had only seconds to vanish before the footman appeared to answer the bell. The door closest to him was the drawing room, alas, a room he cared little enough for, since every time he went near it, his aunt fussed about how likely he was to break something. He had only broken two things since he'd been here, both silly-looking little porcelain gewgaws that shouldn't have been there in the first place. When he was the head of his own household, he would have a rule that there would be no silly little gewgaws lurking about, waiting for innocent people to bump into them so that they could break and cause uproar.

He slipped into the drawing room and silently shut the door behind him, hoping the footman had not noticed the movement. He stood with his ear pressed against the thick panel of the door, barely able to hear through it. He heard a mumble of what sounded like male voices. It had to be a toff, or somebody special. Tradesmen and servants were not allowed to use the front door, not ever. That left Harry with no choice but to hide himself with deliberate speed, since any guest would be ensconced in the drawing room to await the beastly presence of Harry's cousin or aunt. Drat! Why couldn't he have ducked into the dining room instead? No one would be shown into there any time soon. Of course, it was well down the hall, away from the foot of the stairs, so he never could have gotten there in time. He looked carefully around the drawing room for a hiding place, well aware that there were no other doors leading out. Nothing but dreadful little fancy carved bits and pieces of furniture met his eye, all high-legged, curlicued, and insubstantial, not enough to hide a mouse, much less a half-grown miscreant. He bolted for the heavy brocaded curtains, mercifully pulled shut at this hour. Aunt Bettina did not wish to be accused by the landlord of allowing the furnishings to fade in the sun. He found the opening and stepped into the musty, dusty dark. He took a deep breath, determined to hold it as long as possible. If he sneezed, all was lost.

Edgar felt his stomach dropping like a stone as he made his way behind the silent footman to Bettina Quinn's drawing room. He felt almost as sick as Julian, although he hadn't had so much as a drop to drink. Not yet, anyway. How, precisely, did he think to present this matter to Caroline? *Look here, old girl, I've had second thoughts. Let's just forget all this marriage-to-Julian business, shall we?* He rather thought she wouldn't be having any of that. His alternative idea was downright terrifying, but it was the only one that stood a chance.

"If you'll wait here, sir, I'll see if Miss Quinn is receiving this morning. Would you care for some refreshment while you wait?" the footman asked with that distant hauteur common to the finer households. These folk could outdo royalty on the haughty scale.

Although rarely loath to grab a free bite wherever he could, Edgar was quite sure he could not, at this time, swallow a morsel. "Thank you, no," he said, waving negligently, as if he hardly cared when he ate again. The footman nodded and withdrew, closing the door behind him. The note the man carried upstairs to Caroline was brief, but to the point. *Must see you immediately. Absolutely urgent. Come downstairs at once, please.* Edgar had added the "please" as an afterthought. No point in irritating the easily irritated Caroline any more than necessary. He cast an eye about the gloomy room. The late Lord Ewell had had a heavy, dark taste and the furnishings reflected it. He paced the room, noting out of habit, with a practiced eye, the value of this and that. He could feel the annoyance rising in him as it always did at the unfairness of it all. Why were some blessed with so much, while others made do with so little? Were it not for the negligent largesse of the finer households, which passed out refreshment without regard to cost, there would be days when Edgar simply did not eat at all, and not by choice. His propensity for visiting had more to do with a desire for basic sustenance rather than any real enjoyment of these rattlebrains. It did tend to make him a good gossip, however, a talent and perception he nurtured carefully, so as to keep up his entrée.

With a sinking feeling he heard hurried footsteps and the turning of the door handle. Didn't sound like the footman. Perhaps the note had been a little too alarming. Why couldn't Caroline have been "not at home," as ladies often were when they just dratted well wanted some peace and quiet?

The great doors opened with a whoosh and slammed shut peremptorily. Must be the lovely Caroline. With an affected nonchalance, Edgar gave a flick to his lace cuff, then turned casually, as if he did not know she was there.

"Oh, there you are, my dear. Nice of you to be so prompt," he said, with what he hoped was a chilly smile. The ice in his voice was the only thing not affected. He gave her a cool appraisal. If not a disheveled mess, Caroline was certainly not the exquisitely turned-out fashion plate he was used to seeing. She looked, if anything, a bit haggard; a bit—he dared think—older than she was used to appearing. There was a wariness about her, as if she did not know what to expect from him. He arched an eyebrow at her gown—a near cast-off, much mended and faded from its original royal blue, several Seasons gone, a gown she wouldn't be caught in at a cock fight. Thus stood he, the coconspirator, in her estimation, eh? Not important enough to keep up appearances for.

"Whatever do you want, Edgar?" she spat out. "I've a great deal to do today and I've no time for your inanities." She did not ask him to sit. He very nearly sat anyway, just to make a point, then thought better of putting himself in the position of having to look up at her. As it was, she had an inch or so on him. She and most everyone else in the world. Another point that rankled.

"I've been doing some difficult thinking, Caroline," he began, in what he hoped was a reasonable tone. "I find myself highly dissatisfied with the result of our collaboration. When I embarked on this venture with you, I had no idea that my dear Julian was truly so in love with the little country cousin. I supposed he was just being kind in that direction." He paused at the look of growing incredulity on Caroline's face, but she did not speak. "As it turns out, the man is quite devastated. I'm sure it has not escaped your notice that he has no desire whatsoever to marry you?"

"I believe you've prattled nonsense at me long enough, Mr. Randall. Kindly remove yourself from the premises. Our further—association"—she let the word drip with contempt for their financial arrangements, as if paying him for nefarious services rendered was far beneath her dignity—"need only be conducted by post."

"I must differ with you, Caroline. While I may be suffering from a woefully laggard attack of conscience, I do consider the matter most serious. I do not think it fair or wise for you to marry a man whose heart is entirely engaged elsewhere."

"And you expect me to cry off, just like that?" she asked, as if he had suggested she sprout wings and fly. "Give up the match of the Season so that you can rest easy on your pillow?"

"Come now, Caroline," he began, thinking to reason with her. "Surely you noted his behavior last night. The man is near dead of drink. And what of your cousin? Have you no feeling for her? You must know she loves him. Indeed, I feel rather strongly that they had an arrangement, if only informally and privately between them."

"As if I could be brought to care a fig about that insipid fool!" Caroline nearly shrieked. "Not a penny to her name, and the only claim to family she has in this world comes from her thin association with me. Why, that little chit is lucky not to be a scullery maid! In fact," Caroline stopped, a slow smile playing over her face, "I understand that if she doesn't marry well—something most unlikely at this juncture—she may be reduced to just that!"

Edgar could think of no retort. It was dawning on him that this was a woman of no conscience whatsoever, a true *belle-dame sans merci*. Might as well argue right and wrong with the Devil, himself. Very well, he had one more arrow in his quiver, although it frightened him down to his soul even to contemplate its launch.

"Caroline, regardless of whether or not you can be

brought to see what's right, I feel I cannot be a party to this vile plan any longer. You may consider our—ah—association at an end." She raised her eyebrow at him, a cool smile playing across her face, as if this were just what she wanted to hear.

"Hear me out, Caroline," he went on, determined to see it through, whatever the cost to himself. "I am prepared to denounce you, to expose that ugly little scene you played out in Sydney Gardens for the fraud that it was." He stopped, waiting for his threat to sink in. He was disappointed. If anything, her smile grew broader.

"I see," she said, her voice almost a purr. "And how would you disguise your part in our little scene?"

"Well, I—" he began. This was the weak point in his plan. Trust Caroline to focus right in on it. Nothing for it but to bluff it out. "I am prepared to confess all," he stated baldly. He was not quite, actually. This was the part he hadn't dared think all the way through to its logical conclusion, hoping against hope that Caroline would fold before he got so far. This was, of course, one of the chief reasons he did not play cards often at the clubs, and then only with good friends for low stakes. Couldn't bluff worth a damn.

"Are you?" she purred. "Are you, indeed? You will, of course, be persona non grata in the better circles all over England. The continent, for that matter. Perhaps you might emigrate to our ungrateful former Colonies. I understand they have great fun there—shooting bears and hoeing crops. Perhaps you could find some out-of-the-way frontier spot where news of this little fiasco has not penetrated. Perhaps. But I doubt it."

"Caroline, I am well aware of the social risks involved," he said quickly, hoping to stem her words. She conjured up scenarios to make him shudder. "That should tell you how important I think this matter is. We simply cannot, either of us, allow this farce to go on. Surely you can see that!" He knew he was beginning to sound a bit desperate. Wasn't sure he'd like a bear up close. "There are dozens of other men you can marry. What about poor Ledbetter? Word has it in the King's Bath that he is prostrate at the news of your engagement."

"Mr. Ledbetter is a fool. I could eat him for my breakfast. Besides, he isn't nearly well enough set up. I intend to be a very expensive wife." She was purring again. He was getting nowhere. Was he prepared to expose her—and himself—as the evildoers that they were? Never again to grace an elegant ball, a musicale? Unwelcome in every gentlemen's club the length and breadth of England? Even the public rooms would be off limits for someone who could expect only the Cut Direct from every member of the *ton*.

"Nevertheless, Caroline, there are others. Why, whatever happened to Lord Rokeby? He was over the moon about you last Season." It was an exaggeration, to be sure, but there had been something between them, or so the *on dit* had had it at the time.

"He seemed to find his cattle more interesting than I," she answered, her voice sour. "In any event, Edgar, this conversation is at an end. The answer to your asinine question is a resounding 'no.' I am engaged to Julian Thorpe and I intend to marry him—the sooner the better, since there seem to be so many interested in the wedding not going forward. Everyone will live, I, best of all. Julian has plenty of scratch. He can afford me. I will set up in his London house and he can go to ground in the country. I don't care whether I ever lay eyes on him after the wedding. Just so long as I have unlimited access to his prodigious accounts. I'd be mad to give all that up, just so you and your conscience can be on speaking terms. Since when have you a conscience anyway? I've heard you shred perfectly innocent young ladies with gossip even you knew to be preposterous."

"And lived to regret it," Edgar replied. He did, too, at this moment. All his malfeasance come back to haunt him now, on this one thing that mattered so much. "Caroline, I am begging you. Do not do this thing."

"Show yourself out, Mr. Randall. I wouldn't wish to trouble the footman. He has more important things to tend to. Like shining my brother's boots." Caroline swept out of the room without a backward glance.

Edgar sat down with a heavy thump on one of the few sturdy chairs in the room. It gave off a cloud of dust. What to do? He had shown his hand and it had not a winning card in it. Of course, he could do as he threatened—tell the world the truth. And be on the next boat to the new United States. In steerage with the pigs, swine with swine. Well, no point in staying here. At the very worst, Bettina Quinn would come sailing in and find some reason to flay the skin off him. The thought propelled him from the chair and through the door. There was no one in the hallway, mercifully, to witness his skulking, ignominious retreat. He paused at the door. He had no alternative plan. He'd been a sad excuse for a human being all his life, and today marked his nadir. At least things could not get any worse, he thought, as he reached for the front door handle and gave it a pull.

When he was wrong, he was very wrong indeed.

The Viscountess Alderson was startled when the door flew open just as she had touched the large brass door knocker. She did not like being startled. It put one at a visible disadvantage. She was, however, heartened to note that if she was startled, this—what was his name?—oh, yes, Edgar Randall, of the Oxfordshire Randalls—mother, a lovely gel, father, an absolute wastrel—was shocked down to his slippers to find her standing in front of him, hand raised as if to strike.

"Oh, er, ah, I declare! If it isn't Lady Alderson! Good day to you, again, ma'am. Won't you come in?"

"Are you in Bettina Quinn's employ as her footman these days, Mr. Randall?" she asked, stepping over the threshold as he scrambled back.

"Er, well, no, ma'am. I was just letting myself out," he stammered.

"You do seem to be traveling in my circles today, Mr. Randall. Whom, may I ask, did you see here?" Having left him a bare hour ago at poor Julian's, it was obvious he was here on the same mission as she herself. She proceeded to the late Lord Ewell's dreadful drawing room, pausing before the great mahogany doors so that this puppy could open them for her.

"Oh, I thought to have a few words with Miss Quinn, ma'am, Caroline, that is." Edgar stood goggling at her, obviously at a loss as to whether he should offer her a seat in someone else's drawing room.

"Shall I take it that the chit has refused to call off this charade of an engagement?" the viscountess asked. Might do well to get to the facts before they alerted a servant to their presence and that idiot Bettina Quinn bore down on them. She seated herself on one of Ewell's particularly uncomfortable little occasional chairs. She cared about comfort only in her own bed. All other positions were for show only.

"I'm afraid so, ma'am," came his simple reply.

"Perhaps, now that we are alone, you would be so kind as to enlighten me. How does Julian find himself in this dreadful stew?"

Edgar fairly gaped at her. He opened his mouth, then closed it again several times, looking for all the world like a fish out of water. She arched an eyebrow at him, giving no quarter. If she were to involve herself in this fiasco—and she rarely bestirred herself for this sort of thing these days—she'd best have the truth of it. If Julian had compromised the girl, as gossip had it, then he would marry her, if the viscountess, herself, had to march him by the ear to the altar. After all, there were rules, and where a gentleman was fool enough to behave badly, he must pay for it. "I'm waiting, Edgar," she finally said, when it appeared he had run out of air entirely. "Oh, do sit down, boy. You're making me nervous," she snapped.

Edgar sat on a little settee, upholstered in a dreadful brocade, its color and pattern out of style these past forty years and more. Old Ewell always was one to get his money's worth. The boy looked, if anything, even more uncomfortable, pitched forward as if he were about to tumble over his feet. He stared earnestly at her, although he still seemed disinclined to speak.

"Out with it, boy. You're in this little mess up to your neck—sticking it out too far, I'll warrant. I've all the time in the world today, and if you cannot tell me alone, perhaps I should summon Bettina and have you tell us both."

Edgar, who never had much color to him, now paled to the color of parchment. "Lady Alderson . . ." he began, and she had to lean forward to hear him. He could not go on.

"Oh, for heaven's sake, boy! Did Julian compromise Caroline Quinn or not? Surely you can answer a yes or no question."

"Well, not exactly," stammered Edgar.

"That's nonsense! Either he did or he didn't. There is no middle ground where these matters are concerned. Yes or no, Mr. Randall?"

"No," he answered simply; then he sat back, and breathed a great breath, looking almost relieved. So, the boy had some hand in this, indeed. And something to get off his chest, as well.

"Then how does it happen that it is bruited all over Bath that the two of them were caught out in a dreadful indiscretion, and that they are therefore engaged?"

Edgar took a moment, drawing in another deep breath, but she waited him out. If this fish was gasping on her hook, he was hers, nonetheless, and would not free himself and swim off. "Well, there was a—a—contretemps in that regard, ma'am, but Julian was—was . . ." Edgar trailed off, looking stricken.

"If, young man, you are about to tell me that Julian is innocent, you had better be able to prove it. It's the oldest dodge in the book to compromise a young lady beyond all reparation, and then say things were not what they seemed. No one has ever believed that sort of thing."

"But it's true in this case!" Edgar burst out. "Julian knew nothing of it. Caroline set him up. He thought he was meeting Elspeth in the maze, but it was Caroline waiting for him there instead, all disheveled and crying. She'd made a muss of herself, you see. And when I came through a minute later with Lady Haverford—well, you can imagine what it looked like. I mean, Julian was comforting Caroline, after all. She told him she'd been attacked!"

Now it was the viscountess's turn to sit back. The tale might even be true, at that. At least this scenario fit with what she knew of Julian's character—and Caroline's. "How did it happen that you and Lady Haverford, of all people, should wander into that particular part of the maze at that precise moment, Mr. Randall?"

Now the boy looked as though he might sick up all over Lord Ewell's dark and gloomy carpet. There was something very wrong here. She stared, waiting for him to speak. At last he closed his eyes and took a deep breath. "I, myself, had a hand in this, my lady," he said. He rose and began to pace. She did not order him to seat himself again. If what he said was true, things might not go well with him among the *ton* in the future. Again, she waited. Let him finish what he had begun.

"Caroline was hideously jealous of the success her country cousin seemed to be having with Julian. I think she rather viewed Julian as her conquest, since they had been an item a Season or two back. She seemed to feel the competition more keenly this year—I suppose several years of near-misses does take its toll on a demoiselle. In any event, she asked for help in landing him . . ." He broke off again, searching for words. "I thought it sounded like a lark, really. I guess, to be truthful, I didn't think at all. I agreed to help her." Now he hung his head and rubbed at his temples. She was afraid she heard something of a sob escape him. "You must believe me, Your Ladyship. I had no idea that Julian and Elspeth were so in love with each other. I thought it was a simple flirtation, the likes of which we see all year long among the *ton*. Nothing serious. Now I seem to have broken two hearts for . . ." He sat heavily on one of the chairs, dropping his head into his hands.

"What did you do it for, Edgar?" she asked simply.

"A bit of scratch," he replied, not looking up. "I betrayed my best friend for money. Caroline and I came to a—a financial arrangement. You may as well know, ma'am. My father gambled away most of our assets. Mother and I lived like paupers until she died. I received the merest pittance as an inheritance from her, and was lucky she had managed to save that from his debtors. I've been on the edge of ruin ever since." He said it simply, as if he were not telling a shameful family secret. She supposed the truth about his involvement in Caroline's malevolent scheme was shame enough.

She had no doubt of the truth of what he said. Were Julian of a different character, she could well believe he had put his best friend up to such an absurd tale to worm his way out of his fix. But Julian, bless his integrity, was Julian, raised by one of the most decent of women, and by a father of iron character. Besides, the situation didn't make sense any other way. She had seen what passed between Julian and this Elspeth chit last night, and she had no doubt they were well and truly smitten with each other.

But how to fix this awful mess? And what to do about Edgar Randall? Expose him for the traitor that he was, or allow him a chance to mend the hearts that he had helped to break so badly?

She was saved from an immediate decision by a whirling blur that darted past her, and launched itself, full tilt, against the slightly built Edgar Randall, who landed on the awful carpet with a whoosh, a small flailing figure atop him, pummeling him and shouting.

"You've ruined my sister's life, sir!" the blur shrieked. "I challenge you to a duel with pistols! No! Swords! You'll fight me like a man, sir!"

For the first time in as many years as she could remember, the viscountess began to laugh. Not just a polite little chuckle, not a sardonic titter—but a real, from the belly, gasping laugh. She clutched her cane for dear life, afraid that if she let go, she would fall right over, still laughing, and not be able to get up. She wasn't entirely sure what was so funny—the child was not the least bit amused, nor, indeed, was poor Mr. Randall, who waved his hands about trying to protect his face, which, unfortunately, had nevertheless taken something of a beating. There was blood already collecting at his nose and a small cut at the eye. Well, perhaps she had best do something. She took a deep breath and raised her cane.

"Unhand Mr. Randall at once, young man!" she announced, giving several sharp, carefully placed raps to what she hoped was the boy's head. It took a moment, but finally the boy sat up, still straddling the hapless Mr. Randall. The boy rubbed at his scalp and glared balefully at his attacker. Mr. Randall just moaned.

"Stand up immediately, you young ruffian!" she said, giving her cane a sharp crack on the floor for emphasis. "You have committed so many social transgressions in my presence, I don't know where to begin castigating you." The boy got to his feet, still rubbing his head. Well, really, she had barely tapped him to get his attention. At least he had the grace to look sheepish. Edgar Randal, too, came to his feet, albeit far more slowly. He pulled out a linen square and mopped at his face. She was relieved to see very little actual damage—just the small cut that seemed to have already stopped bleeding. Fortunately she was not one of those women who went about shrieking and swooning at the least sign of blood. Dashed inconvenient that would be!

"Perhaps you might make the introductions, Mr. Randall," she asked mildly. Best to maintain the veneer of civilized behavior, even if one did find oneself planted in the middle of an impromptu boxing match. Edgar opened his eyes, the one more slitted than the other, she noted.

"Lady Alderson, may I present to you Harry Quinn. He is Bettina Quinn's nephew, and Miss Elspeth's Quinn's brother, late of Weston-under-Lizard, I believe. Mr. Quinn, you have the honor of addressing the Viscountess Alderson." Edgar went through the introductions flawlessly, as if he were not standing there, sleeve torn and pressing a bloody handkerchief to his eye.

"How d'y'do, Mr. Quinn?" she asked

"Very well, Your—um—Viscountesship," he stammered, sketching a boy's clumsy bow. "And you, ma'am?" he went on.

Acceptable. Some stab at good manners even in the face of extraordinary circumstances, notwithstanding his perfectly dreadful address. "Your Viscountesship," indeed!

"Well, I am somewhat distressed, sir, that you would treat a woman of my sensibilities to such a dreadful display." She rather thought she heard a snort from Edgar, which she chose to ignore.

"But he—he's hurt my sister!" the boy wailed, turning a malevolent glare on Edgar, and scrabbling rather angrily at his face as a lone tear coursed down his cheek.

"Gentlemen take their disputes outside, out of the presence of ladies, Mr. Quinn. No matter what the provocation."

The boy opened his mouth, then shut it again, standing red-faced and glum. It was apparent he knew he was in the wrong, and to his credit dared offer no further argument to an obvious Personage.

"I believe we have some business to tend to, Mr. Randall," she ventured. "Do you suppose you could tidy yourself enough to make a call with me? There's a mirror over there, although I declare it's old enough to be dark as pitch, and not much good to anyone." Edgar moved haltingly over to the grim mirror, gold carved and rather overdone. Fortunately, he did not limp.

"Now, then, young Harry, is it?" She turned her gaze back to the other culprit in the room. "I appreciate your loyalty to your sister. That does you just enough credit to prevent me from treating you to the Cut Direct in society for the rest of whatever life is left to me. You would not enjoy that, I assure you," she went on, when it appeared that the boy was not entirely sure what she meant. "Nevertheless, there are ways that a gentleman may go about setting right a great wrong—ways that do not involve fisticuffs or distasteful scenes in front of perfectly respectable strangers."

The boy squirmed a bit, but stood his ground. His eyes shimmered with tears he obviously was holding back. He was red-faced and breathing hard, but he was listening. "Now, Mr. Randall and I are . . ." She broke off as the door fairly flew open.

"Master Harry, you'd better show yourself this instant! Your aunt is . . ." A mobcapped kitchen girl stood quivering in the door, mouth stopped in mid-word, agape at the sight of unexpected Quality infesting the drawing room.

"Well, come in, gel, and fetch your miscreant," the viscountess said, rising majestically on her gold-tipped walking stick.

"Yes, mum, excuse me, mum, I didn't know you was 'ere, mum. . . ." the girl babbled on, bobbing repeatedly, like a daisy buffeted in a breeze.

"Quite enough, gel," her ladyship snapped. "We are just leaving, aren't we, Mr. Randall?" She cast an eye in his direction and was relieved to see that although he was a bit the worse for wear, he would do for her purposes. She could take a stab at his neckcloth in her carriage, after all. She had, quite in private, enjoyed certain intimacies with her several husbands, and fiddling with neckcloths had been one of them.

"Young Harry, a word with you before we go," she said, gesturing peremptorily with her cane for him to come close. He took a few tentative steps, eyeing the cane with some trepidation. She bent down and put her lips close to his ear. "In the first place, I am properly addressed as 'madam,' or 'Lady Alderson,' not 'Your Viscountesship.' " She barely repressed a shudder. "Further, we are leaving now, Mr. Randall and I," she said, her voice low enough so the servant, who still bobbed frantically in the doorway, could not overhear. "I—and he—will be making every effort to set this sorry mess with your sister to rights. In the meanwhile, I think you would be very wise to button that pouting little lip of yours. Say nothing of our visit, and nothing of what you have overheard. Do I make myself clear, young man?"

"Yes, Lady Alderson," he whispered back. His eyes were still tearful, but there was a creeping hope, and a great deal of awe in them now, instead of sullen helplessness.

She rose and bestowed her gaze on the hapless kitchen maid. "And you, gel, stop your bobbing. I declare I shall have mal de mer just watching you." The girl stopped in mid-bob, then straightened in obvious terror. "We were just taking our leave, gel. We've finished our business with this household. It's quite private. You would do well to hold your tongue regarding my visit. I trust you need no further warning?"

"N—no, Your Ladyship, no indeed. I—I . . ." She started bobbing again.

"Quite! Ready, Mr. Randall?" Not bothering to wait for his answer, she sailed past the goggling, bobbing kitchen girl, who would not hold her tongue in the kitchen, of course. It hardly mattered. She simply hoped Bettina and her viper of a daughter would not hear of her visit before she could start the wheels in motion. The girl at least had enough wits about her to come flying past and pull the front door open, bobbing and gasping out an apology about the footman being unavailable. Now for the difficult part . . .

Chapter Eleven

It wasn't so much the headache. He'd earned it and he could live with it. Or die of it. One or the other, he deserved that much. It was that if he couldn't convince Elspeth he was not a hopeless bounder, there was no point to going on at all. With or without the infernal headache.

A hot bath had worked wonders. By not so much as the flicker of a glance had Forbush, *domestique extraordinaire* that he was, indicated that he was near dying of curiosity as to the morning's remarkable events. Or last evening's, at that. Edgar had been most emphatic that Julian had appeared at the Viscountess Alderson's—at THE ball of the Bath Season—in his afternoon attire, and much the worse for wear, indeed. Julian knew that this would cost Forbush some ribbing in the vast servant world, but he couldn't bring himself to care particularly as he lay back in the big hip bath and attempted, futilely, to soak away his pain.

She wouldn't see him. Of that he was certain. Nor, indeed, did he wish to see Caroline or her mother. If he could get to Harry, now. . . . But, no, the boy was probably as angered and bewildered as his sister. His only hope lay in getting Elspeth alone, somewhere where she'd have to at least listen. His carriage swung ponderously, turning onto the street where the Quinns currently resided. It pulled past another carriage and Julian caught a glimpse of an ornate coat of arms on the door. A hurried look back confirmed the worst. The Viscountess Alderson was calling at the Quinns. The woman was making quite a nuisance of herself. One more dose of the viscountess today, not to mention Bettina Quinn, and this would be the second-worst day of his life.

Well, he hadn't exactly planned on ringing the front doorbell anyway, so perhaps the viscountess's formidable presence would be a blessing in disguise, focusing, as it would, the entire household's attention on the Personage in the drawing room at the front of the house. His coachman had been instructed to drive by the house, then keep going till he rounded the next corner. The carriage made another turn, then slowed to a halt, around the corner from the Quinn house. Julian took a quick look from the window, then jumped out. As agreed, the carriage lumbered on. His man would wait, hours, if necessary, several blocks away. Quite casually, as if out for a leisurely stroll, Julian ambled down the side street. Some yards away he came upon the entryway to the mews serving the houses on the Quinn household's block. With a quick look he stepped into the mews.

So far, so good. No one about. The afternoon was quiet. He heard a horse whinny, then another, but none of the shouting and harness clanking that preceded a carriage about to depart. The mews were clean and well kept, as he would expect in such a neighborhood. He'd been in some, in London, where it wasn't worth one's life to step through the muck and refuse. He glanced up at the back facades of the townhouses. Excellent. It was easy enough to see, by judging the windows and drain pipes, where one house left off and the next began. The Quinn house, he had taken pains to note, was the fourth house in from the side street. He stopped at the house next door, between its windows. All remained quiet. Which way did the Quinn kitchen or scullery look out? Into the mews, no doubt, but it was also likely, as he examined the stairs that led, at each house, down into a well area with a door, that the windows at this level were low enough that only his well-shod feet would be visible by servants. A gentleman of the Quality did not generally wander through mews, but it was not unknown. One did, after all, occasionally have to check on a horse, or some other problem arising with stable matters. Across the way, the stables stood silent, black carriages tucked away, awaiting the evening's call to revelry.

He glanced up at the Quinns' rear facade. As he had expected, vines grew up the bricks. There was gutter piping as well, but it did not look sturdy enough to hold his weight. The bricks, themselves, however, were old enough to have pulled loose in some places. He moved nearer and examined them more closely. Yes, a foothold here, a handhold there. It was just possible to pull one's way up, with the Devil's own luck. The library and dining room were on the first floor, a good ten feet from street level, but the windows were near flush with the wall, and latched tight, by the looks of them. The next floor up would be the family bedrooms. Each window there had a small iron half-enclosure like a balcony, decorative only, enough to give him a place to balance, but not enough to block entrance. These town households feared fire above all things, and would bar only the lowest windows. The topmost floor would house the servants and storage. Unlikely anyone would be up there at this time of the afternoon, but since linens and other useful things were kept there, it was not wise to count on that floor being empty. A servant would set up an unholy ruckus seeing his head pop through a window, while any of the family residents would be, if initially shocked, at least cognizant of his identity. That would present its own set of problems, of course, but anything was better than having a maidservant screaming hysterically and bringing folks running from every direction. The servant's windows were unadorned in any event—and likely fastened tight.

His best bet would be one of the family bedrooms, then. How many would there be? These houses were good-sized, but they were townhouses, not large country estates. The architects tended to make the most of whatever windowed space they had. There would be, at best, only four bedrooms on this floor, two forward and two to the rear. The boys either shared a room, or Harry slept on the servants' level. Caroline and Elspeth did not share a room, of that he could be absolutely certain. How would the various bedrooms be situated? Front bedrooms were noisier than those in the rear, as a rule, but rear windows suffered from stable and kitchen odors, and the rear rooms were therefore generally the less desirable. Front rooms, on the other hand, offered occupants a window onto the world, or, at least, as much of the world as strolled or rolled by. So, if his best guess was correct—a big if—Bettina and Caroline occupied the two front bedrooms and Elspeth and the boys, the rear.

If, of course, he was wrong, there'd be hell itself to pay. Caroline screaming her outrage at him, or Bettina, or any number of serving girls. Not a soothing thought, all that shrieking.

What would Elspeth do? What would any gently reared young lady, who thought herself recently jilted and humiliated throughout all Bath society, do, if the gentleman—or cad—in question appeared, suddenly, in her bedroom window, two stories up?

Scream the place down.

Well, perhaps she wasn't there. Perhaps she was downstairs—in the library maybe, among her blessed books. Perhaps they were out—in Milsom Street, shopping for Caroline's trousseau, but then he seriously doubted Elspeth would go along for that outing. Of course, they could be out calling—or in the Ladies Bath. He'd have a long wait for her if they were out for the afternoon.

He'd wait forever, if need be. He could gain his entrance, bide his time in her room, perhaps, and approach her—gently—when she appeared. If he found her room. If no one else found him first. If she would stay to listen. Lots of ifs.

He took another careful look at the bricks, noting the specific holds. Some were little more than wishful thinking. Others, he suspected, would require the assistance of the ivy to get him to the next one. Once climbing, it would be difficult, if not impossible, for him to look down, so he'd have to rely on his memory as to their placement. Were this a boxing match at Gentleman Jackson's, he would consider these long odds, indeed.

On the second floor, the choice of windows was obvious, as one was slightly ajar, the better to catch a freshening breeze now and then. All right, then . . . no time like the present. . . . He seized a piece of vine and gave it a sharp tug. It held. Placing his foot in a crevice about two feet off the ground, he heaved himself aloft. His foot found the next foothold easily, and then the next. Bless the tenacity of nature, the vine held strong. Halfway there, his foot found its perch, only to have the brick crumble to dust beneath his weight. Only the sturdiness of the vine kept him from a nasty fall. He clung with the strength of his arms, praying the vine would not tear away from the brick. Slowly, so as not to put too much stress on the vine, he moved his feet here and there. Ah, finally, just as he thought his arms would give way entirely, one foot found a small protuberance. He tested it against his weight. It would do. Now, where was the next foothold? He risked a glance to one side and the other. Nothing much that he could see from this angle, but there had been several in this area. He brought his right leg up, pressing against the brick, and found an indentation large enough to hold his weight. A few more steps and he'd have it.

Just then the sound he most dreaded came, a clattering of the cobblestones indicating a carriage approaching. How long before it reached a point where he'd be noticeable? Not too long, by the sounds of it. He was not, by nature, a flamboyant man. Perhaps that would stand him in good stead. As the sound of the carriage grew alarmingly close, he pressed himself as flat as he could to the vine-covered bricks. Dressed as he was in buff-colored breeches and a dark frock coat, he might very well pass for the usual brick-and-vine native to the mews, if no one looked too closely. If there were passengers in the carriage, they'd have to crane their necks a good bit up to see him, although it was most likely the occupants had been disgorged at the front of the house. The real danger came from the coachman, who sat high on his seat. But even there, Julian clung a good several feet above the driver's eye level. Now if only the man would keep his eyes on his team and not look up. . . .

The carriage rumbled past, Julian hardly daring to

breathe. No sounds of a shout or recognition reached him. The carriage kept on its lumbering way, not slowing until it had passed three or four more houses. Julian had to move now, before the various stable boys came tumbling forth into the mews to get everything settled away. He found the next foothold and pulled up. Perhaps two more and he'd gain the ironwork that wrapped around the open bedroom window. Naturally, because he had only a few feet to go, the next foothold seemed not to exist. Try as he might, he could not find a knob or crevice to hold his weight. Now he did hear shouts coming from the end of the mews where the carriage had ground to a halt. He heaved himself up, taking all his weight on his arms and hauled himself hand over hand on the vine. If it pulled loose now he was a dead man. At last the toe of his boot found the iron railing and he allowed his weight to rest again on his foot. With a deep breath, he climbed over the railing. It was rusty, and not built to take any weight. He held quiet for just a moment, still clutching at the vine, lest the ironwork give way entirely. So far, so good.

The window was open but only a bit, not enough for him to crawl through without pushing it open further. Draperies blocked his view into the room but he leaned toward the heavy curtain to listen. As he expected, all was silent from within. That did not mean, of course, that there was no one inside. Holding his weight now against the windowsill, he examined the draperies for a seam that would indicate an opening. Nothing. They appeared to be an unbroken swath of heavy, dusty stuff that most fortunately reached all the way to the floor. He tested the window, aware that as he pushed it up, his weight pushed down on the rusty ironwork that held him, now without the vine for safety. The window did not budge, but the ironwork creaked most ominously and shifted just enough to knock his heart around in his chest a bit. Leaning forward, he wedged his head and neck into the window, and with most of his weight on his hands, he pressed the back of his neck against the bottom of the window, pushing up. The window began to climb, inch by inch, until, finally, there was enough room for him to slide himself forward and through. He hesitated a moment, aware that although the window had slid without much noise, enough rustling must be coming from his efforts that if there were anyone in the room, he'd be discovered.

But all was stillness within. He pushed himself forward on his hands, just as the ironwork gave a last rusty gasp and pulled loose from the bricks. As his feet dropped precariously, he caught his weight on his elbows, which shot pain up his arms. Feet dangling, he heaved himself forward, catching his leg on the windowsill, then lowering it to the safety of the floor below.

Now he was in the room, hiding like a naughty boy behind the draperies, aware that every muscle in his body was annoyed with him. It was a safe bet that had the room been tenanted, his presence would have been noted and bruited about the house by now, so he fumbled for the drapery edge and pulled it to the side. . . .

He was in a large linen closet. What he had taken for fancy drapery was just an old bedspread, obviously tacked up to keep the light from fading the linens, while the open window kept the small room from getting musty. Grateful that his luck had landed him in a safe place, he was nevertheless aware that now more problems lay ahead. The door to the closet was slightly ajar, probably to pull the breeze from other windows open in the house. Dim light spilled into the closet from what must be a central hallway. The bedrooms would be arrayed up and down the hall, two in front, two in back. He leaned forward to look around the door. It took a moment for his eyes to adjust to the dim light after the bright sun outside, but it did appear that the hallway was deserted.

As he had expected, there appeared to be four bedrooms. At least, there were four closed doors, two forward and two rear on either side of the wide hall. The hall itself was covered with a thick, dark carpet, the better to muffle his steps. With a deep breath he moved quickly to the door closest to him on the left. A quiet twist of the handle proved it to be unlocked. Slowly he pushed the door open. The room was in darkness—obviously Bettina Quinn did not wish to pay damages to the landlord for faded carpets and draperies—but he had a sense it was empty. The bed was made up neatly. He looked about for some sign of who the usual occupant might be and spotted it in the corner—a large, gaily decorated wooden rocking horse. A boy's room then, no doubt. He closed the door swiftly and cast a glance down the hall. All was still quiet, but he was mindful that the carpet that so fortunately muffled his own steps could muffle those of anyone else as well. He made for the door on the right of the linen closet.

The handle turned. He pushed the door open slowly, and stepped into the room, quietly shutting the door behind him.

The draperies had been pulled back, so this room was not as dark as the one across the hall. He stood for a brief moment, quickly eyeing the surroundings. The bed, neatly made, was unoccupied. So, too, was the large wing chair that sat near the fireplace. Needlework lay on the little table next to the chair, but any lady in the house would be expected to do some needlework when otherwise unoccupied—even Caroline, he supposed. He peered into the corners, and saw no sign of movement. There was a large privacy screen standing in front of one corner, but not a sound came from behind its ornate panels. He let out the breath he hadn't realized he was holding, and surveyed the furnishings, looking for that telltale clue that would give away the occupant's identity. There was a dress laid out on the bed, either recently doffed or waiting to be donned. It was plain, a dark green silk. Hadn't he seen Elspeth in such a gown? He could hardly remember. It seemed, now that he thought of it, that he always focused on her beautiful face, her luminous eyes. She could have been wearing sacking for all he would have noticed.

Caroline wouldn't be caught dead out in such a plain gown, but who knew what ladies wore in the privacy of the home, upstairs? There were dark slippers by the bed, but these, too, were nondescript afternoon walking shoes. Every lady he knew had one pair, if not several. He had crept forward into the room, the better to eye the dress, and now he sat on the edge of the bed. His muscles had let him know again that his exertions with regard to scaling brick walls were not appreciated. It was odd, being uninvited in the bedroom of a lady of the *ton*. Actually, it was quite unprecedented. While he could not pretend to be utterly ignorant with regard to the female boudoir, all those he had frequented in the past had been ladies of a certain sort, certainly not Quality. This transgression, alone, would be enough to see him married forthwith, if not banned from society altogether.

His eye fell on the nightstand by the bed. On it was a candle, half burned down. And a book, with a marker in it, about halfway through. And—a pair of spectacles. His breath caught. He picked them up carefully. Though he could not say for certain that neither Bettina nor Caroline Quinn wore spectacles to read in the privacy of her boudoir, he was fairly certain he had seen these before—perched on the lovely nose of his beloved. Not too long ago they had resided some days, forgotten, in his pocket. He held them up to his eyes. Blind as a bat, his beloved was, and so, too, the owner of these. He set them back down where they had been.

He wondered how long he'd have to wait for her return. His hastily conceived plan of accosting her in her room was not terribly well thought out, he realized. She could be anywhere—at the Baths, at the Pump Room, shopping, paying calls. Still, her spectacles were here, and he was aware she rarely stirred forth without them.

Elspeth could come up to the room at any minute—or, hours from now if he was unlucky. It wouldn't do for him to be planted firmly on her bed as she entered. Might give her the wrong impression as to his intentions, and he did not need her jumping to any more unfavorable conclusions. A servant might enter as well, and that would truly be a disaster for Elspeth's reputation. Few servants the length and breadth of England could be expected to hold such a tidbit from their colleagues.

He glanced around the room again. He dismissed the draperies out of hand. He would not stand hiding behind dusty, fusty curtains for who knew how many hours, like a cat watching a mouse. The ornate privacy screen, then. He eyed it. Yes, it was large enough to hide him comfortably. He might even find a footstool to place behind it and sit on while he waited. He moved, still softly, toward the screen, aware that his heavier tread might be noted if anyone were in the room below, the library, he thought. He stepped behind the screen and froze.

There was a large hip bath, full of water and soap bubbles. The water still steamed slightly, although it was obviously no longer piping hot. And in the tub, lying back, freshly washed hair falling back onto a towel behind her head, lay his love, eyes closed, fast asleep.

* * *

There was a part of her, distant and annoying, that told Elspeth she was only dreaming. She ignored it. The part of her that was content and comfortable knew very well that waking up had nothing to recommend it. In the dream, she was home with her brother and sisters and everyone loved her and no one sneered at her and she was warm and cozy and. . . .

It was no use. With a shiver she realized that she was not home, not loved and definitely not warm. In a bath, she was, and the water was cooling rapidly. Now where exactly was she? Oh, yes, at Aunt Bettina's in cursed, awful Bath. A bath in Bath. Well, nothing for it but to get out and dry off. She opened her eyes. . . .

She gave a start, splashing water out of the tub. Heaven only knew her vision was limited without her glasses, but even through the blur she could see there was someone standing there. The figure appeared in silhouette, the window behind. Elspeth had never been one to castigate servants, but, really, sneaking up on a lady naked and sleeping in her bath was enough to frighten the wits out of anyone.

"Bessie, you gave me quite a start," she said. "Can you hand me my dressing gown? I'm ready to get out."

There was a pause. And then a voice spoke.

"Elspeth, please forgive me. Please don't scream. I had to see you. Actually, I'm not seeing you at this moment. I'm not looking." He spoke rapidly, obviously noting that she had nearly jumped out of her skin at the sound of his voice.

It was he. Proving once and for all that he was not just a mere rake, but a Peeping Tom and possibly a despoiler, to boot.

Ruined. Utterly and completely lost. She might as well parade naked through the Assembly Rooms this evening soliciting a lover. She opened her mouth to speak and nothing came out—not a syllable. For the life of her she could not recall what a lady's proper response should be under these circumstances. Let's see—having a bath in the presence of a toff betrothed to one's cousin—no . . . no . . . nothing came to mind . . . well, there it was—she was bereft of words for the occasion, a shocking faux pas in itself, no doubt. On the other hand, she was noticing that what she could see through her normally blurry vision had suddenly gone into black and white, colors oddly reversed from what they normally were, and things seemed so very quiet and faraway . . . and. . . .

Oh, please God, don't faint! Julian thought as Elspeth's eyes closed and she began slipping ever so slowly sideways into the water. He floundered forward, knocking into the bath and slopping water onto the floor. Plunging his hands into the tepid water, he grabbed her slippery shoulders and pulled her up. She was light, but the angle was merciless. His booted foot slipped in the sudsy water on the floor and he pitched forward, landing with a splash, shoulder and chest submerged. How could this get any worse? He held a very naked, limp Elspeth up by the shoulders with one hand, and with the other pushed himself up from the bottom of the tub. His body caught on the edge and made it tip dangerously, so he pushed against it with his feet, scrambling for purchase. At last he steadied the tub, took a deep breath, and for one brief moment seemed to have everything under control. Such as it was, of course.

Inches from his own eyes, Elspeth's beautiful eyes opened slowly. He watched as comprehension dawned in their swimming emerald depths. Confusion changed to horror and she opened her mouth. The scream that began as a squeak ended abruptly as he closed his hand over her mouth. Soft wonderful lips that he had longed for days to taste again. . . .

"Elspeth, please, I beg of you! Don't scream. I mean you no harm."

She bit him. Hard. Gritting his teeth against the pain, he heaved himself away, kneeling against the tub, careful to keep his hand over her mouth so that she wouldn't carry through on her obvious intention to scream. "Elspeth, I'm not trying to hurt you! You fainted and I had to pull you up or you'd drown." She released his hand but glared her fury at him. This was not going well.

"I'm leaving, I swear it, but please don't scream when I move my hand," he said, low in her ear. "It will cause more harm than good. You know that." She smelled of fresh-washed wet hair, light and lilac. He was aware of the softness of her beneath his hands. He waited. At last she nodded, slowly, but the rage in her eyes had not diminished a whit. He moved his hand away from her mouth, slowly, ready to clamp down again if necessary. It was unforgivable, and he knew it, but he also knew he was right to keep her from screaming. He could leave the same way he'd come, with no one the wiser and, but for the fact that Elspeth would never speak to him again and he'd probably be married to Caroline for all his days, everything would be fine.

She stayed silent, still staring mutinously into his face. Oh, God, how he wanted to lean forward and kiss her! He turned his head away. No good could come of that line of thinking.

"I—I did not know you were in the bath, Elspeth. I only wanted to talk to you," he began. It was lame, and he knew it. He could not, for the life of him, remember what it was he had planned to say to her. In the original plan, he had come upon her sweetly sewing some bit of lacy stuff in a nice wing chair by a small fire. She had listened, raptly, avidly, to his eloquent explanation, and fallen, weeping tears of joy, into his waiting arms. So far, nothing had gone according to plan.

"I have—I have seen nothing improper, Elspeth, I promise you. The water kept you covered completely. I'll leave immediately, and no one will ever know . . ." he faltered. The ice in her eyes was not melting a bit. "I came to tell you," he made himself go on, "that I did not lay an improper hand on Caroline, that it's you I love. . . ." he trailed off. It was hopeless. Here he was, draped and dripping over a naked lady he'd accosted in her bath, trying to explain the unexplainable. Her look of furious incredulity told him to stop.

He stood, slowly, and stared down at the face of his lady love. She was ice. She was fire. She was not, and now never would be, his.

He looked up at the window. It was closed, but it should open. With more luck than he deserved, he could scale down the wall the way he had come up. He stepped toward the window, then froze. Behind him he heard, unmistakably, the sound of the door to Elspeth's bedroom opening, then shutting softly. No doubt Bessie had come to check on whether it was time to remove the bath. Their eyes met. He had thought Elspeth's rage unbearable, but her horror was so much worse. So far, he was hidden behind the screen, but as soon as the maid stepped around it. . . .

"Elspeth, are you here? Bessie said you were having your bath," came Harry's loud and sibilant whisper. Children, Julian thought, could make more noise with a whisper than most adults could with a shout.

"I—I'm still in the tub, Harry," said Elspeth, haltingly. "Why don't you come back in a—a half an hour?" She looked desperate.

"Can't. I'm punished for thrashing that pig Roderick. I had to sneak out of the scullery as it is. I need to talk to you now!"

"Well," she began, then looked shrewdly at Julian. "As long as you're here, why don't you hand me my dressing gown? It's hanging on the fire screen. Just close your eyes and hand it in behind the screen."

Julian held his breath while he heard fumbling from the other side of the screen. Then a small hand appeared, holding her white lawn dressing gown. Not taking her glare off of Julian, Elspeth reached up and seized the robe.

"Thank you, dear. I'll be out in a minute," she said, far more lightly than her look. She held up her other hand and gestured imperiously for Julian to turn around. He did so, as quietly as he could. Behind him, he heard splashing and rustling, a towel being rubbed over soft, beautiful skin. It was hard keeping his mind off of what was going on back there. Paintings by the very sensual Botticelli came to mind. . . .

He felt a light tap on his shoulder, and he turned around, half expecting a hard slap across the face. She stood before him, robed from neck to toe, a large fluffy towel wrapped around her hair, and a more beautiful, desirable sight he had never seen. The light from the window fell on her face. If only that were love instead of blazing fury he saw in her green eyes. She placed her finger over her lips in an exaggerated gesture for silence, a deadly warning in her gaze. He nodded his understanding. Throwing him a look of pure venom, she stepped from behind the screen and out of his sight. He could feel his shoulders sag, and he let out his breath.

"Owl Eyes! You won't believe what I just found out!" came the expostulation from Harry, who stood looking his usual disreputable self in the center of the room.

"Hush, dear, not too loudly," Elspeth answered quickly. It was bad enough that the cad had seen her in the bath, and was still hiding behind the screen, holding her reputation in the palm of his perfidious hand. He need not hear any of her private business, even if it were prattle from a nine-year-old boy.

"Oh, you'll want everyone to hear this, Owl Eyes," boasted the boy, not lowering his voice a bit. "Servants and all!"

"Let me be the judge of that, please, Harry," she said, trying to sound stern and cool. Her heart pounded furiously in her chest as she made her way over to one of the two small chairs placed near the fireplace. "Come and tell me, dear," she said, seating herself and gesturing him over. It occurred to her that she could ask Harry to tell Bessie to leave her be for a time—to leave the bathwater for later—that she had the headache and was lying down. She was desperate to buy time until she could solve this monumental problem. Absently, she removed the towel from around her head and began to squeeze the water from her long tresses.

"Well, I was just in the drawing room, you see . . ." Harry began. Children had little enough ability to modulate their piercing tones, but Elspeth put her finger to her lips quickly nevertheless. "And, well, you see, I had to hide, because I was . . . well, I was running from Bessie because I, well, I sort of hit Roderick and he fussed the place down, and these people came in, and you'll never guess what I heard . . ." He had lowered his voice to something that passed for a whisper.

"Harry, you know I cannot be a party to your eavesdropping," Elspeth interrupted, almost by rote. It was so hard, being surrogate mother to this wonderful, maddening boy. And it was, if she were blunt with herself, impossible to care a whit for these banal social niceties, such as a distaste for eavesdropping, particularly if one were undressed and had a man hidden in one's boudoir.

"Oh, bother that, Elspeth! Just listen! There was a man there and Caroline, and they had a fight about her marrying Mr. Thorpe. Then Caroline left and I tried to sneak out, but then a lady came, and I had to hide again, really fast—a real lady she was, Viscountess Something-or-Other, I forget—and the man said, well, he said Julian did not com . . . compromise Caroline. Caroline made it look that way, and they tricked Mr. Thorpe into coming into the maze, and this Mr. Randall was a part of it, and he brought you into the maze on purpose to see it! And he said Mr. Thorpe loves you, not Caroline!" He broke off his nonstop recital suddenly. "What does 'compromise' mean, anyway, Owl Eyes?" he asked, as if realizing that he had no idea what he was talking about.

Harry held his silence expectantly, obviously proudly waiting for her to hug him and tell him what a wonderful boy he was. "What's the matter, Owl Eyes?" he finally asked, sounding less certain of himself. "Does compromise mean something awful? I thought you'd be happy about what I told you . . ." Elspeth only heard him from a distance. It seemed impossible for her to open her mouth and speak. She was aware that the child stood looking at her, concerned now, and confused.

"Elspeth, are you all right?" he said in a very small, frightened voice.

"Yes. Yes, darling, I'm just fine," she made herself say. Her head was buzzing and she felt as though she really might faint, twice in a quarter of an hour at that! As dreadful as this situation was, if she could just go away knowing that Julian had loved her after all—well, she could live with that secret joy for the rest of her lonely life. She took Harry's hand gently. "I just need a little time to myself now." She couldn't help glancing at the screen, then looked hurriedly back at Harry's anxious little face. "Darling, thank you for telling me this. It makes me feel much better, it really does. But I want you to go and tell Bessie that I'm lying down now with the headache and don't wish to be disturbed about the bath just yet. . . ."

Too late.

A light rap on the door and then the sound of the handle turning froze Elspeth's heart. "Miss Elspeth?" said Bessie, stepping through the door with a bob. "Is Master Harry in 'ere?"

Elspeth, still holding Harry's hands, gave them a squeeze. She smiled at him. "Go with Bessie, just for now, Harry. I'll come and rescue you shortly, I promise." She turned to Bessie. "Here he is, but don't be too hard on him, Bessie. I suspect strongly that there are two sides to the story."

"Oh, indeed, miss," said Bessie, holding out her hand to the reluctant Harry. "Now, we'll see to removing your bath, miss."

"Oh, no, not yet!" Elspeth said hurriedly, standing. "I have the headache . . . I want to lie down. . . ."

"We'll just be a moment, Miss Elspeth," said Bessie, who turned and gestured to someone outside the bedroom door. "Miss Caroline is back from shopping with her mother and she wants her bath now."

Elspeth just stood there, with her heart pounding out of her chest. Two of the other maids scurried from the hallway into the room, bobbing quickly and smiling timidly at Elspeth; then before she could so much as bolt toward the screen to head them off, they were there before it, efficiently picking it up, folding it and whisking it to the side to reveal . . .

Nothing.

No one.

Just an open window and a cooling bathtub.

Elspeth sank back into the chair, her legs no longer able to support her. Almost in slow motion the maids mopped up the spills and moved in to lift the tub. It took the three of them to lift it, but they seemed to do so with no ill effect. Nodding briskly to Harry to follow, Bessie and the other two maids made their way out of the door, the boy following sluggishly behind. He cast a look of exasperation at Elspeth, but she shooed him away with a tight smile. One of them managed to shut the door behind her. Elspeth waited half a minute, then sprang forward, shooting the lock home. It wasn't much of a lock, but then, no one was likely to attempt to force it, either.

She turned. The room was empty, privacy screen folded and off to the side. The window curtain was pulled aside, but it had been so while she bathed. She frowned. Had he jumped? Most unlikely. She would have heard the splat and so would everyone else. Had she dreamed him? Was she destined to be one of those spinsters who so feared ravishment that she imagined men standing over her in the bath? No, he'd been real enough; she knew that much. She made her way over to the window. Hadn't it been closed while she bathed? While the light from the window was soothing, surely she would have noticed a chilling breeze over her in the tub. Well, it was open now, wide enough for a man to have climbed through. Holding her breath, she approached the window and peered out carefully.

"Have they gone, then?" Julian asked from just below, startling her. He sat crouched in the narrow iron work that decorated the window. For a mad moment, Elspeth contemplated slamming the window down on him, and letting him find his way down the way he'd come. She moved forward, but heard, at the same instant he did, the unmistakable sounds of a carriage rattling down the narrow lane.

"Oh, bother! Come in then, but if you take one step toward me, I shall personally throw you back out of the window."

He clamored quickly through. The carriage was still

some distance away. With a deft twist, he pulled the window draperies closed, then turned and looked at her. It was all there—in his eyes. In a rush, it came over her—what Harry had said. Julian did love her! Harry had overheard it all. She took one step toward him, then stopped abruptly. It didn't really matter, did it? Julian was still engaged to Caroline, and under the circumstances, there was no place for her in his life. Having him here in her bedroom, betrothed to another woman as he was, would do nothing but harm.

"You had best have a plan to remove yourself, unseen from my bedroom immediately, Mr. Thorpe," she said, trying to keep her voice level. "There is nothing left to be said." Why, oh why did he have to be so handsome? Why did his eyes speak to her of regret, love, yearning? She knew now, as her own eyes drank their fill, that this would be their last moment alone together, their last chance for. . . .

Before she could finish the thought, he had crossed the short distance between them. He reached out and gathered her to his chest. She should pull away. She should slap him. She should scream. She should. . . .

His mouth closed on hers, warm and soft, hungry and delicious. She could hardly remember how to breathe. Somewhere in the back part of her mind, a small voice, very small, indeed, was trying to remind her that this wouldn't do, that no lady would ever permit such indecencies. . . . His tongue ran gently over her lips and she shushed the little voice to silence. His arms were around her, pulling her closer and closer. Now his hand ran up her back, then down, down, stopping again at her waist. Almost without thinking she raised her arms and embraced him. With a ragged moan, he pulled her yet closer. Now she was sure she could not breathe, and yet, that made no difference as she allowed her lips to part.

And just as she thought she would drown in his kiss, his lips left hers abruptly, tracing softly, slowly down her cheeks, her throat. He pulled her closer still, his lips now in her hair.

"I love you so much," he whispered. "Only you, Elspeth. Always you."

"Julian," she answered, her voice ragged. Her fingers unsure, she traced a line down his chest.

He moaned and grabbed her hand, pressing it against his mouth. His lips traveled down her arm, to her shoulder, lingering there. She could smell the freshness of him, clean cotton, clean hair. He moved his lips slowly to the base of her throat. Her head fell back and a moan escaped her. His hands traveled down to her hips and he pressed her to him. She gasped as she felt his hardness. Her light lawn wrapper hid nothing from him, and nothing from her. Never had she dreamed lovemaking could feel like this. His whole body quivered as he pressed his hardness against her.

His lips found hers again and she marveled that they could be so soft, and yet so hard at the same time. Gently, slowly, his tongue found hers and again she gasped as a shudder ran through her. His hand strayed from her back around, slowly, up . . . up, and came to rest lightly on her breast, fingers circling her nipple. The shock ran through her as she pushed against him, now unsure of what it was she so desperately sought.

"Ah, Elspeth, you are so magnificent!" he whispered in her hair. "I could love you like this forever. I need no sustenance but you!" As if to demonstrate his words, his lips devoured hers again. But now his hands moved around her again, lightly touching, rubbing her back. And his lips were soft and gentle now, not demanding and insistent as but a moment before.

Again he slid his mouth to her cheek and then to her hair. Then he pulled back, and regarded her.

There was no doubt of the love that lit his eyes. His hands cupped her face with great tenderness. "Let's sit down, my heart," he whispered. "If I keep on like this I cannot vouch for my control." He slipped his hands down her shoulders, her arms, then clasped her hands, as chastely as he would a child's. He drew her gently away from the window, toward the small divan placed to one side of the room. He sat her down, then stood over her, regarding her softly.

"Will you marry me, my love?" he asked gently.

Her heart gave an impossible twist. Love him as she did, there could be no honorable marriage between them. The die was cast. He was engaged to the perfidious Caroline. She could not find her voice.

"Ah," he said quickly, possibly mistaking her silence. "I haven't done that right, have I? Forgive me, please. I've had no practice whatsoever." Practice or no, he slid with a fluid grace to his knee and clasped her hand in his own. "Would you, Miss Quinn, do me the ultimate honor, and consent to be my wife?"

"But, Julian, how can this be?" she finally stammered in answer. "I do believe you now, and I'm sorry I ever doubted you, but you are betrothed to my cousin, however that came to be and that, I think, is that. You cannot cry off now. You'd be shunned forever."

"Why would I care what any of these fools think, Elspeth?" he asked, simply.

She withdrew her hand and looked away. It was hard to think with him right there before her, knee bent. She could still feel the heat of him, up and down the length of her. It made thinking so difficult. "You perhaps do not care now, Julian," she began, trying to marshal her thoughts. "But, later, it will matter. When your children are shunned for it. When your wife is branded a loose and designing woman. You might even"—her voice caught in her throat—"you might even begin to believe those lies . . . to feel I had trapped you and doomed you to a life of ostracism. I should hate to have you despise me. That would be worse than anything else. . . ."

She broke off because he pulled her down. Before she could catch her balance he had steadied her astride him. Now she could indeed feel the heat, the madness of desire—her own and his.

"Then I shall compromise you past all redemption, Elspeth. And you'll have to say yes," he groaned, pulling her down to the floor. He covered her mouth with his own, hard, savage, demanding. His tongue probed her mouth. Hungrily, she responded, probing back with her own. He groaned and rolled over, taking her with him. Now he straddled her, and the heat and hardness of him felt so right. His hand moved from her back, caressing her shoulder, moving down till it cupped her breast through the thin lawn of her gown. Impatiently, he pushed the flimsy stuff aside. The heat of his hand sent a wave of shock through her as his fingers cupped her breast, then circled her nipple gently. Without volition, she gasped and felt herself straining against him, their bodies touching hard and insistent, there, where it mattered. His lips forsook her own and traveled down, down her cheek, to the base of her neck, coming to rest on her breast. He seized her nipple between his teeth, teasing it gently, his tongue tracing circles around it. Liquid fire coursed through her and she heard herself moan.

His hand moved down again, slowly, lingering on her soft skin. She felt him fumbling with the tie of her gown and made no move to stop him. The gown fell open. His hand moved across her belly, teasing, caressing lightly, then moved to pull at his own shirt. He tugged it free from his breeches and ripped it open. Now there was nothing between them, no fine lawn, no fancy lace, no veneer of civilization, just naked flesh, as it was meant to be.

He sat up and his eyes drank their fill. "You are so beautiful, Elspeth," he said with a moan, sinking back down to cover her. Now they were flesh to flesh, breast to chest, and she gasped at the searing heat of him. Again his lips moved to nuzzle against her neck, but now his hand slid still lower, down, down to cup her hip. He pulled her roughly to him, and she could feel the impossible bulge pushing against her. Some instinct she did not recognize made her push back, push hard against him. She needed the pressure, craved it now in some way she could not understand. Slowly, maddeningly, his hand moved now across her belly and down. No, no, he mustn't touch her there. The brief thought flashed through her mind and was lost in an instant as a bolt of pleasure like lightning shot through her. She gasped and reared back. Still, she could not stop herself from pushing against him, the craving relentless, insistent. She drove hard against him now, not knowing what she sought, feeling something she could not put a name to, until, at last, waves of pleasure washed over her again and again and again.

His fingers left her and she could feel him tugging at his breeches. She could not, would not stop him. Now she was lost, indeed. There was no turning back. He was mad to say he would marry her—Caroline would permit no such thing—but if Elspeth couldn't marry him, she would marry no one. And she would carry the joy of this love to sustain her down the long, lonely years to come.

"Do you love me, Julian? Before we do this thing, tell me that you really love me," she heard herself gasp.

He stilled. He lifted his face from where he had nuzzled her breast and gazed into her eyes. He lay on top of her, his breeches open enough that she could feel him now, soft, yet hard, hot and wonderful. Slowly he moved his hands to either side of her head, then pushed himself back from her. She could see the reluctance, feel the war he waged within himself.

"I love you more than my life, Elspeth," he finally whispered, his voice ragged. "I love you too much to do this thing to you now, to take you this way. I will take you as my bride and not before." He lowered his lips to hers once more, but this time he was soft with her, gentle, lingering and loving. At last he pulled back, drawing his kiss down her cheek. He sat up, and lifted his weight from her, rolling to the side.

He took a long, lingering look down the length of her. She should be mortified, she knew, to be so exposed, so naked under his gaze, but all she could think of was how she still craved the heat of his touch. With an obvious reluctance, he broke his gaze and looked into her eyes.

Heaven help her, she could not resist. Her eyes traveled now the length of him, coming to rest there where his breeches gaped open. She gasped at the sight of him, then raised her eyes in alarm to his own. He was so large! How could he possibly . . . ?

He smiled at her, then reached down and brought the sides of the placket together. "Not now, my heart. We shall save those delightful mysteries for our wedding night." He rolled quickly to his knees, then reached for her hands. Together, they stood. He gazed at her for a moment, then crushed her to him.

"I must be mad to turn away from you now," he whispered fiercely, burying his face in her hair. "It's all I can do not to throw you onto the bed and have you now, my own, forever."

He pulled away again, and with a last, long look, pulled her dressing gown chastely together, tying the sash in place. Odd, she felt more naked now, here in her boudoir covered by her robe, than she had felt supine and utterly undone, but a moment before.

He seated her again on the couch and took a step back.

"Now, we will set about solving this sorry mess, my heart," he said, holding both of her hands in his own. "First, I think, I owe you an apology for being so beforehand with my attentions. But I beg you to forgive me. You are so very beautiful it's a wonder I can keep my hands from you even now. In fact . . ." Smiling, he traced a naughty finger down her throat, stopping just shy of her cleavage.

"Oh, Julian!"she gasped, pulling back. She could feel a hot blush spreading over her cheeks and involuntarily reached up to make sure her dressing gown was closed. "I don't know how I could have so forgot myself . . ." she trailed off, at a loss as to how to explain herself further.

"I do, my love," he said simply, seating himself next to her. "I love you, and you love me. We are made to be together. This is just as it should be, forever." He sealed his statement with a chaste kiss on the tip of her nose.

"But now, I think, is the time for me to make my escape," he said, looking at her with tender regret. "Shall I go down the back wall, or try to skulk unseen through the hallways?"

"Oh dear, I think either choice is a dreadful one," she replied, uncertainly. "My cousin and aunt are home now, and, of course, the boys, unless they are locked away in the dungeon as they so often are, roam the house at will. And the servants—they're always running to and fro. Why, anyone at all could see you."

"The wall it is, then," he pronounced. "It will be easier going down than up—faster at any rate."

"Are there vines for you to hold onto?" she asked. "I've never really been back to the mews now that I think of it."

"Indeed, the vines are what got me up here. I shall tell your aunt to have them cut down at once. Can't risk Sir Richard wending his way up to your bedroom in hopes of a delightful interlude."

"Julian, good heavens, what a dreadful thought!" Elspeth couldn't help laughing at the idea of the very elderly Sir Richard, working his inexorable way up the vines, hand over hand. . . .

"I must go now, my love. I've taken too many risks with your reputation as it is." He took her hands again and squeezed them tight.

"Julian, what are we going to do?" she asked. "I know you think you can cry off, and I love you beyond all things, but I cannot for the life of me. . . ."

He silenced her with a kiss. This time it was not gentle, but hard, demanding, possessive, his tongue circling hers, lips devouring her own.

At last, he lifted his face from hers. "Now, then. You must trust me, my love," he whispered. "I will solve the problem, I promise you that. One way or another you will be my wife, not Caroline. Sooner rather than later. Believe me." He brushed his lips past hers one more time, then in a heartbeat lifted himself over the windowsill. For a brief moment she saw him outside the window; then he was gone.

She stood rooted to the spot, hardly daring to breath, listening to the faint rustling that came from outside the window. Then there was silence. She crossed over to the window, took a deep breath and leaned out. Scanning up and down the length of the mews, she saw nothing, no Julian, no carriages, no stable hands. She closed the window and made her way over to the bed, stretching herself out on it. She smiled slowly, deliciously to herself as the memory of his wayward hands and lips washed over her. He loved her. And he would find a way. She knew it.

Chapter Twelve

Edgar admired the way the Viscountess Alderson snapped her card onto the somewhat tarnished silver tray held at a precarious slant by a somewhat disheveled, somewhat unnerved footman. "At once, my man," she announced. "Tell . . . Her Ladyship"—Edgar noted the marked hesitation that fairly dripped condescension—"that I haven't all day." The queen herself should be taking lessons in intimidation from this woman.

"Yes, ma'am, of course, Your Ladyship. At once." The boy nearly fell over trying to bow and work out the correct form of address at the same time, not to mention hanging onto the silver tray bearing its precious card. Given the state of affairs in the dim and dusty household, it was apparent he was not used to afternoon calls from the Quality.

The footman turned to go, then, obviously in a moment of horror, realized he couldn't very well walk off and leave an actual viscountess leaning on her cane in the hallway in the dark. "If I might show Your Ladyship to the drawing room, ma'am?" he offered, in something of a squeak. The boy seemed barely out of leading strings, and had no business having charge of the front door.

"Indeed," came the dry reply. At least the boy seemed to remember which room was the drawing room, and he moved to throw open the double doors, or, at least, he attempted to do so, since they seemed to stick abominably. At last the hinges gave up the fight, and the doors creaked very noisily open.

The viscountess stepped through with a sniff, waving her hand at the hapless footman. "Be off with you, boy, and find your mistress. We can see to ourselves here." Bowing and murmuring, the boy took himself off. The Viscountess Alderson, true to her word, seemed perfectly capable of seating herself sans formal invitation. She did so, on a nasty little occasional chair, but the cloud of dust that resulted was not encouraging to Edgar, who rather suffered from an unfortunate allergy. He moved to the mantlepiece and stood with a hand cast negligently upon it, attempting to look urbane and at ease but failing somewhat, he had no doubt.

Gnarled and elegantly thin hands gripped the gold ball atop her cane; the Viscountess Alderson neither spoke nor looked at him. He could be on the moon for all she appeared to notice or care. The woman was terrifying under the best of circumstances, and these must certainly be among the worst. She held his fate in her bony, aristocratic hands. She could, if she so chose, destroy him socially this very afternoon, and he would have no reasonable course or entrée open to him after that. She had said nothing in the carriage on the way here, either encouraging or discouraging. Not for the first time today, Edgar blessed the poverty that had kept him from breakfast and lunch. He wouldn't have wanted to add fearsome nausea to the discomfort he was feeling.

"Now then, Mr. Randall . . ." she finally began. When she did speak, it made him start like a guilty schoolboy. Well, he was guilty, when it came to that. "You are likely to hear things during this visit that I emphatically do not wish repeated. If these things become the current *on dit* in the Baths and Assembly Rooms, I shall know precisely whom to blame, and it will not go well with you. I hope I make myself perfectly clear?"

"Why, of course, Lady Alderson. In spite of all appearances to the contrary, I am very good at holding my tongue when necessary." A raised eyebrow was the only reply. Edgar did feel a bit insulted, but, then again, it was the curse that went along with being known as an exquisite gossip. No one would ever believe he could keep a secret. Still, his finely honed curiosity had pricked up. Something deliciously wicked was coming, he had no doubt.

From above he heard a few thumps and bumps, as if someone were rushing about slamming drawers. No doubt Lady Haverford had been taken unawares by the very August Presence of the Viscountess Alderson in her drawing room. Such an unprecedented Appearance would no doubt cause havoc and consternation upstairs. While one was expected to keep a visitor waiting, particularly an unexpected one, there were unwritten rules about how long the wait should be, all relative to one's respective position in society. If he knew nothing else, Edgar knew his Dugdale's *Baronage*, and also knew, therefore, that Lady Haverford, as a widow of a mere baronet, had better find her way posthaste to the drawing room, where the widow of a viscount was cooling her satin-shod heels at this moment.

It seemed to take longer than it should have, although, to be sure, time certainly crawled under the fish-eye stare of an annoyed viscountess, but finally Lady

Haverford made flustered and very nearly disheveled appearance at the balky drawing room doors.

"My dear Viscountess Alderson!" she exclaimed as she rushed, breathless, into the room. "How extraordinarily kind of you to call. And Mr. Randall. What a pleasant surprise." That the woman was utterly baffled and discommoded was apparent from the expression on her face. She started over to one of the infernal small tables that infested drawing rooms all over England, then stopped in some obvious confusion. "And so remiss of my staff not to have provided you with refreshment! How dreadful you must think me! Hanley!" she shouted, having turned back to the doors, which stood open.

"Now then, we'll have tea in just a moment!" the baronet's widow proclaimed, as if that were the solution to all of life's difficulties. Quite often that was so, although, Edgar feared, not this time.

There was a short, awkward silence. Edgar could almost see Lady Haverford trying to work out in her mind what this could possibly be about, and what her next remark should be. He'd feel sorry for her if the scene weren't so amusing to watch. She seemed like a butterfly trapped in a naughty boy's jar. And for once, he was not the naughty boy, at least not directly. The viscountess, if not enjoying herself, was certainly making no effort to be agreeable or helpful. She sat rigidly upright, balanced on the gold tip of her cane, as if she had been planted there for the last millennia, staring haughty holes in her hapless hostess.

"Ah, well, the weather has been simply lovely for this time of year, hasn't it, madam?" Lady Haverford finally ventured.

"I prefer it warmer," came the viscountess's icy reply. What was the woman up to? She had not cared to share her plans with Edgar in the carriage ride on the way over, and he was at something of a loss. Surely there must be some purpose to making this poor woman so very uncomfortable, but Edgar had not yet divined what it could be.

"And when will you be returning to London, Lady Alderson?" Lady Haverford inquired. Edgar had to at least give the woman credit for making a game attempt.

"When I tire of Bath," came the unhelpful response.

There was a stir as the benighted footman came teetering in, precariously carrying a large silver tray, on which balanced a variety of pots, teacups, spoons, little cakes, and linen squares. The boy managed to get the thing deposited onto the small table. Edgar was quite sure Lady Haverford breathed a sigh of relief as the tray came to rest without mishap. He watched as she did the honors. Her hand shook just enough to rattle the porcelain teacups. To his practiced eye, it was apparent the tray and pots were plate and not silver, but well enough crafted to pass for good. On the other hand, they could use a good polish.

The cups got handed around, along with the little plates of teacakes. Edgar was feeling well enough again to partake of some nourishment. Heaven only knew when he'd get his next meal. The cakes were gritty and not fresh, but he had long ago learned not to be choosy. For a few moments there was only the sound of the faintest chinks from teacups knocking against saucers. He fancied Lady Haverford viewed this as something of a reprieve.

"Dolly, I understand you saw something unfortunate the other evening in the maze at Sydney Gardens." Obviously choosing her own moment, the Viscountess Alderson sallied forth like a knight riding to war. Deliberately or not, she caught her hostess in mid-chew, with the unfortunate result of a small choking sound, and a hurried press of a small square of linen to the lips.

"I—I beg your pardon, Your Ladyship?" Lady Haverford finally stammered in response.

"Don't play around the bush with me, Dolly. You know exactly what I'm talking about." The viscountess took a small sip of her tea, not omitting a slight grimace. It did taste a bit stewed, at that. Probably had been hastily reheated below stairs.

"I—er—I assume you refer to that little incident with the Quinn girl?" Lady Haverford ventured timidly.

"What, precisely, do you think you saw, Dolly?" asked the viscountess. She set down her cup and stared pointedly at the woman, eyebrows raised. Edgar had been on the receiving end of that particular stare not so long ago, and he did not envy Lady Haverford.

He could almost see the wheels turning inside Dolly Haverford's head. Was the viscountess here for a naughty natter, or did she have a bone to pick with Dolly, herself, on the subject? Edgar watched while she gathered her thoughts.

"Well, I'm sure it was all such a blur, Your Ladyship . . ." Lady Haverford temporized, allowing herself to trail off. If she thought the Viscountess Alderson could be fobbed off with an inane remark like that, she did not know the viscountess terribly well.

"And what do you recall of the blur, Dolly?" The woman would have made an excellent interrogator for the Bow Street Runners.

"Er—well, Mr. Randall and I wandered into the maze . . ." She trailed off again, and glanced hopefully at Edgar, as if he would gallantly pick up the narrative. He would not. She turned her attention back to the viscountess, perhaps hoping that the old woman had taken a stroke and died in the last few seconds, obviating the necessity to go on. Alas, no. The viscountess continued to gaze upon her victim, eyebrows ascendant. Edgar would give a tidy sum to know how she did that.

It was a marvelous look. He turned to the dim mirror over the mantlepiece and wiggled his eyebrows. No luck. Just looked like puny caterpillars having a nice frolic on his forehead.

Dolly Haverford took a deep breath. "And, well, it was nothing, really, just young people getting a bit ahead of themselves, that's all." She stopped and stared brightly at the viscountess.

"And how many people have you told this story, Dolly?" the viscountess asked.

"Oh, well, I may have mentioned it here or there, but they were engaged to be married, after all. . . ." Lady Haverford stammered. It was clear to her now she was on the carpet, but she still was not certain why.

There was a long pause while the viscountess picked up her cup and took a tepid sip gazing coldly over the rim at the hapless baronet's widow. After what seemed an eternity, she set the cup down.

"I seem to recall your own wedding, Dolly . . ." the viscountess ventured, in what sounded like pleasant, reminiscent tones.

The effect of this seemingly innocuous remark on Dolly Haverford was something along the order of a lightning bolt. The woman sat up suddenly, suppressing almost instantaneously a look of alarm, and stifling a small gasp that just managed to escape her lips.

"Do you, indeed, madam?" she squeaked. Her hands were suddenly busy in her lap, dry-washing themselves, and she licked her lips, holding them in what passed for a smile, but looked more like a rictus.

"I recall there was some question . . . ?" The viscountess allowed her voice to trail off.

Now there was no doubt that the baronet's widow looked fit to burst into tears, or faint, or do whatever it was ladies thought to do when confronted with some matter they emphatically did not wish to address. She slanted her eyes at Edgar, then looked imploringly at the viscountess, working her mouth, with no sound coming out.

"Oh, you needn't worry about our dear Mr. Randall, Dolly. He can be a veritable tomb when he chooses to be. Isn't that right, Mr. Randall?"

"Oh, indeed, madam," he replied cheerily. He was beginning to see where this was going and was mightily entertained. Too bad it would never be shared. Imagine Dolly Haverford, the most wagging tongue in the *ton*, having been a bit beforehand herself, as far as her wedding had been concerned. What a delicious piece of blackmail for the Viscountess Alderson to have so handy. The fact that such a thing had never crossed the ears or lips of his set suggested that great pains had been taken long ago to disguise the fact; hence, Dolly's obvious shock and discomfort at hearing the matter broached, even so obliquely, especially in the presence of himself, the second-most wagging tongue in the *ton*.

"People can be so unkind, can't they, Dolly? Especially when they've got things all wrong. Isn't that so?" The viscountess nibbled daintily on a stale cake as if it were quite the most delicious thing she'd had to eat all week.

"Oh, indeed, yes, Lady Alderson, most unkind!" Lady Haverford managed to gasp out. She was breathing in air in great gulps and had turned quite red in the face. Edgar was beginning to fear she might really faint, at that.

"In fact, I'm going to let you in on a great secret, Dolly," the viscountess said, lowering her voice to a near whisper, and leaning in conspiratorially. Edgar was agog to hear what would come next. He had thought himself a player in the gossip game, but he was a novice compared to this woman, who, he would have sworn, had nothing but disdain for the whole scene.

"Indeed," the viscountess continued, "you saw only part of what happened. It was, in fact, much worse than you thought." She paused for effect and got it. Dolly forgot her own predicament so far as to lean in to the viscountess, lips slightly parted, hanging on the next word.

"Caroline Quinn was, indeed, attacked, but not by Julian Thorpe. The dear boy had come upon her quite unexpectedly just before you did. He was wandering in the maze himself and heard an outcry. He ran toward the sound and came upon Caroline under attack by some low miscreant, some employee of the Gardens. She'd been lured there, apparently—you know what a beauty she is. Most disgusting, really. If one is to be compromised, it should at least be by someone of one's own social standing, don't you agree, Dolly?"

"Why—er, yes, of course." If Dolly Haverford seemed less than certain of this astounding bit of choplogic, he could hardly blame her.

"Dear Julian chased the churl, but lost him quickly in the maze. The employees know the maze quite well, of course. . . ."

"Of course. . . ."

"Julian had just returned to the center of the maze to aid poor, dear Caroline when you and Mr. Randall happened along. Most unfortunate for poor Caroline, wouldn't you agree, Dolly? The child was utterly innocent and yet things appeared so . . . ?"

"Oh, yes, yes, of course, Your Ladyship. The poor, dear child. Now that I think of it, she seemed most distraught. . . ."

"Well, naturally. The man had a knife, which he held at her side. It actually left a cut in her dress—I saw it myself. It is a wonder she did not die of the heart attack right there on the spot."

"Oh, indeed! I should have done so!" Dolly Haverford was fairly gasping with delighted horror.

"Julian was apparently holding the poor thing up, to keep her from falling to the ground when you came upon them. That's why things appeared so . . ." The viscountess allowed the innuendo to suggest itself. The woman seemed to have no difficulty piling one preposterous bit of nonsense on the last. To be sure, Dolly Haverford was hanging on every word.

"Indeed, Mr. Randall, you sensed something amiss immediately, did you not?" The viscountess turned her basilisk gaze upon him.

"Oh, yes, indeed, Your Ladyship. I most certainly did. Most irregular. Julian and Caroline would never. . . ."

"Quite, Mr. Randall!" She cut him off, obviously planning to control the flow of information herself. Just as well. He had no idea where they were headed with this outlandish tale. Not that it was any more outlandish than the truth.

"Mr. Randall went back later and found the knife where the miscreant had dropped it, did you not, Mr. Randall?"

"Ah, I did, yes. And a wicked looking thing it was, madam, I'm sure."

"Oooh, you found the knife?" Dolly Haverford was fairly shivering with delight.

"And turned it over to the authorities, did you not, Edgar?"

"Why, of course. Glad to get the evil-looking thing out of my hands, you know," he offered. "A low, criminal thing. I don't know when I've seen such a. . . ." He broke off under an irritated glare from the viscountess. She clearly was writing this script and would stand for no improvisation from the lesser cast.

"Have they caught the fellow?" Dolly Haverford asked eagerly.

"Not yet, but when they do, he'll hang at Tyburn, you mark my words."

"Oh, my!"

The viscountess allowed the horror of it all to echo in the silence while she took another sip of tea that had to be stone cold by now. Dolly Haverford had so far forgot her hostess duties as to fail to notice, or to offer a fresh cup.

"But why, then, did Julian . . . ?" Lady Haverford began.

"Why did Julian allow the blame to fall upon his innocent shoulders?" the viscountess interrupted. She had a plan here and was obviously not to be diverted. "Pure chivalry, Dolly! Nothing less!" she announced triumphantly. "He is most quick-witted, you see, and he knew Caroline's reputation would be in shreds by morning were it known she had been attacked by a ruffian. That's why he kissed her, you see, to divert attention from the hideous truth. Why, no decent woman could speak to her ever again if the truth were to come out. As it is, only a very few of us know what actually happened. And we know, as well, that dear Julian managed to arrive in time to thwart any . . . ah . . . actual . . . ah, well, of course, you know that to which I refer. The girl was, quite simply, unharmed at the point at which Julian frightened the criminal away. I shudder to think of what might have happened had he been otherwise detained or engaged. Poor Caroline would be deranged by now. Locked away in an asylum, for certain." The viscountess went so far as to give a small shudder. Edgar rather thought she was laying it on a bit thick, although, to be sure, Dolly Haverford was eating it up.

"I mention this to you, Dolly, only because I know you to be a woman of great discernment. I am sure you would never allow such a miscarriage of fate to befall poor, dear Caroline, as you . . . could . . . have suffered yourself."

"I—I . . ." Dolly Haverford was doing her excellent impersonation of a gasping fish again.

"Exactly! Now, here is the slight difficulty. . . ." Viscountess Alderson leaned forward again and reduced her voice to a near whisper. Dolly Haverford nearly toppled out of her seat trying to get close enough to hear. "You see, Julian now finds himself engaged to the wrong girl. He had reached an agreement with the cousin—it was to be announced as soon as arrangements were made. And Caroline—why the poor girl is over the moon about young Rokeby—you remember him, Dolly, he's Estelle's son—he's not here yet for the Season. So we have two young women heartbroken, one gentleman engaged to the wrong girl, and one waiting in the wings while his demoiselle is married to the wrong man. All because you and Mr. Randall happened into the maze quite a moment too soon."

"Yes, but . . ."

"Ah, you are probably going to suggest that it's simply too late to undo this damage," the viscountess continued on, implacably. "Or, that the truth will do Caroline more harm than an unhappy marriage would." Dolly Haverford looked a bit befuddled. Clearly she had not been about to suggest any such thing.

"Well, I have an idea, and, with your cooperation, and, of course, that of Mr. Randall, I think it will work." The viscountess paused again. Edgar could hardly wait to hear this one. "You will go to the Assembly Rooms this evening, Dolly, and casually mention to one or two of your dearest friends, with luck those to whom you originally spoke of the incident, that you are most upset to find you have been the unwitting pawn in a very naughty practical joke."

"I—I don't understand . . ." Lady Haverford ventured.

"Oh, it's quite simple, Dolly, although, to be sure, you must act most aggrieved. You must let on that you were the butt of a jest. That the young people had arranged for you to happen upon a most awkward scene, just to see how far the *on dit* would spread in a few days."

"Oh, but no one would believe that, Lady Alderson. . . ." Dolly stammered out.

"Why, of course they will, Dolly, if you are convincing enough. Of course, you must also play down a bit of what you originally reported—Caroline not terribly disheveled or upset—that sort of thing. All a grand joke at our generation's expense, don't you see? I shall back you, of course. I shall report that I came upon them laughing about it a few moments later."

"But in the last few days, no one has set things to rights—Julian and Caroline are acting as if they are engaged. . . ."

"Ah, but they are not, are they? There has been no formal announcement. Indeed, Julian danced only with the cousin at my soiree." The viscountess leaned forward. Edgar had the sudden notion that he was watching a great cat stalk its intended victim. "Dolly, it all depends on you. You are a good dissembler, are you not? I seem to recall. . . ." She let the remark hang unfinished. Edgar would have given the earth to know what lay unspoken between them.

"I suppose I could try. . . ." Dolly Haverford managed to squeak out. She had resumed the dry-washing of her hands.

"Excellent, Dolly. I knew I could count on you to set things to rights. It all depends on you. And Mr. Randall, of course. He will be there to back your story, won't you, Mr. Randall?"

"Why, of course, madam. How could I not, under the circumstances?"

"How could you not, indeed, Mr. Randall," she replied, dryly. She stood suddenly, hoisting herself regally on her gold-tipped cane. "I will take my leave of you, Dolly. Delicious tea, thank you." She turned and walked a few steps to the door. Dolly Haverford stood staring, nonplused, at her stiff back. The viscountess turned once again. "Incidentally, Dolly," she said, "I'm having a small dinner party in a few days. I shall send round an invitation for you. I hope you'll find it amusing."

"W—why, I should be honored, Lady Alderson. It's so kind of you to include me." Dolly Haverford had certainly never received a better invitation in her life. She was quite pink in the cheeks about it.

"Then that's all settled. Mr. Randall?" the viscountess threw over her shoulder as she turned again for the doors. Sketching a quick bow in Lady Haverford's direction, Edgar strode off behind the viscountess. A fascinating afternoon this was turning out to be.

The Viscountess Alderson's well-sprung carriage wended its way through the streets of Bath. Edgar kept a sharp look out for any of his friends. It never hurt to be seen tête-à tête with a peeress, particularly the one who set the social tone every Season. But, alas, one could never find a friend when one needed one. Even in the privacy of her own carriage, the viscountess's back did not touch the seat. She sat, ramrod stiff, gnarled hands atop the gold ball on her cane, but her usual austere expression was decidedly improved by a sly smile.

"Well, that was a difficult but profitable visit, wouldn't you agree, Mr. Randall?"

"Yes, it certainly was, Lady Alderson. Quite admirably done, I must say. I am in awe of you."

She gave a sniff and turned her attention to the small window.

He could not stand the silence. Particularly when he positively had to know what on earth had been left hanging, unspoken, between the two women. "But, madam, if you please, what was Lady Haverford so frightened of? I've never seen anyone look so horrified as she did when you mentioned her marriage."

"Well, since you've obviously surmised a part of it, I will tell you, Mr. Randall. But first, I must remind you of your vow of silence. I never blackmail anyone if I don't intend to keep my part of the bargain." She waited with a chilly expectance.

"Oh, indeed, I remember and re-avow, madam."

"Well, then. I will tell you that Dolly Haverford was born into this world a shop girl. Parents in service, that sort of thing. Mortimer Haverford's second son, Charles, who was, not to put too fine a point on it, quite possibly the stupidest boy ever born, fell head over heels in love with one Miss Dolly Snipes, and, when thwarted by the paterfamilias in his efforts to make an honest woman of her, simply took matters into his own hands, carried her off, and wed her—eventually—without the blessing of the family. As you might imagine, old Sir Mortimer hushed the matter up, and cut the boy off immediately, only to quite sadly lose his first born, and only other, son in a hunting accident shortly thereafter. It became necessary, of course, to bring the hapless Charles back into the good graces of the family, but he wouldn't come without his dear Dolly. So, the girl was fixed up, tutored in the finer social graces, and passed off as a distant cousin. There was an enormous country wedding, and everything was quite all right after that. Most fortunately, there was no child on the way or it never could have been managed so neatly."

"But how on earth did they manage to pull off something that bold? Surely one or two must have known . . . even servants will talk amongst themselves." Edgar knew his gossip and knew that it, like water, would find a way to run out.

"There were a very few who knew, and no one outside the family. Sir Mortimer's household was not overlarge, and most of the retainers had been with the family all their lives. You know how it is in the country—servants hold the same position from one generation to the next, terribly loyal. I believe a few received rather generous pensions, and that, as they say, was that."

"But how did you know, madam?"

The old woman gave a wicked chuckle. "I was one of those few inside the family who knew. Oh, yes," she went on, obviously noting his confusion. "The Haverfords are distant cousins on my mother's side. It was their good fortune that I was close to one of the sisters and visiting at the time." She gazed out of the carriage window, and he fancied she was looking rather smug.

"And I'll venture to say you had something of a hand in all this social chicanery, didn't you, Lady Alderson?" he prodded. Even if he could never in his lifetime repeat this story, it was worth hearing every word of it.

"Who on earth do you think it was taught her the niceties, Mr. Randall? Certainly no one in Sir Mortimer's household was up to the task."

"And you've kept it secret all these years," he said, more to himself. That, alone, was astonishing.

"I liked the girl, liked her pluck. And make no mistake, she's a sharp one. Twice, no, thrice the intellectual capability of poor Charles, for all that they positively adored one another. I thought she could pull it off, and have considered it a great joke on the *ton* all these years that she has. And you may not believe it, but I am quite the romantic at heart. She loved Charles and was a good wife to him all those years. Gave him several fine sons, each one the intellectual superior of their dear father, thank heaven. Indeed, I've always thought a little infusion of sturdy peasant blood greatly improves our stale, arrogant set. And why"—she turned those eyebrows on him again—"why would anyone seek to disturb a perfectly lovely marriage and family out of sheer malice?"

Edgar felt his cheeks burn at the slight sting in her words. He deserved it, he supposed. He had been willing to sell his friend's soul to the she-devil to put a few pounds in his pocket. Didn't get more malicious than that.

"I—I should say that I appreciate your vote of confidence in me, Lady Alderson. To share this story with me, after all I've done. . . ."

"My dear Mr. Randall, I trust you above all at the moment. I'm certain you have not forgotten that I know your part in this ugly little mess. Surely you will not disappoint me in this little confidence."

"Most assuredly not, madam," he said, and he meant it with every fiber of his being. Torture wouldn't pull this information, delicious as it was, from his lips. Besides, having lived something of a charade for most of his life, he had to appreciate a fellow sham artist. He had known Lady Haverford for much of his adult life and never had she let slip so much as a hint that she was not quite what she seemed.

"She seemed rather upset when you made a glancing reference to—er—to the situation," he offered.

"Indeed, and I do regret the necessity. I've let her be all these years. To her credit, she has not pushed the acquaintance. She has probably been discomfitted knowing that I knew her secret. However, she has never had anything to fear from my tongue. Unfortunately, today I did feel that an oblique reference was the most expedient way to get her attention. She has made her way in society somewhat the same way you have, Mr. Randall, by being the consummate gossip. Opens a great many doors, as I am sure you are aware. But, by the same token, you both know what it's like to live on the edge of the abyss, do you not?"

It was uncanny, the look in her eye. How could this viscountess, born to privilege and honor as she had been, never so much as a blush of scandal associated with her name, know anything about the abyss? She was a sharp old dame; he had to give her credit for that.

"Well, I believe she took the point, don't you? I'm sure there won't be a soul in Bath by this evening who does not understand that Julian is most decidedly not going to marry Caroline Quinn. Dolly will manage it somehow. And I will make it up to her. I will, indeed, invite her to a little dinner party. That will raise her several notches in the *ton*. And you, my dear Mr. Randall, will be there as well."

"I will?" he asked, not knowing whether to be flattered or horrified.

"Of course. And you will find a moment in private with Dolly to play the absolute fool—I know you can do it—and assure her you haven't the slightest idea what I was going on about this afternoon. That should put this whole matter to rest, once and for all, and right neatly, too, don't you think?" She turned a triumphant look on him. Military strategists had missed a good bet in not recruiting this woman.

"Well, yes," he responded. "But," he could not help adding, "there is still the matter of convincing Caroline to go along with this new scenario. I fancy that part won't be so easy."

"And that, Mr. Randall, will be Julian's problem to solve. I cannot be expected to take care of everything, now can I?" the Viscountess Alderson announced, as she put her gloved hand into the gloved hand of her liveried footman, and stepped lightly from the carriage, without so much as a farewell nod.

Chapter Thirteen

It was not the fashionable time of day to call, as Julian well knew and cared less. He paced up and down in the Quinn drawing room, waiting impatiently for the infernal Caroline to make an appearance. He had presented himself to a startled footman of the Quinn household a few moments ago, and now he wondered how long he would have to wait. This part of the early evening was usually reserved among the *ton* for readying oneself for the rigors of the evening's entertainments to come, not for making inane chitchat with vapid visitors. While he doubted Caroline would find his chitchat vapid, he was quite certain she would not enjoy it.

His nerves fairly sang with exhilaration. Thanks to Harry, the dear boy, beautiful Elspeth no longer believed that Julian was a philandering cad. He could see now, as he would not allow himself to see then, that Harry was the only one Elspeth could possibly have trusted at the time. He must have been mad to have scaled the back wall of the townhouse, to have even thought to approach a gentle lady like his Elspeth in her boudoir, but thank heaven he had. A smile played lightly around his lips as, unbidden, the thought of Elspeth, pink and naked in her bath, rose before him. She was so lovely, and so passionate. And she loved him. The world could not have found him a better life's partner. Which left only Caroline to convince of the pointlessness of this malevolent sham of an engagement to her.

Of Edgar Randall, there had been no sign all afternoon, and if what Harry recounted was correct, as Julian had no doubt it was, Edgar had better stay scarce for some time to come. He had thought the man one of his best friends, from their early childhood at school, when the slight, nervous boy had been well on his way to becoming the target and punching bag of the school's bullies. Julian, one of the larger and more intelligent of the bunch, had recognized in the cowering boy an intelligence that matched his own. Under Julian's protection, Edgar had blossomed as quite an entertaining toff. What he lacked in physical attraction, he made up for in sharp and perceptive wit, a welcome addition to any gathering.

But Edgar had betrayed Julian, pure and simple, nearly causing him and his beloved Elspeth a lifetime of misery. How could Edgar have done such a thing? How could Julian have thought him a friend? To be sure, Edgar seemed to have confessed all, in front of a viscountess, no less, the Viscountess Alderson, Julian had no doubt. But knowing the viscountess, the confession had been stripped out of him, word by painful word. Julian was sure Edgar would have some glib explanation. He was equally sure he would not be inclined to listen to it.

How long would the witch keep him waiting? He had sent up an imperious note, requesting her attention at her earliest convenience. She was unlikely to ignore it, under the circumstances. Julian pulled out his gold timepiece and checked it against the ormolu clock on the carved marble mantle. They matched precisely. He heard running footsteps and turned expectantly. His heart pounded in anticipation. There would be a battle with Caroline, he had no doubt, but it was one he would win. He was holding all the cards, was he not? He had nothing to gain by following through with this sham engagement, and everything to lose. Elspeth was counting on him. Therefore, he would win.

He did not intend it to be a clean fight. It had not begun as such.

The doors flung themselves open. Julian didn't know whether to laugh or cry when there stood Harry, dear Harry, who was always turning up at the worst, or, sometimes, indeed, the best, moments. The boy's hair, as usual, stuck up all over his head, and his shirt front was soup-stained, creased, and missing several buttons. Nor were the tails tucked properly into his breeches. His boots were missing entirely. He must have left off battling Roderick long enough to have picked up from a servant that his erstwhile hero was taking up space in the drawing room. Turning this scamp into a gentleman in the short years to come would be quite a challenge, and Julian regretted that it would be necessary. Harry was much more interesting the way he was.

"Good afternoon to you, Mr. Thorpe," the boy said, somewhat out of breath.

"Well, it's probably more evening now, Harry," Julian offered affably. "And good evening to you."

Harry threw an anxious glance over his shoulder, then advanced into the room. "I owe you an apology, sir," he began, making an awkward, and unnecessary bow.

"For what do you apologize, Harry?" Julian asked. He

could have picked up the boy and hugged him, considering the child had virtually saved his life, but he thought Harry would prefer a more formal, manly exchange.

"Well, I'm not quite sure, really, but I thought you had hurt Elspeth, and then it turned out everyone else had hurt her instead. What does 'compromise' mean, anyway?"

"Ah, 'compromise.' Well, assuming you do not mean in the sense of coming to some middle ground in a dispute, compromise means—well, it means—well, in the sense I think you mean, it means . . ." Julian took a deep breath. He was not used to explaining sexual innuendo to children. The boy stared at him expectantly.

Julian sat himself on one of the numerous settees. "All right, Harry, let's see if I can explain. A gentleman should never encourage a lady to behave in such a way that other people can criticize her behavior. If he does do that, then he has 'compromised' the lady." There. That should do it.

"That's all?" asked Harry in dubious tones.

"Well, it's more complicated than that really, but that's the gist of it. You'll understand it better when you're older." He regretted those words the moment they left his lips. It was one of those remarks he had loathed as a child. It meant that there was a lot of juicy stuff going unsaid. Harry, looking aggrieved, was on top of it in a crack.

"Does this have anything to do with the way you're always kissing my sister?"

Julian sighed. Children were relentless. "Well, in a way, yes, rather, but it's really a different thing," he began, wondering where he would take it from here. He was saved, if that was the right word, by the sight of Caroline swooping furiously into the room.

She took one murderous look at Harry. "Out of my

sight, brat!" she screeched. "And don't set foot into this room again. You always break something, you clumsy little bumpkin, and Mama has to pay the landlord for it!" She advanced on him menacingly, but, obviously being a clever child, he saw the wisdom in beating a hasty retreat.

"And close the doors after you!" she cried after him. Harry came to a skidding stop on the carpet just outside the room, turned, grabbed the door handles, and, with a look of pity at Julian, slammed them shut.

So now he was alone with the dragon. Good. "You are utterly charming with children, Caroline. What a fine mother you'll make." As opening sallies went it was weak, but better than an awkward silence.

"In case you haven't heard, Julian, there are such things as nurses and boarding school. One gives birth, and then attends their weddings. Nothing more is required than that."

He could not have asked for a better opening. "Oh, you wouldn't find that true in my family, Caroline. We are very attentive to our young. No nurses and no boarding schools. Just good, old-fashioned parents rearing their own children."

"I did not know you came from such lumpish peasant stock, Julian," she sneered. "Well, it's irrelevant, in any event. I do not intend to raise your child. I will be in London and you will be in the country. You can raise him, or her, by yourself."

"One, only, Caroline?" he asked benignly. This was turning out to be more fun than he had expected it to be.

"One only, Julian, if that. The estate is not entailed, I understand. You can leave it to cousins for all I care. I shall not blow myself up like a balloon every nine months to suit your precious lineage."

"Since you mention it, Caroline, I have put the London house on the market. My estate agent has already received two promising offers."

She gaped at him. "But—but, you cannot do that, Julian!" she finally got out. "I like that house. I wish to live in it."

"Ah, but I do not wish to live there, and it's mine, isn't it?" He had spent the past few hours carefully analyzing the enemy's weak points, and found the battle more entertaining than he had hoped.

"Your father is still alive, Julian. The house is surely his, still."

"It's been signed over to me, Caroline, every brick of it."

"But the house is in Mayfair, for heaven sake! Those properties are difficult to come by!"

"Precisely why I received several offers within the first few hours."

"I won't have it, do you hear me?" She was fairly sputtering with rage. "I won't sign any of the sale documents!"

"Not in the least bit necessary, my dear Caroline." He sauntered over to a little table under the window that held a crystal decanter and several snifters, hoping Mrs. Quinn's household brandy was better than he expected it to be. "I will have the property well sold before this wedding you seem to be planning, Caroline. Your signature will not be necessary. Brandy, my dear? You look as if you could use a snort." She did not answer. He poured himself a full snifter and turned. She was eying him the way a hooded cobra might peruse its intended next meal. Well, he intended to be the mongoose, not the meal. He took a small sip of the brandy. Not half bad, it was. Must be left over from the late Lord Ewell's collection. Tasted like victory, come to think of it. He took a long, deep draught and gave her a pleasant smile.

It was like throwing a flaming torch into hot oil. "I

will live in London, Julian!" she flared at him. She began to pace, her slippers stomping alarmingly, the floorboards creaking under the unusual assault. "I shall let a house, an expensive one, mind, in the best neighborhood. You would do well to take your house off the market at once!" She turned back to him with a malevolent smile of triumph.

"And how do you intend to pay for this, Caroline?" he asked, drawing deeply again from the snifter.

"I shall not pay for it, Julian. You will!" she announced, Victory Rampant.

"Ah, but I shall not, Caroline. I have already sent round communication to all of the London estate agents that I will not be held financially responsible for any leases you sign, before, or after, any wedding." He finished off the snifter and turned to pour himself some more. "I think you'll find, Caroline, that no one will accept your signature on a lease," he remarked, his back to her.

"Then I'll live with friends! I'll live with Mama. But I will live in London, Julian. You'll not see my face at that farmhouse you call a country estate!"

"I'm merely curious, you understand, but since you've brought it up, how would you be planning to live in London, Caroline? Will your dear Mama continue to support you?"

"You know perfectly well who will support me, Julian. The bills—and there will be a great many of them . . ." she paused and smiled again. "Very large bills, Julian, very large, will be sent to you in the country. You will have to pay them." She was feeling confident enough to drape herself over one of the hideous little settees, and give him a spiteful smile.

"Ah, but you may not be aware, Caroline, that a husband has options where these matters are concerned. I have already written to my solicitor. All of the London merchants will be notified that they are not to extend you credit—that any credit they do extend to one Caroline Thorpe will not be honored with payment. It's perfectly legal, if they have proper notice. Done all the time in the lower classes, I understand. You'll find that all of the finer, and the less fine, establishments will close their doors to you." He smiled to himself and took another sip. He had no idea whether or not this was true, but it certainly had sounded right when he thought it up this afternoon. The house wasn't on the market, either, come to that, but it certainly could be, and would be snapped up in a heartbeat. That much was true, at least.

He took another deep draught of the brandy and smiled at her. "I think you'll find us Thorpes to be a frugal lot. I keep quite a tight rein on the finances. Everything has to be approved by me, down to the smallest purchase. Won't tolerate a lot of frivolous spending. But not to despair, Caroline. You have an excellent wardrobe, I've noticed, and more than enough jewelry. Your clothing should last you, assuming you take care of it properly, for many years to come. And, of course, you won't have much need of frippery in the country. No, plain and simple, that's our country life."

She sat in dark silence, staring at nothing, ignoring him as if he were not there. He could almost see the thoughts chasing around in her head. Finally, she looked up at him. He almost stepped back, so potent was the loathing in her eyes.

"You think you have me trapped, don't you, Julian?" she said slowly. She was trying to appear relaxed, but her hands were clenched into white-knuckled fists.

"I prefer not to think of it as 'trapped,' Caroline. Such an unpleasant concept, don't you agree? For example, you, indeed, think you have trapped me into making a loveless marriage. You cannot sit there and look me in the face and tell me you and Edgar Randall didn't set a vicious trap for me in Sydney Gardens the other night. . . ." He had scored with that one. He could see the flare in her eyes. "So I prefer to think of this as my turn to exert a few reasonable conditions, as the head of the household. You wish to marry me? So you shall, but on my terms. We will live on my estates in the country, all the time. No London, no Bath. I'm really a simple family man, Caroline, early to bed, early to rise. I enjoy riding around the estates, visiting my tenants. I shall expect you to accompany me, the way my mother always did my father. It's charming, really, quite bucolic. Chucking babies under the chin, drinking stewed tea in dark kitchens, admiring pigs, urchins wiping their adorable little noses on your pants leg, or, in your case, your skirt. You'll get used to it, you'll see. Of course, you won't be able to do that all the time. I don't hold with breeding women gadding about the countryside on horseback. Too much danger of bleeding to death. And"—he smiled conspiratorially at her—"I won't accept for a minute all this modest, missish nonsense about having only one child." He took another deep swig. Perhaps he shouldn't drink too much. He was beginning to enjoy himself too much. "No, indeed," he went on, appreciating the look of horror that was dawning in her face, "I know my breeding stock when I look it over"—he allowed his eyes to rake her body, appraising, weighing, evaluating—"and you're a fine brood mare, if I do say so. Wonderful teats, hips, and belly on you. You can grow a baby the size of a calf in there and pop it right out, one a year. Until your womb drops, of course. Messy and painful, that is, or so I understand, but happens to the best of them, unfortunately."

"Julian, please. . . ." Caroline said faintly. She sat back against the chair, eyes closed. She looked positively green around the gills.

"Of course, people aren't like animals, fortunately for us men. We have to work at getting babies. Night after night—all that humping and pumping, no rest for the weary." He paused and gave her a gleaming smile. "I'm sure your delicate sensibilities are shocked at all this, Caroline, but you'll be pleased to know all this infernal delicacy and tiptoeing around disappears in the privacy of the marital bedroom. Why, we can say anything we please to one another. Very relaxing and great fun, really. No secrets, at all. Chamber pots, bleeding cycles, what-have-you. Have you ever heard a man break wind, Caroline? Most entertaining, I assure you. We have contests sometimes at White's when we're foxed. The staff has to air the place out by morning. . . ."

"Julian, that's enough!" Caroline lurched to her feet, literally shaking all over. "I will not be spoken to like this! You are beneath contempt!"

"Oh, sorry, Caroline, I get like this when I drink. I drink too much, have you noticed? Can't control myself at all. But I have a damned fine time of it. Damned fine!" He raised the snifter and drained off the rest of it. He tossed the empty glass to the table. The delicate crystal shattered into a million pieces. "Hah, there's another damned thing busted for your mama to pay for. Don't blame little Harry for that one, Caroline."

He turned and perused her carefully, looking her up and down, his eyes coming to rest on her own. He moved toward her slowly, not allowing his eyes to leave hers. Now there was more fear than rage mirrored in their depths. "I get quite randy when I drink, as well, Caroline," he said, allowing his voice to sound husky, as if with desire. "Can't get enough of it. Usually use whores for my pleasure, but it'll be nice having a wife to service me whenever I want. And I want it often." He gave her a slow, knowing smile and continued his advance. "Give us a little kiss, Caroline. I can teach you what to do. First, I stick my tongue in your mouth. . . ."

With a shriek, she bolted, ripping at the door handles as if the hounds of hell were on her heels. The doors slammed shut behind her, rattling the bric-a-brac around the room. He could hear her footsteps pounding up the staircase. He stood for a moment and stared at the door, a small smile playing around the corners of his mouth. He should, by rights, be utterly disgusted with himself. He wouldn't dare talk to even one of London's whores like that, much less to a demoiselle of the *ton*. But Caroline deserved it, he had to admit. And he strongly suspected it had been a most profitable few minutes' effort. She would cry off after this. She would have to. . . .

Chapter Fourteen

"Oh, my dear Mrs. Carberry. You would not believe how distressed I am to be the butt of such a poor jest at my own expense. I ask you, what have I ever done to deserve this utter lack of respect from these young people? Why, I am the very soul of kindness to them, nothing less! Isn't that true, Mr. Randall?"

"Oh, indeed it is, Lady Haverford, indeed it is." Edgar refrained from rolling his eyes, but it was difficult. The woman had been nattering on in this vein for a good quarter hour. She'd collected quite a crowd of ladies by this time, all cluck, clucking and tsk, tsking. Every time a new lady arrived, Lady Haverford obligingly started her tale all over again from the beginning. It grew more elaborate with each telling, and with each telling, Dolly Haverford's enjoyment grew as well. She loved being the center of attention.

They had arrived rather early at the Assembly Rooms this evening, and staked out a good position where they could see and be seen by all entering and leaving. Edgar had duly escorted her in her carriage. At least they had had time to work out some of the more difficult details of the tale on the way over. In the meanwhile, Edgar had managed to extricate himself as one of the villains of the piece. He was now a sad and unwilling dupe just like poor Dolly. He didn't much fancy being a dupe, but it certainly beat being a villain.

"But, Dolly, I thought you said at the time that Caroline was all mussed about, and Julian Thorpe had his arms around her," argued a tenacious newcomer to the scene. Edgar felt sorry for the poor orchestra players who were playing their hearts out in the small musicians' balcony, to no effect. The room grew more and more crowded with each passing moment. There were, as far as Edgar knew, no competing fancy private entertainments scheduled this evening, which would mean the large rooms would be fair to bursting at the seams in an hour or so.

"Oh, good heavens, nothing so naughty as that, Miss Worth. Caroline's attire was quite perfectly intact, such as it was, of course. You know my opinion of how these young girls today go about with entirely too much bosom. . . ."

"But, Dolly, I know you said you saw Julian with his arms about her. I distinctly remember because it made me feel quite faint."

"Miss Worth, you feel faint at the suggestion of rain coming," Dolly said dryly, clearly unwilling to give up the center of attention, not to mention control of the story. "I did, indeed, see Julian put his arms about Caroline, and, of course, I said so. But you will recall I said that he did so after Mr. Randall and I, and, of course, her mother, Bettina Quinn, had arrived on the scene. Apparently they deliberately waited until we arrived to stage this little scene. Why, the very idea that I should be the butt of this wicked little joke. . . ." and she was off again, full circle. Lady Haverford had great stamina, Edgar had to give her credit for that.

"But why on earth, would they do such a thing?" Mrs. Blanchard mused. "Caroline Quinn, I grant you, is a headstrong girl, but such a poor hoax makes no sense at all. Why, she has most of the *ton* toasting her upcoming nuptials, I declare. And Julian Thorpe seems a levelheaded sort. I can't see why they would put themselves in such a silly, not to mention dangerous, position."

"Exactly, Henrietta! Precisely why I did not wish to believe it myself," Dolly Haverford crowed, as if she had been waiting for this very point to be raised. Edgar had been waiting for it, as well, but with far more trepidation than Dolly seemed to feel. It was, of course, the absurd part of the tale.

"Well, I'll let you in on a little secret. . . ." She leaned forward and lowered her voice to a stage whisper. All dozen or so ladies leaned in toward her. From the musicians' balcony, it must have looked like a flower closing up at dusk.

"It seems Caroline has her heart quite set on young Rokeby—you remember—they were all but declared last year when his stable burned down, and he had to leave suddenly. But you all know Bettina. It seems she favors young Thorpe—saw him as a bird in the hand, don't you know. Julian and Caroline found that quite amusing, as they have been friends since childhood, and want nothing to do with each other in that regard. . . ."

Edgar did so wish she'd stick to the script. One could get in trouble with this free-wheeling invention. . . .

"But, apparently Bettina has been relentless in her attempts to throw them together, nauseatingly so. So, they decided to teach her a lesson. Threw themselves together right in front of her. Although I must say, I do not see why I had to be the butt. . . ."

And she was off again. Actually, the story had gotten pretty good at that. Most of the ladies were nodding, thin-lipped, quite ready to condemn an entire generation for dreadful judgment and antics unworthy of the better bred. Miss Worth still looked a bit confused, however. Perhaps he might have a go at her, himself, later this evening, to make sure she climbed into the lifeboat with everyone else.

"Bettina must have been beside herself," one of the old biddies, a Mrs. Carberry, he thought, offered helpfully.

"Oh, indeed. Why we nearly had to carry her out of the maze, prostrate."

"Oh, that's right, Lady Haverford, didn't you say the country cousin had fainted in the maze? Was she a part of the scheme, or a dupe?"

"Oh, a dupe, no doubt, Mrs. Carberry. She was quite insensible for a few minutes. In fact, that's when I should have realized something was up. Recall that I said at the time that Julian went immediately to the cousin when she fainted; most attentive, he was. I suspect he had not realized she would be lured into the maze as well. I believe he's quite smitten with the cousin, you know, certainly not Caroline."

"I suspect Caroline's hand in that part," Edgar found himself offering. "She's been quite jealous over all the attention Miss Elspeth Quinn has garnered this Season. Personally—" He leaned in and lowered his voice to make sure they would all pay rapt attention, and he was not disappointed. "I think Caroline had Elspeth imported from the country to make herself look young and fresh by comparison. I think she has been greatly annoyed that the ploy had quite the opposite effect." He observed the group, weighing their reaction to this bit of salacious *on dit*. As he hoped, he saw heads nodding and lips thinning. Caroline deserved their censure for more than they knew, and Elspeth deserved their alliance.

"But this naughty little escapade nearly caught them in their own trap. Why, Bettina has all but said the two are betrothed," Miss Worth put in. At least she seemed to be coming round to the new version.

"Indeed. Why it would serve the two of them right to be leg-shackled together for the rest of their lives," Dolly Haverford pronounced. They had all pitched their voices a bit louder to compete with the musicians, who were, in turn, competing with an ever-growing crowd. It was growing warm, too. Or, perhaps Edgar was feeling he'd been on the griddle a bit too long. At least they hadn't focused on his part in all this.

"Why, Mr. Randall, you were there with Lady Haverford, weren't you?" Henrietta Blanchard announced loudly. All eyes turned to him. The room got suddenly very hot, indeed. "What did you think of all this nonsense?"

"Well, I must say I thought it quite queer at the time. Didn't ring true at all. Why, I know full well that Julian Thorpe and Miss Quinn want nothing to do with one another in that regard. The girl is over the moon about Rokeby—can't think why—he has the wit of a brick, but you know how *les demoiselles* can be. And dear Julian is, indeed, quite smitten with the Quinn cousin. He's already written to the mother to offer for her." He paused briefly, waiting for this stone to sink. He saw the light go on in several pairs of eyes. "And, too, it simply did not look right. I believe my eyesight is a bit stronger than that of the dear ladies, who were, as they will, nattering to one another as we entered the maze. . . ." He paused and bestowed a conspiratorial smile on Dolly Haverford, one inveterate gossip saluting another. "But it appeared to me at first glance that Julian and Caroline were just waiting for something, not standing particularly close. They sprang into action on sight of her mother and Lady Haverford. And Julian looked positively horrified to find Miss Elspeth Quinn there. I must say"—he was warming to his role now—"that I, too, feel that I have been unfairly singled out as the butt. . . ."

"Did you say young Julian is smitten with the Quinn cousin, Mr. Randall?" one of the biddies interrupted peremptorily, getting, as he had hoped they would, to the heart of the matter.

"Oh, indeed, so I understand, Jane." Lady Haverford seized control of the floor again. "That was part of the reason Caroline and Julian decided to act when they did, although to be sure, they had intended for Bettina to be so outdone with Julian's alleged ungentlemanly behavior that she would foist him, herself, onto the cousin. But, as you can see, the best-laid plans . . ."

From something of a distance, Edgar could see that Thomas and Robert had entered the Assembly Rooms. Indeed, they were hard to miss. Every lady in the place should look to her own comparatively drab attire in shame. His feet itched to take him away. He looked around at the group. It had grown in the last few moments by another half dozen ladies, and he could hear it all starting over again. "Oh, I have been sadly abused, Tabitha," Lady Haverford was saying. "To have been the butt . . ."

Surely he could make his escape now. With a general bow in the direction of precisely no one, he spun, gracefully, he hoped, and very nearly knocked into Herself, the Viscountess Alderson. Gad, but the woman knew how to turn up at the most inopportune times!

"Mr. Randall," she said, doing that marvelous thing

with her eyebrows. He simply must figure out how it was done.

"Ah, and a good evening to you, madam. I do so hope you are well, this evening."

"Wouldn't be here if I weren't, of course," she snapped.

By now, naturally, all conversation among the biddies had ceased. A viscountess preceded everyone in the ladies' circle, and her appearance at Edgar's shoulder was more interesting, even, than the subject at hand. Scandals, after all, could be so short-lived. Or revived, if boredom necessitated.

"Good evening, Dolly, Henrietta," she said, nodding distantly around the rest of the circle.

"Oh, good evening, Lady Alderson." Lady Haverford beamed around the circle, clearly delighted at the personal recognition.

"Please do not allow me to interrupt your animated discussion. Do go on," she announced, as if calling for a performance. To Edgar, who was at least mariginally a part of these doings, the cue was obvious, but no one else seemed to pick up on it.

"Oh, madam," gushed Dolly, "we were just discussing how sadly abused I have been by these young people and their sorry little jest. You all may remember"—she beamed around the circle again—"that it was Viscountess Alderson, herself, who explained to me that what I had seen was a charade, nothing less! Isn't that right, Your Ladyship?"

"Indeed, it is." Viscountess Alderson gave a slight tap with her cane for emphasis. "Why, I feel much abused myself in this matter. I had thought that there was to be an announcement of Miss Caroline Quinn's betrothal to Julian Thorpe at my ball last night, but what the young people had secretly planned was to announce his engagement to the cousin instead—what's that child's name, Mr. Randall? Sweet thing, very mannerly."

"That would be Miss Elspeth Quinn, madam, lately of Weston-under-Lizard," he replied without missing a beat. Deftly done, m'lady, thought Edgar, giving the Imprimatur to the heretofore ignored Elspeth. The biddies would fall all over her after this rare sanctification.

"It was meant to be a surprise, and, I must say, a cut down, to all of us," the viscountess went on. "Bettina Quinn most of all. Apparently some sort of set down to Bettina for what Caroline considered untoward meddling—the very idea that a mother has not the right to meddle in her daughter's marriage plans! I declare, I don't know what these young people today can possibly be thinking. Why, civilization, itself, is on the very brink of destruction, if a mother is not to select her daughter's husband. . . ."

He edged himself out of the circle. His work was done here. The biddies were hanging on the viscountess's every word, nodding and frowning at the perfidies of the Younger Generation. Elspeth was Saved. Caroline was in the briers, as was Julian, apparently, but it was the sort of high-handed escapade that was to be expected of Young People, and soon forgotten. He supposed there would be some confusion and skepticism among the young people themselves. But in the face of a united front of old biddies determined to believe the viscountess's version, they would have to yield. Speaking of whom, perhaps now would be a good time to bring Thomas and Robert into the new version. And, besides, he had a bet he needed to call off. It seemed no one had won after all. . . .

It had been, Elspeth thought to herself, a most uncomfortable carriage ride from the Quinn home to the Assembly Rooms. Barely a word spoken among the three Quinn ladies, none of them civil. Caroline sat in a corner of the carriage huddled in a dark ball of rage. Elspeth had even heard her cousin muttering to herself along the way. Aunt Bettina was befuddled and alarmed by Caroline. She had attempted several light remarks and had been utterly rebuffed. Now she, too, sat in a huddled ball, as if afraid to make further social effort. Elspeth, herself, could hardly bring herself to notice. The two ladies could have been riding stark naked on the top of the carriage for all Elspeth could care. She could barely keep from singing out loud. Again and again, the most unmaidenly images from this afternoon's most unorthodox bath rose before her mind's eye. She was grateful that the dark of the carriage prevented her companions from seeing the blush and smile that seemed to have taken up permanent residence on her face. Julian loved her! He would set everything to rights; he had promised. Indeed, she had reason to believe he had already set the wheels in motion. Harry had come sneaking into her room again, early this evening, and had reported that Mr. Thorpe was downstairs in the drawing room speaking to Caroline. Elspeth would have given the world to eavesdrop, but she couldn't, for the life of her, figure out how to manage it without running a terrible risk of being caught out. Elspeth had waited by her door inside her bedroom after shooing Harry away. The boy had gotten entirely too much of an education on this visit, she thought, ruefully. He had left her bedroom door slightly ajar, and she did not shut it. Her patience was rewarded a few moments later by the sound of heavy footsteps pounding up the stairs. Elspeth peeked out into the dark hallway in time to see her cousin flying by, her face a mask of rage. Caroline ran full tilt into her own bedroom and slammed the door shut behind her. Elspeth could hear the sound of the bolt being shot home. Oh, how she longed to find out what had transpired, but she knew she would have to be patient. Best to let dear Julian handle matters himself. After all, they would have the rest of their lives for him to regale her with the details.

She dipped her head as the carriage passed under a street lamp that threw its light into the dark interior. Again, came the feel of him pressed hot and hard up and down the length of her, and she nearly gasped at the thought, as her stomach fluttered with a heretofore unknown pleasure. A lifetime of Julian touching her. . . .

"We need not stay long if you are indisposed, Caroline," Aunt Bettina offered somewhat timidly.

"I am perfectly 'disposed,' Mama. We will stay as long as I wish to," Caroline snarled in the dark, and Aunt Bettina held her peace.

The street lanterns were spaced more closely together now, and Elspeth could feel the carriage slowing as they neared their destination. She schooled her face into what she hoped was a cool, composed mask, glad that the world could not see inside her, where her stomach was turning Catherine wheels, and her mind reviewed scenes no decent maiden should know enough to conjure. Julian would be there tonight, she just knew it. She could not imagine how the evening would progress—something was bound to happen—but she could walk into the room knowing that Julian loved her, and only her. That was enough to raise her chin high.

The carriage stopped and the door was flung open by the Quinn footman. Was it Elspeth's imagination, or did he give her a veiled grin as he handed her down? Oh, heavens, was her private business to be the talk of Bath, below stairs? At least they could not possibly know about the interlude with Julian in her boudoir!

Despite her joy, her heart pounded as she walked behind her aunt and cousin. Caroline, Elspeth noted, seemed to undergo a remarkable transformation. By the time her cousin stepped into the Assembly Rooms, one would have thought her to be the most delightful, carefree demoiselle in England. Aunt Bettina cast several anxious looks in her daughter's direction, and seemed satisfied that Caroline would behave herself.

Elspeth took a quick look about the room, seeking a certain tall, handsome gentleman. Her heart dropped a little when she could not spot him, although, to be sure, there were several rooms available to the public, including card rooms, and he could be in any of them.

A low voice at her elbow made her start. "I wonder, Miss Quinn, if you aware that things have taken a decided turn for the better since the ball last night." It was Edgar Randall. She hardly knew how to react. Harry's jumbled version of events had cast Edgar as one of the chief villains of the piece, although it seemed he might have had a change of heart. At least he had attempted to get Caroline to cry off, and had then confessed all to Viscountess Alderson this afternoon. Of course, the most hardened criminal in all of England would spill everything to Viscountess Alderson, should she set her mind to obtaining the confession. So was Edgar Randall friend or foe? And either way, could she trust him to stay that way for long?

He smiled rather wanly at her. "I can see you are trying to work out where I stand in all this glorious mess, Miss Quinn," he offered. He seemed rather subdued compared to his usual self.

"I can't quite think what to say, Mr. Randall," she offered, unable to keep her tone from sounding chilly.

"I understand, really I do," he said. "I don't know that this is the place to explain myself—indeed, I hardly can explain some of my actions—but it is the place to offer you my abject apologies for the pain I've caused you. The only defense I have at all is that I truly did not understand that you and Julian love each other—I thought it was simply one of those mindless, fan-tapping flirtations that one engages in several times a day in Bath. Of course, that's still no defense at all . . ." he trailed off, staring intently at her. He was terribly uncomfortable. The smooth and urbane Mr. Randall looked as if he couldn't find the next word to utter. Elspeth was not ready to forgive him. Considering the pain he had caused her, not to mention Julian, she was not sure she ever would. She held her tongue.

"Well, I cannot blame you if you never forgive me. I wouldn't if I were you. But please allow me to say that I am shamed beyond measure, that I've wished a thousand times to undo everything, and, indeed, I have done so. Or,"—he looked around hurriedly—"I must say, I've had help in the matter. Viscountess Alderson and Lady Haverford, between them, have set the story straight."

Elspeth could sense from his face and words that he was truly abject in his apology. It was not like her to hold a grudge. On the other hand, no one in her entire lifetime in Weston-under-Lizard had ever attempted to ruin every shred of happiness for her. She supposed it was only fair to forgive him. Forgetting was another matter.

"I shall take you at your word, Mr. Randall, and accept your apology," she said. But she could produce no smile to go along with the words.

"Well, I shall have to settle for that, then, shan't I? Better than I deserve, I must say." He took the opportunity to offer her his arm. "Shall we take a stroll around the room? I should catch you up on where things stand at the moment."

"Have you seen Mr. Thorpe?" Elspeth asked, placing her hand as lightly as she could on his arm.

"Any number of times today, actually. The man is beginning to take up quite a great deal of my time—not"—he held up his other hand in response to the look that crossed Elspeth's face—"that I don't owe him every minute of it."

They had begun their stately ambling. Heads were turning in her direction, Elspeth noticed, but while there had been knowing smirks and elbow-punching last night, tonight there were looks of confusion, speculation, a few conspiratorial, inclusive nods. Something had changed all right.

"Let's see, where should I began? Have I mentioned that it is you who are now engaged to Julian, and not Caroline?" He seemed to delight in her obvious confusion. "No? Then perhaps we should begin at the beginning. It seems, for reasons I am not at liberty to disclose, that the voluble-tongued Lady Haverford owes a debt of discretion to the Viscountess Alderson. . . ."

Julian never enjoyed these squeezes—too crowded, too hot, too inane—but tonight he had absolutely no desire to attend. Viscountess Alderson had been adamant that he appear at the Assembly Rooms this evening. He was sure the evening would be a crush—these things always were—but he was also quite certain he would be one of the main attractions. As a man who prided himself on his privacy, he did not appreciate knowing that he might as well be decked out in a Punch costume for everyone's entertainment.

And it appeared he was right. Heads turned and mouths went to ears as he passed. Last night, at least, he had been drunk enough, and intent enough on Elspeth, that he had not noticed the jibes and japery. She, on the other hand, had been stone sober last night. Every whisper must have cut through her like a knife. Well, he would have a lifetime to make up for the pain his stupidity had caused her.

Not that Caroline Quinn and Edgar Randall weren't mostly to blame. He caught sight of Caroline dancing with the poor benighted Mr. Ledbetter. Well, he wished him joy of her, although he rather thought that if Mr. Ledbetter were so unfortunate as to gain her hand, she would eat him alive. The music brought the couple close to where he stood and she caught sight of him. A look of pure loathing crossed her face. Good. He felt the same way about her.

Now where was Elspeth? After all, what did any of it matter beside Elspeth? It had been all he could do to concentrate on anything this evening—going through the motions of dressing, shaving, et cetera. Poor Forbush had been near to gibbering at the state of Mr. Thorpe's attire this afternoon. Mr. Thorpe refrained from mentioning to his valet that he had scaled a brick wall, and had an unexpected partial dip in a hip bath before returning home, and the state of his cravat bore no discussion at all.

He spotted the Viscountess Alderson in a knot of biddies and dragons, Lady Haverford among them. Ducking behind a column, he continued scanning the room for Elspeth. It was always possible she had stayed at home—all the better, he decided, since he would simply join her there, propriety be damned.

At last, she swam into his view, like something out of Greek legend, the personification of beauty. Praxiteles would have considered himself a lucky sculptor, indeed, to have had the likes of Miss Elspeth Quinn for a model. Gad, how she made his heart thud. She would be his, if they had to hie for Gretna Green by morning. She was walking on the arm of a toff, who it was he couldn't clearly see. They were walking toward him, and as they grew closer, he could see that it was Edgar Randall. Drat! He wanted to talk to Elspeth now, not deal with Edgar's perfidies. That subject could be explored at another time. He watched their slow progress, made all the slower by the beckonings and greetings from others.

It was apparent that Elspeth had risen considerably in the eyes of the other attendees this evening. Far from hiding in the corner as she had been inclined to do, very much shadowed by her cousin, Elspeth now seemed to be the center of attention. She nodded and smiled and was obviously making pleasant small talk. She hadn't spotted him yet; at least he didn't think so. He stepped out from behind the column to catch her eye. Right into the path of Thomas and Robert, in outfits that should be the envy of every lady there.

"Ooh, Julian!" gushed Thomas—or was it Robert? "I've heard the most delicious prattle about you!"

"You naughty boy!" said Robert—or was it Thomas? "You had everyone fooled! Neatly done, my dear sir."

Julian sighed audibly. "To what do you refer, gentlemen?" he asked. "I find it very difficult to keep up with the rumors about myself. I must be exceedingly fascinating, considering the amount of time the gentry spends discussing my every movement." Might as well find out what was being said at this point. He supposed it was too much to hope that Caroline had told everyone she was not betrothed to him after all.

"Silly man! As if you didn't know!" giggled one of the two popinjays.

"Such a taradiddle, Julian! Brilliant of you, I must say!" giggled the other.

"Gentlemen, please," he interrupted, holding up his hand. They would stretch this out for hours for the sheer entertainment value, knowing these two. "I've only a minute or two to spare. Enlighten me as to the details, if you please, so that I may know whether tonight I should play the villain, the hero, the clown, or the boozer. It gets confusing, you know."

"Oh, you were marvelous last night as the jug-bitten Julian! But we noticed—didn't we?"—the one smirked at the other—"that you weren't the least bit foxed when you danced the waltz with Miss Elspeth Quinn! That's when we suspected something was afoot—didn't we, Robert?" Must have been Thomas speaking, then.

Julian remained silent. It seemed that whatever he said veered them off in another direction.

"Well, dear boy, what we want to know is—just how angry is Bettina Quinn with the lovely, if headstrong, Caroline? Why the girl is lucky the dragons seem to find it all so amusing. Otherwise, she'd be ruined. You, too, for that matter! Whatever possessed you to play such a dangerous little scene in the maze?" tittered one.

"I declare, Bettina could still take a horsewhip to you, if she chose!" tittered the other.

"She'd have to catch me first," growled Julian, hoping they would continue with their prattle. He liked where this was going.

"Ah, Mr. Thorpe?" came a timid voice at his elbow. Trying not to show his exasperation, he turned around. It was one of the elderly ladies—a biddy, rather than a dragon, he noted. "Ah, good evening to you, Miss . . . Worth," he caught at the name at the last possibly polite moment. "I trust you are well, this evening?"

"Why certainly, sir, thank you for inquiring, indeed. But it's Viscountess Alderson. She wishes for you to attend her at once, she says." She cast her eyes nervously in the direction he had last seen the clutch of dragons.

Well, there was nothing for it. He cast a quick look around for Elspeth, and saw that she and Edgar were caught up in a small knot of his contemporaries, many of them *les demoiselles* of the Season. He could hear squeals and giggles from that direction. Between the devil and the deep blue sea, indeed.

"Humble yourself abjectly, Julian!" cried Thomas, or was it Robert? He'd got them confused again.

"Let us know if she treats you to the Cut Direct immediately, Julian, so we can shun you as well!" cried the other. They all but waved lace handkerchiefs as he moved away with Miss Worth on his arm.

This falling in love business let one in for a great deal of difficulty, he thought as he closed on the clutch of dragons. He therefore intended to do it only this once in his life.

Elspeth had caught a glimpse of Julian a good five minutes ago, and she longed to be on her way to him. Edgar Randall, however, appeared to have other plans for her this evening, and getting away from him had proved, thus far, to be an insurmountable challenge. In small whispered bits and pieces, Edgar had filled her in on how things stood. Quite remarkably, they had managed to turn the whole scene in the labyrinth into a big jest, if a sorry one at that. Elspeth endured knowing smiles and winks and murmured noncommittal pleasantries as they made an aimless progress through the room.

"You mustn't look confused," he had whispered, as they had started out. "I'll explain everything as we go. Look like the cat who swallowed the cream, and leave everything to me."

That was harder than it sounded. From what Elspeth had gleaned from the quick, whispered remarks, Caroline was alleged to have played a dreadful hoax on her mother and Lady Haverford. Julian was coming in for some censure for having agreed to assist her in the matter. Sympathy did not seem to run high, however, for the duped ladies. One might gather much of the *ton* thought they had it coming to them. It was apparent that everyone appreciated the mid-Season diversion and would dine on it for weeks to come.

"What are these mysterious, veiled references to Lord Rokeby, Mr. Randall?" she whispered, through a tightly held smile, as they threaded their way from one group to another.

"A red herring, my dear, or, at least, what we came up with as motivation for Caroline. As it turns out, she may be lucky at that. I heard through the grapevine this evening that he is, indeed, returning to Bath. Can't wait to watch what unfolds when he arrives. He's all but betrothed to Caroline, and he doesn't even know it."

"What's he like, this Lord Rokeby?" she asked. They were coming upon another group and she knew she would lose his ear for a time.

"Oh, arrogant, mean-spirited and demanding. Thick as mud. He and she are made for each other, never you fear. If he winds up leg-shackled to the malevolent Miss Caroline Quinn, it will be nothing less than either of them deserves."

Elspeth wasn't sure she should take comfort in that. She would still have to feel some pity for the unsuspecting Lord Rokeby, who, at least, was one of the few in all this who had done her no ill. Caroline went sailing by, on the arm of the devoted, if ill-fated, Mr. Ledbetter. She looked to be in high spirits, laughing and tapping at his arm with her fan. She did not spare her country cousin so much as a glance.

Right in the middle of some inane remark someone was making in her ear, she spotted Julian again. Tall and utterly handsome, he stood in a clutch of dragons, right next to Thomas and Robert. The contrast couldn't have been more striking. Where they wore a veritable rainbow of amazing colors, Julian was attired in his usual buff and black. She could see him only from the back, but the way his breeches molded his rear was enough to bring a dark blush to her cheeks. Was she indeed a wanton that every glimpse of him produced such unmaidenly thoughts? There was more to this marital relations business than she had ever guessed, she was beginning to understand. And that thought, too, made her blush anew. Thank heavens no one could read her mind.

At that moment, Julian shifted slightly to make room for yet another dragon who bore down on the clutch. Their eyes met across the space that separated them. It was like a jolt of lightning between them. His face lit up at the sight of her, and he smiled a broad smile. She was a fish caught on his hook. She could do nothing but allow him to reel her in. Her hand still lightly topping Edgar's arm, she pushed slightly, signaling that it was time to move on. Maddeningly the man continued his nattering. Oh, yes, he had been sadly abused by the perfidious and manipulative Miss Caroline Quinn, but wasn't it all so terribly amusing, and didn't the old biddies deserve their comeuppance? It would serve the chit right if Rokeby would have nothing whatsoever to do with her, and had they heard that Rokeby, himself, was on his way to Bath? Quite possibly in haste to stop this supposed betrothal. Oh, wasn't it all just too diverting?

She pushed again with her hand, and that earned her a knowing and amused glance from Mr. Randall, who nevertheless continued his chatter. Half the room away, Julian gazed at her, his love clear for her to read. Enough was enough! She moved first one foot, then the other, keeping a grip on Edgar's arm. It was now up to him to make a graceful exit from the group, and, consummate toff that he was, he did so, extricating them with his smooth and witty excuses.

"Mustn't appear too eager, my dear," he murmured in her ear. "I declare, we are near to sprinting."

"Mr. Randall, so help me if you stop and talk to one more of these scandalmongers, I shall haul you bodily away," she said, although to be sure, she was near to panting from their speed.

"Do I take it we are on the way to seeing our dear

Julian?" he asked, nodding cordially at several interested sorts.

"Of course we are," she replied. "He's been signaling me these past ten minutes to come over to him."

"Why hasn't he come to you, then . . . oh, no, he's with Lady Haverford and the viscountess! Oh, please have mercy, Elspeth. I had only just managed to escape them when you came in!"

"Not on your life, Edgar," she replied, continuing to steer him with great determination toward Julian. "Don't forget, you still owe us great penance for your part in this."

"But, Julian, well, that is . . ." He hesitated, then stopped dead in his tracks. No amount of tugging could budge him.

"Oh, what is it, Mr. Randall?" she asked with great exasperation.

"I haven't made my peace with Julian, Elspeth," he replied, sounding truly miserable. "I doubt he would be speaking to me at all. . . ."

"Well, no time like the present, Mr. Randall. Let's go." He gave up the fight and shambled along next to her, but the spring was most emphatically gone from his step, and his bubbling repartee had vanished.

In less than a moment they had reached the clutch of dragons. Belatedly, Elspeth saw that Aunt Bettina was among them, hidden behind several of the stouter ladies. She looked as though she had just swallowed something gone terribly off. Seeing Elspeth at last, Julian's eyes lit up. Ignoring Edgar, Julian offered her his arm. With a smile that came from her heart, she placed her hand on his arm, and he covered it with his other hand. She could not take her eyes from his.

"Ah, I believe Mr. Thorpe has an announcement to make," rang out the viscountess's powerful voice. Elspeth could feel her heart start to pound and she was glad of his arm supporting her.

"Indeed, I do, Your Ladyship," Julian said. He had not yet taken his eyes from Elspeth's own, but his hand tightened on hers. "Allow me to announce that to my undying joy, Miss Elspeth Quinn has consented to be my wife."

The collective "ahhhh" from the ladies was music to Elspeth's ears.

Chapter Fifteen

"I thought this moment would never come, Elspeth," Julian said, holding her as tightly as he dared. They spun through the room to the lilting strains of a waltz. He had never much cared for the dance before—always made him feel as if it gave the lady unrealistic expectations with regard to his intentions—but tonight, his intentions had never been clearer. And never more beautiful and welcome was the lady in his arms.

"Everyone is staring, Julian," she said, looking about with some apprehension.

"Let them stare," he pronounced grandly. "I am dancing with the most beautiful woman in the room, so naturally the men are envious and the women jealous."

"Promise me you'll never get stronger spectacles, Julian," laughed Elspeth.

"Are you suggesting that I see you with eyes of love, my heart?"

"I am merely saying that I should be very unhappy if you came home one day with new spectacles and found yourself feeling sadly abused by your wife's appearance."

"Impossible. I could look you over, head to toe, attired in Praxitelian fashion, with a magnifying glass and find every inch of you exquisite."

"Julian!" she giggled, her face turning pink. "Someone will hear!"

"In fact, I believe I will do just that, first chance I get," he vowed. He bent his head down to gaze upon her, as thoughts of her naked and exquisite rose in his mind. The music slowed to a halt, and for the first time in his life, Julian was sorry that a dance was ending.

"There's Mr. Randall, Julian," Elspeth said as they left the dance floor. "He's looking truly miserable."

"Well, he should be," Julian snapped, changing their direction abruptly so their path would not intersect with that of Edgar Randall.

"He's really quite contrite, Julian," she said. "And I'm under the impression he's gone to great lengths to set things right. I had Harry sit down and tell me everything he remembered from this afternoon's remarkable events. He told me Edgar came to Caroline first, this afternoon, and begged her to call off the whole thing. Even threatened to expose her at his own risk."

"But why would he do that to me in the first place, Elspeth?" Julian asked. "When have I ever been anything but a good friend to him?"

"Harry said Edgar told the viscountess he is quite without funds. Not really enough to live on at all."

"Good God, is that all? He knows I would bail him out at the drop of a hat. All he needed to do was ask."

"But, Julian, don't you see? That is the most difficult thing of all. You don't know this. You have never been in such a position, but, truly, when one is poor, all one has is one's pride. And that becomes very hard to give up."

"He betrayed me."

"He did. And then, almost immediately, he realized what a terrible thing he'd done and he set about fixing things."

"You have a kind heart and good soul, my darling," he said. "I suppose you'll want me to forgive him?" They had reached the double doors that gave out onto the staircase. He led her down, enjoying the cool breeze that wafted up.

"Oh, we really must, Julian," she replied. "We cannot go through life bitter and angry about this. After all, things have turned out remarkably well, considering. We have each other, and Edgar has . . . well, Edgar has nothing very much, has he?"

"Well, when you put it that way . . ."

"I say, aren't you Julian Thorpe?" A toff coming up the steps stopped and peered closely at Julian.

"I am he. And you're Rokeby, aren't you?" Julian said.

"I say, I heard you were set to marry the Quinn gel. Is that right?" Rokeby asked, a bit bluntly.

"I am, indeed," Julian said. He had an idea where this was going and found himself amused. "May I present my affianced, Miss Elspeth Quinn? Miss Quinn, this is Lord Rokeby."

"Oh, er, I say, how d'ye do, and all that," Rokeby mumbled, looking confusedly at Elspeth. "But I thought . . . well, the gel's name is Caroline, isn't it? And she's not you, is she?"

"Er, no, she's my cousin, Lord Rokeby," Elspeth said. It was obvious she was trying very hard not to laugh.

"So you're not marrying . . . er, Caroline, then?" Rokeby asked Julian.

"No, Lord Rokeby, I am marrying her cousin, Elspeth," Julian replied, enjoying himself immensely. He had forgotten what a muttonhead Rokeby really was. "But Caroline is inside, possibly dancing with a Mr. Ledbetter, who, if I may say so"—he leaned in and lowered his voice, as if to share a great confidence—"seems quite smitten with her. If you are inclined in that direction, I suggest you hurry along."

"Er, well, I'm not sure . . . well, I suppose I should see . . . well, evening to you, Thorpe, and . . . er, felicitations and all that." With the barest of abstracted nods, Rokeby turned his attention to the ballroom, from which emanated the lilting sounds of a quadrille.

By tacit mutual agreement, Julian and Elspeth held their silence until the man had disappeared through the double doors and was beyond earshot. Then they exploded in laughter.

"Oh, Julian, you are not going to tell me that that clodpoll is the magnificent Lord Rokeby, of the burned stables, are you?" Elspeth finally asked, between gasps.

"I am, indeed. I think his horses are more intelligent, actually."

"One almost has to feel sorry for the man," Elspeth said.

"Oh, I don't know. He managed to get away at the last moment last year. And Ledbetter is bound to put up a fight."

"Well, as to that, I'd rather see Rokeby take the prize. Mr. Ledbetter is simply too nice a fellow for my cousin," Elspeth said.

"Indeed. This will be amusing to watch."

He took her arm and they continued down the stairs. The air freshened with every step.

"Let's talk about weddings, my darling," Julian said, as they reached the lower rooms. He steered her toward the doors that led out to a small garden. As crowded as the Assembly Rooms were this evening, there was no hope of getting Elspeth alone somewhere for a kiss or two. "Do you want a large one, or small, or something in-between?"

"Oh, small, please, Julian," Elspeth said. "Unless, of course, your family would prefer something more elaborate?"

"My mother and father would be happy to see me hie off to Gretna Green, so happy will they be to get me married off," he replied. It gave him something of a pang to think about his father. He heard regularly from his mother, and the news was never encouraging. They could not travel to his wedding, but he and his beautiful bride would have their love and best wishes wherever they decided to wed.

"Bath or Weston-under-Lizard, then?" he asked.

"Oh, well, I'd love to have the wedding at home. People . . . well, people there are really my friends. They wish me well all the time, not just when there's something in it for them," Elspeth said with a slight shudder. "But it's terribly rustic. Not at all elegant. If you prefer Bath. . . ."

"Weston-under-Lizard will suit admirably, my love. And I long to meet people who value a real friendship." He felt the twist in his heart again as the thought of Edgar's perfidy rose again. "Let's sit here, and plan the wedding. I must say, I never thought I'd enjoy speaking those words, but I find that I do." He sat her on a small iron bench in the corner of the garden, far enough away from the paths to give them some privacy, but not enough, alas, to allow him to kiss her madly for hours on end. Nevertheless, he leaned over and touched his lips gently to hers. Let people think what they would. He wanted no mistake about who it was he really loved. . . .

* * *

Edgar was truly having a miserable evening. It had been fun spinning the tale to the biddies and dragons. Edgar loved the game, enjoyed the balancing act, and, if he admitted the truth to himself, he reveled in making fools of these vapid denizens of the *ton*, who were manipulated so easily, yet so certain of their own infallibility. But of all his set, it was Julian he really respected; he could see that now. And, of all his set, it was Julian he had sought to ruin. It made no sense at all, now. It was easy enough to blame his own poverty for his astonishing behavior, but that was no excuse at all. Better he had starved in a ditch than sought to ruin all happiness for his best friend.

And to have thought to leg-shackle the man to Caroline Quinn, of all women! He could, at least, give himself a small credit for not having known how truly evil she was at the time they had embarked upon their misbegotten plan. But now that he knew, it was hard not to look at Caroline and see the face of Medusa, snake-haired and malevolent.

Speaking of whom . . . Caroline whirled by in a flash of pink satin. It still amazed him how the face of evil could be so beautiful. The Viscountess Alderson, Herself, had waylaid Caroline upon the demoiselle's entrance, and given her fair warning that her planned betrothal to Julian Thorpe had unraveled completely, and that, if she knew what was good for her future, she would embrace the new tale with a mischievous grin and a shrug of the shoulders. Edgar had watched this exchange from a distance, noting as Caroline's face became a dark and angry red, her thin-lipped scowl visible from across the room. At least the chit was smart enough to know defeat when it stared her in the face. She had then, obviously on command, smiled sweetly at the viscountess, curtsied prettily, and taken herself off in the direction of a clot of her contemporaries. Edgar had been relieved to watch her go through the motions this evening, regaling one friend after another with the naughty escapade and how her mother had so deserved the jest.

And, indeed, they all seemed to accept the tale. It did not hurt that Thomas and Robert had embraced it as their very own, mincing about the room, entertaining and embellishing to their dear hearts' content. He, of course, had avoided Caroline all evening as if she carried the Plague, but, then, Caroline had made no effort to seek him out either. It seemed their little association was at an end. Gad, how he hoped so.

But none of that would help Edgar as far as Julian was concerned. He knew Julian had seen him here this evening. Their eyes had met several times across the room, Edgar's hopeful, Julian's icy cold. Elspeth, gentle soul that she was, had forgiven him, although it had taken some persuasion. Julian, now, Julian would be far more difficult. . . .

Edgar stopped dead in his tracks. His eyes could not be deceiving him. No, they were not. Lord Rokeby, himself, had just come through the double doors into the Assembly Room. What a delicious turn of events! He watched as the baron scanned the room, squinting at the various clots scattered about. It was obvious when the man spotted his quarry. He made his way purposefully, like the nodcock that he was, over to where Caroline now stood with a group of their set. It was equally obvious when Caroline spotted Lord Rokeby bearing down on her. Too clever to let it show, her flare of satisfaction was quickly suppressed, and replaced with a bored lack of recognition. She turned back to her friends, offering the baron the cold shoulder as he approached the group. Oh, this was too good to pass up. Edgar took up a post close enough to catch the exchange and settled down for the second-most entertaining part of the evening. . . .

Chapter Sixteen

Elspeth heard Harry squeal, and with force of long-standing habit, turned to see from what mischief she needed to extricate him.

"Allow me, Mrs. Thorpe," Julian whispered at her ear. "I intend to be a good influence on the little scamp. Someone needs to be. The women in this family have spoiled him dreadfully."

Elspeth snorted at that, and watched as Julian waded into the thick of the fray, separating Harry from the flailing flock of nine- and ten-year-olds. Mothers hastily set down plates of refreshment and came running through the grass, ribbons and bonnets bouncing, each to claim her own miscreant from the noisy pile.

"Oh, dear, Elspeth, I had so hoped he would behave," came Margaret Quinn's breathless voice at Elspeth's side. "I explained to him quite carefully that this was your wedding and that he mustn't spoil it."

"Julian will settle it, Mama," Elspeth replied, looking

fondly on the mayhem. "Harry thinks Julian is the center of the universe. If Julian tells Harry to behave, he will. You watch and see."

Indeed, it was miraculous to watch the transformation. No sooner had Julian snagged Harry from the writhing pile of trouble, and had a short whisper in the boy's ear, than Harry drew himself up, dusted himself off, and stepped away, casting a disdainful look back at the naughty children who still scrambled and squealed in the dust. Julian laughed and ruffled the boy's hair, earning himself an exasperated look from his disciple. But Julian now had eyes only for his bride. He turned a smile on her and headed back in her direction.

She could not tear her eyes from him. Step by step he neared. He was as handsome a man as had ever walked the face of this earth, she was quite sure of it. Even for his wedding, he would not bedeck himself in the gaudy nonsense that passed for fashion among gentlemen these days. He was simply clad, as always, with impeccable, understated elegance. His breeches of fawn-colored kerseymere clung to his muscled thighs in a way to bring a blush to her cheeks, knowing as she did, and should not, what they covered. His frock coat of hunter green was cut superbly to his broad shoulders which, she knew from private moments, needed no padding. His fine lawn shirt was dazzling white, and the neckcloth of infinite complexity suggested a valet beyond price.

By contrast, Thomas and Robert stood in a clutch of friends from Bath, true friends, whom she was genuinely happy to see. The peacocks had left no color untried in their remarkable outfits, and, if the macaronies of London were losing their grip on the most outlandish of men's fashions, Robert and Thomas would certainly be the last to give up the fight. As it was, every flower in Margaret Quinn's garden must hang its head in shame for being so eclipsed.

Not, of course, that women's fashions were any less alarming. Elspeth had seen more turbans and ostrich feathers today than Weston-under-Lizard usually could boast in any given year.

Julian had reached her side again, his eyes drinking in the sight of her. In the month since the Viscountess Alderson's ball, they had scarcely seen one another. She and Harry had deemed it wise to return to Weston-under-Lizard from Bath as soon as the conveyance could be arranged. Thank heaven for the thick-witted Lord Rokeby, whose appearance in Bath had blunted the edge of Caroline's rage, and Aunt Bettina's frosty, ungracious acceptance of Elspeth's betrothal. The last few weeks had been a whirl of preparation. Margaret Quinn had insisted that the proprieties must be observed, the banns posted, and a decent amount of time allowed to elapse between the announcement and the wedding, so that no one would make unkind speculation regarding Unseemly Haste.

A London modiste had arrived in Weston-under-Lizard in the first week of Elspeth's return, and had made it plain that she was a "wedding gift" from Elspeth's soon-to-be mother-in-law, and was not to take "go away" for an answer. Elspeth had submitted to fitting after fitting, as the most astonishing fabrics and laces were spread out before her eyes. Letters of protest to Julian as to the expense were ignored, and now she stood in a wedding dress of elegant perfection, a light and airy confection that seemed more Belgian lace than silk, although, to be sure, there were yards and yards of it all.

Well, at least she had the satisfaction of knowing that as a bride she did not disgrace her elegant, magnificent bridegroom. And the wedding itself had been wonderful, simple and lovely, in the small chapel that served most of the village's population. The vicar, who had christened all of the Quinn babies, Elspeth included, had performed the ceremony, with tears in his eyes, and a very old prayer book in his hands.

"We can leave soon, I hope," Julian whispered in her ear. He had placed his gloved hand on hers and now he gave it a squeeze. "I want to kiss you. I want to rip off your dress and kiss you all over. I'm tired of silks and cotton between us. I want to see you as Praxiteles would."

"Oh, Julian," she whispered back, her stomach doing Catherine wheels. The past month had been maddening. Julian had been able to come to Weston-under-Lizard only once, a day after she had arrived, to ask Mrs. Quinn for her daughter's hand in marriage. A stolen kiss or two then was all they had managed. After that, they had had to content themselves with letters back and forth, letters that had to remain reasonably circumspect, since, with a houseful of younger siblings, most especially Harry, it would not do to pen anything that couldn't be shared with prying nine-year-old eyes and adolescent sisters.

Her dreams this past month had only added to the frustration. Julian kissing her, Julian lying next to her, Julian . . . well, Julian doing things most brides did not know enough to contemplate. She, too, longed for this day, lovely as it was, to end. They would leave this afternoon, journeying to his estate in the country, where his father clung to life in hopes of meeting his son's bride and the future mother of his grandchildren, and where his mother fussed about the house so that all should be welcoming for her wonderful, long-awaited daughter-in-law. But it would take several days to get there—two nights spent in what Julian assured her were among the finest inns in England. Alone with her beloved at last. . . .

"Julian!" Edgar Randall's excited tones pierced her

reverie. "Splendid wedding, dear boy, just splendid. Brought a tear to my eye, I declare. I shall never wed, now that you've gone and married the most beautiful girl in all of England."

"As you've never shown any inclination in that regard, Edgar, I do not feel at all guilty," Julian replied. Edgar held out his hand, and Elspeth was relieved to see Julian accept it. She had been hard pressed convincing Julian to forgive Edgar, but time and his own better nature finally caused his anger to thaw, and if there was a slight strain to the friendship, Elspeth meant to have it all smoothed over eventually. Such happiness as they had been granted would not permit the canker of bitterness to lurk within it.

"I do have a secret to tell you both," Edgar said, brightly, "but you must swear on your lives not to repeat it, or I shall be ruined, absolutely ruined, I swear it."

"Oh, Mr. Randall, do not breach any confidences on my account," Elspeth said, with a laugh. She'd long ago learned that secrets one wasn't supposed to know had a way of tripping one up, eventually.

"Oh, this confidence is mine and mine alone to breach, my dear Mrs. Thorpe." It gave her such a jolt of joy to hear herself addressed as such. She had so feared something would rise up and snatch her happiness away before this day could arrive.

Edgar leaned in and lowered his voice to what passed for a whisper. "I find myself, for the first time in my life, gainfully employed," he announced, with a wicked smile.

"You're working?" Julian replied, sounding shocked.

"I am, indeed. Tell no one, or I'll be drummed out of the *ton* forever. I am—well, I'm still not sure what I am, but I take care of things for the Viscountess Alderson. She has, most miraculously, not to mention fraudulently, uncovered a connection between our families, distant, but creditable. As her 'cousin,' I have been invited to live with her. No one knows that I also act as her social secretary. It's most entertaining, really. I now know everything there is to know about the upper, upper echelons, I'm included in all the very best entertainments, I have a stipend that would seem modest to most, but is a king's ransom to me, and, in short, I am the best set up toff in all of the *ton*, and I did not have to marry to get myself there," he finished with a flourish.

"Oh, Mr. Randall, I'm so happy for you," Elspeth said, and she meant it.

"Keep you out of mischief, won't it?" Julian said, a trifle pointedly, she thought.

Edgar had the grace to look a bit abashed. Julian put his hand on his friend's shoulder. "I am happy for you, old man," Julian said, keeping his voice low. "This is perfect for you, and perfect for the viscountess as well. She's got a gem in you for what she needs. In a way, I suppose I owe you an apology—no, no." He held up his hand as Edgar registered astonishment. "I should have recognized your financial woes. It was careless and negligent of me to ignore what should have been obvious. The viscountess, dragon that she may be, was more perspicacious than I, and set about helping you to resolve your difficulties. I should have been a better friend to you, Edgar," he finished, simply.

Julian grunted as Edgar launched himself forward, and enveloped him in a bear hug. They patted each other on the back for an awkward moment, while Elspeth looked on, a wide grin splitting her face. *This breach is mended*, she thought to herself.

"Oh, I haven't had a chance yet to tell you that *on dit* has it Rokeby hasn't yet come up to scratch. Caroline does lead him a merry dance, at poor Mr. Ledbetter's expense, but I suspect strongly she'd rather be Lady Rokeby than Mrs. Ledbetter. Bettina Quinn keeps quiet these days, but one can see she is all but holding her breath, hoping the Season does not end before a betrothal can be accomplished. I have a nasty feeling that Rokeby's days as a bachelor are numbered. One does have to feel sorry for the man. I see," he said, looking about, "that your cousins have not graced your wedding with their presence," he said.

"No. Aunt Bettina wrote and said her health would not permit the journey," Elspeth said. "There was not a damp eye in the house at the news."

They broke off laughing as Wesley Ames and his wife strolled over to offer their felicitations. Elspeth had been delighted that some of Julian's good friends had braved a trip to Weston-under-Lizard on Julian's behalf. They had all enjoyed several lovely days of visiting and wedding preparation. Everyone would return to their respective homes tomorrow, and Weston-under-Lizard would go back to being its sleepy little self.

Behind her back, where no one could see, Julian gave her backside an expectant squeeze, then defiantly left his hand exactly where it was.

"Julian!" she giggled.

"Mr. Thorpe! Unhand my sister at once," cried Harry from somewhere to the rear of them.

Julian rolled his eyes and smiled at Elspeth. "We can leave shortly, can't we, my love?" he asked, his eyes dancing with love.

"Any minute, my heart," she answered, simply, smiling back.

Chapter Seventeen

"We should be there within the half hour, Elspeth," Julian murmured as he felt his sleeping bride stir against his chest. The well-sprung carriage had provided a smooth enough ride to permit them both a bit of a nap. It had been a tiring few days and he looked forward to spending the next few alone for hours on end with his dearly beloved.

"Mmmm," she replied, and snuggled deeper against him. It was warm and comfortable under the thick woolen carriage wraps, and as he had never stinted on quality when ordering a new carriage, the seats were comfortable enough to sleep on. If, indeed, one were tired enough, as they both certainly were.

They had finally gotten away from Weston-under-Lizard, in a flurry of tears and well wishes, later than he had hoped, but earlier than he had expected. Now the twilight descended rapidly, and it seemed they would make Leicester before nightfall as he had hoped. The small medieval town, like Bath, dated back to the Romans, and it boasted enough trade to have several well-appointed inns, safe, clean, and comfortable.

And private.

Julian had been firm that they should not spend their first night as husband and wife either under Elspeth's mother's roof, or that of his own parents. Family was all well and good, but there were times when one decidedly wished to be alone. And now was certainly one of those times. He bent his head and kissed the top of hers, inhaling the sweet scent of her clean hair. She stirred again, and stretched, opening her eyes and blinking sleepily.

"Are we nearly there?" she murmured, sitting up and looking around.

"Nearly, I think," he replied. His hand lingered in her hair, and he played with her soft tresses. His fingers moved down her neck with the lightest touch. She sat against him, their hips and thighs touching. He could feel the burn of her through the silks and wools and infernal cottons that separated them.

She turned and looked at him, a tenuous smile touching her lips. But her eyes—her enormous, beautiful, green eyes looked a bit shadowed, a bit apprehensive.

"What is wrong, my heart?" he asked, gently, fingers still moving on her warm, soft skin.

"Oh, heavens, nothing, really, nothing at all," she stammered, but her eyes gave the lie to her words, and she looked away quickly.

"I think you'd better tell me," he said, solemnly. It was amazing how the smallest thought that she might be regretting her decision to marry him could bring his heart to a thudding stop.

"Well, I . . ." She stopped. Her fingers were twisting in the woolen carriage robe. Something was very wrong, indeed, when Elspeth was bereft of speech.

"Yes?" he prodded, growing more anxious.

She opened her mouth, then closed it again. He waited. Finally, after what seemed an eternity, she turned to him.

"I am worried about—well, I'm worried that I—that you—oh, dear. . . ."

"Go on, sweetheart," he said. He took her hands in his own, to stop them from twisting in the wool.

"Oh, Julian. I don't know what to think about—about what will happen tonight. You know what they say—'a little knowledge is a dangerous thing.' I'm afraid. . . ." She had begun in a rush and now trailed off. Her eyes were large and luminous, swimming in confusion. He was beginning to get a glimmering here.

"You're afraid of our bedding, Elspeth?" he asked gently. It was like holding a bird in his hands. He was so afraid she would startle and fly away.

"No—I mean, yes! Oh, Julian, I don't know what I mean. On the one hand, it's all I've been able to think about these last few weeks. My heart pounds at the thought of your touch. I can hardly wait for your next kiss! It is most unmaidenly. I'm so afraid you'll be disappointed, thoroughly disgusted, really, to think me a wanton. On the other hand—well, Julian . . ." She stopped again and took a deep breath. He wanted desperately to speak, but, aware that she had more to say, and that getting it out was so difficult for her, he held his silence, and waited for her to continue. "Julian, you're so large!" she finally stammered out. "However will this work?"

"Well," he said, gently, thinking furiously as to how best to approach this. "First of all, my darling, what passes between us in the bedroom is between us, alone. How we behave toward each other in that regard is our own business and no one else's. Are you possibly not aware . . ." Now he had to pause and draw a deep breath.

While he had been willing, even enthusiastic about disgusting Caroline with gross and inaccurate details about the sexual act, he had no wish whatsoever to frighten his beloved, most particularly on the brink of their first bedding.

". . . Has no one shared with you that lovemaking can and should be pleasurable for the lady, Elspeth?" he finished.

"Well, no, Julian," she said, looking away again, out of the carriage window where the darkness gathered. "At our last dinner together in Bath, Aunt Bettina was telling Caroline that—well—that it was something to be gotten through—that a lady must simply close her eyes, and plan her next party, and wait for her husband to finish. She said no real lady should ever stoop so low as to express, or, worse, experience any enthusiasm for the—ah—for the act—and that any woman who did was nothing more than a—a trollop. And so I've felt, well, I've felt that I might disgust you in some way. I should hate that, Julian!" she cried, launching herself into his arms. "I should so hate for you to be disgusted with me. I don't know what to do!"

He could feel his blood boiling, and for once, it was not with passion for his beloved. The evil of that household knew no bounds. "Elspeth, my own, my love, look at me!" he said. He pulled her back gently, keeping a tight hold on her shoulders. She trembled beneath his fingers. "You have been victimized enough by that malevolent family. That woman drips poison from her tongue. There is no truth, no truth, whatsoever, to what she said. Indeed, I'm certain that she held that little conversation in front of you on purpose—to spoil your wedding night and my own, possibly to spoil our marital relations for the rest of our lives." He stopped and took another deep breath. "Did your mother not speak of these things to you, Elspeth?" he asked.

"Oh, she meant to, she really did. Kept saying we'd get to it. But the children were always underfoot, and there was so much to do, and then the houseguests came, and then, well, we just never managed to have the time to talk. As she helped me dress this afternoon, she whispered that I should trust you, and all would be well, and she just laughed, but there were so many ladies in the room that I couldn't ask her anything else. . . ." She trailed off and buried her face in the folds of his neckcloth again.

So it all came down to how he managed the next few minutes. It seemed the carriage had grown suddenly very warm. Very warm, indeed. "Elspeth, do you remember the afternoon when I came upon you in your bath?" he asked, keeping his voice soft. He slid his hand to the back of her neck and rubbed it gently.

"Oh, I do!" she said breathlessly. In the dim of twilight he could still see the deep blush that suffused her cheeks. "You must have thought me a dreadful wanton. . . ." She looked so apprehensive, it was all he could do not to crush her to him.

"I thought then, and still do, that you are the most beautiful, the most passionate, the most desirable woman I have ever known, Elspeth," he said simply. Unable to stop himself, he pulled her face close and touched his lips to hers, gently at first. She tasted so delicious; her lips were so soft and yielding against his own. He drank in the taste of her, deepening the kiss. Then he pulled away. Holding her head in his hands, he looked into the green depths of her eyes. "I love you exactly the way you are, my darling. From the beginning, I knew you for a deep intellect and rare wit, but it is utter joy to find passion in you as well. A woman, a real lady, is permitted to take her pleasure with her husband. I should be terribly disappointed if you did not find making love with me pleasurable for you. In fact, I intend to explore every inch of you as I promised once to do, to learn what gives you pleasure. I want you to look forward to our lovemaking, not fear it, or, worse"—he broke off with a mock shiver—"plan your next party. My God, Elspeth, I want you to want me the way I want you!" he cried, and pulled her to him again, crushing her in his embrace.

For a moment he just held her, feeling her heart beat beneath his own. Had he frightened her? Very gently, he pulled back, keeping his hands on her shoulders. He peered into her eyes, barely visible in the darkness. In their swimming green depths, he read only love. He lowered his lips to hers, again, slowly, carefully, letting them brush against her softness. Her lips yielded to his, and he could feel her hands moving around his waist to his back, until she held him as closely as he held her. For a moment he played against her lips with his own, then deepened the kiss, his tongue lightly brushing hers, then probing more deeply the warmth of her mouth. She tightened her arm about him, and he groaned and pulled her closer. Now his lips left hers, tracing down her cheek, to her neck. She threw her head back, and he heard her soft moan as he drew his lips down, down her neck, coming to rest where her flesh met the top of her decolletage. More silk, more lace! Never had he been so sick of the stuff!

He moved his hand up to her neckline. Where his fingers brushed against her skin, they burned with the heat of her. It was difficult to control himself, but he made his hands move softly, slowly, as he pulled down gently on the material, freeing her breast from the silks. She gasped as his fingers found the nipple and circled it. He lowered his lips yet again from her neck to the pink bud, taking it gently into his mouth, as his tongue found it and teased it to tautness.

"Oh, Elspeth," he gasped, breathing against her skin.

His tongue continued to tease her nipple as his hand moved down, down to her waist, across her hip. He pulled at the silken fabric that seemed to encase her everywhere, pulling it up, up, seeming yards and yards of it, till he could feel the flesh of her thigh against his fingers. And now his hand moved again across her silken belly, down to that place he had so long wanted to touch. She gasped and pulled back as his fingers found her place of secrets, but with his other hand he held her close. He probed gently, feeling her silky and damp beneath his touch. She arched her back and moaned, now pushing against him. It was almost a shock to feel that now her hand was moving as well, down his back, over his hip, coming to rest at the front placket of his breeches. He could feel her fumbling at the fastenings and could hardly think as the blood pounded in his head. He moved his hand to help her and got himself undone. His tumescence was apparent as his shaft leaped from its too tight confinement. He could feel her hand close around him and he could not stop himself from pushing forward, hard, against her touch.

"Oh, Julian!" she cried out, gasping, as she sat up, and pulled her hand away. He could see her face now, her eyes large as saucers, the question in them plain.

"Oh, my darling," he said, but it came out more as a gasp. "I know what you fear, but please do not worry. . . ." His voice froze in his throat as he heard the carriage door being opened behind him. How on earth had he not noticed the carriage coming to a halt?

"We're here, Mr. Thorpe," came the cheery voice of his driver. Julian moved not a muscle, calculating quickly that his back hid most of their activities from view, relieved that it was dark enough, at least, that they must appear to be a dark blur inside the carriage. "I'll see to finding the ostler, sir," the man said, hurriedly. Julian strongly suspected the fellow could see well enough to know there was some canoodling going on twixt bride and groom, but he also knew the man valued his position in the Thorpe household enough to let no hint of this knowledge cross his lips.

Julian heard his man's footsteps fading in the gravel of the inn yard, and raised his head carefully. Elspeth, too, raised hers, eyes wide.

"Oh, Julian!" she began, then choked with a giggle. "Do you suppose he could see what we were doing?" she went on, nearly breathless, when she could speak again.

"I think he could see nothing in the dark, my heart," Julian assured her, hoping desperately he spoke the truth. "My back was to him, and I was blocking his view, after all." He fiddled with her neckline, pulling the silk up, and, with a lingering, regretful look, watched her breast disappear into its lacy confines. Ah, but there would be later. . . . He then had to fiddle, rather ignominiously, he thought, with the placket of his breeches, which somehow did not wish to fasten. He was further hampered by the fact that Elspeth was watching his efforts with some amusement.

At last the beastly thing buttoned up. He cast a quick eye over his beloved, relieved to see that she had got herself to looking every inch the lady, except for the naughty merriment that still danced in her eyes. Oh, she was a wanton, indeed, and that knowledge set his heart to racing all over again. But, alas, the game was up for now, so he stepped from the carriage.

He surveyed the inn yard, quickly, pleased to see no one about, at least anywhere close. Perhaps his man was sharper than Julian gave him credit for. He turned back to the open door of the carriage. "If we are presentable, I believe our supper awaits, Mrs. Thorpe," he said, for all the world as if they had not been devouring one another but a moment ago.

"I believe I could use a bite at that, Mr. Thorpe,"

replied his bride, her tone as proper as any duchess. He presented his now-gloved hand and she placed her gloved hand in it, stepping gracefully from the carriage.

"Now then," he said, presenting his arm to her.

As she reached for him, her eyes, straying down, widened in alarm, "Julian, wait!" she choked out, and gestured frantically with her fingers toward his nether regions. He looked down and, to his horror, saw a good-sized bit of white shirttail protruding quite obviously from the front of his breeches placket.

"Oh, the devil," he expostulated, turning back to face the carriage, and pushing frantically at the infernal stray piece, tucking it back where it belonged. He straightened himself, took a deep, calming breath, and turned back to Elspeth, who wasn't helping matters in the least by being purple in the face, and snorting with an effort not to collapse in fits of giggles.

"Madam?" he said coolly, offering her his arm again.

"Sir," she replied loftily. She took his arm, and they dared not so much as a glance at one another as they made their stately way into the inn.

Chapter Eighteen

It seemed to take forever to finish the lavish dinner presented to them by the innkeeper himself, in the small but nicely appointed private dining room. Elspeth found that she was ravenous, and for a short while feared that she could hardly get enough to eat as several fine dishes were set before the bride and bridegroom with a flourish. And then after the first few mouthfuls, she could hardly swallow a bite. Julian had attempted a little conversation here and there, and she gamely tried to be responsive, but for the life of her, she could hardly mind what he said. All she could think of was the large, tastefully appointed bedchamber that awaited them upstairs. And the large bed.

Oh, when would this supper end? And just when she thought the meal would, indeed, go on eternally, like something out of Norse mythology, the dishes were being cleared away and he was standing, holding out his hand to her. In a few moments, she would be upstairs . . . alone . . . with Julian. . . .

She was on fire. She was cold as ice. She was terrified down to the very toes of her slippers.

With one hand on her elbow and one resting lightly on her back, he helped her up the narrow wooden stairs. The inn was old, dating back, or so they said, to the great Tudor era. Good Queen Bess, herself, was said to have slept in this very room. That did not seem important now. She did find herself hoping it hadn't been on the very same mattress.

Julian pushed the door open and helped her through. He seemed aware that she was nervous. He was very gentle with her. She saw that their bags had been brought up and a few things unpacked. Her silk nightgown lay out on the bed. Next to it was a fine lawn garment—Julian's nightshirt, of course.

He stood behind her as she gazed about the room. She was aware that she was trembling slightly and was mightily annoyed with herself. The man must think her a perfect fool! She felt his hands touch her, very softly on her shoulders. She leaned back against him with a sigh. It felt so good to lean against his big, broad chest, to know he was there, and that he loved her, indeed.

"Are you still worried, my heart?" he whispered in her ear, following the question with a nibble and a light kiss on the back of her neck.

She shivered with delight. "I—I suppose I am, Julian," she said simply. Gently, he turned her to him. He gazed deep into her eyes.

"Would you feel more comfortable if you could actually see, Elspeth?" he asked, the teasing obvious in his smile. "You can put on your spectacles, if you feel the need."

"Oh, Julian," she laughed. "I'm nervous enough without actually being able to see . . . things," she finished, somewhat lamely. He gave a laugh, deep in his throat, almost like a growl, and pulled her toward him. Carefully, he leaned forward, and brought his lips to hers. It felt like a bolt of lightning, every time he kissed her. That she went mad, and lost all reason when he touched her was beyond doubt. She could feel him deepen the kiss, moving his lips against hers, as he gently ran his tongue against her soft mouth, pushing, just slightly. Her lips parted against his and she felt herself sigh. His tongue sought hers, and a thrill ran through her as she felt her own response, deep within. She shifted in his arms to push herself closer, so that they touched, up and down the length of their bodies, and a low moan escaped her.

At last he drew his head back from hers. He turned her in his arms, and with fingers as nimble as any lady's maid, he undid her buttons, one by one, down the length of her back. He lifted the dress over her head and tossed it negligently over the back of a chair.

She stepped out of her slippers and now she stood wearing nothing but her chemise and silk stockings. He turned her around to face him, holding her away a bit, his eyes drinking their fill. With hands that trembled, she reached up and began untying the intricate twists of his neckcloth. He threw back his head with a smile and let her fingers do the work. It came loose at last, and with a mischievous grin, she pulled it free of his neck, and tossed it atop her dress on the chair. She reached up and divested him of his frock coat, then went to work on his waistcoat buttons. He stood very still, a small smile playing about his lips, and let her undress him.

The waistcoat went the way of the dress, the neckcloth, and the frock coat.

And then she looked down. "Julian,"she whispered breathlessly, unable—or was it unwilling—to take her eyes from the obvious bulge in his breeches.

With a growl, he swung her into his arms, and carried her over to the bed. He laid her down in the middle, then sat down next to her. His eyes, starting at the top of her head, took her all in, down to the tip of her toes. She could feel herself tingling all over, as if she could feel his very look.

"You are exquisite," he whispered, as his hand reached around her waist. The light cotton chemise rode up under his fingers. He lay down alongside her and gathered her to him. Now they were touching, every inch along the length of their bodies, thin cotton and the kerseymere breeches all that lay between their flesh. He pulled her closer still, and dropped his mouth to hers for another searing kiss that left her gasping. He moved his hand to her thigh, rubbing it, teasing her sensitive skin. He lifted his mouth from hers, and her head fell back. She was breathing in rapid pants now, and so was he. He traced a line from her lips, down her neck. His lips inched down, down, his tongue tracing a path along the soft, milk-white skin of the swell of her breasts. His hand moved up, up along the side of her, coming to rest on her bosom. She gasped, and pressed closer, moaning. His hand found her nipple under the cotton of her chemise and he pulled the thin stuff away impatiently. His hand cupped her naked breast, and he moaned soft and low in her ear as she arched against him. Behind him, her hands moved down his back, then up again, rather frantically, as she sought something . . . something, but she did not know what.

He moved his hand again to her thigh, and then her calf, where he came to the edge of her chemise. He moved his hand on her silk stocking, rubbing her leg, then moving his hand up slowly. Just over the knee, the silk stocking came to an end at its lace garter. He did not stop. She could feel the soft, warm flesh of his chest pressed against her, and still, his hand traced upward on her thigh.

She did not flinch when his fingers found her moistness, but she threw back her head and moaned his name. And now her hand slid down his chest, tracing over his belly, and coming to rest just shy of . . . of. . . .

"Ah, Elspeth, sweetheart!" he moaned, taking her hand in his and pressing it against his hardness. It was like touching fire. He reared back, a low moan escaping his lips, and pushed hard, hard against her. She fumbled with the buttons on his breeches, and he let her. After a seeming eternity, the fastenings came loose and he sprang forth, hard and hot.

"Let me see," she whispered close to his ear, feeling the shivers of pleasure that rippled through him.

He rolled away, and lay on his back, gasping for breath, his eyes raking her. She looked down.

"Ah, Julian," she whispered, with a long look. Then she reached for him. As her fingers grasped him, he cried out, and grabbed her hand, holding it still.

"Elspeth, wait!" he gasped out. "I want you so much, I have almost no control!"

"It's so soft, and yet so hard," she whispered, wonder in her voice. He did not answer.

"That is what goes inside me?" she asked, moving her fingers gently along his shaft.

"Yes," he croaked out.

"Will it hurt terribly? It seems so large," she said. She could hardly keep the fear from her voice.

"Oh, my darling," he whispered against her hair. "It does hurt the first time, I am sorry to say. But after that, it does not hurt again. After that first time, I think you'll find it pleasurable."

"Then do it now, Julian," she said, urgently. "Take me now. Let's get the hurt over with, and then I can feel the pleasure."

"Are you sure, my heart? We can wait, if you are fearful of the pain."

"I will never forgive you if you don't do it now, Julian. I would rather get the pain over with. I am most anxious to get on with the pleasure." Her hand grasped him tightly, and he fell back against the pillows again, with a low moan.

She rubbed him, tentatively like the virgin that she was, not really knowing what to do. Her hand closed tight against him and she began to rub him harder. "Julian," she whispered urgently, "show me what to do." He wrapped his hand around hers, showing her, without telling, how to touch him. His other hand slid down again . . . "Julian," she gasped as his fingers found the secret place. She could feel herself grow wet and hot. He slid his finger into the moistness, and she fell against him, moaning. "Oh, what are you doing?" she cried. She moved hard against him, faster and faster, gasping in each breath. He pressed his fingers hard against her, sliding them into her wet sheath, using his thumb to press where he knew, as she did not, that she needed the pressure.

"Don't stop," she moaned, moving faster and harder against his hand. But, maddeningly, he did just that. He stopped, and rolled over, reaching for her and pulling her atop him. Her thighs now straddled his hips, and she was astonished at the pleasure that flooded her at the feel of it. His hard shaft pressed against her moistness, and all rational thought fled.

"I'll go quickly," he gasped, reaching down to guide himself into her. "It will only hurt for a moment, I promise."

She stopped his words with a long, deep kiss, her tongue thrusting deep into his mouth, just as he thrust hard inside her. She felt the barrier give against his assault and could not stop herself from crying out, as her sheath closed tight around him.

"Are you all right, my love?" he whispered.

"Yes, oh, yes," she said, her voice ragged. Slowly, gently, he began to move again. She knew that she was wet and slippery and tight. He moved faster, thrusting deep and hard. With a cry, he arched upward, the seed bursting from him as he pumped again and again into her wetness. He placed his finger against the hot nub, and she gave a great cry, feeling waves of pleasure washing over her. And then she lay still, panting. She could not move.

Gradually, she felt herself come back, as if from a distant place. Tentatively, he moved his lips against her hair and then to her cheek. "I'm sorry, my darling," he whispered. "Did I hurt you badly?" he asked, his eyes clouded with worry.

"You were right, Julian," she whispered. "I barely felt the pain, because the pleasure was so great."

In answer he gave a laugh and rolled her over, keeping their bodies locked tightly together. "Well, that's a relief, Mrs. Thorpe," he said in between the kisses he rained down all over her face, in her hair, on her neck, on her breasts. "Because I intend to do that to you every chance you give me for the rest of our lives."

"I will find that a suitable arrangement, Mr. Thorpe," she said, playfully, nipping at his nose. Gently, he settled her in the crook of his arm. She was surprised to find herself yawning. Nestled there in the warmth of his arms, held fast in his love, she found herself drifting off, the swirl of her thoughts settling around the joy of this union, and it was all she could do to keep her owl eyes open. . . .

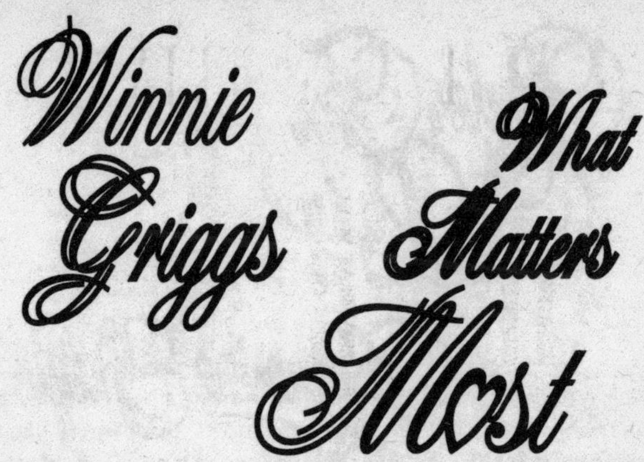

Reed Wilder journeys to Far Enough, Texas, in search of a fallen woman. He finds an angel. Barely reaching five feet two inches, the petite brunette helps to defend him against two ruffians and then treats his wounds with a gentleness that makes him long to uncover all her secrets. But she only has to reveal her name and he knows his lovely rescuer is not an innocent woman, but the deceitful opportunist who preyed on his brother. Reed prides himself on his logic and control, but both desert him when he gazes into Lucy's warm brown eyes. He has only one option: to discover the truth behind those enticing lips he longs to sample.

__4829-9 $4.99 US/$5.99 CAN

Dorchester Publishing Co., Inc.
P.O. Box 6640
Wayne, PA 19087-8640

Please add $2.50 for shipping and handling for the first book and $.75 for each book thereafter. NY and PA residents, please add appropriate sales tax. No cash, stamps, or C.O.D.s. All orders shipped within 6 weeks via postal service book rate. Canadian orders require $2.00 extra postage and must be paid in U.S. dollars through a U.S. banking facility.

Name______________________________
Address______________________________
City__________________ State______ Zip__________
I have enclosed $________ in payment for the checked book(s).
Payment must accompany all orders. ☐ Please send a free catalog.

CHECK OUT OUR WEBSITE! www.dorchesterpub.com

A lady does not attempt to come out in London society disguised as her deceased half-sister. A lady does not become enamored of her guardian, even though his masterful kisses and whispered words of affection tempt her beyond all endurance. A lady may not climb barefoot from her bedroom on a rose trellis, nor engage in fisticuffs with riffraff in order to rescue street urchins. No matter how impossible the odds, a lady always gives her hand and her heart–though not necessarily in that order–to the one man who sees her as she truly is and loves her despite her flagrant disobedience of every one of the rules for a lady.

___4818-3 $4.99 US/$5.99 CAN